英美文学经典赏析

British and American Literary Works: A Reader

主　编　卢　云
副主编　李　慷　冯　迪
　　　　周诗羽　张英贤

中国地质大学出版社
CHINA UNIVERSITY OF GEOSCIENCES PRESS

图书在版编目(CIP)数据

英美文学经典赏析/卢云主编.—武汉:中国地质大学出版社,2019.6
ISBN 978-7-5625-4575-0

Ⅰ.①英…
Ⅱ.①卢…
Ⅲ.①英国文学-文学欣赏②文学欣赏-美国
Ⅳ.①I561.06②I712.06

中国版本图书馆CIP数据核字(2019)第126828号

英美文学经典赏析	卢　云　**主　编** 李　慷　冯　迪　周诗羽　张英贤　**副主编**
责任编辑:马　严	责任校对:周　旭

出版发行:中国地质大学出版社(武汉市洪山区鲁磨路388号)	邮政编码:430074
电　　话:(027)67883511　　　传真:67883580	E-mail:cbb@cug.edu.cn
经　　销:全国新华书店	http://cugp.cug.edu.cn
开本:787毫米×1092毫米 1/16	字数:390千字　　印张:15.25
版次:2019年6月第1版	印次:2019年6月第1次印刷
印刷:荆州鸿盛印务有限公司	印数:1—1500册
ISBN 978-7-5625-4575-0	定价:39.80元

如有印装质量问题请与印刷厂联系调换

前言

　　文学是语言的艺术。在笔者多年的大学英语教学生涯里，无论讲授语言点、篇章修辞还是写作技法，备课过程中从文学经典里选取了大量的语料。笔者发现，优美的文学语言往往能引起学生极大的阅读兴趣。学习大学英语的学生是一个极为广大的群体，他们渴望阅读经典，汲取文学的养分。而纵观国内现有的英美文学类教材，多是面向英语专业本科生和研究生编写的，具有以下两类特点：①以史为纲，按照时间线索，介绍一堆的作家和作品。虽然系统全面，然而内容浩繁，学生难以留下深刻印象；②以文学理论为主，介绍西方文学各门各派的理论主张及其代表人物。这类教材虽然提供了评价文学作品的方法，却因缺乏结合具体文本进行解读使得学生最终对于理论的掌握流于空泛。因此，笔者组织起中国地质大学（武汉）大学英语英美文学课程教学团队，希望根据大学英语学生的特点和需求，推出适用于大学英语学生群体的英美文学教材。几年来，团队成员以全校性的通识课"英美文学经典赏析"作为课程实践的基础，对教学资源不断筛选、论证、整理和编写，通过辛勤的付出，这本书终于付梓面世了。

　　本书定位为大学英语高阶阶段人文类后续课程学习教材，也可以作为通识教育选修课教材。教材在内容上撷取英国和美国文学史上经典作家的代表作品，按照文学传统四大体裁进行编排，包括小说、诗歌、戏剧和散文四大部分，每一篇又设置背景介绍、文本选读、作品赏析、思考题等条目。在作品赏析部分虽然涉及到文学理论，但并非孤立地讨论文学理论或文学批评，而是立足于所选文学文本展开的鉴赏性阅读。赏析往往会从一个或几个具体的点展开，目的在于赋予学生独特的视角，引导学生进入对文本的深度阅读，让他们在阅读体验中有所感悟和收获，进而能够发现和建构意义。众所周知，文学阅读很难产生一言堂的结论,本书中设计的思考题并不存在所谓的"标准答案",目的主要在于调动学生积极思考,发挥想象,从更广阔的角度去挖掘和诠释作品,最终提高学生的阅读能力和思辨意识。

本书兼具人文性和艺术性,期待能为高等院校众多非英语专业的大学生打开一扇通往文学殿堂的大门。本书同样适用于有一定水平的英语爱好者,通过文学阅读体验,接触丰富的语言现象,提高英语语感,增强英语的学习动力。

由于编者水平有限,书中的不足及偏颇之处在所难免,敬请读者谅解。

卢 云

2019年6月于南望山麓

Contents

Part I Fiction

Chapter 1 Robinson Crusoe *by Daniel Defoe* ··· (3)

Chapter 2 Frankenstein *by Mary Shelley* ·· (13)

Chapter 3 Jane Eyre *by Charlotte Brontë* ··· (24)

Chapter 4 The Gift of the Magi *by O · Henry* ·· (36)

Chapter 5 Ticket, Please *by D. H. Lawrence* ··· (44)

Chapter 6 Kew Garden *by Virginia Woolf* ··· (60)

Chapter 7 The Great Gatsby *by F. Scott Fitzgerald* ·· (70)

Chapter 8 A Rose for Emily *by William Faulkner* ·· (81)

Chapter 9 Joy Luck Club *by Amy Tan* ··· (95)

Part II Poetry

Chapter 1 Sonnet 18: Shall I compare thee to a summer's day? *by William Shakespeare* ·· (113)

Chapter 2 Elegy Written in a Country Churchyard *by Thomas Gray* ··············· (116)

Chapter 3 She dwelt among untrodden ways *by William Wordsworth* ············ (126)

Chapter 4 Ulysses *by Alfred Tennyson* ·· (131)

Chapter 5 "Hope" is the Thing with Feathers-(314) *by Emily Dickinson* ········· (138)

Chapter 6 He Wishes for the Cloths of Heaven *by William Butler Yeats* ········· (142)

Chapter 7   Stopping by Woods on a Snowy Evening *by Robert Frost* ……… (145)

Chapter 8   l(a *by E. E. Cummings* ……………………………………… (149)

Part Ⅲ Drama

Chapter 1   Richard Ⅲ *by William Shakespeare* ……………………… (155)

Chapter 2   Hamlet *by William Shakespeare* …………………………… (165)

Chapter 3   Death of a Salesman *by Arthur Miller* …………………… (177)

Chapter 4   Waiting for Godot *by Samuel Beckett* …………………… (188)

Chapter 5   M. Butterfly *by David Henry Hwang* ……………………… (203)

Part Ⅳ Prose

Chapter 1   Of Studies *by Francis Bacon* ……………………………… (211)

Chapter 2   Walden *by Henry David Thoreau* …………………………… (215)

Chapter 3   Three Days to See *by Helen Keller* ……………………… (226)

Chapter 4   Youth *by Samuel Ullman* …………………………………… (234)

Part I Fiction

Chapter 1 Robinson Crusoe
by Daniel Defoe
(excerpts)

 背景介绍

1704 年,一位名叫亚历山大·塞尔科克(Alexander Selkirk)的英格兰水手由于与船长不和,在航行途中被抛弃到了一座荒岛上。四年后,当一位航海家发现他时,这名水手几乎变成了一个茹毛饮血的野蛮人。回抵英国后,他的事迹被媒体广为报道。小说家丹尼尔·笛福受这一真实事件的启发,通过艺术加工与想象,创作出了《鲁滨逊漂流记》。小说的主人公鲁滨逊为追求财富而出海探险,不幸遇到船难,孤身陷于荒岛之上。面对困境,他没有绝望,而是凭借自己的力量,利用大自然能提供的一切生存所需的资源顽强存活了下来,牢牢掌握了自己的命运。主人公鲁滨逊身上充满了对外探索的好奇心、征服欲和冒险精神。作品高度赞扬了人的坚毅品质和创造精神。

 文本选读

Chapter 23

During the long Time that Friday has now been with me, and that he began to speak to me, and understand me, I was not wanting to lay a Foundation of religious Knowledge in his Mind; particularly I ask'd him one Time who made him? The poor Creature did not understand me at all, but thought I had ask'd who was his Father; but I took it by another handle, and ask'd him who made the Sea, the Ground we walk'd on, and the Hills, and Woods; he told me it was one old Benamuckee, that liv'd beyond all: He could describe nothing of this great Person, but that he was very old; much older he said than the Sea, or the Land; than the Moon, or the Stars: I ask'd him then, if this old Person had made all Things, why did not all Things worship him; he look'd very grave, and with a perfect Look of Innocence, said, All Things do say O to him: I ask'd him if the People who die in his Country went away any where; he said, yes, they all went to Benamuckee; then I ask'd him whether these they eat up went thither too, he said yes.

From these Things, I began to instruct him in the Knowledge of the true God: I told him that the great Maker of all Things liv'd up there, pointing up towards Heaven: That he governs the World by the same Power and Providence by which he had made it: That he was omnipotent, could do every Thing for us, give every Thing to us, take every Thing from us; and thus by Degrees I open'd his Eyes. He listned with great Attention, and receiv'd with Pleasure the Notion of Jesus Christ being sent to redeem us, and of the Manner of making our Prayers to God, and his being able to hear us, even into Heaven; he told me one Day, that if our God could hear us up beyond the Sun, he must needs be a greater God than their Benamuckee, who liv'd but a little way off, and yet could not hear, till they went up to the great Mountains where he dwelt, to speak to him; I ask'd him if ever he went thither, to speak to him; he said no, they never went that were young Men; none went thither but the old Men, who he call'd their Oowocakee, that is, as I made him explain it to me, their Religious, or Clergy, and that they went to say O, (so he called saying Prayers) and then came back, and told them what Benamuckee said: By this I observ'd, That there is Priestcraft, even amongst the most blinded ignorant Pagans in the World; and the Policy of making a secret Religion, in order to preserve the Veneration of the People to the Clergy, is not only to be found in the Roman, but perhaps among all Religions in the World, even among the most brutish and barbarous Savages.

I endeavour'd to clear up this Fraud, to my Man Friday, and told him, that the Pretence of their old Men going up the Mountains, to say O to their God Benamuckee, was a Cheat, and their bringing Word from thence what he said, was much more so; that if they met with any Answer, or spake with any one there, it must be with an evil Spirit: And then I entred into a long Discourse with him about the Devil, the Original of him, his Rebellion against God, his Enmity to Man, the Reason of it, his setting himself up in the dark Parts of the World to be Worship'd instead of God, and as God; and the many Stratagems he made use of to delude Mankind to his Ruine; how he had a secret access to our Passions, and to our Affections, to adapt his Snares so to our Inclinations, as to cause us even to be our own Tempters, and to run upon our Destruction by our own Choice.

I found it was not so easie to imprint right Notions in his Mind about the Devil, as it was about the Being of a God. Nature assisted all my Arguments to Evidence to him, even the Necessity of a great first Cause and over-ruling governing Power; a secret directing Providence, and of the Equity, and Justice, of paying Homage to him that made us, and the like. But there appeared nothing of all this in the Notion of an evil Spirit; of his Original, his Being, his Nature, and above all of his Inclination to do Evil, and to draw us in to do so too; and the poor Creature puzzl'd me once in such a manner, by a Question meerly natural and innocent, that I scarce knew what to say to him. I had been talking a great deal to him of the Power of God, his Omnipotence, his dreadful Nature to Sin, his being a consuming Fire to the Workers of Iniquity; how, as he had made us all, he could destroy us and all the World in a Moment; and he listen'd with great Seriousness to me all the while.

Chapter 24

It was after this some considerable Time, that being upon the Top of the Hill, at the East Side of the Island, from whence as have said, I had in a clear Day discover'd the Main, or Continent of America; Friday, the Weather being very serene, looks very earnestly towards the Main Land, and in a kind of Surprise, falls a jumping and dancing, and calls out to me, for I was at some Distance from him: I ask'd him, What was the Matter? O joy! Says he, O glad! There see my Country, there my Nation!

I observ'd an extraordinary Sense of Pleasure appear'd in his Face, and his Eyes sparkled, and his Countenance discover'd a strange Eagerness, as if he had a Mind to be in his own Country again; and this Observation of mine, put a great many Thoughts into me, which made me at first not so easy about my new Man Friday as I was before; and I made no doubt, but that if Friday could get back to his own Nation again, he would not only forget all his Religion, but all his Obligation to me; and would be forward enough to give his Countrymen an Account of me, and come back perhaps with a hundred or two of them, and make a Feast upon me, at which he might be as merry as he us'd to be with those of his Enemies, when they were taken in War.

But I wrong'd the poor honest Creature very much, for which I was very sorry afterwards. However as my Jealousy encreased, and held me some Weeks, I was a little more circumspect, and not so familiar and kind to him as before; in which I was certainly in the Wrong too, the honest grateful Creature having no thought about it, but what consisted with the best Principles, both as a religious Christian, and as a grateful Friend, as appeared afterwards to my full Satisfaction.

While my Jealousy of him lasted, you may be sure I was every Day pumping him to see if he would discover any of the new Thoughts, which I suspected were in him; but I found every thing he said was so Honest, and so Innocent, that I could find nothing to nourish my Suspicion; and in spight of all my Uneasiness he made me at last entirely his own again, nor did he in the least perceive that I was Uneasie, and therefore I could not suspect him of Deceit.

    One Day walking up the same Hill, but the Weather being haizy at Sea, so that we could not see the Continent, I call'd to him, and said, Friday, do not you wish your self in your own Country, your own Nation? Yes, he said, he be much O glad to be at his own Nation. What would you do there said I, would you turn Wild again, eat Mens Flesh again, and be a Savage as you were before? He lookt full of Concern, and shaking his Head said, No no, Friday tell them to live Good, tell them to pray God, tell them to eat Corn bread, Cattleflesh, Milk, no eat Man again: Why then said I to him, They will kill you. He look'd grave at that, and then said, No, they no kill me, they willing love learn: He meant by this, they would be willing to learn. He added, they learn'd much of the Bearded-Mans that come in the Boat. Then I ask'd him if he would go back to them? He smil'd at that, and told me he could not swim so far. I told him I would make a Canoe for him. He told me, he would go, if I would go with him. I go! says I, why they will Eat me if I come there! No, no, says he, me make they no Eat you; me make they much Love you: He meant he would tell them how I had kill'd his Enemies, and sav'd his Life, and so he would make them love me; then he told me as well as he could, how kind they were to seventeen White-men, or Bearded-men, as he call'd them, who came on Shore there in Distress.

    From this time I confess I had a Mind to venture over, and see if I could possibly joyn with these Bearded-men, who I made no doubt were Spaniards or Portuguese; not doubting but if I could we might find some Method to Escape from thence, being upon the Continent, and a good Company together, better than I could from an Island 40 Miles off the Shore, and alone without Help. So after some Days I took Friday to work again, by way of Discourse, and told him I would give him a Boat to go back to his own Nation; and accordingly I carry'd him to my Frigate which lay on the other Side of the Island, and having clear'd it of Water, for I always kept it sunk in the Water, I brought it out, shewed it him, and we both went into it.

    I found he was a most dextrous Fellow at managing it, would make it go almost as swift and fast again as I could; so when he was in, I said to him, Well now, Friday, shall we go to your Nation? He look'd very dull at my saying so, which it seems was, because he thought the Boat too small to go so far. I told him then I had a bigger; so the next Day I went to the Place where the first Boat lay which I had made, but which I could not get into Water: He said that was big enough; but then as I had taken no Care of it, and it had lain two or three and twenty Years there, the Sun had split and dry'd it, that it was in a manner rotten. Friday told me such a Boat would do very well, and would carry much enough Vittle, Drink, Bread, that was his Way of Talking.

Upon the whole, I was by this Time so fix'd upon my Design of going over with him to the Continent, that I told him we would go and make one as big as that, and he should go home in it. He answer'd not one Word, but look'd very grave and sad: I ask'd him what was the matter with him? He ask'd me again thus; Why, you angry mad with Friday, what me done? I ask'd him what he meant; I told him I was not angry with him at all. No angry! No angry! says he, repeating the Words several Times, Why send Friday home away to my Nation? Why, (says I) Friday, did you not say you wish'd you were there? Yes, yes, says he, wish be both there, no wish Friday there, no Master there. In a Word, he would not think of going there without me; I go there! Friday, (says I) what shall I do there? He turn'd very quick upon me at this: You do great deal much good, says he, you teach wild Mans be good sober tame Mans; you tell them know God, pray and live new Life. Alas! Friday, (says I) thou knowest not what thou sayest, I am but an ignorant Man my self Yes, yes, says he, you teachee me Good, you teachee them Good. No, no, Friday, (says I) you shall go without me, leave me here to live by my self as I did before. He look'd confus'd again at that Word, and running to one of the Hatchets which he used to wear, he takes it up hastily, comes and gives it me, What must I do with this? says I to him. You take, kill Friday; (says he.) What must I kill you for? said I again. He returns very quick, What you send Friday away for? take, kill Friday, no send Friday away. This he spoke so earnestly, that I saw Tears stand in his Eyes: In a Word, I so plainly discover'd the utmost Affection in him to me, and a firm Resolution in him, that I told him then, and often after, that I would never send him away from me, if he was willing to stay with me.

马斯洛需求层次理论在《鲁滨逊漂流记》中的体现

《鲁滨逊漂流记》于1719年4月25日首次出版。该作品以日记体的形式呈现,是英国第一部现实主义长篇小说。主人公鲁滨逊荒岛求生的传奇经历强烈地吸引了一代代的读者,使得《鲁滨逊漂流记》成为世界文学宝库中一部不朽的名著。本文运用马斯洛需求层次理论分析该作品,对小说中主人公的需求及需求层次的发展过程进行梳理,剖析鲁滨逊的心路历程和命运发展轨迹，希冀为读者开辟一个新的解读视角。

马斯洛需求层次理论是人本主义科学的理论之一，由美国心理学家亚伯拉罕·马斯洛于1943年在一篇名为《人类激励理论》的论文中提出。文中将人类需求从低到高按层次分为五种：生理需求、安全需求、社交需求、尊重需求和自我实现需求。一般来说，这五种需求像阶梯一样从低到高，按层次逐级递升。当某一层次的需要相对满足了，就会向高一层次发展，追求更高一层次的需求就成为了行为的驱动力。马斯洛提出的人类需求五种层次在《鲁滨逊漂流记》这部作品中的主人公鲁滨逊身上均有体现。

一、生理需求

生理需求属于级别最低的需求，是人类维持自身生存的最基本要求，包括对呼吸、水、食物、睡眠、生理平衡、分泌和性的需求。如果这些需求（除性以外）任何一项不能得到满足，个体的生理机能就无法正常运转。换而言之，个体的生命就会因此受到威胁。从这个意义上来说，生理需求是推动人们行动的首要动力。只有当最基本的生理需求得到了必要的满足，其他的需求才能成为新的激励因素。鲁滨逊刚漂流到荒岛上时，首先要考虑的就是如何存活下来。为此，他想尽了一切办法来满足吃、喝、住这样一些基本的生理需求。

1659年9月1日，鲁滨逊乘坐的船遭遇风暴失事。他被海浪卷上了一个不知名的小岛。当劫后余生的欣喜过去后，他的情绪很快陷入了低谷。此刻的他又饥又渴，却没有任何东西可以解渴充饥。他在岛上寻找淡水，又将随身带的烟草放进嘴里以应对不断袭来的饥饿感。为了填饱肚子，他甚至游回大船，通过绳子攀爬上甲板，果然在舱室里发现了许多可供充饥果腹的食品：面包、三大块荷兰奶酪、腌羊肉、饼干、朗姆酒。除此之外，他还找到了锯子、斧头、锤子以及枪支弹药。他自制木筏把这些物资运回岛上。在岛上最初的日子里，他每天都去打猎，通过捕获野兔、山羊、鸟等动物来充饥。有一天，他不经意地在地上随手扔了一些作物的种子。几个月后，这片土地上居然长出了麦子。经过一年的试验，他掌握了岛上农业耕作的规律，于是他每年都种植小麦和稻谷，在收获的季节将收获的农作物剥皮并存放在陶罐中。经过多次试验，鲁滨逊甚至还做出了面包。在一次徒步旅行中，他发现了野甘蔗、甜瓜、葡萄、柠檬、柑橘等野生水果。他把一串葡萄带回来，将它晒成葡萄干以便长久储存。他还制造陷阱并困住了几只羊，在草地上圈养它们。几年后，羊已经繁殖到了43只。牧场能够产出足够的羊奶、黄油和奶酪。所有这些农作物、牲畜、葡萄干等为他提供了丰富的食物。

鲁滨逊一直在为自己积极营造一个稳定安逸的居住环境。他在一处水源地附近就地取材，搭建自己的屋子。为了避免塌方，屋子安有天花板，并用柱子予以支撑加固。他还自己动手建造简单的家具：桌子、椅子、床、沙发、毯子和其他必需品。鲁滨逊没有助手，工具不全，缺乏经验，做每一样物件都需要付出大量的精力和时间。正是在生存目标的驱动下，荒岛上的鲁滨逊一刻不歇地辛勤劳作，创造出所有的生活必需品。正如他亲口所说:"这一切足以说明我从来都没游手好闲过,为了丰衣足食、生活舒适,凡是需要做的事情,我都会不遗余力为之。"鲁滨逊在荒岛上用自己的双手和智慧创造了一个文明人所必需的生活条件,这不得不说是一个奇迹——人类生存的伟大奇迹。

二、安全需求

安全需求同样属于低级别的需求,其中包括对人身安全、生活稳定以及免遭痛苦、威胁或疾病等。安全需求反映了个体希望能够在安全有序的环境中工作和生活,并保证自身的生命和财产安全。当个体的生理需求得到实现后,需要进一步获取安全感的满足。

鲁滨逊初次登岛时就表现出了很强的安全意识。为了防范野兽,他选择爬到一棵长有刺的枝叶繁茂的大树上栖身。他还截下一段树枝,削成短棍用作防身的武器。在修建固定居所的选址上,鲁滨逊不但考虑到了日晒和滑坡等因素,更是将如何防范抵御野兽和食人生番的进攻作为重点。为此,他刻意在高耸的山峰后面选了一块小平地。山坡如墙壁一样陡峭,因而野兽和生番都无法冲下来攻击他。他又将链条安置在木桩之间,以防野兽和生番偷袭。晚上睡觉时,他习惯性地会在枕头下放置枪械以防不测。此外,他的住所没有安装门,仅用梯子进出房屋。这些举措极大地满足了他的安全感。

在荒岛上独自生活了 18 年后,鲁滨逊有一天在海滩上偶然发现了人类的足迹,这让他感到无比的恐惧。回到家后,他立即为住所赶制了双层屏障并用锚链加固,还将栅栏加厚到 10 英尺的墙上。他将 7 只火枪全部填充火药,以便随时射杀进犯的敌人。为了隐蔽他的帐篷,他用树枝填满了房子,秘密地转移了羊群,就这样过了两年胆战心惊的生活。又过了一年之后,他在海边看到了人的骷髅之后,变得更加谨慎。他停止了射击捕猎,只是设陷阱来猎获动物。在此期间,他极度缺乏安全感,神经始终处于紧绷状态。直到鲁滨逊杀死了两名野蛮人并救下了一名俘虏(鲁滨逊将这名俘虏称为"星期五")。星期五对他的忠诚和爱令他慢慢放下戒心,这才重获安全感,真正在岛上过上了幸福的生活。

三、社交需求

社交需求属于较高层次的需求,例如:对友谊、爱情以及归属关系的需求。人类不但具有自然属性,也具有社会属性。在满足生理需求和安全需求后,个体将渴望与周围的人建立各种社会关系,在人际交往中建立爱的需求和归属感的需求。其中,爱的需求包括给予他人爱和接受他人的爱。归属感则指人们希望从属于一定的群体并被群体所接纳和认同。

在岛上的 23 年里,孤寂困扰着鲁滨逊。他没有任何人可以交流,只有一只狗和两只猫与他做伴。身边的那只鹦鹉似乎都对他充满同情,总是调侃般地喊着:"可怜的鲁滨逊"。因为无人诉说,他只能通过记日记的方式来排遣自己的情绪。有一天,他看到一艘失事的船。尽管顾忌船上或许有食人生番攻击他,但他仍旧不假思索地去救人,因为他无比渴望与人交流。他希望船上有幸存者,他太想把自己的一切说给别人听了!但他的希望落空了,船上空无一人,他只得失望地回家了。

当鲁滨逊从食人族手中救下星期五,他教星期五说的第一个词就是"主人",并且让星期五记住"这是我的名字",由此确立了二人之间的主仆关系。鲁滨逊最初对星期五保持警惕心理,睡觉时与他相距甚远。但在与星期五相处的过程中,鲁滨逊发现这个仆人忠诚、可爱、诚恳,便逐渐与他成为好朋友。正是源于这种友谊,鲁滨逊甚至觉得:只要平平安安,哪怕永远和星期五待在这个地方,他都不介意。鲁滨逊愉快地教星期五打谷子、做面包、烤面包、打枪、捕猎、造船等技能。没过多久,星期五就变成了一个能干的帮手。鲁滨逊教授星期五英语,等到星期五慢慢能够表达,鲁滨逊终于在岛上有了一个可以倾诉与交流的伙伴。在鲁滨逊眼中,和星期五相处的日子是岛上最愉快的时光。

鲁滨逊回到英国结婚成家后,家人的爱及他对家庭的责任使他一度放弃了海外历险的想法。他的婚姻生活按他自己的话说"还算不错"。妻子去世后,他再次回到了岛上,除了带上工人、木匠和铁匠,还带了武器、火药、子弹、衣服及工具来建设他的领地。他将带来的物资分发给岛上的居民,还与他们签署了书面文件去划分土地,让精明能干的人制定规章制度进行管理。这样一来,岛上秩序井然,居民们各司其职,安居乐业,共同价值也渐渐凝聚起来,以至于当 300 个加勒比土著乘船来进犯时,岛上居民同仇敌忾不惜血战来捍卫他们的家园。振奋他们士气的正是融入居民们内心的归属感。

四、尊重需求

尊重需求属于较高层次的需求。人人都希望自己有稳定的社会地位,希望个人的能力和成就得到社会的承认。尊重的需求又可分为内部尊重和外部尊重。内部尊重是指一个人希望在各种不同情境中有实力、能胜任、充满信心、能独立自主。总之,内部尊重就是人的自尊。外部尊重是指一个人希望有地位、有威信,受到别人的尊重、信赖和高度评价。马斯洛认为,尊重需求得到满足,能使人对自己充满信心,对社会满腔热情,体验到自己活着的用处和价值。

鲁滨逊尽管流落荒岛,他仍然利用一切条件来保持着文明人的尊严。登岛伊始,他就在岛上树立起一个作为基督教标志物的十字架,并通过在木桩两侧刻下凹痕以计算星期和年月。而宗教与历法正是人类文明的典型代表。他没有像土著人那样赤身裸体,而是用布或羊皮制作的外套来遮蔽身体;他也没有像土著人般茹毛饮血,而是将食物烤熟后撒上盐再进食。他还制作面包、奶酪、陶器、家具、独木舟来不断提高自己的生活质量。他对各种野蛮行径深恶痛绝。当看到土著架起篝火吃人时,鲁滨逊谋划去攻击血腥的宴会。当察觉星期五依旧垂涎人肉时,鲁滨逊警告星期五要是吃人肉就杀了他。从始至终鲁滨逊都没有选择与土著人为伍,堕落到他们的生存状态。虽然他在这 28 年里遭受过疾病的折磨和生存的困难,但他一直保持勤奋,充满自信,不怨天尤人,表现出强大的自尊和自信。他的智慧、勇敢和勤劳不仅保障了他在岛上文明体面的生活,还收获了别人对他的尊重。

首先,他对星期五的救援和帮助赢得了星期五对他的尊重和忠诚。获救后,星期五跪在地上,吻着地面,把鲁滨逊的脚放到头上,宣誓终身为奴。之后,出于善良和扩充荒岛人口,鲁滨逊带领星期五拯救了星期五的父亲和西班牙人。在救他们之前,鲁滨逊已经让他们庄严起誓,保证绝对听从他的指挥,对他忠心耿耿,也不准觊觎他的位置。对于获救的人来说,鲁滨逊对他们的恩情就像他们的再生父母一般。船长第一个向他起誓:保证一生都不离开他,并保证永远站在他这边,终身不会忘记他的大恩大德。返回大船之后,船长给岛上留下了丰富的物资,并遵守诺言将鲁滨逊和星期五带回英国。多年后当鲁滨逊重返荒岛,岛上的居民(英国人、西班牙人和土著)恭敬地迎接他,称赞鲁滨逊对岛上所有的改造活动,对他表现出无与伦比的崇拜。鲁滨逊俨然像一位德高望重的君王一样凝视着这个岛。岛上居民毕恭毕敬,心甘情愿地接受他的管辖。鲁滨逊的权威正是建立在岛上居民对他的信任和尊重的基础之上。

五、自我实现需求

自我实现需求是最高层次的需求,指实现个人理想、抱负,发挥个人的能力到最大程度,完成与自己能力相称的一切事情的需求。自我实现需求也包括实现真善美这样至高人生境界的愿望。马斯洛提出,为满足自我实现需求所采取的途径是因人而异的。而达到自我实现层次的人不仅接受自己,也接受他人。鲁滨逊对荒岛从经济建设到制度建设,再到文化建设的全方位改造正体现了他"衣带渐宽终不悔,为伊消得人憔悴"的追梦过程。他的精神境界也在这个过程中不断提升,从而满足了自我实现的需求。

鲁滨逊的父亲期待自己的儿子过中产阶级的生活,并早已替鲁滨逊做好了人生规划。但鲁滨逊并不满足于稳定的生活状态。他的内心一直渴望航海,因此他坚定地选择了出海冒险以实现自己的梦想。前两次航行使他积累了丰富的航海经验,第四次出海由于船只失事,他漂流到了荒岛。但他勇敢地接受了现实,并利用他的智慧和创造力解决了一个个难题,将荒岛打造成为一个宜居的地方。他利用破船上留下的简单工具,亲手建造房屋,制造工具,打猎觅食,生产粮食,驯养动物,缝制衣物。经过鲁滨逊的努力,荒岛逐渐变得兴旺起来。为了管理庞大的人口,他与居民们签署了书面文件,明确规定了各人土地的位置和界限以及自己授予给他们的权力;他还在法国神父的指引下完善了岛上的婚姻法。制度建设保障了岛上生产和生活秩序有条不紊。除此之外,鲁滨逊还在岛上推行了文化建设。鲁滨逊解救了星期五后,还将欧洲的基本情况说给星期五听,有计划地向他灌输欧洲文化价值观,让他适应欧洲的生活方式。鲁滨逊不但成功改造了星期五,还对此后来到岛上的其他土著人进行同样的文化改造。他在荒岛上所做的一切,不但解决了自身生存的难题,并且积累了远远超出他预期的财富,诠释了鲁滨逊实现自我价值的过程。

鲁滨逊的自我实现还体现在他精神境界的提升上。经过多年的磨砺,鲁滨逊认识到:"我所追求的将不只是人间的快乐,而是一种至善至美的幸福,而且我也会得知,在这人间,生活毕竟还是有着高于这些情况的目的和意义,而这正是人们应该拥有的。"回到英国后,他没有独自享受种植园为他带来的巨额利润,而是果断决定用这笔钱回馈社会,例如建造修道院和接济穷人。他每年还给老船长100个葡萄牙金币来报恩。这些典型事例体现了鲁滨逊的责任感以及他对于至善至美人生境界的不断追求。

鲁滨逊的荒岛求生经历,使他从一个天真单纯的年轻人成长为一个成熟坚毅的男子汉。运用马斯洛需求层次理论去理解无数磨难锤炼下的主人公,将有助于丰富对这部经典作品的解读,也赋予了对《鲁滨逊漂流记》新的思考角度和解构空间。虽然鲁滨逊的荒岛生活距离我们已经过去数个世纪,但故事在今天仍有现实意义。我们应该学习鲁滨逊,即使身处逆境,也要心怀希望,勇敢地追求和实现自我价值。

主要参考文献

丹尼尔·笛福.鲁宾逊漂流记[M].梁遇春译.长春:吉林出版集团有限责任公司,2013.
刘炳善.英国文学简史[M].郑州:河南人民出版社,2007.
刘烨.马斯洛的人本哲学[M].呼和浩特:内蒙古文化出版社,2008.
秦玉杰.劳动者、资产者和殖民者三重身份的统一[J].延边教育学院学报,2008(6):16-18.
ABRAHAM H M. Motivation and Personality[M]. Beijing:China Social Sciences and Publishing House & Cheng Publisher,2008.

思考题

(1)谁是贝纳默基(Benamuckee)?他在土著人中起着怎样的作用?

(2)鲁滨逊为什么要给星期五灌输宗教信仰,让他信仰上帝?

(3)小说第24章中描写了一段鲁滨逊试探星期五的情节:鲁滨逊伴装要让星期五独自乘舟返回大陆,星期五却误以为主人对自己不满要赶走自己,情急之下甚至举起斧子表示与其让他离开主人不如让他结束自己的生命。你怎样理解这个部分?

Chapter 2　Frankenstein

by Mary Shelley

（*excerpts*）

 背景介绍

　　玛丽·雪莱的《弗兰肯斯坦》(全名《弗兰肯斯坦——现代普罗米修斯的故事》，其他译名有《科学怪人》《人造人的故事》等)，是文学史上的第一部科幻小说，作者也因此被誉为"科幻小说之母"。故事的灵感源于一次文学游戏。1816年，玛丽·雪莱同丈夫和拜伦等友人在日内瓦郊外聚会，大家提议每人讲一个恐怖故事，由此《弗兰肯斯坦》应运而生。自面世以来，该作已经被翻译成100多种语言，根据它改编的舞台剧和电影多达几十个版本。

　　小说主人公弗兰肯斯坦是个热衷于研究生命起源的生物学家。他怀着挑战和征服死亡的强烈渴望，频繁出没于藏尸间，尝试用从不同尸体上截取的肢体部分拼凑成一个巨大人体。当这个怪物终于获得生命睁开眼睛时，弗兰肯斯坦被他狰狞的面目吓得魂飞魄散夺路而逃。人造人饱受苦难和煎熬后，躲在村民家的棚屋内，透过墙上的缝隙暗中观察一家人的生活，了解人类的情感，学习人类的语言。他默默地行善，却无法得到人们的接纳，甚至遭到鄙视和唾弃。他继而决定向弗兰肯斯坦索要女伴、温暖和友情；但在弗兰肯斯坦违背了为他创造伴侣的承诺后，怪物掐死了弗兰肯斯坦的挚友并在弗兰肯斯坦新婚之夜杀死了新娘伊丽莎白。弗兰肯斯坦发誓要报仇，他一路追踪怪物到北极，直至奄奄一息，最终被在北极探险的沃尔顿船长发现。

 文本选读

Chapter 16

　　Cursed, cursed creator! Why did I live? Why, in that instant, did I not extinguish the spark of existence which you had so wantonly bestowed? I know not; despair had not yet taken possession of me; my feelings were those of rage and revenge. I could with pleasure have destroyed the cottage and its inhabitants, and have glutted myself with their shrieks and misery.

"When night came, I quitted my retreat, and wandered in the wood; and now, no longer restrained by the fear of discovery, I gave vent to my anguish in fearful howlings. I was like a wild beast that had broken the toils; destroying the objects that obstructed me, and ranging through the wood with a stag-like swiftness. O! what a miserable night I passed! the cold stars shone in mockery, and the bare trees waved their branches above me: now and then the sweet voice of a bird burst forth amidst the universal stillness. All, save I, were at rest or in enjoyment: I, like the arch-fiend, bore a hell within me; and, finding myself unsympathized with, wished to tear up the trees, spread havoc and destruction around me, and then to have sat down and enjoyed the ruin.

"But this was a luxury of sensation that could not endure; I became fatigued with excess of bodily exertion, and sank on the damp grass in the sick impotence of despair. There was none among the myriads of men that existed who would pity or assist me; and should I feel kindness towards my enemies? No: from that moment I declared everlasting war against the species, and, more than all, against him who had formed me, and sent me forth to this insupportable misery.

"The sun rose; I heard the voices of men, and knew that it was impossible to return to my retreat during that day. Accordingly, I hid myself in some thick underwood, determining to devote the ensuing hours to reflection on my situation.

"The pleasant sunshine, and the pure air of day, restored me to some degree of tranquility; and when I considered what had passed at the cottage, I could not help believing that I had been too hasty in my conclusions. I had certainly acted imprudently. It was apparent that my conversation had interested the father in my behalf, and I was a fool in having exposed my person to the horror of his children. I ought to have familiarized the old De Lacey to me, and by degrees to have discovered myself to the rest of his family, when they should have been prepared for my approach. But I did not believe my errors to be irretrievable; and, after much consideration, I resolved to return to the cottage, seek the old man, and by my representations win him to my party.

"These thoughts calmed me, and in the afternoon, I sank into a profound sleep; but the fever of my blood did not allow me to be visited by peaceful dreams. The horrible scene of the preceding day was forever acting before my eyes; the females were flying, and the enraged Felix tearing me from his father's feet. I awoke exhausted; and, finding that it was already night, I crept forth from my hiding-place, and went in search of food.

Chapter 2 Frankenstein *by Mary Shelley*

"When my hunger was appeased, I directed my steps towards the well-known path that conducted to the cottage. All there was at peace. I crept into my hovel, and remained in silent expectation of the accustomed hour when the family arose. That hour passed, the sun mounted high in the heavens, but the cottagers did not appear. I trembled violently, apprehending some dreadful misfortune. The inside of the cottage was dark, and I heard no motion; I cannot describe the agony of this suspense.

"Presently two countrymen passed by; but, pausing near the cottage, they entered into conversation, using violent gesticulations; but I did not understand what they said, as they spoke the language of the country, which differed from that of my protectors. Soon after, however, Felix approached with another man: I was surprised, as I knew that he had not quitted the cottage that morning, and waited anxiously to discover, from his discourse, the meaning of these unusual appearances.

"'Do you consider,' said his companion to him, 'that you will be obliged to pay three months' rent, and to lose the produce of your garden? I do not wish to take any unfair advantage, and I beg therefore that you will take some days to consider of your determination.'

"'It is utterly useless,' replied Felix; 'we can never again inhabit your cottage. The life of my father is in the greatest danger, owing to the dreadful circumstance that I have related. My wife and my sister will never recover their horror. I entreat you not to reason with me anymore. Take possession of your tenement, and let me fly from this place.'

"Felix trembled violently as he said this. He and his companion entered the cottage, in which they remained for a few minutes, and then departed. I never saw any of the family of De Lacey more.

"I continued for the remainder of the day in my hovel in a state of utter and stupid despair. My protectors had departed, and had broken the only link that held me to the world. For the first time the feelings of revenge and hatred filled my bosom, and I did not strive to control them; but, allowing myself to be borne away by the stream, I bent my mind towards injury and death. When I thought of my friends, of the mild voice of De Lacey, the gentle eyes of Agatha, and the exquisite beauty of the Arabian, these thoughts vanished, and a gush of tears somewhat soothed me. But again, when I reflected that they had spurned and deserted me, anger returned, a rage of anger; and, unable to injure anything human, I turned my fury towards inanimate objects. As night advanced, I placed a variety of combustibles around the cottage; and, after having destroyed every vestige of cultivation in the garden, I waited with forced impatience until the moon had sunk to commence my operations.

"As the night advanced, a fierce wind arose from the woods, and quickly dispersed the clouds that had loitered in the heavens: the blast tore along like a mighty avalanche, and produced a kind of insanity in my spirits, that burst all bounds of reason and reflection. I lighted the dry branch of a tree, and danced with fury around the devoted cottage, my eyes still fixed on the western horizon, the edge of which the moon nearly touched. A part of its orb was at length hid, and I waved my brand; it sunk, and, with a loud scream, I fired the straw, and heath, and bushes, which I had collected. The wind fanned the fire, and the cottage was quickly enveloped by the flames, which clung to it, and licked it with their forked and destroying tongues.

"As soon as I was convinced that no assistance could save any part of the habitation, I quitted the scene, and sought for refuge in the woods.

"And now, with the world before me, whither should I bend my steps? I resolved to fly far from the scene of my misfortunes; but to me, hated and despised, every country must be equally horrible. At length the thought of you crossed my mind. I learned from your papers that you were my father, my creator; and to whom could I apply with more fitness than to him who had given me life? Among the lessons that Felix had bestowed upon Safie geography had not been omitted: I had learned from these the relative situations of the different countries of the earth. You had mentioned Geneva as the name of your native town; and towards this place I resolved to proceed.

"But how was I to direct myself? I knew that I must travel in a south-westerly direction to reach my destination; but the sun was my only guide. I did not know the names of the towns that I was to pass through, nor could I ask information from a single human being; but I did not despair. From you only could I hope for succour, although towards you I felt no sentiment but that of hatred. Unfeeling, heartless creator! you had endowed me with perceptions and passions, and then cast me abroad an object for the scorn and horror of mankind. But on you only had I any claim for pity and redress, and from you I determined to seek that justice which I vainly attempted to gain from any other being that wore the human form.

"My travels were long, and the sufferings I endured intense. It was late in autumn when I quitted the district where I had so long resided. I travelled only at night, fearful of encountering the visage of a human being. Nature decayed around me, and the sun became heatless; rain and snow poured around me; mighty rivers were frozen; the surface of the earth was hard and chill, and bare, and I found no shelter. Oh, earth! how often did I imprecate curses on the cause of my being! The mildness of my nature had fled, and all within me was turned to gall and bitterness. The nearer I approached to your habitation, the more deeply did I feel the spirit of revenge enkindled in my heart. Snow fell, and the waters were hardened; but I rested not. A few incidents now and then directed me, and I possessed a map of the country; but I often wandered wide from my path. The agony of my feelings allowed me no respite: no incident occurred from which my rage and misery could not extract its food; but a circumstance that happened when I arrived on the confines of Switzerland, when the sun had recovered its warmth, and the earth again began to look green, confirmed in an especial manner the bitterness and horror of my feelings.

"I generally rested during the day, and travelled only when I was secured by night from the view of man. One morning, however, finding that my path lay through a deep wood, I ventured to continue my journey after the sun had risen; the day, which was one of the first of spring, cheered even me by the loveliness of its sunshine and the balminess of the air. I felt emotions of gentleness and pleasure, that had long appeared dead, revive within me. Half surprised by the novelty of these sensations, I allowed myself to be borne away by them; and, forgetting my solitude and deformity, dared to be happy. Soft tears again bedewed my cheeks, and I even raised my humid eyes with thankfulness towards the blessed sun which bestowed such joy upon me.

"I continued to wind among the paths of the wood, until I came to its boundary, which was skirted by a deep and rapid river, into which many of the trees bent their branches, now budding with the fresh spring. Here I paused, not exactly knowing what path to pursue, when I heard the sound of voices, that induced me to conceal myself under the shade of a cypress. I was scarcely hid, when a young girl came running towards the spot where I was concealed, laughing, as if she ran from someone in sport. She continued her course along the precipitous sides of the river, when suddenly her foot slipped, and she fell into the rapid stream. I rushed from my hiding-place; and, with extreme labour from the force of the current, saved her, and dragged her to shore. She was senseless; and I endeavoured, by every means in my power, to restore animation, when I was suddenly interrupted by the approach of a rustic, who was probably the person from whom she had playfully fled. On seeing me, he darted towards me, and tearing the girl from my arms, hastened towards the deeper parts of the wood. I followed speedily, I hardly knew why; but when the man saw me draw near, he aimed a gun, which he carried, at my body, and fired. I sunk to the ground, and my injurer, with increased swiftness, escaped into the wood.

"This was then the reward of my benevolence! I had saved a human being from destruction, and, as a recompense, I now writhed under the miserable pain of a wound, which shattered the flesh and bone. The feelings of kindness and gentleness, which I had entertained but a few moments before, gave place to hellish rage and gnashing of teeth. Inflamed by pain, I vowed eternal hatred and vengeance to all mankind. But the agony of my wound overcame me; my pulses paused, and I fainted.

"For some weeks I led a miserable life in the woods, endeavouring to cure the wound which I had received. The ball had entered my shoulder, and I knew not whether it had remained there or passed through; at any rate I had no means of extracting it. My sufferings were augmented also by the oppressive sense of the injustice and ingratitude of their infliction. My daily vows rose for revenge—a deep and deadly revenge, such as would alone compensate for the outrages and anguish I had endured.

"After some weeks my wound healed, and I continued my journey. The labours I endured were no longer to be alleviated by the bright sun or gentle breezes of spring; all joy was but a mockery, which insulted my desolate state, and made me feel more painfully that I was not made for the enjoyment of pleasure.

"But my toils now drew near a close; and, in two months from this time, I reached the environs of Geneva.

"It was evening when I arrived, and I retired to a hiding-place among the fields that surround it, to meditate in what manner I should apply to you. I was oppressed by fatigue and hunger, and far too unhappy to enjoy the gentle breezes of evening, or the prospect of the sun setting behind the stupendous mountains of Jura.

"At this time a slight sleep relieved me from the pain of reflection, which was disturbed by the approach of a beautiful child, who came running into the recess I had chosen, with all the sportiveness of infancy. Suddenly, as I gazed on him, an idea seized me, that this little creature was unprejudiced, and had lived too short a time to have imbibed a horror of deformity. If, therefore, I could seize him, and educate him as my companion and friend, I should not be so desolate in this peopled earth.

"Urged by this impulse, I seized on the boy as he passed, and drew him towards me. As soon as he beheld my form, he placed his hands before his eyes, and uttered a shrill scream: I drew his hand forcibly from his face, and said, 'Child, what is the meaning of this? I do not intend to hurt you; listen to me.'

"He struggled violently. 'Let me go,' he cried; 'monster! ugly wretch! you wish to eat me, and tear me to pieces—You are an ogre—Let me go, or I will tell my papa.'

"'Boy, you will never see your father again; you must come with me.'

"'Hideous monster! let me go, My papa is a Syndic—he is M. Frankenstein—he will punish you. You dare not keep me.'

"'Frankenstein! you belong then to my enemy—to him towards whom I have sworn eternal revenge; you shall be my first victim.'

"The child still struggled, and loaded me with epithets which carried despair to my heart; I grasped his throat to silence him, and in a moment, he lay dead at my feet.

"I gazed on my victim, and my heart swelled with exultation and hellish triumph: clapping my hands, I exclaimed, 'I, too, can create desolation; my enemy is not invulnerable; this death will carry despair to him, and a thousand other miseries shall torment and destroy him.'

"As I fixed my eyes on the child, I saw something glittering on his breast. I took it; it was a portrait of a most lovely woman. In spite of my malignity, it softened and attracted me. For a few moments I gazed with delight on her dark eyes, fringed by deep lashes, and her lovely lips; but presently my rage returned: I remembered that I was forever deprived of the delights that such beautiful creatures could bestow; and that she whose resemblance I contemplated would, in regarding me, have changed that air of divine benignity to one expressive of disgust and affright.

"Can you wonder that such thoughts transported me with rage? I only wonder that at that moment, instead of venting my sensations in exclamations and agony, I did not rush among mankind, and perish in the attempt to destroy them.

"While I was overcome by these feelings, I left the spot where I had committed the murder, and seeking a more secluded hiding-place, I entered a barn which had appeared to me to be empty. A woman was sleeping on some straw; she was young: not indeed so beautiful as her whose portrait I held; but of an agreeable aspect, and blooming in the loveliness of youth and health. Here, I thought, is one of those whose joy-imparting smiles are bestowed on all but me. And then I bent over her, and whispered, 'Awake, fairest, thy lover is near—he who would give his life but to obtain one look of affection from thine eyes: my beloved, awake!'

"The sleeper stirred; a thrill of terror ran through me. Should she indeed awake, and see me, and curse me, and denounce the murderer? Thus would she assuredly act, if her darkened eyes opened, and she beheld me. The thought was madness; it stirred the fiend within me—not I, but she shall suffer: the murder I have committed because I am forever robbed of all that she could give me, she shall atone. The crime had its source in her: be hers the punishment! Thanks to the lessons of Felix and the sanguinary laws of man, I had learned now to work mischief. I bent over her, and placed the portrait securely in one of the folds of her dress. She moved again, and I fled.

"For some days I haunted the spot where these scenes had taken place; sometimes wishing to see you, sometimes resolved to quit the world and its miseries forever. At length I wandered towards these mountains, and have ranged through their immense recesses, consumed by a burning passion which you alone can gratify. We may not part until you have promised to comply with my requisition. I am alone, and miserable; man will not associate with me; but one as deformed and horrible as myself would not deny herself to me. My companion must be of the same species, and have the same defects. This being you must create."

傲慢之罪——《弗兰肯斯坦》中的上帝情结和反智主义

这部科幻色彩浓厚的作品充满了作者对于"七宗罪"之首傲慢（hubris）的反思。傲慢不仅表现在主人公弗兰肯斯坦志在操控生死的内心渴望，同时也表现在对于知识和科学近乎狂热的追求所带来的毁灭性结果的反思。上帝情结和反智主义可以视作解读该作品的两个视角。

一、弗兰肯斯坦的上帝情结

上帝情结，指的是对于个人能力（ability）、个人特权（privilege）和个人绝无错误（infallibility）的不断膨胀且无法动摇的信念。如果说上帝情结在沃尔顿身上只是通过"elevates me to heaven"等语言有所影射，在主人公弗兰肯斯坦身上可谓是体现得淋漓尽致。弗兰肯斯坦在向沃尔顿叙述的一开始就介绍了自己早年强烈的求知欲（"I desired to learn; ... my enquires were directed to the metaphysical, or in its highest sense, the physical secrets of the world."），并且希望获得驱逐疾病和违抗死亡的个人特权（"what glory would attend the discovery, if I could banish disease from the human frame, and render man invulnerable to any but a violent death!"）。通过钻研和反复尝试，弗兰肯斯坦终于通过其个人能力创造出生命。尽管心怀恐惧，但此刻的他似乎俨然成了上帝的化身。他所造的"怪物"（Monster）多次称其为造物主"creator"或父亲"father"（影射"The Holy Father"）。怪物自认为像亚当一般被带到这个世界（"Like Adam, I was apparently united by no link to any other being in existence"），但自己并未得到过造物主对亚当一般的眷顾（"Remember, that I am thy creature; I ought to be thy Adam; but I am rather the fallen angel, whom thou drivest from joy for no misdeed."）。

该作采用了书信体和记叙体相穿插的形式，作为小说开头和结尾处书信的撰写者同时又是弗兰肯斯坦经历的倾听者和见证者，探险航海家沃尔顿（Walton）一方面是用来隐藏作者的叙事形象(narrative persona)同时又可以理解为弗兰肯斯坦的镜像(mirror image)。沃尔顿对于人类从未涉足的地理领域的好奇,本质上和弗兰肯斯坦对于人类从未成功涉足的知识领域——生死的挑战如出一辙。在与姐姐的书信中,沃尔顿谈到了自己前往北极探险的航海旅程,字里行间毫不隐晦地透露了他对于自然的强烈好奇和对险恶自然的征服欲望("I shall satiate my ardent curiosity with the sight of a part of the world never before imprinted by the foot of a man.")以及笃定的目标对炽烈的灵魂带来的抚慰和镇静作用。("I feel my heart glow with an enthusiasm which elevates me to heaven; for nothing contributes so much to tranquillize the mind as a steady purpose—a point on which the soul may fix its intellectual eye.")所以,对于用个人能力挑战自然且化身上帝在弗兰肯斯坦及其镜像叙述者沃尔顿身上均有体现。

二、作品透射的反智主义

该小说的全名《弗兰肯斯坦——现代普罗米修斯的故事》(*Frankenstein; or, The Modern Prometheus*)包含了希腊神话中的人物普罗米修斯。在希腊神话中,普罗米修斯是最具智慧的神明之一,名字有"先见之明"(forethought)的意思,他为人类盗取智慧之火的行为受到了宙斯的惩罚。作为弗兰肯斯坦的原型(archetype),不仅因为普罗米修斯是希腊神话中的"造物主",同时他的智慧及其智慧带来的严惩也呼应了本作品中透射出的反智主义思想。

反智主义,由美国历史学家理查德·霍夫斯塔特(Richard Hofstadter)于1962年出版的《美国生活中的反智主义》一书提出,该书描述了反智主义是如何贯穿于整个历史和"实用性的"美国文化,深入剖析了美国反智主义的历史渊源,说明教育、政治和商业等不同领域中知识分子与大众的矛盾。虽然反智主义这一概念的提出比《弗兰肯斯坦》的出版晚了近一个半世纪,但其提出的知识分子对于科技和知识的过分追求所带来的与大众的矛盾,在主人公弗兰肯斯坦博士身上有着更为极端化的呈现。

知识带来的除了进步还有理性和思考的痛苦,这一点在小说中不仅通过弗兰肯斯坦的叙述得到体现,在怪物的自白中也有提及。在怪物饱受人类的唾弃和鄙视之后,他说道:

"I cannot describe to you the agony that these reflections inflicted upon me; I tried to dispel them, but sorrow only increased with knowledge. Oh, that I had for ever remained in my native wood, nor known nor felt beyond the sensations of hunger, thirst, and heat!"

"我无法向你描述当我的脑子里盘旋着这些想法的时候,我有多么痛苦。我试图抛开这些想法,但是知道的事情越多,就越难过。哎,我真想永远待在原来的那片树林中,除了饥渴和冷暖这些感觉外,对其他一切都无知无觉啊。"

"Of what a strange nature is knowledge! It clings to the mind, when it has once seized on it, like a lichen on the rock. I wished sometimes to shake off all thought and feeling..."

"知识的特性太奇妙了!它一旦钻进了你的头脑,就会死死缠着你不放,好像粘在岩石上的地皮菜一样。有时候,我真希望把所有的思想和感觉都统统抛开……"

怪物的痛苦由于知识的"催化"显得尤为刻骨,连他自己都体会到知识仿佛像石头上生长的苔藓般紧紧地吸附于人的思想中。怪物被创造之初主要表现的是求生的本能,但随着知识的积累,它的内心平添了许多欲望和痛苦。它表现出对爱、伴侣以及被人们所接纳的渴望,而这些幻想最终破灭,他的诉求也未得到实现。由此,怪物的心中充斥着对造物主弗兰肯斯坦的仇恨,从而踏上了犯罪和复仇的不归路。

弗兰肯斯坦对于知识的追求在早年就表现得淋漓尽致:

"My temper was sometimes violent, and my passions vehement; but by some law in my temperature they were turned not towards childish pursuit but to an eager desire to learn."

他偶尔"暴躁的性格和炽烈的激情"全都导向了"学习(知识)的渴望"。弗兰肯斯坦在造人产生恶果之后,其后的自述中充斥着反思和忏悔之情。在怪物要求他再造一个女性伴侣的时候,他开始心生恐惧。

"I shuddered to think that future ages might curse me as their pest, whose selfishness had not hesitated to buy its own peace at the price, perhaps, of the existence of the whole human race."

他已经意识到自己所掌握的能力意味着什么。如果为了一己私欲,再造一个怪物,将会危及到整个人类。最终在弥留之际,弗兰肯斯坦更是意识到他傲慢的追求将其置于万劫不复之地:

"All my speculations and hopes are as nothing; and, like the archangel who aspired to omnipotence, I am chained in an eternal hell. My imagination was vivid, yet my powers of analysis and application were intense; by the union of these qualities I conceived the idea, and executed the creation of a man.... I trod heaven in my thoughts, now exulting in my powers, now burning with the idea of their effects. From my infancy I was imbued with high hopes and a lofty ambition; but how am I sunk!"

"我所有对未来的远大理想和抱负都化为泡影。我就像那个天使长,一心渴望获得万能的权威,到头来却被永远禁锢在地狱之中……那时,我在想象的世界里尽情遨游,时而为自己过人的才干而自鸣得意,时而又为自己的能力所能产生的影响而兴奋不已。从幼时起,我就有远大的理想,对自己寄予了崇高的期望,可是现在,我却如此潦倒落魄。"

在"追求全能"的过程中,他"永堕地狱"。丰富的想象力和理性分析能力,促成他去执行造人,他的至高期望和勃勃野心,他的傲慢和对于"天堂"的践踏最终导致了他的堕落和毁灭。

主要参考文献

高亮华.技术失控与人的责任——论弗兰肯斯坦问题[J].科学与社会,2016(3):128-135.

李伟昉.《弗兰肯斯坦》叙事艺术论[J].外国文学研究,2005(3):70-74.

张国庆.霍桑小说中的知识分子与科学家形象及其反智主义倾向[J].长江学术,2010(1):37-41.

HOFSTADTER R. Anti-Intellectualism in American Life[M]. New York:Vintage Books,2012.

SHELLEY M. Frankenstein[M]. New York:Pocket Books,2004.

思考题

(1)小说在开头和结尾采用了书信体叙事,这种叙事方法产生了什么叙事效果?如果是作者玛丽·雪莱亲自叙事,会产生什么样的叙事效果差异?

(2)弗兰肯斯坦称其所创造的生物为"怪物"(Monster),英文中表示"像怪物般的残暴"有 Monstrosity 一词。Monstrosity 这一主题,在小说中是否仅仅在被创造的怪物身上体现?

(3)小说中数次描写主人公弗兰肯斯坦在意志消沉时会选择外出游荡,且有非常细致的自然风光描写,作者对于大自然的描绘有何用意?

Chapter 3　Jane Eyre

by Charlotte Brontë

（*excerpts*）

 背景介绍

　　《简·爱》是英国女作家夏洛蒂·勃朗特（Charlotte Brontë, 1816—1855）创作的一部带有自传色彩的长篇小说。女主人公简·爱（简称"简"）出身卑微、相貌普通，但却意志坚定、独立自强、充满智慧，展现出了强大的人格魅力。当尊严受到挑衅时，她勇于反抗；在爱情降临时，她毅然冲破世俗的偏见，大胆追求属于自己的幸福。在作家勃朗特创作《简·爱》的时代，英国通过工业革命已然成为世界头号大国，但英国社会女性的从属地位仍无改观。在当时，婚姻是女性生存的唯一出路，妇女唯有依附于男性才能获得财富和地位，而简敢于向传统观念挑战，主动向她爱慕的异性倾诉衷情，并没有因阶级、地位、财富的不平等而胆怯退缩。女作家通过简的经历向世人宣告：女性并不是只能永远处于被动地位。她可以，也应该主动掌握自己的命运！这是19世纪英国文学史上一个全新的女性艺术形象。英国作家萨克雷对这部作品予以了高度的评价，称《简·爱》是"一位伟大天才的杰作"。

 文本选读

Chapter 26

　　I know not whether the day was fair or foul; in descending the drive, I gazed neither on sky nor earth: my heart was with my eyes; and both seemed migrated into Mr. Rochester's frame. I wanted to see the invisible thing on which, as we went along, he appeared to fasten a glance fierce and fell. I wanted to feel the thoughts whose force he seemed breasting and resisting.

　　At the churchyard wicket he stopped: he discovered I was quite out of breath. "Am I cruel in my love?" he said, "Delay an instant: lean on me, Jane."

　　And now I can recall the picture of the grey old house of God rising calm before me, of a rook wheeling round the steeple, of a ruddy morning sky beyond. I remember something, too, of the green grave-mounds; and I have not forgotten, either, two figures of strangers straying amongst the low hillocks and reading the mementoes graven on the few mossy head-stones. I noticed them, because, as they saw us, they passed round to the back of the church; and I doubted not they were going to enter by the side-aisle door and witness the ceremony. By Mr. Rochester they were not observed; he was earnestly looking at my face, from which the blood had, I daresay, momentarily fled: for I felt my forehead dewy, and my cheeks and lips cold. When I rallied, which I soon did, he walked gently with me up the path to the porch.

We entered the quiet and humble temple; the priest waited in his white surplice at the lowly altar, the clerk beside him. All was still: two shadows only moved in a remote corner. My conjecture had been correct: the strangers had slipped in before us, and they now stood by the vault of the Rochesters, their backs towards us, viewing through the rails the old times-stained marble tomb, where a kneeling angel guarded the remains of Damer de Rochester, slain at Marston Moor in the time of the civil wars, and of Elizabeth, his wife.

Our place was taken at the communion rails. Hearing a cautious step behind me, I glanced over my shoulder: one of the strangers-a gentleman, evidently-was advancing up the chancel. The service began. The explanation of the intent of matrimony was gone through; and then the clergyman came a step farther forward, and, bending slightly towards Mr. Rochester, went on.

"I require and charge you both (as ye will answer at the dreadful day of judgment, when the secrets of all hearts shall be disclosed), that if either of you know any impediment why ye may not lawfully be joined together in matrimony, ye do now confess it; for be ye well assured that so many as are coupled together otherwise than God's Word doth allow, are not joined together by God, neither is their matrimony lawful."

He paused, as the custom is. When is the pause after that sentence ever broken by reply? Not, perhaps, once in a hundred years. And the clergyman, who had not lifted his eyes from his book, and had held his breath but for a moment, was proceeding: his hand was already stretched towards Mr. Rochester, as his lips unclosed to ask, "Wilt thou have this woman for thy wedded wife? -" when a distinct and near voice said-"The marriage can not go on: I declare the existence of an impediment."

The clergyman looked up at the speaker and stood mute; the clerk did the same; Mr. Rochester moved slightly, as if an earthquake had rolled under his feet: taking a firmer footing, and not turning his head or eyes, he said, "Proceed."

Profound silence fell when he had uttered that word, with deep but low intonation. Presently Mr. Wood said-"I can not proceed without some investigation into what has been asserted, and evidence of its truth or falsehood."

"The ceremony is quite broken off," subjoined the voice behind us. "I am in a condition to prove my allegation: an insuperable impediment to this marriage exists."

Mr. Rochester heard, but heeded not: he stood stubborn and rigid, making no movement but to possesshimself of my hand. What a hot and strong grasp he had! and how like quarried marble was his pale, firm, massive front at this moment! How his eye shone, still watchful, and yet wild beneath!

Mr. Wood seemed at a loss. "What is the nature of the impediment?" he asked. "Perhaps it may be got over-explained away?"

"Hardly," was the answer. "I have called it insuperable, and I speak advisedly."

The speaker came forward and leaned on the rails. He continued, uttering each word distinctly, calmly, steadily, but not loudly.

"It simply consists in the existence of a previous marriage. Mr. Rochester has a wife now living."

My nerves vibrated to those low-spoken words as they had never vibrated to thunder-my blood felt their subtle violence as it had never felt frost or fire; but I was collected, and in no danger of swooning. I looked at Mr. Rochester: I made him look at me. His whole face was colourless rock: his eye was both spark and flint. He disavowed nothing: he seemed as if he would defy all things. Without speaking, without smiling, without seeming to recognise in me a human being, he only twined my waist with his arm and riveted me to his side.

"Who are you?" he asked of the intruder.

"My name is Briggs-a solicitor of- Street, London."

"And you would thrust on me a wife?"

"I would remind you of your lady's existence, sir, which the law recognises, if you do not."

"Favour me with an account of her- with her name, her parentage, her place of abode."

"Certainly." Mr. Briggs calmly took a paper from his pocket, and read out in a sort of official, nasal voice:-

"'I affirm and can prove that on the 20th of October, A. D. -, (a date of fifteen years back) Edward Fairfax Rochester, of Thornfield Hall, in the country of-, and of Ferndean Manor, in-shire, England, was married to my sister, Bertha Antoinetta Mason, daughter of Jonas Mason, merchant, and of Antoinetta his wife, a Creole, at-church, Spanish Town, Jamaica. The record of the marriage will be found in the register of that church-a copy of it is now in my possession. Signed, Richard Mason.'"

"That- if a genuine document- may prove I have been married, but it does not prove that the woman mentioned therein as my wife is still living."

"She was living three months ago," returned the lawyer.

"How do you know?"

"I have a witness to the fact, whose testimony even you, sir, will scarcely controvert."

"Produce him- or go to hell."

"I will produce him first- he is on the spot. Mr. Mason, have the goodness to step forward."

Mr. Rochester, on hearing the name, set his teeth; he experienced, too, a sort of strong convulsive quiver; near to him as I was, I felt the spasmodic movement of fury or despair run through his frame. The second stranger, who had hitherto lingered in the background, now drew near; a pale face looked over the solicitor's shoulder- yes, it was Mason himself. Mr. Rochester turned and glared at him. His eye, as I have often said, was a black eye: it had now a tawny, nay, a bloody light in its gloom; and his face flushed- olive cheek and hueless forehead received a glow as from spreading, ascending heart-fire: and he stirred, lifted his strong arm- he could have struck Mason, dashed him on the church-floor, shocked by ruthless blow the breath from his body- but Mason shrank away and cried faintly, "Good God!" Contempt fell cool on Mr. Rochester- his passion died as if a blight had shrivelled it up: he only asked- "What have you to say?"

An inaudible reply escaped Mason's white lips.

"The devil is in it if you cannot answer distinctly. I again demand, what have you to say?"

"Sir-sir," interrupted the clergyman, "do not forget you are in a sacred place." Then addressing Mason, he inquired gently, "Are you aware, sir, whether or not this gentleman's wife is still living?"

"Courage," urged the lawyer,- "speak out."

"She is now living at Thornfield Hall," said Mason, in more articulate tones: "I saw her there last April. I am her brother."

"At Thornfield Hall!" ejaculated the clergyman. "Impossible! I am an old resident in this neighbourhood, sir, and I never heard of a Mrs. Rochester at Thornfield Hall."

I saw a grim smile contort Mr. Rochester's lips, and he muttered-"No, by God! I took care that none should hear of it- or of her under that name. " He mused- for ten minutes he held counsel with himself: he formed his resolve, and announced it:-"Enough-all shall bolt out at once, like the bullet from the barrel.- Wood, close your book, and take off your surplice; John Green (to the clerk), leave the church: there will be no wedding to-day."The man obeyed.

Mr. Rochester continued, hardily and recklessly: "Bigamy is an ugly word! -I meant, however, to be a bigamist; but fate has out-manoeuvred me, or Providence has checked me,- perhaps the last. I am little better than a devil at this moment; and, as my pastor there would tell me, deserve no doubt the sternest judgments of God, even to the quenchless fire and deathless worm. Gentlemen, my plan is broken up:- what this lawyer and his client say is true: I have been married, and the woman to whom I was married lives! You say you never heard of a Mrs. Rochester at the house up yonder, Wood; but I daresay you have many a time inclined your ear to gossip about the mysterious lunatic kept there under watch and ward. Some have whispered to you that she is my bastard half-sister: some, my cast-off mistress. I now inform you that she is my wife, whom I married fifteen years ago,-Bertha Mason by name; sister of this resolute personage, who is now, with his quivering limbs and white cheeks, showing you what a stout heart men may bear. Cheer up, Dick! - never fear me! - I'd almost as soon strike a woman as you. Bertha Mason is mad; and she came of a mad family; idiots and maniacs through three generations! Her mother, the Creole, was both a mad-woman and a drunkard! - as I found out after I had wed the daughter: for they were silent on family secrets before. Bertha, like a dutiful child, copied her parent in both points. I had a charming partner- pure, wise, modest: you can fancy I was a happy man. I went through rich scenes! Oh! my experience has been heavenly, if you only knew it! But I owe you no further explanation. Briggs, Wood, Mason, -I invite you all to come up to the house and visit Mrs. Poole's patient, and my wife! You shall see what sort of a being I was cheated into espousing, and judge whether or not I had a right to break the compact, and seek sympathy with something at least human. This girl," he continued, looking at me, "knew no more than you, Wood, of the disgusting secret: she thought all was fair and legal, and never dreamt she was going to be entrapped into a feigned union with a defrauded wretch, already bound to a bad, mad, and embruted partner! Come, all of you, follow!"

Still holding me fast, he left the church: the three gentlemen came after. At the front door of the hall we found the carriage.

"Take it back to the coach-house, John," said Mr. Rochester coolly: "it will not be wanted to-day."

At our entrance, Mrs. Fairfax, Adele, Sophie, Leah, advanced to meet and greet us.

"To the right-about- every soul!" cried the master; "away with your congratulations! Who wants them? Not I! - they are fifteen years too late!"

He passed on and ascended the stairs, still holding my hand, and still beckoning the gentlemen to follow him, which they did. We mounted the first staircase, passed up the gallery, proceeded to the third storey: the low, black door, opened by Mr. Rochester's master-key, admitted us to the tapestried room, with its great bed and its pictorial cabinet.

"You know this place, Mason," said our guide; "she bit and stabbed you here."

He lifted the hangings from the wall, uncovering the second door: this, too, he opened. In a room without a window, there burnt a fire guarded by a high and strong fender, and a lamp suspended from the ceiling by a chain. Grace Poole bent over the fire, apparently cooking something in a saucepan. In the deep shade, at the farther end of the room, a figure ran backwards and forwards. What it was, whether beast or human being, one could not, at first sight, tell: it grovelled, seemingly, on all fours; it snatched and growled like some strange wild animal: but it was covered with clothing, and a quantity of dark, grizzled hair, wild as a mane, hid its head and face.

"Good-morrow, Mrs. Poole!" said Mr. Rochester. "How are you? and how is your charge to-day?"

"We're tolerable, sir, I thank you," replied Grace, lifting the boiling mess carefully on to the hob: "rather snappish, but not "rageous."

A fierce cry seemed to give the lie to her favourable report: the clothed hyena rose up, and stood tall on its hind-feet.

"Ah! sir, she sees you!" exclaimed Grace: "you'd better not stay."

"Only a few moments, Grace: you must allow me a few moments."

"Take care then, sir! - for God's sake, take care!"

The maniac bellowed: she parted her shaggy locks from her visage, and gazed wildly at her visitors. I recognised well that purple face,- those bloated features. Mrs. Poole advanced.

"Keep out of the way," said Mr. Rochester, thrusting her aside: "she has no knife now, I suppose, and I'm on my guard!"

"One never knows what she has, sir: she is so cunning: it is not in mortal discretion to fathom her craft."

"We had better leave her," whispered Mason.

"Go to the devil!" was his brother-in-law's recommendation.

"Ware!" cried Grace. The three gentlemen retreated simultaneously. Mr. Rochester flung me behind him: the lunatic sprang and grappled his throat viciously, and laid her teeth to his cheek: they struggled. She was a big woman, in stature almost equalling her husband, and corpulent besides: she showed virile force in the contest- more than once she almost throttled him, athletic as he was. He could have settled her with a well-planted blow; but he would not strike: he would only wrestle. At last he mastered her arms; Grace Poole gave him a cord, and he pinioned them behind her: with more rope, which was at hand, he bound her to a chair. The operation was performed amidst the fiercest yells and the most convulsive plunges. Mr. Rochester then turned to the spectators: he looked at them with a smile both acrid and desolate.

"That is my wife," said he. "Such is the sole conjugal embrace I am ever to know- such are the endearments which are to solace my leisure hours! And this is what I wished to have" (laying his hand on my shoulder): "this young girl, who stands so grave and quiet at the mouth of hell, looking collectedly at the gambols of a demon. I wanted her just as a change after that fierce ragout. Wood and Briggs, look at the difference! Compare these clear eyes with the red balls yonder- this face with that mask- this form with that bulk; then judge me, priest of the gospel and man of the law, and remember with what judgment ye judge ye shall be judged! Off with you now. I must shut up my prize."

再谈阁楼上的疯女人——后殖民女性主义视角解读《简·爱》

自小说《简·爱》(*Jane Eyre*, 1847) 问世以来, 评论界对此书的解读俯仰皆是, 视角各异。如认为简体现了一个贫苦女性的奋斗史, 有着"灰姑娘"般的传奇色彩; 或认为小说揭露了资本主义社会制度对底层群体个性的压抑, 抨击了资产阶级慈善机构的虚伪; 也有评论家从妇女解放的立场分析简的抗争在男权社会下的积极意义。20 世纪 70 年代英美女性主义的代表桑德拉·吉尔伯特(Sandra Gilbert)和苏珊·格芭(Susan Gubar)推出了专著《阁楼上的疯女人: 女作家与 19 世纪的文学想象》(*The Mad Woman in the Attic*, 1979)。该书从女性主义的角度评析了《简·爱》, 一个以往很少被评论家提及的人物——罗切斯特的疯妻子伯莎·梅森(简称"伯莎")被放在了聚光灯下。在心理分析模式下, 简和疯女人伯莎被解读为一个女性的两面。疯女人伯莎所具有的反抗精神和报复力正是简身上潜藏的对男性中心主义的反抗能力。

印度裔美国女学者加亚特里·斯皮瓦克(Gayatri Chakravorty Spivak)是当今著名的后殖民主义批评家,在阐述其文化批评观的过程中也把对西方经典文学作品的重读和解构放在极其重要的位置。她在《三位女性的文本以及对帝国主义的批判》(*Three Women's Texts and a Critique of Imperialism*,1986)一文中对《简·爱》的重读,成为后殖民文学批评的经典之作。斯皮瓦克同样也将关注的目光聚焦到了罗切斯特的疯夫人伯莎身上,让她再一次从隐秘的暗处走到了前台。

一、《简·爱》对女主人公简大加称颂,而对疯女人伯莎进行了妖魔化处理。这体现了作者文明/野蛮、西方/他者的二元对立思想

斯皮瓦克指出,伯莎的形象是在帝国主义的原则下塑造出来的,就如同萨义德所说是西方人根据自己的想象和需求幻构出来的。早在伯莎现身之前,小说就不断地在做出铺垫,极力渲染她给这所庄园所带来的麻烦和恐怖。

例如简刚到桑菲尔德庄园时,她对所处的新环境非常满意。可是惬意的生活很快就被庄园里发生的一系列离奇的事扰乱了。比如宁静的月夜响彻桑费尔德的嚎叫、夜深人静时走廊上的癫笑、男主人卧室神秘着火、陌生人梅森意外造访后被咬伤。甚至婚礼前夕,她的卧室被人意外闯入。一个身材高大、容貌可憎的女人在她房中对着镜子戴她的婚纱。罗切斯特告诉简,那不过是她的幻觉,可第二天早晨,她在房间里发现了婚纱的碎片。可以说,整部小说都在传递着一个信息:伯莎的存在就是对庄园秩序的威胁。

在小说第26章,正当罗切斯特与简举办婚礼时,来自加勒比的梅森先生带着律师闯入教堂终止了婚礼的进行。律师当着众人的面道出了一个惊人的秘密:罗切斯特15年前娶了梅森先生的妹妹伯莎·梅森为妻,这个女人至今还活着。罗切斯特承认了这一事实,并带领众人到桑菲尔德庄园看他的合法妻子——那个被关在三楼的疯女人。这个谜一样的女人终于现身了,小说这样描写伯莎的出场:

"In a room without a window, there burnt a fire guarded by a high and strong fender, and a lamp suspended from the ceiling by a chain. Grace Poole bent over the fire, apparently cooking something in a saucepan. In the deep shade, at the farther end of the room, a figure ran backwards and forwards. What it was, whether beast or human being, one could not, at first sight, tell: it grovelled, seemingly, on all fours; it snatched and growled like some strange wild animal: but it was covered with clothing, and a quantity of dark, grizzled hair, wild as a mane, hid its head and face."

"在一间没有窗户的房间里,燃着一堆火,外面围着一个又高又坚固的火炉围栏,从天花板上垂下的铁链子上悬挂着一盏灯。格雷斯·普尔俯身向着火,似乎在平底锅里炒着什么东西。在房间另一头的暗影里,一个人影在前后跑动,那究竟是什么,是动物还是人?粗粗一看难以辨认。它好像四肢着地趴着,又是抓又是叫,活像某种奇异的野生

动物,只不过有衣服蔽体罢了。一头黑白相间、乱如鬃毛的头发遮去了她的头和脸。"

斯皮瓦克以其敏锐的文学批评眼光从原著中摘出了这段文字,作者勃朗特在刻画伯莎外型特征时所使用的措辞不能不引发读者的思考。作家在这段短短的文字中分别使用了"beast(野兽)"和"wild animal(野生动物)"来描绘伯莎,并且使用"mane(马鬃)"来形容她的头发。行为上,"grovel(爬行,匍匐)""snatch(抓)""growl(嚎叫,咆哮)"等一系列动词的应用使得伯莎呈现出明显动物化的特征。正如斯皮瓦克所指出的,"通过刻画伯莎这个牙买加的克里奥尔人,勃朗特混淆了人与动物的界限"。伯莎是来自于加勒比地区的"非西方人",她的形象是经西方固定了的野蛮文化的代表。或者用斯皮瓦克的话来说,她是根据帝国主义原则创作出来的。因此她必须像野兽一样。一旦作为疯女人的她的身份介于人与兽之间变得模糊不清,她在法律条文或法律精神之下作为"人"的应有地位随即相应地得以削弱。

在小说接下来对伯莎与罗切斯特搏斗场景的描述中,勃朗特进一步对伯莎进行了妖魔化:

". . . the lunatic sprang and grappled his throat viciously, and laid her teeth to his cheek: they struggled. She was a big woman, in stature almost equalling her husband, and corpulent besides: she showed virile force in the contest-more than once she almost throttled him, athletic as he was."

"疯子猛扑过来,凶恶地卡住他喉咙,往脸上就咬。他们搏斗着。她是大个子女人,腰圆膀粗,身材几乎与她丈夫不相上下。厮打时显露出男性的力量,尽管罗切斯特先生有着运动员的体质,但不止一次险些儿被她闷死。"

伯莎的搏击方式也呈现出某些动物化特性——攻击对方的咽喉并利用牙齿进行撕咬。作为一个女人,她的身上不仅看不到一星半点女性应有的温顺与克己,甚至缺乏人的特征和意识。读者所看到的只有她的野蛮和兽性,因此对她的悲惨境遇不会产生丝毫的同情,甚至欲除之而后快,这样才能消除简内心的梦魇。可是这样的想法对伯莎公平吗?又有谁曾经跳出文本预设的立场之外想过这些问题:伯莎到底是一个怎样的人?罗切斯特为什么会同她结婚?她经历过怎样的遭遇才变成了野兽般的存在?

二、在西方的叙述话语中,克里奥尔女人被剥夺了自我表述的能力

自《简·爱》问世以来,简始终是一代代读者阅读的中心,勃朗特将她刻画成一个特立独行、自尊自强的女性。她出身卑微,却乐观积极;身材弱小,却不屈不挠。在与罗切斯特的相处中,简并未因罗切斯特的地位、财富而迁就取悦于他,而是始终追求一种平等的爱情。在父权制传统依旧强大的维多利亚时代,这样一个新女性形象的横空出世,颇有宣告女性解放的先声,作品表现出明显的社会进步意义。而在小说中疯女人伯莎是作为简的对立面出现的。这个人物形象被塑造得极度扭曲,就像一个恶魔横亘在简和罗切斯特之间,阻碍了他们爱情的发展。

然而通过细读文本,我们会发现一个秘密,女作家勃朗特对于这两名女性的叙述话语所做的安排是不一样的。女作家对简的大篇幅正面描述自不必提,疯女人伯莎的形象则多是通过她丈夫——罗切斯特从反面叙述的(也可以说是罗切斯特的一面之词)。整个小说中没有来自于伯莎的只言片语,她的话语权被作者剥夺了。在小说第27章中,罗切斯特对于自己的第一段婚姻有一段叙述:

"Well, Jane, being so, it was his resolution to keep the property together; he could not bear the idea of dividing his estate and leaving me a fair portion: all, he resolved, should go to my brother, Rowland. Yet as little could he endure that a son of his should be a poor man. I must be provided for by a wealthy marriage. He sought me a partner betimes. Mr. Mason, a West India planter and merchant, was his old acquaintance. He was certain his possessions were real and vast: he made inquiries. Mr. Mason, he found, had a son and daughter; and he learned from him that he could and would give the latter a fortune of thirty thousand pounds: that sufficed. When I left college, I was sent out to Jamaica, to espouse a bride already courted for me..."

"好吧,简,出于贪婪,我父亲决心把他的财产合在一起,而不能容忍把它分割,留给我相当一部分。他决定一切都归我哥哥罗兰,然而也不忍心我这个儿子成为穷光蛋,还得通过一桩富有的婚事解决我的生计。不久之后他替我找了个伴侣。他有一个叫梅森先生的老相识,是西印度的种植园主和商人。他作了调查,肯定梅森先生家业很大。他发现梅森先生有一双儿女,还知道他能够,也愿意给他的女儿三万英镑的财产,那已经足够了。我一离开大学就被送往牙买加,跟一个已经替我求了爱的新娘成婚。"

根据罗切斯特的描述,他的婚姻是家族利益的产物。由于在家中并非长子,他无法继承父亲留下的财产。而与伯莎的婚姻意味着这个克里奥尔女人带来的三万英镑嫁妆能确保他过上衣食无忧的生活。在小说中,罗切斯特声称他对于这桩婚事的安排并非是情愿的,只是出于"幼稚无知,没有经验,以为自己爱上了她。",再加上"她的亲戚们怂恿我;情敌们激怒我;她来勾引我。"而罗切斯特绝口不提的一个事实是当时的法律剥夺了已婚妇女支配嫁妆的权利,嫁妆只能由丈夫掌管。所以结婚之后,他顺理成章地霸占了这笔钱财。这一点无疑再现了帝国主义殖民暴力的寓言。罗切斯特通过婚姻手段攫取了伯莎的财富,正如大英帝国在加勒比对殖民地人民的掠夺。两者同样都是通过不光彩的手段完成了资本的原始积累。可以想象,如果没有这笔从殖民地掠夺的财富,也许就没有庞大的桑菲尔德庄园,罗切斯特也就没有资本出入各类名流的交际场所,更不会到欧洲各地旅行浪荡。而一旦目的达到,罗切斯特开始露出了虚伪的面孔,他开始诋毁自己的妻子:

"I never loved, I never esteemed, I did not even know her. I was not sure of the existence of one virtue in her nature: I had marked neither modesty, nor benevolence, nor candour, nor refinement in her mind or manners- and, I married her:- gross, grovelling, mole-eyed blockhead that I was!"

"我从来没有爱过她,敬重过她,甚至也不了解她。她天性中有没有一种美德我都没有把握。在她的内心或举止中,我既没有看到谦逊和仁慈,也没有看到坦诚和高雅。而我娶了她——我是多么粗俗,多么没有骨气!真是个有眼无珠的大傻瓜!"

不但如此,罗切斯特甚至恶语中伤她的家族:

"Bertha Mason is mad; and she came of a mad family; idiots and maniacs through three generations! Her mother, the Creole, was both a mad-woman and a drunkard! - as I found out after I had wed the daughter: for they were silent on family secrets before."

"伯莎·梅森是疯子,而且出身于一个疯人家庭——一连三代的白痴和疯子!她的母亲,那个克里奥人既是个疯女人,又是个酒鬼!——我是同她的女儿结婚后才发现的,因为以前他们对家庭的秘密守口如瓶。"

罗切斯特痛恨与妻子有关的一切,甚至连伯莎成长的西印度群岛,在他眼中也变得有几分魔鬼般的狰狞:

"One night I had been awakened by her yells- (since the medical men had pronounced her mad, she had, of course, been shut up)- it was a fiery West Indian night; one of the description that frequently precede the hurricanes of those climates. Being unable to sleep in bed, I got up and opened the window. The air was like sulphur-steams- I could find no refreshment anywhere. Mosquitoes came buzzing in and hummed sullenly round the room; the sea, which I could hear from thence, rumbled dull like an earthquake- black clouds were casting up over it; the moon was setting in the waves, broad and red, like a hot cannon-ball- she threw her last bloody glance over a world quivering with the ferment of tempest…"

"This life," said I at last, "is hell: this is the air- those are the sounds of the bottomless pit!"

"一天夜里我被她的叫喊惊醒了(自从医生宣布她疯了以后,她当然是被关起来了)——那是西印度群岛火燎似的夜晚,这种天气常常是飓风到来的前奏。我难以入睡,便爬起来开了窗。空气像含硫的蒸气——到处都让人提不起神来。蚊子嗡嗡地飞进来,阴沉地在房间里打转。在那儿我能听到大海之声,像地震一般沉闷地隆隆响着。黑云在大海上空集结,月亮沉落在宽阔的红色波浪上,像一个滚烫的炮弹——向颤抖着正酝酿风暴的海洋,投去血色的目光……"

"'这种生活,'我终于说,'是地狱!这就是无底深渊里的空气和声音!'"

女作家勃朗特帝国意识支配下的话语主导以及罗切斯特单视角的叙事话语呈现给读者的只能是一个在无序、野蛮的殖民地出生的低贱的疯女人。在"西方的凝视"中,被凝视者成了赤裸裸的被审视评判的客体。他们"生理上劣等,文化上落后,奇异怪诞,一成不变。"斯皮瓦克在《贱民能够说话吗》一文中提道:"贱民是不能够说话的。他们即使发表了自己的意见,也是不会被听到的"。因此在小说中,伯莎无法为自己代言和辩解。她的癫笑、咆哮、呐喊所传达的反抗之声不仅不会被关注,还被殖民者建构为癫狂的表征。因此罗切斯特将伯莎禁闭在阁楼上的行为显得合情合理;罗切斯特对自己的妻子不闻不问,跑到欧洲大陆去寻欢作乐,也变成了可以理解甚至值得同情的一种解脱方式。总而言之,罗切斯特的一面之辞就是对伯莎的"缺席审判"。

在《三位女性的文本以及对帝国主义的批判》一文中,斯皮瓦克还对勃朗特为伯莎安排的悲剧性结局提出了质疑。以往读者通常将疯女人看作是阻挡简和罗切斯特幸福婚姻的绊脚石,因此她纵火烧毁庄园,毁灭自己的结局被视为是理所当然的。小说叙事的合理性从来没有受到过怀疑。而斯皮瓦克认为牺牲掉伯莎反映了勃朗特活跃的帝国意识形态。具体来说,罗彻斯特和伯莎的婚姻代表着合法家庭地位,而简与罗彻斯特之间的私情则代表着非法家庭地位。如何让伯莎从合法家庭地位上让位给简呢?唯有她的毁灭才能成全简,让简名正言顺地和罗切斯特组成合法家庭。作者只有通过这种安排才能成全简,令简成为白人世界里自强不息追求平等爱情的典范,最终成为英国乃至世界文学史上闪耀女性主义光芒的个体英雄,这不能不说是典型的帝国主义认知暴力的体现。

主要参考文献

萨义德 E W. 东方学[M]. 王宇根,译. 北京:生活读书新知三联书店,1999.

符海平,刘向辉.《简爱》的后殖民主义视角再解读[J]. 长春师范学院学报(人文社会科学版),2012(4):88-91.

斯皮瓦克. 三位女性的文本以及对帝国主义的批判[A]. 吉尔伯特. 后殖民批评[C]. 杨乃乔,毛荣运,刘须明,译. 北京:北京大学出版社,2001.

勃朗特. 简·爱[M]. 黄源深,译. 南京:译林出版社,1993.

思考题

(1) 你认为简与罗切斯特结合的最大阻碍是什么?

(2) 罗切斯特为什么选择将疯女人伯莎·梅森安置在桑菲尔德,桑菲尔德庄园又有何象征意义?

(3) 罗切斯特曾经说过:"雇一个情妇仅次于购买一个奴隶,两者就本性和地位而言都是低下的",你怎样理解这句话?

(4) 作为女主角,简·爱的身上是否有帝国主义意识的流露?试结合文本进行分析。

Chapter 4　The Gift of the Magi

by O · Henry

 背景介绍

《麦琪的礼物》是"世界三大短篇小说之王"之一的美国作家欧·亨利(O·Henry, 1862—1910)最初于1905年创作并发表的代表作。1906年4月该作品被收录到欧·亨利名为 *The Four Million* 的短片故事集之中。数字"四百万"暗合当时纽约市大约的人口数量,纽约也正是欧·亨利笔下许多故事所发生的背景城市。该小说集囊括了作者许多耳熟能详的短篇作品,包括《警察与赞美诗》("The Cop and the Anthem")、《二十年后》("After Twenty Years")等。而《麦琪的礼物》更是其中最广为流传和收录的经典之作。故事讲述了一对平凡的年轻夫妇在经济拮据的境况下倾其所有地为对方秘密准备圣诞礼物的故事。故事的男主人公Jim是一位收入仅够维系日常生活的工薪阶层,女主人公Della是一位善良贤惠的家庭主妇。他们分别为对方舍弃了自己最为珍贵的"宝物",而换来的礼物却因此变得似乎"毫无作用"。

 文本选读

One dollar and eighty-seven cents. That was all. And sixty cents of it was in pennies. Pennies saved one and two at a time by bulldozing the grocer and the vegetable man and the butcher until one's cheeks burned with the silent imputation of parsimony that such close dealing implied. Three times Della counted it. One dollar and eighty-seven cents. And the next day would be Christmas.

There was clearly nothing left to do but flop down on the shabby little couch and howl. So Della did it. Which instigates the moral reflection that life is made up of sobs, sniffles, and smiles, with sniffles predominating.

While the mistress of the home is gradually subsiding from the first stage to the second, take a look at the home. A furnished flat at $8 per week. It did not exactly beggar description, but it certainly had that word on the look-out for the mendicancy squad.

In the vestibule below was a letter-box into which no letter would go, and an electric button from which no mortal finger could coax a ring. Also appertaining thereunto was a card bearing the name "Mr. James Dillingham Young."

The "Dillingham" had been flung to the breeze during a former period of prosperity when its possessor was being paid $30 per week. Now, when the income was shrunk to $20, the letters of "Dillingham" looked blurred, as though they were thinking seriously of contracting to a modest and unassuming D. But whenever Mr. James Dillingham Young came home and reached his flat above he was called "Jim" and greatly hugged by Mrs. James Dillingham Young, already introduced to you as Della. Which is all very good.

Della finished her cry and attended to her cheeks with the powder rag. She stood by the window and looked out dully at a grey cat walking a grey fence in a grey backyard. To-morrow would be Christmas Day, and she had only $1.87 with which to buy Jim a present. She had been saving every penny she could for months, with this result. Twenty dollars a week doesn't go far. Expenses had been greater than she had calculated. They always are. Only $1.87 to buy a present for Jim. Her Jim. Many a happy hour she had spent planning for something nice for him. Something fine and rare and sterling—something just a little bit near to being worthy of the honour of being owned by Jim.

There was a pier-glass between the windows of the room. Perhaps you have seen a pier-glassin an $8 Bat. A very thin and very agile person may, by observing his reflection in a rapid sequence of longitudinal strips, obtain a fairly accurate conception of his looks. Della, being slender, had mastered the art.

Suddenly she whirled from the window and stood before the glass. Her eyes were shining brilliantly, but her face had lost its colour within twenty seconds. Rapidly she pulled down her hair and let it fall to its full length.

Now, there were two possessions of the James Dillingham Youngs in which they both took a mighty pride. One was Jim's gold watch that had been his father's and his grandfather's. The other was Della's hair. Had the Queen of Sheba lived in the flat across the airshaft, Della would have let her hair hang out of the window some day to dry just to depreciate Her Majesty's jewels and gifts. Had King Solomon been the janitor, with all his treasures piled up in the basement, Jim would have pulled out his watch every time he passed, just to see him pluck at his beard from envy.

So now Della's beautiful hair fell about her, rippling and shining like a cascade of brown waters. It reached below her knee and made itself almost a garment for her. And then she did it up again nervously and quickly. Once she faltered for a minute and stood still while a tear or two splashed on the worn red carpet.

On went her old brown jacket; on went her old brown hat. With a whirl of skirts and with the brilliant sparkle still in her eyes, she cluttered out of the door and down the stairs to the street.

Where she stopped the sign read: 'Mme Sofronie. Hair Goods of All Kinds.' One Eight up Della ran, and collected herself, panting. Madame, large, too white, chilly, hardly looked the 'Sofronie.'

"Will you buy my hair?" asked Della.

"I buy hair," said Madame. "Take yer hat off and let's have a sight at the looks of it."

Down rippled the brown cascade.

"Twenty dollars," said Madame, lifting the mass with a practised hand.

"Give it to me quick." said Della.

Oh, and the next two hours tripped by on rosy wings. Forget the hashed metaphor. She was ransacking the stores for Jim's present.

She found it at last. It surely had been made for Jim and no one else. There was no other like it in any of the stores, and she had turned all of them inside out. It was a platinum fob chain simple and chaste in design, properly proclaiming its value by substance alone and not by meretricious ornamentation—as all good things should do. It was even worthy of The Watch. As soon as she saw it she knew that it must be Jim's. It was like him. Quietness and value—the description applied to both. Twenty-one dollars they took from her for it, and she hurried home with the 78 cents. With that chain on his watch Jim might be properly anxious about the time in any company. Grand as the watch was, he sometimes looked at it on the sly on account of the old leather strap that he used in place of a chain.

When Della reached home her intoxication gave way a little to prudence and reason. She got out her curling irons and lighted the gas and went to work repairing the ravages made by generosity added to love. Which is always a tremendous task dear friends—a mammoth task.

Within forty minutes her head was covered with tiny, close-lying curls that made her look wonderfully like a truant schoolboy. She looked at her reflection in the mirror long, carefully, and critically.

"If Jim doesn't kill me," she said to herself, "before he takes a second look at me, he'll say I look like a Coney Island chorus girl. But what could I do-oh! what could I do with a dollar and eighty-seven cents?"

At 7 o'clock the coffee was made and the frying-pan was on the back of the stove hot and ready to cook the chops.

Jim was never late. Della doubled the fob chain in her hand and sat on the corner of the table near the door that he always entered. Then she heard his step on the stair away down on the first flight, and she turned white for just a moment. She had a habit of saying little silent prayers about the simplest everydaythings, and now she whispered: "Please, God, make him think I am still pretty."

The door opened and Jim stepped in and closed it. He looked thin and very serious. Poor fellow, he was only twenty-two—and to be burdened with a family! He needed a new overcoat and he was with out gloves.

Jim stepped inside the door, as immovable as a setter at the scent of quail. His eyes were fixed upon Della, and there was an expression in them that she could not read, and it terrified her. It was not anger, nor surprise, nor disapproval, nor horror, nor any of the sentiments that she had been prepared for. He simply stared at her fixedly with that peculiar expression on his face.

Della wriggled off the table and went for him.

"Jim, darling," she cried, "don't look at me that way. I had my hair cut off and sold it because I couldn't have lived through Christmas without giving you a present. It'll grow out again—you won't mind, will you? I just had to do it. My hair grows awfully fast. Say 'Merry Christmas!' Jim, and let's be happy. You don't know what a nice—what a beautiful, nice gift I've got for you."

"You've cut off your hair?" asked Jim, laboriously, as if he had not arrived at that patent fact yet, even after the hardest mental labour.

"Cut it off and sold it," said Della. "Don't you like me just as well, anyhow? I'm me without my hair, ain't I?"

Jim looked about the room curiously.

"You say your hair is gone?" he said, with an air almost of idiocy.

"You needn't look for it," said Della. "It's sold, I tell you—sold and gone, too. It's Christmas Eve, boy. Be good to me, for it went for you. Maybe the hairs of my head were numbered," she went on with a sudden serious sweetness, "but nobody could ever count my love for you. Shall I put the chops on, Jim?"

Out of his trance Jim seemed quickly to wake. He enfolded his Della. For ten seconds let us regard with discreet scrutiny some inconsequential object in the other direction. Eight dollars a week or a million a year—what is the difference? A mathematician or a wit would give you the wrong answer. The magi brought valuable gifts, but that was not among them. This dark assertion will be illuminated later on.

Jim drew a package from his overcoat pocket and threw it upon the table.

"Don't make any mistake, Dell," he said, "about me. I don't think there's anything in the way of a haircut or a shave or a shampoo that could make me like my girl any less. But if you'll unwrap that package you may see why you had me going a while at first."

White fingers and nimble tore at the string and paper. And then an ecstatic scream of joy; and then, alas! a quick feminine change to hysterical tears and wails, necessitating the immediate employment of all the comforting powers of the lord of the flat.

For there lay The Combs—the set of combs, side and back, that Della had worshipped for long in a Broadway window. Beautiful combs, pure tortoise-shell, with jewelled rims—just the shade to wear in the beautiful vanished hair. They were expensive combs, she knew, and her heart had simply craved and yearned over them without the least hope of possession. And now, they were hers, but the tresses that should have adorned the coveted adornments were gone.

But she hugged them to her bosom, and at length she was able to look up with dim eyes and a smile and say: "My hair grows so fast, Jim!"

And then Della leaped up like a little singed cat and cried, "Oh, oh!"

Jim had not yet seen his beautiful present. She held it out to him eagerly upon her open palm. The dull precious metal seemed to flash with a reflection of her bright and ardent spirit.

"Isn't it a dandy, Jim? I hunted all over town to find it. You'll have to look at the time a hundred times a day now. Give me your watch. I want to see how it looks on it."

Instead of obeying, Jim tumbled down on the couch and put his hands under the back of his head and smiled.

"Dell," said he, "let's put our Christmas presents away and keep 'em a while. They're too nice to use just at present. I sold the watch to get the money to buy your combs. And now suppose you put the chops on."

The magi, as you know, were wise men—wonderfully wise men—who brought gifts to the Babe in the manger. They invented the art of giving Christmas presents. Being wise, their gifts were no doubt wise ones, possibly bearing the privilege of exchange in case of duplication. And here I have lamely related to you the uneventful chronicle of two foolish children in a flat who most unwisely sacrificed for each other the greatest treasures of their house. But in a last word to the wise of these days let it be said that of all who give gifts these two were the wisest. Of all who give and receive gifts, such as they are wisest. Everywhere they are wisest. They are the magi.

暗藏于动人真情背后的玄机
——欧·亨利《麦琪的礼物》中的叙事策略

欧·亨利创作的短篇小说情节丰富多彩,语言诙谐幽默,悬念设计巧妙,结尾多有出人意料的反转(后被称为"欧·亨利式的结尾")。《麦琪的礼物》可谓是囊括了其文学创作特色的最富代表性的作品。但是,灵光一现的情节创意必须辅以精妙的叙事策略,才能突出故事的艺术感染力。读者在被《麦琪的礼物》中主人公夫妇真挚的爱情打动之余,理应细细品读欧·亨利在此作中运用的叙事视角和叙事线索等策略。

一、第三人称全知视角和有限视角的交替

叙述视角也称叙述聚焦,是指叙述语言中对故事内容进行观察和讲述的特定角度。《麦奇的礼物》从大体上来看,采用了经典的第三人称全知视角(Third-Person Omniscient Point of View)。所谓全知视角,也就是叙述者比任何人物知道的都多(叙述者>人物),他全知、全觉、全在。申丹在她的视角模式中则将传统的全知视角归于"零视角"类型,并指出全知视角(零视角)的特点是"'上帝'般的全知全能叙述者可以从任何角度、任何时空来叙述;既可以高高在上地鸟瞰概貌,也可以看到在其他地方同时发生的一切;对人物的过去、现在和未来均了如指掌,也可任意透视人物的内心"。全知视角能够超越限制地去剖析和展示人物的内心活动以及情节的发展。

《麦琪的礼物》中大部分场景描写、心理描写用的是第三人称全知视角。在故事开篇描绘到 Della 数钱的场景时,便是第三人称全知视角的运用。"One dollar and eighty-seven cents. That was all. ... Pennies saved one and two at a time by bulldozing the grocer and the vegetable man and the butcher until one's cheeks burned with the silent imputation of parsimony that such close dealing implied."这里全知的叙述者,不仅知道确切的金额,更是交代了这看起来微不足道的一笔存款是女主人公与商贩们一分一厘地讨价还价所得来的。Della 因为经济的拮据掩面而泣时,作者更是提到了"生活正是由一系列的啜泣、抽噎和笑容构成。但抽噎是绝对的主导地位"("life is made up of sobs, sniffles, and smiles, with sniffles predominating.")。"在全知模式中,叙述声音与叙述眼光常常统一于叙述者。全知叙述者通常与人物保持一定的距离,具有一定的权威性和客观性"。从开篇的措辞中我们便可对叙述者的权威性有所体会,"silent imputation of parsimony"以及"instigates the moral reflection"这样的表达和后文夫妇对话中的语体风格截然不同,叙述者站在客观的角度用权威的口吻揭示了作为人生主旋律的苦难和悲伤,让读者能够清晰体会到女主人公生活中的无奈。此外,第三人称全知叙述也能帮助读者获取更多的细节信息。第三段开篇"While the mistress of the home is gradually subsiding from the first stage to the second, take a look at the home."这一句似乎是全知叙述者在引导读者一起来"看看这个家",继而展开对家居环境的细节描写。无人问津的信箱和损坏的门铃更是让读者领略到主人公近乎"贫民窟"(mendicancy squad)一般的生活境况。随着情节的展开,接下来 Della 忍痛割爱卖掉长发和为丈夫 Jim 挑选购买礼物的场景,同样是用第三人称全知视角进行呈现,从而刻画出 Della 为爱而做出的舍弃和牺牲。

但是,全文并非无一例外地用到了第三人称全知视角,欧·亨利在文中也运用到了叙述视角的切换——第三人称全知视角会有选择性地切换为第三人称有限视角(Third-Person Omniscient Point of View)。在第三人称有限视角的叙述中,叙述者一般采用故事中人物的眼光来叙事,从而不再是全知全在。在《麦琪的礼物》戏剧冲突进入高潮之际,作者将叙述视角切换为女主人公 Della 的视角。所以在丈夫回来见到她剪短了的头发时,脸上流露出的神情被描绘为:"那既不是愤怒,也不是惊讶,又不是不满,更不是嫌恶,不是她所预料的任何一种。他只带着那种奇特的神情凝视着德拉。"("It was not anger, nor surprise, nor disapproval, nor horror, nor any of the sentiments that she had been prepared for. He simply stared at her fixedly with that peculiar expression on his face.")当 Della 拿出精心挑选的表链要求带到怀表上时,Jim 的反应却是"没有照着她的话去做,却倒在榻上,双手枕着头,笑了起来。"("Instead of obeying, Jim tumbled down on the couch and put his hands under the back of his head and smiled.")这里通过 Della 的视角看到的 Jim 的表情和反应使她自己和读者都充满疑惑甚至隐约地不安,似乎自己巨大牺牲所换来的礼物,没有达到期待中的效果。而这层层递进的悬念,正是为最后意料之外而又温馨感人的"欧·亨利式的结尾"作出铺垫。

第三人称全知视角能够让读者客观地领略到故事场景和人物内心等点滴细节,而偶尔地切换到第三人称有限视角又让叙事变得更为"个人化"从而增强了艺术感染力和悬念的张力。欧·亨利巧妙地在两种视角中切换以达到其不同的叙事目的。当然,全文最后一段作者再次回到了全知视角,点出了标题中蕴含的圣经典故以及叙述者对于"wise gifts and wisest gifts givers"的褒赞。

二、双线叙事中的叙事省略和叙事留白

《麦琪的礼物》中的情节悬念并非仅仅依赖于叙事视角的切换。欧·亨利对于叙事线索的巧妙构思更是突出了故事悬念的张力和吸引力。《麦琪的礼物》中分明有两个主要人物,两个珍贵的宝物,两份重大牺牲所换来的礼物。但似乎本文中仅仅讲述了 Della 一方所呈现的一半的故事。这正是作者采用的另一重要的叙事策略——明线叙事和暗线叙事的融合。

欧·亨利在明线叙事(Della 准备礼物)的过程中运用了叙事省略来强化故事的悬念。叙述省略是指"叙述者故意对读者隐瞒一些必要的信息",而在读者的阅读中造成空

白,因而营造出阅读紧迫感和悬念的效果。前文提到本文主要运用了第三人称全知视角进行叙述,在全文的一开始叙述者完全具备足够的能力和信息来告诉读者,Della 数钱时哭泣背后的原因是希望为丈夫准备一件精致的圣诞礼物。但如此一来故事未免会变得过于平铺直叙。所以,叙述者先是"引导"读者了解主人公的家庭境况和阴郁的情绪,Della 生活中和眼前似乎一片"灰暗"("a grey cat walking a grey fence in a grey backyard"),继而着墨描绘家中两件最值钱的"珍宝"(尤其是 Della 富有光泽的及腰长发"rippling and shining like a cascade of brown waters")。对于 Della 卖掉长发后的两个小时中所发生的事,作者更是刻意地一笔带过。("Oh, and the next two hours tripped by on rosy wings.")这样的叙事省略,一方面让故事保有悬念,另一方面能更好地聚焦在对礼物的细节描绘,从而影射出 Della 心中的期待——她和读者都认为丈夫看到礼物后"理应"表现出的喜悦和感动。

Della 返回公寓后,作者并未将焦点放在丈夫 Jim 的活动上,而是接着描述 Della 精心地烫自己的短发和为丈夫准备晚餐的"琐事"。至此,整个过程中,处在叙事另一端的 Jim 有没有数钱,他的苦恼,他当掉怀表和挑选礼物时的心理活动等,作者都刻意避免提及。这便是欧·亨利隐藏在文中的暗线叙事。正是上述的这些叙事留白促成了本文的暗线叙事,将 Jim 的心理活动和所作所为埋为暗线,让故事的悬念和核心戏剧冲突保留到了最后。读者未能从叙述者的文字中去了解 Jim 回家前的经历,但是读者获得了叙事留白所赋予的巨大想象空间。因此,在文末悬念揭晓后,读者仿佛能在脑海中刻画出一个同样为钱所困、忍痛割爱、满心期待地回到家中准备送妻子礼物的丈夫形象。

纵观《麦琪的礼物》的叙事策略,作者一是借助叙述视角的切换,增强故事的戏剧性,为"欧·亨利式"的结尾营造气氛、埋下伏笔,二是双线叙事中所运用的叙事省略和叙事空白,通过隐藏部分信息从而设置了一连串的悬念,使整个故事波澜迭起又难以预料,让读者兴致盎然又潜移默化地参与到文本互动之中。

主要参考文献

林雪萍.《麦琪的礼物》的叙述视角透视[J].福建教育学院学报,2008(7):64-66.
申丹.叙述学与小说文体学研究[M].北京:北京大学出版社,2004.
童庆炳.文学理论教程[M].北京:高等教育出版社,1998.
朱宾忠.英美短篇小说精粹——从斯各特至福克纳[M].武汉:武汉大学出版社,2010.

思考题

(1) 如果作者将丈夫 Jim 为妻子 Della 购买礼物的过程作为叙事明线,而隐藏妻子的叙事线索,故事的艺术效果和感染力是否会受到影响?

(2) 欧·亨利的故事经常令我们"笑中含泪",《麦琪的礼物》中有哪些让我们"笑中含泪"的细节?

(3) 小说结尾处,叙述者似乎在证明和褒扬主人公夫妇选择了"最智慧的礼物",对于故事的主题和文中夫妇的行为,有没有可能运用非褒赞的视角来分析?

Chapter 5　Ticket, Please

by D. H. Lawrence

背景介绍

大卫·赫伯特·劳伦斯(David Herbert Lawrence, 1885—1930)是20世纪英国著名的现代主义作家,也是最具争议性的现代主义作家之一。劳伦斯一生创作了10部长篇小说、11部短篇小说集、4部戏剧、10部诗集、4部散文集、5部理论论著、3部游记和大量的书信。劳伦斯出生于英国诺丁汉郡的煤矿小镇。父亲是煤矿工人,母亲来自中产阶级家庭,当过教师。父母的阶层差异和由此导致的关系恶化是劳伦斯早年作品的创作来源。劳伦斯的名作《儿子与情人》(1913)出版后曾引起"恋母情结"的巨大争议。1928年他出版了最有争议的长篇小说《查泰莱夫人的情人》,欧美国家直到20世纪60年代初才解除对此书的禁令。在劳伦斯的短篇小说《请买票》里,有轨电车的检票领班约翰试图勾引年轻的检票员安妮,却在意识到安妮开始认真对待他们的关系后抛弃了安妮。安妮召集了约翰曾经勾引过的其他女检票员,她们一起商议教训约翰一顿。但在她们痛打了约翰一顿后,却并没有感到开心,反而感到了茫然和恐惧。

文本选读

Here is in the Midlands a single-line tramway system which boldly leaves the county town and plunges off into the black, industrial countryside, up hill and down dale, through the long ugly villages of workmen's houses, over canals and railways, past churches perched high and nobly over the smoke and shadows, through stark, grimy cold little market-places, tilting away in a rush past cinemas and shops down to the hollow where the collieries are, then up again, past a little rural church, under the ash trees, on in a rush to the terminus, the last little ugly place of industry, the cold little town that shivers on the edge of the wild, gloomy country beyond. There the green and creamy coloured tram-car seems to pause and purr with curious satisfaction. But in a few minutes—the clock on the turret of the Co-operative Wholesale Society's Shops gives the time—away it starts once more on the adventure. Again there are the reckless swoops downhill, bouncing the loops: again the chilly wait in the hill-top market-place:

Chapter 5 Ticket, Please *by D. H. Lawrence*

again the breathless slithering round the precipitous drop under the church: again the patient halts at the loops, waiting for the outcoming car: so on and on, for two long hours, till at last the city looms beyond the fat gas-works, the narrow factories draw near, we are in the sordid streets of the great town, once more we sidle to a standstill at our terminus, abashed by the great crimson and cream-coloured city cars, but still perky, jaunty, somewhat dare-devil, green as a jaunty sprig of parsley out of a black colliery garden.

To ride on these cars is always an adventure. Since we are in war-time, the drivers are men unfit for active service: cripples and hunchbacks. So they have the spirit of the devil in them. The ride becomes a steeple-chase. Hurray! we have leapt in a clear jump over the canal bridges—now for the four-lane corner. With a shriek and a trail of sparks we are clear again. To be sure, a tram often leaps the rails—but what matter! It sits in a ditch till other trams come to haul it out. It is quite common for a car, packed with one solid mass of living people, to come to a dead halt in the midst of unbroken blackness, the heart of nowhere on a dark night, and for the driver and the girl conductor to call, 'All get off—car's on fire!' Instead, however, of rushing out in a panic, the passengers stolidly reply: 'Get on—get on! We're not coming out. We're stopping where we are. Push on, George.' So till flames actually appear.

The reason for this reluctance to dismount is that the nights are howlingly cold, black, and windswept, and a car is a haven of refuge. From village to village the miners travel, for a change of cinema, of girl, of pub. The trams are desperately packed. Who is going to risk himself in the black gulf outside, to wait perhaps an hour for another tram, then to see the forlorn notice 'Depot Only', because there is something wrong! Or to greet a unit of three bright cars all so tight with people that they sail past with a howl of derision. Trams that pass in the night.

This, the most dangerous tram-service in England, as the authorities themselves declare, with pride, is entirely conducted by girls, and driven by rash young men, a little crippled, or by delicate young men, who creep forward in terror. The girls are fearless young hussies. In their ugly blue uniform, skirts up to their knees, shapeless old peaked caps on their heads, they have all the sang-froid of an old non-commissioned officer. With a tram packed with howling colliers, roaring hymns downstairs and a sort of antiphony of obscenities upstairs, the lasses are perfectly at their ease. They pounce on the youths who try to evade their ticket-machine. They push off the men at the end of their distance. They are not going to be done in the eye—not they. They fear nobody—and everybody fears them.

'Hello, Annie!'

'Hello, Ted!'

'Oh, mind my corn, Miss Stone. It's my belief you've got a heart of stone, for you've trod on it again.'

'You should keep it in your pocket,' replies Miss Stone, and she goes sturdily upstairs in her high boots.

'Tickets, please.'

She is peremptory, suspicious, and ready to hit first. She can hold her own against ten thousand. The step of that tram-car is her Thermopylae.

Therefore, there is a certain wild romance aboard these cars—and in the sturdy bosom of Annie herself. The time for soft romance is in the morning, between ten o'clock and one, when things are rather slack: that is, except market-day and Saturday. Thus Annie has time to look about her. Then she often hops off her car and into a shop where she has spied something, while the driver chats in the main road. There is very good feeling between the girls and the drivers. Are they not companions in peril, shipments aboard this careering vessel of a tram-car, for ever rocking on the waves of a stormy land?

Then, also, during the easy hours, the inspectors are most in evidence. For some reason, everybody employed in this tram-service is young: there are no grey heads. It would not do. Therefore the inspectors are of the right age, and one, the chief, is also good-looking. See him stand on a wet, gloomy morning, in his long oil-skin, his peaked cap well down over his eyes, waiting to board a car. His face is ruddy, his small brown moustache is weathered, he has a faint impudent smile. Fairly tall and agile, even in his waterproof, he springs aboard a car and greets Annie.

'Hello, Annie! Keeping the wet out?'

'Trying to.'

There are only two people in the car. Inspecting is soon over. Then for a long and impudent chat on the foot-board, a good, easy, twelve-mile chat.

The inspector's name is John Thomas Raynor—always called John Thomas, except sometimes, in malice, Coddy. His face sets in fury when he is addressed, from a distance, with this abbreviation. There is considerable scandal about John Thomas in half a dozen villages. He flirts with the girl conductors in the morning, and walks out with them in the dark night, when they leave their tram-car at the depot. Of course, the girls quit the service frequently. Then he flirts and walks out with the newcomer: always providing she is sufficiently attractive, and that she will consent to walk. It is remarkable, however, that most of the girls are quite comely, they are all young, and this roving life aboard the car gives them a sailor's dash and recklessness. What matter how they behave when the ship is in port. Tomorrow they will be aboard again.

Annie, however, was something of a Tartar, and her sharp tongue had kept John Thomas at arm's length for many months. Perhaps, therefore, she liked him all the more: for he always came up smiling, with impudence. She watched him vanquish one girl, then another. She could tell by the movement of his mouth and eyes, when he flirted with her in the morning, that he had been walking out with this lass, or the other, the night before. A fine cock-of-the-walk he was. She could sum him up pretty well.

In this subtle antagonism they knew each other like old friends, they were as shrewd with one another almost as man and wife. But Annie had always kept him sufficiently at arm's length. Besides, she had a boy of her own.

The Statutes fair, however, came in November, at Bestwood. It happened that Annie had the Monday night off. It was a drizzling ugly night, yet she dressed herself up and went to the fair ground. She was alone, but she expected soon to find a pal of some sort.

The roundabouts were veering round and grinding out their music, the side shows were making as much commotion as possible. In the coco-nut shies there were no coco-nuts, but artificial war-time substitutes, which the lads declared were fastened into the irons. There was a sad decline in brilliance and luxury. None the less, the ground was muddy as ever, there was the same crush, the press of faces lighted up by the flares and the electric lights, the same smell of naphtha and a few fried potatoes, and of electricity.

Who should be the first to greet Miss Annie on the showground but John Thomas? He had a black overcoat buttoned up to his chin, and a tweed cap pulled down over his brows, his face between was ruddy and smiling and handy as ever. She knew so well the way his mouth moved.

She was very glad to have a 'boy'. To be at the Statutes without a fellow was no fun. Instantly, like the gallant he was, he took her on the dragons, grim-toothed, round-about switchbacks. It was not nearly so exciting as a tram-car actually. But, then, to be seated in a shaking, green dragon, uplifted above the sea of bubble faces, careering in a rickety fashion in the lower heavens, whilst John Thomas leaned over her, his cigarette in his mouth, was after all the right style. She was a plump, quick, alive little creature. So she was quite excited and happy.

John Thomas made her stay on for the next round. And therefore she could hardly for shame repulse him when he put his arm round her and drew her a little nearer to him, in a very warm and cuddly manner. Besides, he was fairly discreet, he kept his movement as hidden as possible. She looked down, and saw that his red, clean hand was out of sight of the crowd. And they knew each other so well. So they warmed up to the fair.

After the dragons they went on the horses. John Thomas paid each time, so she could but be complaisant. He, of course, sat astride on the outer horse—named 'Black Bess'—and she sat sideways, towards him, on the inner horse—named 'Wildfire'. But of course John Thomas was not going to sit discreetly on 'Black Bess', holding the brass bar. Round they spun and heaved, in the light. And round he swung on his wooden steed, flinging one leg across her mount, and perilously tipping up and down, across the space, half lying back, laughing at her. He was perfectly happy; she was afraid her hat was on one side, but she was excited.

He threw quoits on a table, and won for her two large, pale-blue hat-pins. And then, hearing the noise of the cinemas, announcing another performance, they climbed the boards and went in.

Of course, during these performances pitch darkness falls from time to time, when the machine goes wrong. Then there is a wild whooping, and a loud smacking of simulated kisses. In these moments John Thomas drew Annie towards him. After all, he had a wonderfully warm, cosy way of holding a girl with his arm, he seemed to make such a nice fit. And, after all, it was pleasant to be so held: so very comforting and cosy and nice. He leaned over her and she felt his breath on her hair; she knew he wanted to kiss her on the lips. And, after all, he was so warm and she fitted in to him so softly. After all, she wanted him to touch her lips.

But the light sprang up; she also started electrically, and put her hat straight. He left his arm lying nonchalantly behind her. Well, it was fun, it was exciting to be at the Statutes with John Thomas.

When the cinema was over they went for a walk across the dark, damp fields. He had all the arts of love-making. He was especially good at holding a girl, when he sat with her on a stile in the black, drizzling darkness. He seemed to be holding her in space, against his own warmth and gratification. And his kisses were soft and slow and searching.

So Annie walked out with John Thomas, though she kept her own boy dangling in the distance. Some of the tram-girls chose to be huffy. But there, you must take things as you find them, in this life.

Chapter 5 Ticket, Please *by D. H. Lawrence*

There was no mistake about it, Annie liked John Thomas a good deal. She felt so rich and warm in herself whenever he was near. And John Thomas really liked Annie, more than usual. The soft, melting way in which she could flow into a fellow, as if she melted into his very bones, was something rare and good. He fully appreciated this.

But with a developing acquaintance there began a developing intimacy. Annie wanted to consider him a person, a man; she wanted to take an intelligent interest in him, and to have an intelligent response. She did not want a mere nocturnal presence, which was what he was so far. And she prided herself that he could not leave her.

Here she made a mistake. John Thomas intended to remain a nocturnal presence; he had no idea of becoming an all-round individual to her. When she started to take an intelligent interest in him and his life and his character, he sheered off. He hated intelligent interest. And he knew that the only way to stop it was to avoid it. The possessive female was aroused in Annie. So he left her.

It is no use saying she was not surprised. She was at first startled, thrown out of her count. For she had been so very sure of holding him. For a while she was staggered, and everything became uncertain to her. Then she wept with fury, indignation, desolation, and misery. Then she had a spasm of despair. And then, when he came, still impudently, on to her car, still familiar, but letting her see by the movement of his head that he had gone away to somebody else for the time being, and was enjoying pastures new, then she determined to have her own back.

She had a very shrewd idea what girls John Thomas had taken out. She went to Nora Purdy. Nora was a tall, rather pale, but well-built girl, with beautiful yellow hair. She was rather secretive.

'Hey!' said Annie, accosting her; then softly, 'Who's John Thomas on with now?'

'I don't know,' said Nora.

'Why tha does,' said Annie, ironically lapsing into dialect. 'Tha knows as well as I do.'

'Well, I do, then,' said Nora. 'It isn't me, so don't bother.'

'It's Cissy Meakin, isn't it?'

'It is, for all I know.'

'Hasn't he got a face on him!' said Annie. 'I don't half like his cheek. I could knock him off the foot-board when he comes round at me.'

'He'll get dropped-on one of these days,' said Nora.

'Ay, he will, when somebody makes up their mind to drop it on him. I should like to see him taken down a peg or two, shouldn't you?'

'I shouldn't mind,' said Nora.

'You've got quite as much cause to as I have,' said Annie. 'But we'll drop on him one of these days, my girl. What? Don't you want to?'

'I don't mind,' said Nora.

But as a matter of fact, Nora was much more vindictive than Annie.

One by one Annie went the round of the old flames. It so happened that Cissy Meakin left the tramway service in quite a short time. Her mother made her leave. Then John Thomas was on the qui-vive. He cast his eyes over his old flock. And his eyes lighted on Annie. He thought she would be safe now. Besides, he liked her.

She arranged to walk home with him on Sunday night. It so happened that her car would be in the depot at half past nine: the last car would come in at 10:15. So John Thomas was to wait for her there.

At the depot the girls had a little waiting-room of their own. It was quite rough, but cosy, with a fire and an oven and a mirror, and table and wooden chairs. The half dozen girls who knew John Thomas only too well had arranged to take service this Sunday afternoon. So, as the cars began to come in, early, the girls dropped into the waiting-room. And instead of hurrying off home, they sat around the fire and had a cup of tea. Outside was the darkness and lawlessness of wartime.

John Thomas came on the car after Annie, at about a quarter to ten. He poked his head easily into the girls' waiting-room.

'Prayer-meeting?' he asked.

'Ay,' said Laura Sharp. 'Ladies only.'

'That's me!' said John Thomas. It was one of his favourite exclamations.

'Shut the door, boy,' said Muriel Baggaley.

'On which side of me?' said John Thomas.

'Which tha likes,' said Polly Birkin.

He had come in and closed the door behind him. The girls moved in their circle, to make a place for him near the fire. He took off his great-coat and pushed back his hat.

'Who handles the teapot?' he said.

Nora Purdy silently poured him out a cup of tea.

'Want a bit o' my bread and drippin'?' said Muriel Baggaley to him.

'Ay, give us a bit.'

And he began to eat his piece of bread.

'There's no place like home, girls,' he said.

They all looked at him as he uttered this piece of impudence. He seemed to be sunning himself in the presence of so many damsels.

'Especially if you're not afraid to go home in the dark,' said Laura Sharp.

'Me! By myself I am.'

They sat till they heard the last tram come in. In a few minutes Emma Houselay entered.

'Come on, my old duck!' cried Polly Birkin.

'It is perishing,' said Emma, holding her fingers to the fire.

'But—I'm afraid to, go home in, the dark,' sang Laura Sharp, the tune having got into her mind.

'Who're you going with tonight, John Thomas?' asked Muriel Baggaley, coolly.

'Tonight?' said John Thomas. 'Oh, I'm going home by myself tonight—all on my lonely-O.'

'That's me!' said Nora Purdy, using his own ejaculation.

The girls laughed shrilly.

'Me as well, Nora,' said John Thomas.

'Don't know what you mean,' said Laura.

'Yes, I'm toddling,' said he, rising and reaching for his overcoat.

'Nay,' said Polly. 'We're all here waiting for you.'

'We've got to be up in good time in the morning,' he said, in the benevolent official manner.

They all laughed.

'Nay,' said Muriel. 'Don't leave us all lonely, John Thomas. Take one!'

'I'll take the lot, if you like,' he responded gallantly.

'That you won't either,' said Muriel, 'Two's company; seven's too much of a good thing.'

'Nay—take one,' said Laura. 'Fair and square, all above board, and say which.'

'Ay,' cried Annie, speaking for the first time. 'Pick, John Thomas; let's hear thee.'

'Nay,' he said. 'I'm going home quiet tonight. Feeling good, for once.'

'Whereabouts?' said Annie. 'Take a good 'un, then. But tha's got to take one of us!'

'Nay, how can I take one,' he said, laughing uneasily. 'I don't want to make enemies.'

'You'd only make one' said Annie.

'The chosen one,' added Laura.

'Oh, my! Who said girls!' exclaimed John Thomas, again turning, as if to escape. 'Well—good-night.'

'Nay, you've got to make your pick,' said Muriel. 'Turn your face to the wall, and say which one touches you. Go on—we shall only just touch your back—one of us. Go on—turn your face to the wall, and don't look, and say which one touches you.'

He was uneasy, mistrusting them. Yet he had not the courage to break away. They pushed him to a wall and stood him there with his face to it. Behind his back they all grimaced, tittering. He looked so comical. He looked around uneasily.

'Go on!' he cried.

'You're looking—you're looking!' they shouted.

He turned his head away. And suddenly, with a movement like a swift cat, Annie went forward and fetched him a box on the side of the head that sent his cap flying and himself staggering. He started round.

But at Annie's signal they all flew at him, slapping him, pinching him, pulling his hair, though more in fun than in spite of anger. He, however, saw red. His blue eyes flamed with strange fear as well as fury, and he butted through the girls to the door. It was locked. He wrenched at it. Roused, alert, the girls stood round and looked at him. He faced them, at bay. At that moment they were rather horrifying to him, as they stood in their short uniforms. He was distinctly afraid.

'Come on, John Thomas! Come on! Choose!' said Annie.

'What are you after? Open the door,' he said.

'We shan't—not till you've chosen!' said Muriel.

'Chosen what?' he said.

'Chosen the one you're going to marry,' she replied.

He hesitated a moment.

'Open the blasted door,' he said, 'and get back to your senses.' He spoke with official authority.

'You've got to choose!' cried the girls.

'Come on!' cried Annie, looking him in the eye. 'Come on! Come on!'

He went forward, rather vaguely. She had taken off her belt, and swinging it, she fetched him a sharp blow over the head with the buckle end. He sprang and seized her. But immediately the other girls rushed upon him, pulling and tearing and beating him. Their blood was now thoroughly up. He was their sport now. They were going to have their own back, out of him. Strange, wild creatures, they hung on him and rushed at

Chapter 5 Ticket, Please by D. H. Lawrence

him to bear him down. His tunic was torn right up the back, Nora had hold at the back of his collar, and was actually strangling him. Luckily the button burst. He struggled in a wild frenzy of fury and terror, almost mad terror. His tunic was simply torn off his back, his shirt-sleeves were torn away, his arms were naked. The girls rushed at him, clenched their hands on him and pulled at him: or they rushed at him and pushed him, butted him with all their might: or they struck him wild blows. He ducked and cringed and struck sideways. They became more intense.

At last he was down. They rushed on him, kneeling on him. He had neither breath nor strength to move. His face was bleeding with a long scratch, his brow was bruised.

Annie knelt on him, the other girls knelt and hung on to him. Their faces were flushed, their hair wild, their eyes were all glittering strangely. He lay at last quite still, with face averted, as an animal lies when it is defeated and at the mercy of the captor. Sometimes his eye glanced back at the wild faces of the girls. His breast rose heavily, his wrists were torn.

'Now, then, my fellow!' gasped Annie at length. 'Now then—now—'

At the sound of her terrifying, cold triumph, he suddenly started to struggle as an animal might, but the girls threw themselves upon him with unnatural strength and power, forcing him down.

'Yes—now, then!' gasped Annie at length.

And there was a dead silence, in which the thud of heart-beating was to be heard. It was a suspense of pure silence in every soul.

'Now you know where you are,' said Annie.

The sight of his white, bare arm maddened the girls. He lay in a kind of trance of fear and antagonism. They felt themselves filled with supernatural strength.

Suddenly Polly started to laugh—to giggle wildly—helplessly—and Emma and Muriel joined in. But Annie and Nora and Laura remained the same, tense, watchful, with gleaming eyes. He winced away from these eyes.

'Yes,' said Annie, in a curious low tone, secret and deadly. 'Yes! You've got it now! You know what you've done, don't you? You know what you've done.'

He made no sound nor sign, but lay with bright, averted eyes, and averted, bleeding face.

'You ought to be killed, that's what you ought,' said Annie, tensely. 'You ought to be killed.' And there was a terrifying lust in her voice.

Polly was ceasing to laugh, and giving long-drawn Oh-h-hs and sighs as she came to herself.

'He's got to choose,' she said vaguely.

'Oh, yes, he has,' said Laura, with vindictive decision.

'Do you hear—do you hear?' said Annie. And with a sharp movement, that made him wince, she turned his face to her.

'Do you hear?' she repeated, shaking him.

But he was quite dumb. She fetched him a sharp slap on the face. He started, and his eyes widened. Then his face darkened with defiance, after all.

'Do you hear?' she repeated.

He only looked at her with hostile eyes.

'Speak!' she said, putting her face devilishly near his.

'What?' he said, almost overcome.

'You've got to choose!' she cried, as if it were some terrible menace, and as if it hurt her that she could not exact more.

'What?' he said, in fear.

'Choose your girl, Coddy. You've got to choose her now. And you'll get your neck broken if you play any more of your tricks, my boy. You're settled now.'

There was a pause. Again he averted his face. He was cunning in his overthrow. He did not give in to them really—no, not if they tore him to bits.

'All right, then,' he said, 'I choose Annie.' His voice was strange and full of malice. Annie let go of him as if he had been a hot coal.

'He's chosen Annie!' said the girls in chorus.

'Me!' cried Annie. She was still kneeling, but away from him. He was still lying prostrate, with averted face. The girls grouped uneasily around.

'Me!' repeated Annie, with a terrible bitter accent.

Then she got up, drawing away from him with strange disgust and bitterness.

'I wouldn't touch him,' she said.

But her face quivered with a kind of agony, she seemed as if she would fall. The other girls turned aside. He remained lying on the floor, with his torn clothes and bleeding, averted face.

'Oh, if he's chosen—' said Polly.

'I don't want him—he can choose again,' said Annie, with the same rather bitter hopelessness.

'Get up,' said Polly, lifting his shoulder. 'Get up.'

He rose slowly, a strange, ragged, dazed creature. The girls eyed him from a distance, curiously, furtively, dangerously.

'Who wants him?' cried Laura, roughly.

'Nobody,' they answered, with contempt. Yet each one of them waited for him to look at her, hoped he would look at her. All except Annie, and something was broken in her.

He, however, kept his face closed and averted from them all. There was a silence of the end. He picked up the torn pieces of his tunic, without knowing what to do with them. The girls stood about uneasily, flushed, panting, tidying their hair and their dress unconsciously, and watching him. He looked at none of them. He espied his cap in a corner, and went and picked it up. He put it on his head, and one of the girls burst into a shrill, hysteric laugh at the sight he presented. He, however, took no heed, but went straight to where his overcoat hung on a peg. The girls moved away from contact with him as if he had been an electric wire. He put on his coat and buttoned it down. Then he rolled his tunic-rags into a bundle, and stood before the locked door, dumbly.

'Open the door, somebody,' said Laura.

'Annie's got the key,' said one.

Annie silently offered the key to the girls. Nora unlocked the door.

'Tit for tat, old man,' she said. 'Show yourself a man, and don't bear a grudge.'

But without a word or sign he had opened the door and gone, his face closed, his head dropped.

'That'll learn him,' said Laura.

'Coddy!' said Nora.

'Shut up, for God's sake!' cried Annie fiercely, as if in torture.

'Well, I'm about ready to go, Polly. Look sharp!' said Muriel.

The girls were all anxious to be off. They were tidying themselves hurriedly, with mute, stupefied faces.

欲望的双重性——《请买票》的心理分析解读

《请买票》这个短篇故事情节并不复杂。年轻的电车检票员领班约翰·托马斯试图勾搭一位名叫安妮的年轻女检票员。而当他知道安妮开始认真对待他们的关系时，又抛弃了她。于是安妮联系了其他曾受过约翰同样对待的姑娘们，大家一起商定揍他一顿。在车场的休息室里，姑娘们一拥而上，把约翰狠狠教训了一番。安妮在被约翰追求而又抛弃的过程中，心理显然发生了变化，而姑娘们在痛打约翰后并没有感到报复的痛快。由此可见,心理变化在这篇故事里是非常重要的。下面从心理分析的视角解读这个短篇故事。

一、欲望的双重性

可以说,即使是在这部短篇小说里,劳伦斯也在这些人物身上清楚地表现了心理矛盾之处:即那种被姑娘们认为是爱情,但其实应该是被弗洛伊德称之为"欲望"(desire)所具有的双重性。

比如,女主人公安妮就表现出那种既主动又被动、既残忍又温柔、既想占有又想背弃的奇怪而复杂的感情。这里作者通过一系列生动的描写展示出安妮丰富的内心世界。在约翰最初和安妮调情时,安妮可以说是洞若观火:

"She could tell by the movement of his mouth and eyes, when he flirted with her in the morning, that he had been walking out with this lass, or the other, the night before. A fine cock-of-the-walk he was. She could sum him up pretty well."

"根据他的嘴角和眼神,说出他在前一天晚上曾和这个或那个姑娘出去过。他真可谓是个唐璜式的人物。安妮算是把他看透了。"

在那个时候,安妮是冷静的。因此,她和约翰保持着一定的距离。但在十一月份的游艺会上,约翰请她去玩了小火车(一条绕来绕去的铁龙),还骑了木马,并且每次都是约翰买票:

"After the dragons they went on the horses. John Thomas paid each time, she could but be complaisant."

"乘完铁龙,他们又去骑木马。每次都是约翰·托马斯付钱,所以,她只能表现得很温顺了。"

这里可以看出,虽然安妮作为女售票员在电车上卖票时向来说一不二,谁也别想从她那里逃票。但到了游乐场,她从电车上接收乘客票款的角色变成了要向别人给票的人,她变得顺从和被动。所以,到了两人一起看完电影之后,安妮心理起了变化:

"Annie wanted to consider him a person, a man; she wanted to take an intelligent interest in him, and to have an intelligent response."

"安妮想将他作为一个人,一个男人来看待,她要从各个方面了解他,也希望约翰·托马斯同样了解她。"

可以说故事里其他的人物都或多或少存在这些矛盾的感情,但是安妮这个女主人公比其他人更深地卷入了与约翰的感情纠纷中。

二、本我的创造和毁灭

安妮不仅比其他人对这种感情纠葛更有感受,而且在这种纠葛里比其他人更加无可奈何地受着相互矛盾的支配:

"For a while she was staggered, and everything became uncertain to her. Then she wept with fury, indignation, desolation, and misery. Then she had a spasm of despair."

"有一段时间,她不知所措,一切事物对她都变得捉摸不定。随后,她怀着一腔怒气、怨恨、凄凉和悲痛哭了一场。接着,她感到一阵绝望。"

在安妮意识到约翰离开她之后,安妮变得惊慌失措。那么安妮究竟想从她对约翰·托马斯的恶作剧中得到什么呢?可以说,安妮把其她的姑娘召集起来,起初只是想让约翰出丑而已。但是,按照弗洛伊德的无意识分析,安妮其实还有更深的欲求。弗洛伊德将人的潜意识分为本我(id)、自我(ego)和超我(super-ego)。弗洛伊德认为人的自我要服从本我和超我这两个主人,所以会产生精神方面的问题。本我同时具有创造和毁灭的双重冲动。对安妮来说,她创造了与约翰的爱情,而在她意识到要失去爱情的时候,就产生了毁灭的冲动。这从小说的后半部分发生的情节可以得到印证:

"But at Annie's signal they all flew at him, slapping him, pinching him, pulling his hair, though more in fun than in spite of anger."

"随着安妮的信号,姑娘们一起扑上来,又是抽,又是掐,又是揪头发。她们虽然满腔怨恨,但更多的是出于好玩。"

由此可见,安妮本能地希望能有机会发泄一下自己因受伤而产生的愤恨之感,姑娘们抱团参与的群殴给她提供了泄愤的机会。安妮打在约翰脸上的那一拳是非常狠的:

"Annie went forward and fetched him a box on the side of the head that sent his cap flying and himself staggering."

"安妮就像一只猫,飞身上前,对着他的太阳穴狠狠一击,把他的帽子打飞了,人也踉跄了几步。"

接下来,姑娘们一拥而上,与约翰厮打起来。而当约翰停止抵抗时,姑娘们却不知道接下来该做什么。"虽然满腔怨恨,但更多的是出于好玩(though more in fun than in spite of anger)",这一句更像是为姑娘们恶作剧背后的动机提供的注解。这样的报复究竟能达到什么目的?从安妮和别的姑娘的话语和行动来看,实际上她们都没有考虑过。姑娘们参与到群殴中,陷入了她们自己也不明白的疯狂。

而在安妮的内心深处,她仍心存侥幸希望能和约翰在一起。比如安妮在给了约翰一记耳光之后,还在不依不饶地问他:

"Choose your girl, Coddy. You've got to choose her now. And you'll get your neck broken if you play any more of your tricks, my boy. You're settled now."

"挑你的姑娘,科迪,你必须现在就挑。你要是还不老实,小子,就拧断你的脖子。你已经完了。"

三、感情的困境

可见,安妮和她的同伴们虽然开启了这场殴斗,但并不知道应当以怎样的方式结束这场殴斗。她们殴打了约翰，但仍然提出希望约翰选择她们中的一位带走。安妮或许期待约翰能够选择自己，她的行为实际上是出于感情冲动的需要。安妮的诉求也是这一群姑娘的愿望，而正是这种想法又使得姑娘们感到惶惑甚至害怕。在约翰回答说他选了安妮之后，安妮的反应是"站起身，带着令人感到陌生的厌恶和痛苦朝后退去（she got up, drawing away from him with strange disgust and bitterness）"，并且她并没有丝毫得意高兴的感觉，相反"她的脸由于痛苦而抽搐着，仿佛要跌倒（her face quivered with a kind of agony, she seemed as if she would fall）"。

在约翰离开之后，姑娘们却并没有感到出了一口恶气，而是带着"痴呆麻木的表情（with mute, stupefied faces）"离开了。这个故事的结尾比较突兀，可以说是用一句悬而未决的话来结束的。就是这种貌似突然中断的结尾，表现出人物剧烈的心理变化。在女检票员们实施了报复行为后，她们其实进入了一种困境，因为她们发现自己对约翰依然还是有感情的，她们要求约翰在离开之前挑一个姑娘带走。这种感情甚至超过了报复时那种狂热。所以在小说的最后一句里，女检票员们是带着麻木的表情离开的。

由此可见，对于参加群殴的任何一个姑娘来说，报复并不可能带来令人满意的解决办法，尤其对于这次报复行动的领导者安妮来说更是如此。因为她和约翰的关系在感情上是自相矛盾的。这种复杂的感情从表面上看似乎是要迫使约翰做出选择，然而由于这是在约翰被痛打之后做出的选择，并非是他个人意愿的真实体现，所以约翰的"选择"本身已变得没有实际意义，安妮的报复也就没有达到预期的效果。

主要参考文献

杜卿.图式理论视角下《请买票》中典型场景的特征和作用分析[J].长春工程学院学报(社会科学版)，2016,17(3):77-79.

丰蕴.本我与超我的碰撞——浅析劳伦斯短篇小说《请买票》[J].山西煤炭管理干部学院学报,2010(2):113-114.

劳伦斯.请买票[M].邢历,译//布鲁克斯,华伦编.小说鉴赏.主万,冯亦代,译.北京:中国青年出版社,1986.

王建文.谈非理性主义的艺术审美—从《请买票》看劳伦斯创作中的非理性因素[J].开封教育学院学报,2009(12):21-23.

姚金璐,王斌.从认知文体学看D.H.劳伦斯《请买票》[J].戏剧之家,2016(10):246-247.

游潺.结构主义视角下的《请买票》[J].贵阳学院学报(社会科学版),2016(11):96-98.

赵倾国,王耀辉.从《请买票》看劳伦斯的二元对立爱情观[J].文史,2012(11):70-71.

LAWRENCE D H. Tickets, Please[M]//BROOKS C,WARREN R P. Edit. Understanding Fiction. Englewood Clliffs: Prentice-Hall, 1979:152-162.

思考题

（1）作者在第一段用了很长的篇幅描写有轨电车的行驶路线，电车的行驶被描写成像一只猫一样，这有何意义？

(2)为什么安妮在听到约翰选她带走的时候,回答是"我不要他",神色是"失望至极"的?

(3)小说结束时安妮和其他姑娘们对约翰的感觉如何?

(4)小说前半部分对安妮和约翰之间的调情描写一直是带有喜剧性的,但从姑娘策划报复开始,特别是到了休息室里的群殴部分,故事转向了对暴力冲突的细节描述,这段情节是否表现出人在失去理性后的野蛮性?

Chapter 6　Kew Garden

by Virginia Woolf

背景介绍

弗吉尼亚·伍尔夫(Virginia Woolf, 1882—1941)是英国二十世纪现代主义文学和女性主义文学的代表作家,她的非线性叙事和意识流的写作方法对英美现代主义文学产生了深远的影响。伍尔夫自幼受父母藏书丰富和结交文学名士的影响,从小就表现出非凡的文学天赋。父亲去世后,她和家人搬到了布鲁姆斯伯里(Bloomsbury),并和朋友们创立了名为"布鲁姆斯伯里派"的文人团体,成员多为当时英国文学界、绘画界、经济学界、政治界和法律界的艺术家和知识分子。伍尔夫于1905年开始职业写作生涯,1915年她的第一部小说《远航》(*On the Voyage*)发表。她还和丈夫伦纳德·伍尔夫(Leonard Woolf)一起成立了"霍加斯出版社"(Hogarth Press),出版过T. S. 艾略特(T. S. Eliot)、西格蒙德·弗洛伊德(Sigmund Freud)、E. M. 福斯特(E. M. Forster)和伍尔夫夫妇自己的作品。伍尔夫最有名的小说是《达洛卫夫人》(*Mrs. Dalloway*, 1925)和《到灯塔去》(*To the Lighthouse*, 1927)等。伍尔夫也写了大量的文艺评论和书信,其中在《一间自己的房间》(*A Room of One's Own*, 1929)中,她呼吁女性,要成为一名作家就应该经济独立并拥有自己独立的空间。"二战"爆发后,伍尔夫在伦敦的房子被德国飞机炸毁。目睹了战争的残酷,加上长期遭受精神疾病的折磨,伍尔夫在给她的丈夫留下一封遗书后,于1941年3月28日投河自尽。伍尔夫的《邱园》(*Kew Garden*)最早发表于1919年,后收录于她的《周一或周二》(*Monday or Tuesday*, 1921)以及她去世后出版的《鬼屋》(*A Haunted House*, 1944)中。

文本选读

FROM THE OVAL-SHAPED flower-bed there rose perhaps a hundred stalks spreading into heart-shaped or tongue-shaped leaves half way up and unfurling at the tip red or blue or yellow petals marked with spots of colour raised upon the surface; and from the red, blue or yellow gloom of the throat emerged a straight bar, rough with gold dust and slightly clubbed at the end. The petals were voluminous enough to be stirred by the summer breeze, and when they moved, the red, blue and yellow lights passed one over the other, staining an inch of the brown earth beneath with a spot of the most intricate colour. The light fell either upon the smooth, grey back of apebble, or, the shell of a snail with its brown, circular veins, or falling into a raindrop, it expanded with such intensity of red, blue and yellow the thin walls of water that one expected them to burst and disappear. Instead, the drop was left in a second silver grey once more, and the light now settled upon the flesh of a leaf, revealing the branching thread of fibre beneath the surface, and again it moved on and spread its illumination in the vast green spaces beneath the dome of the heart-shaped and tongue-shaped leaves. Then the breeze stirred rather more briskly overhead and the colour was flashed into the air above, into the eyes of the men and women who walk in Kew Gardens in July.

The figures of these men and women straggled past the flower-bed with a curiously irregular movement not unlike that of the white and blue butterflies who crossed the turf in zig-zag flights from bed to bed. The man was about six inches in front of the woman, strolling carelessly, while she bore on with greater purpose, only turning her head now and then to see that the children were not too far behind. The man kept this distance in front of the woman purposely, though perhaps unconsciously, for he wished to go on with his thoughts.

"Fifteen years ago I came here with Lily," he thought. "We sat somewhere over there by a lake and I begged her to marry me all through the hot afternoon. How the dragonfly kept circling round us: how clearly I see the dragonfly and her shoe with the square silver buckle at the toe. All the time I spoke I saw her shoe and when it moved impatiently I knew without looking up what she was going to say: the whole of her seemed to be in her shoe. And my love, my desire, were in the dragonfly; for some reason I thought that if it settled there, on that leaf, the broad one with the red flower in the middle of it, if the dragonfly settled on the leaf she would say 'Yes' at once. But the dragonfly went round and round: it never settled anywhere—of course not, happily not, or I shouldn't be walking here with Eleanor and the children—Tell me, Eleanor. D'you ever think of the past?"

"Why do you ask, Simon?"

"Because I've been thinking of the past. I've been thinking of Lily, the woman I might have married.... Well, why are you silent? Do you mind my thinking of the past?"

"Why should I mind, Simon? Doesn't one always think of the past, in a garden with men and women lying under the trees? Aren't they one's past, all that remains of it, those men and women, those ghosts lying under the trees,... one's happiness, one's reality?"

"For me, a square silver shoe buckle and a dragonfly-"

"For me, a kiss. Imagine six little girls sitting before their easels twenty years ago, down by the side of a lake, painting the water-lilies, the first red water-lilies I'd ever seen. And suddenly a kiss, there on the back of my neck. And my hand shook all the afternoon so that I couldn't paint. I took out my watch and marked the hour when I would allow myself to think of the kiss for five minutes only—it was so precious—the kiss of an old grey-haired woman with a wart on her nose, the mother of all my kisses all my life. Come, Caroline, come, Hubert."

They walked on the past the flower-bed, now walking fourabreast, and soon diminished in size among the trees and looked half transparent as the sunlight and shade swam over their backs in large trembling irregular patches.

In the oval flower bed the snail, whose shell had been stained red, blue, and yellow for the space of two minutes or so, now appeared to be moving very slightly in its shell, and next began to labour over the crumbs of loose earth which broke away and rolled down as it passed over them. It appeared to have a definite goal in front of it, differing in this respect from the singular high stepping angular green insect who attempted to cross in front of it, and waited for a second with its antennæ trembling as if in deliberation, and then stepped off as rapidly and strangely in the opposite direction. Brown cliffs with deep green lakes in the hollows, flat, blade-like trees that waved from root to tip, round boulders of grey stone, vast crumpled surfaces of a thin crackling texture-all these objects lay across the snail's progress between one stalk and another to his goal. Before he had decided whether to circumvent the arched tent of a dead leaf or to breast it there came past the bed the feet of other human beings.

This time they were both men. The younger of the two wore an expression of perhaps unnatural calm; he raised his eyes and fixed them very steadily in front of him while his companion spoke, and directly his companion had done speaking he looked on the ground again and sometimes opened his lips only after a long pause and sometimes did not open them at all. The elder man had a curiously uneven and shaky method of walking, jerking his hand forward and throwing up his head abruptly, rather in the manner of an impatient carriage horse tired of waiting outside a house; but in the man these gestures were irresolute and pointless. He talked almost incessantly; he smiled to himself and again began to talk, as if the smile had been an answer. He was talking about spirits-the spirits of the dead, who, according to him, were even now telling him all sorts of odd things about their experiences in Heaven.

"Heaven was known to the ancients as Thessaly, William, and now, with this war, the spirit matter is rolling between the hills like thunder." He paused, seemed to listen, smiled, jerked his head and continued:—

"You have a small electric battery and a piece of rubber to insulate the wire—isolate?—insulate?—well, we'll skip the details, no good going into details that wouldn't be understood-and in short the little machine stands in any convenient position by the head of the bed, we will say, on a neat mahogany stand. All arrangements being properly fixed by workmen under my direction, the widow applies her ear and summons the spirit by sign as agreed. Women! Widows! Women in black—"

Here he seemed to have caught sight of a woman's dress in the distance, which in the shade looked a purple black. He took off his hat, placed his hand upon his heart, and hurried towards her muttering and gesticulating feverishly. But William caught him by the sleeve and touched a flower with the tip of his walking-stick in order to divert the old man's attention. After looking at it for a moment in some confusion the old man bent his ear to it and seemed to answer a voice speaking from it, for he began talking about the forests of Uruguay which he had visited hundreds of years ago in company with the most beautiful young woman in Europe. He could be heard murmuring about forests of Uruguay blanketed with the wax petals of tropical roses, nightingales, sea beaches, mermaids, and women drowned at sea, as he suffered himself to be moved on by William, upon whose face the look of stoical patience grew slowly deeper and deeper.

Following his steps so closely as to be slightly puzzled by his gestures came two elderly women of the lower middle class, one stout and ponderous, the other rosy cheeked and nimble. Like most people of their station they were frankly fascinated by any signs of eccentricity betokening a disordered brain, especially in the well-to-do; but they were too far off to be certain whether the gestures were merely eccentric or genuinely mad. After they had scrutinised the old man's back in silence for a moment and given each other a queer, sly look, they went on energetically piecing together their very complicated dialogue:

"Nell, Bert, Lot, Cess, Phil, Pa, he says, I says, she says, I says, I says, I says—"

"My Bert, Sis, Bill, Grandad, the old man, sugar, Sugar, flour, kippers, greens, Sugar, sugar, sugar."

The ponderous woman looked through the pattern of falling words at the flowers standing cool, firm, and upright in the earth, with a curious expression. She saw them as a sleeper waking from a heavy sleep sees a brass candlestick reflecting the light in an unfamiliar way, and closes his eyes and opens them, and seeing the brass candlestick again, finally starts broad awake and stares at the candlestick with all his powers. So the heavy woman came to a standstill opposite the oval-shaped flower bed, and ceased even to pretend to listen to what the other woman was saying. She stood there letting the words fall over her, swaying the top part of her body slowly backwards and forwards, looking at the flowers. Then she suggested that they should find a seat and have their tea.

The snail had now considered every possible method of reaching his goal without going round the dead leaf or climbing over it. Let alone the effort needed for climbing a leaf, he was doubtful whether the thin texture which vibrated with such an alarming crackle when touched even by the tip of his horns would bear his weight; and this determined him finally to creep beneath it, for there was a point where the leaf curved high enough from the ground to admit him. He had just inserted his head in the opening and was taking stock of the high brown roof and was getting used to the cool brown light when two other people came past outside on the turf. This time they wereboth young, a young man and a young woman. They were both in the prime of youth, or even in that season which precedes the prime of youth, the season before the smooth pink folds of the flower have burst their gummy case, when the wings of the butterfly, though fully grown, are motionless in the sun.

"Lucky it isn't Friday," he observed.

"Why? D'you believe in luck?"

"They make you pay sixpence on Friday."

"What's sixpence anyway? Isn't it worth sixpence?"

"What's 'it'—what do you mean by 'it'?"

"O, anything—I mean—you know what I mean."

Long pauses came between each of these remarks; they were uttered in toneless and monotonous voices. The couple stood still on the edge of the flower bed, and together pressed the end of her parasol deep down into the soft earth. The action and the fact that his hand rested on the top of hers expressed their feelings in a strange way, as these short insignificant words also expressed something, words with short wings for their heavy body of meaning, inadequate to carry them far and thus alighting awkwardly upon the very common objects that surrounded them, and were to their inexperienced touch so massive; but who knows (so they thought as they pressed the parasol into the earth) what precipices aren't concealed in them, or what slopes of ice don't shine in the sun on the other side? Who knows? Who has ever seen this before? Even when she wondered what sort of tea they gave you at Kew, he felt that something loomed up behind her words, and stood vast and solid behind them; and the mist very slowly rose and uncovered—O, Heavens, what were those shapes? —little white tables, and waitresses who looked first at her and then at him; and there was a bill that he would pay with a real two shilling piece, and it was real, all real, he assured himself, fingering the coin in his pocket, real to everyone except to him and to her; even to him it began to seem real; and then—but it was too exciting to stand and think any longer, and he pulled the parasol out of the earth with a jerk and was impatient to find the place where one had tea with other people, like other people.

"Come along, Trissie; it's time we had our tea."

"Wherever does one have one's tea?" she asked with the oddest thrill of excitement in her voice, looking vaguely round and letting herself be drawn on down the grass path, trailing her parasol, turning her head this way and that way, forgetting her tea, wishing to go down there and then down there, remembering orchids and cranes among wild flowers, a Chinese pagoda and a crimson crested bird; but he bore her on.

Thus one couple after another with much the same irregular and aimless movement passed the flower-bed andwere enveloped in layer after layer of green blue vapour, in which at first their bodies had substance and a dash of colour, but later both substance and colour dissolved in the green-blue atmosphere. How hot it was! So hot that even the thrush chose to hop, like a mechanical bird, in the shadow of the flowers, with long pauses between one movement and the next; instead of rambling vaguely the white butterflies danced one above another, making with their white shifting flakes the outline of a shattered marble column above the tallest flowers; the glass roofs of the palm house shone as if a whole market full of shiny green umbrellas had opened in the sun; and in the drone of the aeroplane the voice of the summer sky murmured its fierce soul. Yellow and black, pink and snow white, shapes of all these colours, men, women, and children were spotted for a second upon the horizon, and then, seeing the breadth of yellow that lay upon the grass, they wavered and sought shade beneath the trees, dissolving like drops of water in the yellow and green atmosphere, staining it faintly with red and blue. It seemed as if all gross and heavy bodies had sunk down in the heat motionless and lay huddled upon the ground, but their voices went wavering from them as if they were flames lolling from the thick waxen bodies of candles. Voices. Yes, voices. Wordless voices, breaking the silence suddenly with such depth of contentment, such passion of desire, or, in the voices of children, such freshness of surprise; breaking the silence? But there was no silence; all the time the motor omnibuses were turning their wheels and changing their gear; like a vast nest of Chinese boxes all of wrought steel turning ceaselessly one within another the city murmured; on the top of which the voices cried aloud and the petals of myriads of flowers flashed their colours into the air.

失败的交流与坚定的蜗牛——伍尔夫《邱园》的印象派描写

《邱园》的故事发生在英国七月份一个阳光灿烂的日子里,在伦敦著名的花园"邱园"中有一处卵形的花坛,里面鲜花绽放,植被茂盛,有一只蜗牛在缓缓地爬行。先后有四对游人经过了花坛。开始是一对夫妇带着他们的孩子,夫妻俩在追忆往昔。接着是一位年轻人和一位精神错乱的老人出场,老人一直在嘟嘟囔囔。随后是两位中年妇女,两人也是在自说自话,没有听对方在讲什么。最后是一对年轻的情侣,两人在短暂交谈后打算一起喝茶。在人来人往之中,那只蜗牛一直在努力朝着它的目标坚定地爬行。

《邱园》的全文只有 2612 个英文单词,它的情节如此简单,也许很难算作一个完整的故事。但伍尔夫在其中充分发挥了印象主义式的写作手法,将景物描写和人物描写有机地结合在了一起,体现了其现代主义的文学风格。下面就从作者的缺席、交流的困境、重复的意象、空间的转换以及印象派描写这几个方面探讨该作品的独特魅力。

一、作者的缺席

现代主义的一个典型特征就是作者的缺席。这意味着作者不再直接参与到他们的作品中去,不再为读者提供引导和建议,而是站在故事之外。因此,读者不会在故事里得到作者关于人物或事件看法的线索,而是要自己做出判断。作者的缺席增加了作品解读的困难;而另外一个导致阅读困难的因素就是这个故事里只有人物的片段,读者还来不及完整地了解这些人物,他们就在故事里消失了。

比如,经过花坛的第一批游人是西蒙(Simon)和他的妻子爱丽诺(Eleanor)以及孩子们。读者开始并不知道他们的过去,只了解他们两人出场时保持着大约 6 英寸的距离:西蒙是在"无目的地散步"("strolling carelessly"),而爱丽诺则比较"专注"("with greater purpose"),爱丽诺边走边看管她的孩子们。伍尔夫这里并没有加入任何评论,但读者能感受到夫妻俩并不和谐的精神状态。西蒙回忆起 15 年前那个同样炎热的夏日,他向当时的女友莉莉(Lily)求婚。在莉莉拒绝了西蒙之后,西蒙反而认为这是一件好事,因为要不然他就不会与现在的妻子和孩子们在一起了。这是以一种所谓的理性方式进行的自欺欺人。当西蒙告诉妻子他在想另外一个女人时,爱丽诺用沉默回应了丈夫的"荒诞不经"。很明显,任何妻子都无法忍受一个感情不专的丈夫。接着西蒙又拙劣地继续道:那是个"我也许会娶的女人"("the woman I might have married")。西蒙使用的是

"也许"这个词,但真相是莉莉果断拒绝了他,西蒙这里明显在撒谎。伍尔夫用西蒙的故事表现了现代人的自私与自我欺骗。

可见,作为一名现代主义的代表作家,伍尔夫很擅长展示故事里的人物是如何欺骗他们自己的,即他们往往不肯承认有关他们自己或者与他人关系的事实。在缺少作者评论的情况下,这就意味着读者只有根据这些人物的话语去做出判断,虽然这些人物往往并不是一个可靠的叙述者。

二、交流的困境

与人物的自我欺骗相伴随的就是现代主义文学作品中经常出现的人物之间交流的困境。在这个故事里,可以发现出场的人物都在表达自己的想法,但他们的交流往往并不成功。比如,在第一批游人当中,爱丽诺对过去的回忆与西蒙的回忆截然不同:爱丽诺回忆起的是那个在脖颈后的吻,来自那位"鼻子上长着个疣子的鬓发斑白的老太太"("an old grey-haired woman with a wart on her nose")。可以说,西蒙与爱丽诺之间存在精神上的距离,他们的交流是失败的。

而接下来出场的人物尽管分属不同的类型——一对夫妇、一位青年和一位老人、两位妇人及一对情侣,他们之间也都存在着交流失败这一共性的问题。老人精神错乱,完全没法与那位青年交流;两位妇人絮絮叨叨,都没有在听对方讲话;那对情侣则完全沉溺于无关紧要的对话中去了。

交流失败及其所造成的人与人之间产生的距离这一主题始终贯穿于整部作品。但花坛与走过的人们之间却存在对比关系——路过的人们漫无目的,但蜗牛却有着明确的目的地:"它好像有一个明确的目标"("It appears to have a definite goal"),其中的隐喻不言自明。

三、重复的意象

伍尔夫非常擅长用意象传达人物的心情,并且这些意象往往重复出现。比如西蒙出场时注意力是在一只蜻蜓上:蜻蜓不规则的飞舞与花坛里那些在故事最后被称作"活像半截颓败的大理石圆柱"("shattered marble column")的白蝴蝶互为呼应。

在西蒙回忆向莉莉求婚时,还注意到了莉莉鞋子上的装饰扣,而莉莉则是在"不耐烦地"("impatiently")挪动她的脚。伍尔夫并没有交代莉莉在想什么,但读者可以判断莉莉并不打算接受西蒙的求婚。这似乎证明了一点:如同爱丽诺一样,莉莉也是一位与西蒙不协调的女性。西蒙接着把他的希望都寄托在了那只落在了一朵红花之上的蜻蜓身上,这朵红花也回应了故事开头和结尾描述的那些花儿,但蜻蜓并没有停留在那朵红花上面多久。

这些重复出现的"意象"("image")正是伍尔夫用来代替传统线性故事情节的创作手法。

四、空间的转换

故事的开始和结尾都是围绕着花坛与花瓣展开。作者从花坛的细微处开始描写,然后过渡到更大的空间,这样便产生了空间的转换。

比如,伍尔夫在故事的开头描写了花瓣的不同色彩,然后是雨点反射出的不同光线和蜗牛壳的颜色。在第一段的最后,作者是这样描写花朵的:"这时高处的风吹得略微强了些,于是彩色的亮光便转而反射到顶上辽阔的空间里"("Then the breeze stirred rather more briskly overhead and the colour was flashed into the air above")。到了故事最后一段的末尾,伍尔夫也是这样结束的:"万紫千红的花瓣也把自己的光彩都射入了辽阔的空中"("and the petals of myriads of flowers flashed their colours into the air")。

这里从花瓣、雨点、蜗牛到天空的空间转移体现出伍尔夫在故事里将空间从极小描写到极大,这正与英国诗人威廉·布莱克(William Blake,1757—1827)在其《天真的预言》(*Auguries of Innocence*)一诗中提到的"一沙一世界,一花一天堂"("To See the world in a grain of sand, And a heaven in a wild flower")有异曲同工之妙。

五、印象派描写

伍尔夫对绘画非常感兴趣,她的妹妹瓦内萨·贝尔(Vanessa Bell)也热衷于绘画并主动提出为这个故事设计封面和插图。在《邱园》里,伍尔夫试图通过对天空、光线和阴影的描述捕捉住生命的气息。她的《邱园》可以说是典型的莫奈和雷诺阿的印象派画作。

在故事中,除了描写炎热夏天里的花园和路过的人们,伍尔夫还刻画了斑驳的光线和阴影,这些都是典型的印象派创作风格。比如在西蒙和爱丽诺与孩子们走过花坛以后,作者写道:

"They walked on the past the flower-bed, now walking four abreast, and soon diminished in size among the trees and looked half transparent as the sunlight and shade swam over their backs in large trembling irregular patches."

"于是他们四个人并排走过了花坛,不一会儿在大树间就只留下了四个小小的身影,阳光和树荫在他们背上拂动,投下了摇曳不定的大块斑驳的碎影。"

可以看出,这一家人在光线的照射和阴影的衬托下,逐渐变得透明而慢慢消失在花园中。这种效果使得作品中的四组游人之间产生了视觉的过渡。他们经过了花坛,只停留了一会,就继续前行。如果说《邱园》有传统的故事情节,那这个故事就是有关四组游人在一个炎热的夏日午后走过花坛的故事。但实际上,这只是故事的一部分。另外一部分是花坛里面发生了什么。读者们可以注意到伍尔夫对花坛里的昆虫和植物进行了细致的描写,而这与故事里的人物形成了强烈的反差。

花坛里五彩缤纷的花朵和水滴、一只在坚定爬行的蜗牛和四组在交流上缺乏相互理解的游人,这些看上去缺乏关联的事物,在伍尔夫的笔下以印象派绘画方法的方式构成了一个个画面,组成片段,进而连接成一个完整的作品,向读者展示了一个复杂而难以言表的世界,表现了现代人的孤独和异化。伍尔夫是一个具有深邃思想的作家,她始终在思考真理以及生活的本质问题,并在作品中通过尝试个性化的写作风格及诗意的叙述语言去表达自己的观点。而她的小说创作风格客观上也极大地影响了现代小说的发展。

主要参考文献

管淑红.前景化与意识流小说主题的构建——试析伍尔夫短篇小说《邱园记事》[J].外语与外语教学,2007(12):22-41.

刘须明,路琪.论《邱园记事》中女性诗话写作与艺术表现的多样性[J].英美文学研究论丛,2009(11):111-118.

伍尔夫.达洛维夫人[M].孙梁,苏美,译.上海:上海译文出版社,2007.

吴尔夫.普通读者[M].马爱新,译.北京:人民文学出版社,2003.

翟世镜.伍尔夫研究[M].上海:上海文艺出版社,1988.

翟世镜.意识流小说集伍尔夫[M].上海:上海文艺出版社,1989.

BISHOP E L. Pursuing "It" Through "Kew Gardens"[J]. Studies in Short Fiction, 1982,19(3):269.

DREWERY C. Modernist Short Fiction by Women:The Liminal in Katherine Mansfield, Dorothy Richardson, May Sinclair and Virginia Woolf[M]. London:Routledge, 2016.

MARCUS L. Virginia Woolf and the HogarthPress[M]// Willison I, Gould W, Chernaik W. Modernist Writers and the Marketplace. London:Palgrave Macmillan, 1996:124-150.

OAKLAND J. Virginia Woolf's Kew Gardens[J]. English Studies,1987,68(3):264-273.

SMYTHE K. Virginia Woolf's Elegiac Enterprise[C]// Novel:A Forum on Fiction. Durham:Duke University Press, 1992,26(1):64-79.

WOOLF V. A Haunted House and Other Short Stories[M]. Boston:Houghton Mifflin Harcourt, 1972.

WOOLF V. Monday or Tuesday[M]. London:Alma Books, 2018.

思考题

1. 邱园里的自然景观是什么样子的?为什么会对故事里的人物有如此重要的影响力?

2. 如果故事的背景不是在花园而是在市区,故事会有什么不同?

3. 为什么故事里的蜗牛有着与人物同等重要的地位?蜗牛应该被当作故事中的一个人物吗?

Chapter 7　The Great Gatsby

by F．Scott Fitzgerald

（*excerpts*）

 背景介绍

《了不起的盖茨比》是美国作家弗·司各特·菲茨杰拉德（F. Scott Fitzgerald，1896—1940）创作的一部以20世纪20年代的纽约市及长岛为背景的中篇小说，出版于1925年。主人公是一个从小立志出人头地的农家子弟，经过努力成为富人后改名为杰伊·盖茨比。为了看到分别五年的情人黛西，他在长岛西端买下了一幢豪华别墅，与黛西夫妇的房子隔海湾相望，并每晚举办盛大的宴会，希望吸引黛西来参加。但是盖茨比和黛西重逢后的快乐时光没能持续太久，黛西开车碾死了丈夫汤姆的情妇，汤姆嫁祸于盖茨比，盖茨比因此被枪杀。而黛西为了尽早离开是非之地居然拒绝出席他的葬礼。叙述者尼克由此看透了上流社会的冷漠无情，选择离开纽约，回到了中西部的故乡。《了不起的盖茨比》的问世，奠定了弗·司各特·菲茨杰拉德在美国文学史上的地位，成为20年代"爵士时代"的代言人和"迷惘的一代"的代表作家之一。20世纪末，美国学术界权威在百年英语文学长河中选出一百部最优秀的小说，《了不起的盖茨比》高居第二位，并多次被搬上银幕和舞台。

 文本选读

Chapter 9

When I left his office the sky had turned dark and I got back to West Egg in a drizzle. After changing my clothes I went next door and found Mr. Gatz walking up and down excitedly in the hall. His pride in his son and in his son's possessions was continually increasing and now he had something to show me.

'Jimmy sent me this picture.' He took out his wallet with trembling fingers. 'Look there.'

It was a photograph of the house, cracked in the corners and dirty with many

Chapter 7 The Great Gatsby by F. Scott Fitzgerald

hands. He pointed out every detail to me eagerly. 'Look there!' and then sought admiration from my eyes. He had shown it so often that I think it was more real to him now than the house itself.

'Jimmy sent it to me. I think it's a very pretty picture. It shows up well.'

'Very well. Had you seen him lately?'

'He come out to see me two years ago and bought me the house I live in now. Of course we was broke up when he run off from home but I see now there was a reason for it. He knew he had a big future in front of him. And ever since he made a success he was very generous with me.'

He seemed reluctant to put away the picture, held it for another minute, lingeringly, before my eyes. Then he returned the wallet and pulled from his pocket a ragged old copy of a book called 'Hopalong Cassidy.'

'Look here, this is a book he had when he was a boy. It just shows you.'

He opened it at the back cover and turned it around for me to see. On the last flyleaf was printed the word SCHEDULE, and the date September 12th, 1906. And underneath:

Rise from bed ············ 6.00 A. M.

Dumbbell exercise and wall-scaling ······ 6.15—6.30 A. M.

Study electricity, etc ············ 7.15—8.15 A. M.

Work ···················· 8.30—4.30 P. M.

Baseball and sports ············ 4.30—5.00 P. M.

Practice elocution, poise and how to attain it 5.00—6.00 P. M.

Study needed inventions ········· 7.00—9.00 P. M.

GENERAL RESOLVES

No wasting time at Shafters or [a name, indecipherable]

No more smoking or chewing

Bath every other day

Read one improving book or magazine per week

Save $5.00 [crossed out] $3.00 per week

Be better to parents

'I come across this book by accident,' said the old man. 'It just shows you, don't it?'

'It just shows you.'

'Jimmy was bound to get ahead. He always had some resolves like this or something. Do you notice what he's got about improving his mind? He was always great for that. He told me I et like a hog once and I beat him for it.'

He was reluctant to close the book, reading each item aloud and then looking eagerly at me. I think he rather expected me to copy down the list for my own use.

A little before three the Lutheran minister arrived from Flushing and I began to look involuntarily out the windows for other cars. So did Gatsby's father. And as the time passed and the servants came in and stood waiting in the hall, his eyes began to blink anxiously and he spoke of the rain in a worried uncertain way. The minister glanced several times at his watch so I took him aside and asked him to wait for half an hour. But it wasn't any use. Nobody came.

About five o'clock our procession of three cars reached the cemetery and stopped in a thick drizzle beside the gate—first a motor hearse, horribly black and wet, then Mr. Gatz and the minister and I in the limousine, and, a little later, four or five servants and the postman from West Egg in Gatsby's station wagon, all wet to the skin. As we started through the gate into the cemetery I heard a car stop and then the sound of someone splashing after us over the soggy ground. I looked around. It was the man with owl-eyed glasses whom I had found marvelling over Gatsby's books in the library one night three months before.

I'd never seen him since then. I don't know how he knew about the funeral or even his name. The rain poured down his thick glasses and he took them off and wiped them to see the protecting canvas unrolled from Gatsby's grave.

I tried to think about Gatsby then for a moment but he was already too far away and I could only remember, without resentment, that Daisy hadn't sent a message or a flower. Dimly I heard someone murmur 'Blessed are the dead that the rain falls on,' and then the owl-eyed man said 'Amen to that,' in a brave voice.

We straggled down quickly through the rain to the cars. Owl-Eyes spoke to me by the gate.

'I couldn't get to the house,' he remarked.

'Neither could anybody else.'

'Go on!' He started. 'Why, my God! they used to go there by the hundreds.'

He took off his glasses and wiped them again outside and in.

'The poor son-of-a-bitch,' he said.

One of my most vivid memories is of coming back west from prep school and later from college at Christmas time. Those who went farther than Chicago would gather in the old dim Union Station at six o'clock of a December evening with a few Chicago friends already caught up into their own holiday gayeties to bid them a hasty goodbye. I

Chapter 7 The Great Gatsby by F. Scott Fitzgerald

remember the fur coats of the girls returning from Miss This or That's and the chatter of frozen breath and the hands waving overhead as we caught sight of old acquaintances and the matchings of invitations: 'Are you going to the Ordways'? the Herseys'? the Schultzes'?' and the long green tickets clasped tight in our gloved hands. And last the murky yellow cars of the Chicago, Milwaukee and St. Paul Railroad looking cheerful as Christmas itself on the tracks beside the gate.

When we pulled out into the winter night and the real snow, our snow, began to stretch out beside us and twinkle against the windows, and the dim lights of small Wisconsin stations moved by, a sharp wild brace came suddenly into the air. We drew in deep breaths of it as we walked back from dinner through the cold vestibules, unutterably aware of our identity with this country for one strange hour before we melted indistinguishably into it again.

That's my middle west—not the wheat or the prairies or the lost Swede towns but the thrilling, returning trains of my youth and the street lamps and sleigh bells in the frosty dark and the shadows of holly wreaths thrown by lighted windows on the snow. I am part of that, a little solemn with the feel of those long winters, a little complacent from growing up in the Carraway house in a city where dwellings are still called through decades by a family's name. I see now that this has been a story of the West, after all—Tom and Gatsby, Daisy and Jordan and I, were all Westerners, and perhaps we possessed some deficiency in common which made us subtly unadaptable to Eastern life.

Even when the East excited me most, even when I was most keenly aware of its superiority to the bored, sprawling, swollen towns beyond the Ohio, with their interminable inquisitions which spared only the children and the very old—even then it had always for me a quality of distortion. West Egg especially still figures in my more fantastic dreams. I see it as a night scene by El Greco: a hundred houses, at once conventional and grotesque, crouching under a sullen, overhanging sky and a lustreless moon. In the foreground four solemn men in dress suits are walking along the sidewalk with a stretcher on which lies a drunken woman in a white evening dress. Her hand, which dangles over the side, sparkles cold with jewels. Gravely the men turn in at a house—the wrong house. But no one knows the woman's name, and no one cares.

After Gatsby's death the East was haunted for me like that, distorted beyond my eyes' power of correction. So when the blue smoke of brittle leaves was in the air and the wind blew the wet laundry stiff on the line I decided to come back home.

There was one thing to be done before I left, an awkward, unpleasant thing that perhaps had better have been let alone. But I wanted to leave things in order and not just trust that obliging and indifferent sea to sweep my refuse away. I saw Jordan Baker and talked over and around what had happened to us together and what had happened afterward to me, and she lay perfectly still listening in a big chair.

She was dressed to play golf and I remember thinking she looked like a good illustration, her chin raised a little, jauntily, her hair the color of an autumn leaf, her face the same brown tint as the fingerless glove on her knee. When I had finished she told me without comment that she was engaged to another man. I doubted that though there were several she could have married at a nod of her head but I pretended to be surprised. For just a minute I wondered if I wasn't making a mistake, then I thought it all over again quickly and got up to say goodbye.

'Nevertheless you did throw me over,' said Jordan suddenly. 'You threw me over on the telephone. I don't give a damn about you now but it was a new experience for me and I felt a little dizzy for a while.'

We shook hands.

'Oh, and do you remember—' she added, '—a conversation we had once about driving a car?'

'Why—not exactly.'

'You said a bad driver was only safe until she met another bad driver? Well, I met another bad driver, didn't I? I mean it was careless of me to make such a wrong guess. I thought you were rather an honest, straightforward person. I thought it was your secret pride.'

'I'm thirty,' I said. 'I'm five years too old to lie to myself and call it honor.'

She didn't answer. Angry, and half in love with her, and tremendously sorry, I turned away.

One afternoon late in October I saw Tom Buchanan. He was walking ahead of me along Fifth Avenue in his alert, aggressive way, his hands out a little from his body as if to fight off interference, his head moving sharply here and there, adapting itself to his restless eyes. Just as I slowed up to avoid overtaking him he stopped and began frowning into the windows of a jewelry store. Suddenly he saw me and walked back holding out his hand.

'What's the matter, Nick? Do you object to shaking hands with me?'

'Yes. You know what I think of you.'

'You're crazy, Nick,' he said quickly. 'Crazy as hell. I don't know what's the matter with you.'

'Tom,' I inquired, 'what did you say to Wilson that afternoon?'

He stared at me without a word and I knew I had guessed right about those missing hours. I started to turn away but he took a step after me and grabbed my arm.

'I told him the truth,' he said. 'He came to the door while we were getting ready to leave and when I sent down word that we weren't in he tried to force his way upstairs. He was crazy enough to kill me if I hadn't told him who owned the car. His hand was on a revolver in his pocket every minute he was in the house—' He broke off defiantly. 'What if I did tell him? That fellow had it coming to him. He threw dust into your eyes just like he did in Daisy's but he was a tough one. He ran over Myrtle like you'd run over a dog and never even stopped his car.'

There was nothing I could say, except the one unutterable fact that it wasn't true.

'And if you think I didn't have my share of suffering—look here, when I went to give up that flat and saw that damn box of dog biscuits sitting there on the sideboard I sat down and cried like a baby. By God it was awful—

I couldn't forgive him or like him but I saw that what he had done was, to him, entirely justified. It was all very careless and confused. They were careless people, Tom and Daisy—they smashed up things and creatures and then retreated back into their money or their vast carelessness or whatever it was that kept them together, and let other people clean up the mess they had made. . . .

I shook hands with him; it seemed silly not to, for I felt suddenly as though I were talking to a child. Then he went into the jewelry store to buy a pearl necklace—or perhaps only a pair of cuff buttons—rid of my provincial squeamishness forever.

Gatsby's house was still empty when I left—the grass on his lawn had grown as long as mine. One of the taxi drivers in the village never took a fare past the entrance gate without stopping for a minute and pointing inside; perhaps it was he who drove Daisy and Gatsby over to East Egg the night of the accident and perhaps he had made a story about it all his own. I didn't want to hear it and I avoided him when I got off the train.

I spent my Saturday nights in New York because those gleaming, dazzling parties of his were with me so vividly that I could still hear the music and the laughter faint and incessant from his garden and the cars going up and down his drive. One night I did hear a material car there and saw its lights stop at his front steps. But I didn't investigate. Probably it was some final guest who had been away at the ends of the earth and didn't know that the party was over.

On the last night, with my trunk packed and my car sold to the grocer, I went over and looked at that huge incoherent failure of a house once more. On the white steps an obscene word, scrawled by some boy with a piece of brick, stood out clearly in the moonlight and I erased it, drawing my shoe raspingly along the stone. Then I wandered down to the beach and sprawled out on the sand.

Most of the big shore places were closed now and there were hardly any lights except the shadowy, moving glow of a ferryboat across the Sound. And as the moon rose higher the inessential houses began to melt away until gradually I became aware of the old island here that flowered once for Dutch sailors' eyes—a fresh, green breast of the new world. Its vanished trees, the trees that had made way for Gatsby's house, had once pandered in whispers to the last and greatest of all human dreams; for a transitory enchanted moment man must have held his breath in the presence of this continent, compelled into an aesthetic contemplation he neither understood nor desired, face to face for the last time in history with something commensurate to his capacity for wonder.

And as I sat there brooding on the old, unknown world, I thought of Gatsby's wonder when he first picked out the green light at the end of Daisy's dock. He had come a long way to this blue lawn and his dream must have seemed so close that he could hardly fail to grasp it. He did not know that it was already behind him, somewhere back in that vast obscurity beyond the city, where the dark fields of the republic rolled on under the night.

Gatsby believed in the green light, the orgastic future that year by year recedes before us. It eluded us then, but that's no matter—tomorrow we will run faster, stretch out our arms farther.... And one fine morning—So we beat on, boats against the current, borne back ceaselessly into the past.

THE END

"美国梦"的阴影
——从"灰谷"这一地理景观解读《了不起的盖茨比》

"美国梦(American Dream)"是《了不起的盖茨比》的核心主题。"美国梦"集中体现了美国人的理想与信仰,是美国人的价值观和民族精神的标志。从广义上讲,"美国梦"指"民主、平等、自由"的国家理想;从狭义上讲,它指的是个人通过艰苦奋斗而获得成功,改变命运的梦想。美国历史学家詹姆斯·特拉斯诺·亚当斯1931年在他所著的《美国史诗》中提出"美国梦"的概念。所谓"美国梦"是指美国人在建国、开拓过程中形成的,以实现个人理想为目标,通过不懈奋斗"白手起家"的梦想,它是美国价值体系特别是其终极价值目标的通俗表达。亚当斯认为，不论阶层或出身如何，每个人都有机会凭借自己的能力或成就在美国拥有更好的生活。"美国梦"是美国的民族精神，包括一系列理想信念（如民主、权利、自由、机会和平等），内涵极为丰富。以"自由"为例，这一理想包含取得成功的机会，以及在一个障碍较少的社会中通过辛勤工作来实现向上的社会流动的可能性。要理解"美国梦"的丰富内涵，首先我们必须了解"美国梦"这一概念形成和发展的历史。

"美国梦"最早可追溯到第一批欧洲移民登上美洲大陆的 17 世纪。1607 年英国移民在北美弗吉尼亚的詹姆斯顿建立起第一个英属殖民地，其他欧洲国家也相继在北美的大西洋海岸线上占领土地。早期移民以清教徒（Puritans）为主，他们长途跋涉移居到美国是为了摆脱宗教的束缚，自力更生创造一个信仰自由的新天堂。清教徒把自己看作上帝的选民，承担着向世界传播自由和正义的神圣使命，梦想建立一个"山巅之城"（a city upon a hill），也就是人类的希望，国家的典范。清教徒很快积累了大量财富，创造出美国神话，是"美国梦"最早的代言人。正如美国民主运动的先驱杰斐逊在《独立宣言（Declaration of Independence）》中所说"我们认为下面这些真理是不言而喻的：人人生而平等，造物主赋予他们若干不可剥夺的权利，其中包括生命权、自由权和追求幸福的权利。"这些价值观是美国文化的精髓，并以各种方式代代延续。

17 世纪末 18 世纪初在欧洲盛行的启蒙运动思潮在 18 世纪传入了美国。启蒙运动倡导理性和科学，相信人的可完善性和社会的不断进步，强调个人权利。出身贫寒的富兰克林是这一时期"美国梦"的最佳范例。他的成功证明了底层的年轻人凭借智慧和勤奋可以改变命运。相较于清教徒的理想化，这一时期的"美国梦"是实用主义的"美国梦"，强调物质财富的重要性，鼓励自我实现和个人成功。启蒙思想释放了人们的潜能，层出不穷的成功案例极大地鼓舞了美国人民辛勤工作，以期复制白手起家的奇迹。随后，18 世纪末 19 世纪初的"淘金热（Gold Rush）"使美国全国沸腾，进一步刺激了人们对金钱的渴望。加利福尼亚发现金矿的消息传出后，报纸每天刊登淘金的传奇故事，不论在家里还是公共场所，人们的话题都离不开黄金。追求个人成功逐渐演变为追求物质财富，人们也越来越推崇一掷千金的生活方式。随着美国东部居民和后来的移民不断向西部迁移，19 世纪末 20 世纪初声势浩大的"西进运动（Westward Expansion）"不仅催生了一大批敢于冒险的年轻人，也催生了美国的实用主义哲学。就这样，"美国梦"这一起源于清教，富含宗教内涵的理想在历史发展中逐渐世俗化，演变为对物质和利益的追逐。而在菲茨杰拉德所生活的 19 世纪 20 年代，"美国梦"则已经完全蜕变成了赤裸裸的"金钱梦"。盖茨比的故事发生在美国历史上著名的爵士时代（The Jazz Age），也被称为"咆哮的二十年代"（"Roaring Twenties"）。一般指 1918 年"一战"结束后到 1929 年经济大萧条之前的约十年时间。"一战"后的美国经济空前繁荣，自 20 年代中期，北美经济规模开始凌驾于欧洲之上。市场经济发展迅猛，人们被鼓励努力挣钱，尽情享受。资本的激增让传统的价值观念和道德风尚发生了翻天覆地的变化。与物质财富的满足相对的是精神世界的贫瘠。传统的清教徒道德已经土崩瓦解,享乐主义开始大行其道。用菲茨杰拉德自己的话来说,"这是一个奇迹的时代,一个艺术的时代,一个挥金如土的时代,也是一个充满嘲讽的时代(It was an age of miracles, it was an age of art, it was an age of excess, and it was an age of satire)。"菲茨杰拉德称这个时代为"爵士时代",他也因此被称为爵士时代的"编年史家"和"桂冠诗人"。

在这本小说中,主人公盖茨比经常被看作是"美国梦"的象征。他不甘平庸,坚持奋斗,希望靠自己的努力跻身于上流社会,是典型的美国式"白手起家"的英雄形象。但是他的"美国梦"其实是一个梦碎了的故事。从这本书中我们可以看到菲茨杰拉德对"美国梦"的反思,比如金钱决定一切的社会现实,上流社会空虚无聊的浮华生活,一味追求物质带来的人情冷漠和道德沦丧问题,以及貌似自由的阶层流动面纱下掩盖的阶级固化等尖锐矛盾。下面以本书中常被忽略的一个独特的地理空间——灰谷(a valley of ashes)为例阐释"美国梦"的困境。

《了不起的盖茨比》中以汤姆和黛西为代表的传统贵族阶层住在东卵,光彩夺目的豪宅沿着海岸线铺开;盖茨比这样的新富则住在西卵,同样拥有宫殿般壮观的房子,彻夜不停举办宴会。东卵和西卵"外形一模一样,中间隔着一条小湾,一直伸进西半球那片最恬静的咸水",而灰谷就处在西卵到纽约市中心之间。

"About half way between West Egg and New York the motor-road hastily joins the railroad and runs beside it for a quarter of a mile, so as to shrink away from a certain desolate area of land. This is a valley of ashes—a fantastic farm where ashes grow like wheat into ridges and hills and grotesque gardens where ashes take the forms of houses and chimneys and rising smoke and finally, with a transcendent effort, of men who move dimly and already crumbling through the powdery air. Occasionally a line of grey cars crawls along an invisible track, gives out a ghastly creak and comes to rest, and immediately the ash-grey men swarm up with leaden spades and stir up an impenetrable cloud which screens their obscure operations from your sight."

"西卵和纽约之间大约一半路程的地方,汽车路匆匆忙忙跟铁路会合,它在铁路旁边跑上四分之一英里,为的是要躲开一片荒凉的地方。这是一个灰烬的山谷——一个离奇古怪的农场,在这里灰烬像麦子一样生长,长成小山小丘和奇形怪状的园子。在这里灰烬堆成房屋、烟囱和炊烟的形式,最后,经过超绝的努力,堆成一个个灰蒙蒙的人,隐隐约约地在走动,而且已经在尘土飞扬的空气中化为灰烬了。有时一列灰色的货车慢慢沿着一条看不见的轨道爬行,叽嘎一声鬼叫,停了下来,马上那些灰蒙蒙的人就拖着铁铲一窝蜂拥上来,扬起一片尘土,让你看不到他们隐秘的活动。"

作者在第二章的开篇描述了灰谷这个地方。与东卵、西卵的明亮色彩截然不同,这里仿佛被雾霾笼罩,房屋、烟囱、汽车,甚至连人都是灰蒙蒙的。正如它的名字所传达的那样——灰烬的山谷——这是一片阴霾之地,充满了绝望的死气,仿佛与光鲜亮丽,欣欣向荣的东卵、西卵处于两个世界。20世纪末以来人文研究出现了大规模的"空间转向",大批学者开始关注文学作品中的地理景观。研究人与其活动的空间场所之间相互作用关系的文学地理学认为,地理景观不仅是物质性的存在,更集中体现着社会意识形态。灰谷与东卵、西卵的对比与其说是地理环境上的鲜明差异,不如说是生活在其中的人们的阶级地位的强烈反差。

灰谷是真实存在于纽约历史中的一个地理位置,最初的灰谷是皇后区和布鲁克林的沿海湿地中的一片草甸,被称为科罗纳草甸。1910年前后,商人Michael Degnon购买了附近的大片沼泽地,计划修建大型工业港口。为了填平沼泽,Degnon把布鲁克林的家用煤炭、垃圾焚烧剩下的灰烬和街道上的灰土运到此地,并倾倒在草甸里。该港口项目在1917年因资金问题被叫停,但是倾倒灰土的行为并没有停止,数量反而因为城市垃圾的增加而飙升。日积月累的灰烬彻底破坏了科罗纳草甸的环境,原来的草地完全被弥漫的灰色尘土覆盖。"在近30年的灌装期间,大约5000万立方米的灰渣和废物被倾倒在草地上,形成了一个特殊的灰烬堆,最高的那一个达到90英尺(27米)高,被称为'科罗纳山',而其他的土堆也有40~50英尺(12~15米),整个科罗纳地区的灰堆平均厚度为30英尺(9.1米)。"无人管理的草甸最终被城市居民当作了垃圾站,不仅是灰土,各种垃圾也被集中倒在这里,终日尘土飞扬。菲茨杰拉德给这片荒凉之地取名为灰谷,放置在东卵和西卵之间,给看似光彩照人的纽约市蒙上了一层阴影。

菲茨杰拉德还为灰谷找了一个看门人——汤姆情妇的丈夫威尔逊,在灰谷的主街上经营一家破败的车行。他的脸与灰谷一样始终被尘土笼罩,几乎要被周围环境吞噬:"他的身影马上就跟墙壁的水泥色打成一片了。一层灰白色的尘土笼罩着他深色的衣服和浅色的头发,笼罩着前后左右的一切"。19世纪中期开始的纽约城市扩张和工业发展带来了郊区工人阶级生存环境的持续恶化。底层人民每天面对的是狭小的空间和灰蒙蒙的污染,金光闪闪的"美国梦"似乎遥不可及。文化地理学的代表人物迈克·克朗认为城市环境影响居住在其中的人们的知觉和观感,继而影响他们的精神状态和价值观:"城市不仅是故事发生的场地,城市地理景观还作用于对社会和生活的认识"。生活在被城市化进程抛弃的灰谷,威尔逊是这一时期下层居民的典型代表。"他是个头发金黄、没精打采的人,脸上没有血色,样子还不难看。他一看见我们,那对浅蓝的眼睛就流露出一线暗淡的希望。"威尔逊们整日在灰尘笼罩的灰谷机械劳动,把仅存的一丝希望寄托在汤姆这样冷酷无情的富人身上。这一时期繁荣的美国有无数个像灰谷这样的地方,居住在那里的小人物毫无希望,变成死寂的灰烬也许就是他们的结局。

东卵、西卵和灰谷这三个地理空间象征着美国"爵士时代"三个不同的社会阶层,东卵、西卵之间有科罗纳草甸这片荒凉之地,从长岛进入纽约必须经过灰谷。正如詹姆斯·科纳所说:"地理景观是建构,是表征,还是一系列复杂的结构和观念,指引了人们对环境的认识和处于其中的自我的认知,更影响着他们与环境的相互作用。"菲茨杰拉德在20年代歌舞升平、纸醉金迷的纽约中看到了灰谷,敏锐地发现了繁华都市生活背后的一片荒原。人们用赞叹和羡慕的目光望向灯火辉煌的纽约城时,却无法预料到浮华之后是废墟。正如西卵的盖茨比夜夜遥望着黛西船上的那盏绿灯,以为距离自己的梦想只有一步之遥,结果一切努力都是徒劳。作者试图通过盖茨比的故事阐述"美国梦"幻灭的一面:在那个躁动不安,令人头昏目眩的年代,"金钱至上"的价值观扼杀了浪漫的人生理想。曾经的"美国梦"已被人们抛弃。"爵士时代"之后的1929年经济大萧条席卷了整个美国,《了不起的盖茨比》中可怕的灰谷也最终蔓延到现实中的纽约城。

主要参考文献

崔蕾.繁华都市的阴影——灰谷[J].华中师范大学研究生学报,2017(12):62-66.

菲茨杰拉德.了不起的盖茨比[M].李继宏,译.天津:天津人民出版社,2003.

迈克·克朗.文化地理学[M].杨淑华,宋慧敏,译.南京:南京大学出版社,2003.

CULLEN J P. American Dream: A Short History of an Idea That Shaped a Nation[M]. Oxford: Oxford University Press, 2003.

FITZGERALD F S. The Great Gatsby[M]. London: Penguin Books, 1950.

思考题

(1)怎样理解这本小说最后一句话:"So we beat on, boats against the current, borne back ceaselessly into the past."?

(2)你如何看待盖茨比和黛西之间的感情?试结合文本进行分析。

(3)你认为盖茨比为什么了不起?

(4)有关"美国梦"的讨论对于我们的"中国梦"有什么启示?

Chapter 8　A Rose for Emily
by William Faulkner

　　威廉·福克纳(William Faulkner,1897—1962)是美国南方现代文学和意识流文学的代表人物,因其作品对"当代美国小说做出了强有力的和艺术上无与伦比的贡献"而荣获1949年诺贝尔文学奖。福克纳一生创作了19部长篇小说与120多篇短篇小说,其中15部长篇小说与大多数短篇小说都是以作者虚构的约克纳帕塔法县为故事背景。作者围绕着这个县的杰弗森镇及其郊区描述了来自不同社会阶层的家族几代人的故事,叙述时间从1800年起直到第二次世界大战以后,大约600多个有名有姓的人物在各个长篇、短篇小说中穿插交替出现。短篇小说《献给艾米丽的玫瑰》(*A Rose for Emily*)是福克纳最早被译为中文的作品之一。该故事讲述了美国南北战争后一个南方小镇——杰弗森镇(Jefferson)上格里尔森家族的命运。艾米丽·格里尔森(Emily Grierson)的父亲作为家族族长,其父权意识异常强烈,他赶走了所有向艾米丽求爱的男子,剥夺了她追求幸福的权利。父亲去世后,艾米丽爱上了来小镇修路的工头——北方佬荷默·伯隆(Homer Barron)。但当她发现荷默无意与她结婚时,便用砒霜毒死了他。从此,艾米丽在她日渐破败的宅院里过着与世隔绝的生活,并一直与荷默的尸体同床共枕。直到艾米丽去世后小镇居民才在艾米丽家的卧室里发现了这个秘密。

I

　　WHEN Miss Emily Grierson died, our whole town went to her funeral: the men through a sort of respectful affection for a fallen monument, the women mostly out of curiosity to see the inside of her house, which no one save an old manservant—a combined gardener and cook—had seen in at least ten years.

　　It was a big, squarish frame house that had once been white, decorated with cupolas and spires and scrolled balconies in the heavily lightsome style of the seventies, set on what had once been our most select street. But garages and cotton gins had encroached and obliterated even the august names of that neighborhood; only Miss Emily's house was left, lifting its stubborn and coquettish decay above the cotton wagons and the gasoline pumps—an eyesore among eyesores. And now Miss Emily had gone to join the representatives of those august names where they lay in the cedar-bemused cemetery among the ranked and anonymous graves of Union and Confederate soldiers who fell at the battle of Jefferson.

Alive, Miss Emily had been a tradition, a duty, and a care; a sort of hereditary obligation upon the town, dating from that day in 1894 when Colonel Sartoris, the mayor—he who fathered the edict that no Negro woman should appear on the streets without an apron—remitted her taxes, the dispensation dating from the death of her father on into perpetuity. Not that Miss Emily would have accepted charity. Colonel Sartoris invented an involved tale to the effect that Miss Emily's father had loaned money to the town, which the town, as a matter of business, preferred this way of repaying. Only a man of Colonel Sartoris' generation and thought could have invented it, and only a woman could have believed it.

When the next generation, with its more modern ideas, became mayors and aldermen, this arrangement created some little dissatisfaction. On the first of the year they mailed her a tax notice. February came, and there was no reply. They wrote her a formal letter, asking her to call at the sheriff's office at her convenience. A week later the mayor wrote her himself, offering to call or to send his car for her, and received in reply a note on paper of an archaic shape, in a thin, flowing calligraphy in faded ink, to the effect that she no longer went out at all. The tax notice was also enclosed, without comment.

They called a special meeting of the Board of Aldermen. A deputation waited upon her, knocked at the door through which no visitor had passed since she ceased giving china-painting lessons eight or ten years earlier. They were admitted by the old Negro into a dim hall from which a stairway mounted into still more shadow. It smelled of dust and disuse—a close, dank smell. The Negro led them into the parlor. It was furnished in heavy, leather-covered furniture. When the Negro opened the blinds of one window, they could see that the leather was cracked; and when they sat down, a faint dust rose sluggishly about their thighs, spinning with slow motes in the single sun-ray. On a tarnished gilt easel before the fireplace stood a crayon portrait of Miss Emily's father.

They rose when she entered—a small, fat woman in black, with a thin gold chain descending to her waist and vanishing into her belt, leaning on an ebony cane with a tarnished gold head. Her skeleton was small and spare; perhaps that was why what would have been merely plumpness in another was obesity in her. She looked bloated, like a body long submerged in motionless water, and of that pallid hue. Her eyes, lost in the fatty ridges of her face, looked like two small pieces of coal pressed into a lump of dough as they moved from one face to another while the visitors stated their errand.

She did not ask them to sit. She just stood in the door and listened quietly until the spokesman came to a stumbling halt. Then they could hear the invisible watch ticking at the end of the gold chain.

Her voice was dry and cold. "I have no taxes in Jefferson. Colonel Sartoris explained it to me. Perhaps one of you can gain access to the city records and satisfy yourselves."

"But we have. We are the city authorities, Miss Emily. Didn't you get a notice from the sheriff, signed by him?"

"I received a paper, yes," Miss Emily said. "Perhaps he considers himself the sheriff... I have no taxes in Jefferson."

"But there is nothing on the books to show that, you see. We must go by the—"

"See Colonel Sartoris. I have no taxes in Jefferson."

"But, Miss Emily—"

"See Colonel Sartoris." (Colonel Sartoris had been dead almost ten years.) "I have no taxes in Jefferson. Tobe!" The Negro appeared. "Show these gentlemen out."

II

So she vanquished them, horse and foot, just as she had vanquished their fathers thirty years before about the smell.

That was two years after her father's death and a short time after her sweetheart—the one we believed would marry her—had deserted her. After her father's death she went out very little; after her sweetheart went away, people hardly saw her at all. A few of the ladies had the temerity to call, but were not received, and the only sign of life about the place was the Negro man—a young man then—going in and out with a market basket.

"Just as if a man—any man—could keep a kitchen properly," the ladies said; so they were not surprised when the smell developed. It was another link between the gross, teeming world and the high and mighty Griersons.

A neighbor, a woman, complained to the mayor, Judge Stevens, eighty years old.

"But what will you have me do about it, madam?" he said.

"Why, send her word to stop it," the woman said. "Isn't there a law?"

"I'm sure that won't be necessary," Judge Stevens said. "It's probably just a snake or a rat that nigger of hers killed in the yard. I'll speak to him about it."

The next day he received two more complaints, one from a man who came in diffident deprecation. "We really must do something about it, Judge. I'd be the last one in the world to bother Miss Emily, but we've got to do something." That night the Board of Aldermen met—three graybeards and one younger man, a member of the rising generation.

"It's simple enough," he said. "Send her word to have her place cleaned up. Give her a certain time to do it in, and if she don't...."

"Dammit, sir," Judge Stevens said, "will you accuse a lady to her face of smelling bad?"

So the next night, after midnight, four men crossed Miss Emily's lawn and slunk about the house like burglars, sniffing along the base of the brickwork and at the cellar openings while one of them performed a regular sowing motion with his hand out of a sack slung from his shoulder. They broke open the cellar door and sprinkled lime there, and in all the outbuildings. As they recrossed the lawn, a window that had been dark was lighted and Miss Emily sat in it, the light behind her, and her upright torso motionless as that of an idol. They crept quietly across the lawn and into the shadow of the locusts that lined the street. After a week or two the smell went away.

That was when people had begun to feel really sorry for her. People in our town, remembering how old lady Wyatt, her great-aunt, had gone completely crazy at last, believed that the Griersons held themselves a little too high for what they really were. None of the young men were quite good enough for Miss Emily and such. We had long thought of them as a tableau, Miss Emily a slender figure in white in the background, her father a spraddled silhouette in the foreground, his back to her and clutching a horsewhip, the two of them framed by the back-flung front door. So when she got to be thirty and was still single, we were not pleased exactly, but vindicated; even with insanity in the family she wouldn't have turned down all of her chances if they had really materialized.

When her father died, it got about that the house was all that was left to her; and in a way, people were glad. At last they could pity Miss Emily. Being left alone, and a pauper, she had become humanized. Now she too would know the old thrill and the old despair of a penny more or less.

The day after his death all the ladies prepared to call at the house and offer condolence and aid, as is our custom Miss Emily met them at the door, dressed as usual and with no trace of grief on her face. She told them that her father was not dead. She did that for three days, with the ministers calling on her, and the doctors, trying to persuade her to let them dispose of the body. Just as they were about to resort to law and force, she broke down, and they buried her father quickly.

We did not say she was crazy then. We believed she had to do that. We remembered all the young men her father had driven away, and we knew that with nothing left, she would have to cling to that which had robbed her, as people will.

III

She was sick for a long time. When we saw her again, her hair was cut short, making her look like a girl, with a vague resemblance to those angels in colored church windows—sort of tragic and serene.

The town had just let the contracts for paving the sidewalks, and in the summer after her father's death they began the work. The construction company came with niggers and mules and machinery, and a foreman named Homer Barron, a Yankee—a big, dark, ready man, with a big voice and eyes lighter than his face. The little boys would follow in groups to hear him cuss the niggers, and the niggers singing in time to the rise and fall of picks. Pretty soon he knew everybody in town. Whenever you heard a lot of laughing anywhere about the square, Homer Barron would be in the center of the group. Presently we began to see him and Miss Emily on Sunday afternoons driving in the yellow-wheeled buggy and the matched team of bays from the livery stable.

At first we were glad that Miss Emily would have an interest, because the ladies all said, "Of course a Grierson would not think seriously of a Northerner, a day laborer." But there were still others, older people, who said that even grief could not cause a real lady to forget *noblesse oblige*—without calling it *noblesse oblige*. They just said, "Poor Emily. Her kinsfolk should come to her." She had some kin in Alabama; but years ago her father had fallen out with them over the estate of old lady Wyatt, the crazy woman, and there was no communication between the two families. They had not even been represented at the funeral.

And as soon as the old people said, "Poor Emily," the whispering began. "Do you suppose it's really so?" they said to one another. "Of course it is. What else could. . ." This behind their hands; rustling of craned silk and satin behind jalousies closed upon the sun of Sunday afternoon as the thin, swift clop-clop-clop of the matched team passed: "Poor Emily."

She carried her head high enough—even when we believed that she was fallen. It was as if she demanded more than ever the recognition of her dignity as the last Grierson; as if it had wanted that touch of earthiness to reaffirm her imperviousness. Like when she bought the rat poison, the arsenic. That was over a year after they had begun to say "Poor Emily," and while the two female cousins were visiting her.

"I want some poison," she said to the druggist. She was over thirty then, still a slight woman, though thinner than usual, with cold, haughty black eyes in a face the flesh of which was strained across the temples and about the eyesockets as you imagine a lighthouse-keeper's face ought to look. "I want some poison," she said.

"Yes, Miss Emily. What kind? For rats and such? I'd recom—"

"I want the best you have. I don't care what kind."

The druggist named several. "They'll kill anything up to an elephant. But what you want is—"

"Arsenic," Miss Emily said. "Is that a good one?"

"Is... arsenic? Yes, ma'am. But what you want—"

"I want arsenic."

The druggist looked down at her. She looked back at him, erect, her face like a strained flag. "Why, of course," the druggist said. "If that's what you want. But the law requires you to tell what you are going to use it for."

Miss Emily just stared at him, her head tilted back in order to look him eye for eye, until he looked away and went and got the arsenic and wrapped it up. The Negro delivery boy brought her the package; the druggist didn't come back. When she opened the package at home there was written on the box, under the skull and bones: "For rats."

IV

So the next day we all said, "She will kill herself"; and we said it would be the best thing. When she had first begun to be seen with Homer Barron, we had said, "She will marry him." Then we said, "She will persuade him yet," because Homer himself had remarked—he liked men, and it was known that he drank with the younger men in the Elks' Club—that he was not a marrying man. Later we said, "Poor Emily" behind the jalousies as they passed on Sunday afternoon in the glittering buggy, Miss Emily with her head high and Homer Barron with his hat cocked and a cigar in his teeth, reins and whip in a yellow glove.

Then some of the ladies began to say that it was a disgrace to the town and a bad example to the young people. The men did not want to interfere, but at last the ladies forced the Baptist minister—Miss Emily's people were Episcopal—to call upon her. He would never divulge what happened during that interview, but he refused to go back again. The next Sunday they again drove about the streets, and the following day the minister's wife wrote to Miss Emily's relations in Alabama.

So she had blood-kin under her roof again and we sat back to watch developments. At first nothing happened. Then we were sure that they were to be married. We learned that Miss Emily had been to the jeweler's and ordered a man's toilet set in silver, with the letters H. B. on each piece. Two days later we learned that she had bought a complete outfit of men's clothing, including a nightshirt, and we said, "They are married." We were really glad. We were glad because the two female cousins were even more Grierson than Miss Emily had ever been.

So we were not surprised when Homer Barron—the streets had been finished some time since—was gone. We were a little disappointed that there was not a public blowing-off, but we believed that he had gone on to prepare for Miss Emily's coming, or to give her a chance to get rid of the cousins. (By that time it was a cabal, and we were all Miss Emily's allies to help circumvent the cousins.) Sure enough, after another week they departed. And, as we had expected all along, within three days Homer Barron was back in town. A neighbor saw the Negro man admit him at the kitchen door at dusk one evening.

And that was the last we saw of Homer Barron. And of Miss Emily for some time. The Negro man went in and out with the market basket, but the front door remained closed. Now and then we would see her at a window for a moment, as the men did that night when they sprinkled the lime, but for almost six months she did not appear on the streets. Then we knew that this was to be expected too; as if that quality of her father which had thwarted her woman's life so many times had been too virulent and too furious to die.

When we next saw Miss Emily, she had grown fat and her hair was turning gray. During the next few years it grew grayer and grayer until it attained an even pepper-and-salt iron-gray, when it ceased turning. Up to the day of her death at seventy-four it was still that vigorous iron-gray, like the hair of an active man.

From that time on her front door remained closed, save for a period of six or seven years, when she was about forty, during which she gave lessons in china-painting. She fitted up a studio in one of the downstairs rooms, where the daughters and granddaughters of Colonel Sartoris' contemporaries were sent to her with the same regularity and in the same spirit that they were sent to church on Sundays with a twenty-five-cent piece for the collection plate. Meanwhile her taxes had been remitted.

Then the newer generation became the backbone and the spirit of the town, and the painting pupils grew up and fell away and did not send their children to her with boxes of color and tedious brushes and pictures cut from the ladies' magazines. The front door closed upon the last one and remained closed for good. When the town got free postal delivery, Miss Emily alone refused to let them fasten the metal numbers above her door and attach a mailbox to it. She would not listen to them.

Daily, monthly, yearly we watched the Negro grow grayer and more stooped, going in and out with the market basket. Each December we sent her a tax notice, which would be returned by the post office a week later, unclaimed. Now and then we would see her in one of the downstairs windows—she had evidently shut up the top floor of the house—like the carven torso of an idol in a niche, looking or not looking at us, we could never tell which. Thus she passed from generation to generation—dear, inescapable, impervious, tranquil, and perverse.

And so she died. Fell ill in the house filled with dust and shadows, with only a doddering Negro man to wait on her. We did not even know she was sick; we had long since given up trying to get any information from the Negro. He talked to no one, probably not even to her, for his voice had grown harsh and rusty, as if from disuse.

She died in one of the downstairs rooms, in a heavy walnut bed with a curtain, her gray head propped on a pillow yellow and moldy with age and lack of sunlight.

V

The Negro met the first of the ladies at the front door and let them in, with their hushed, sibilant voices and their quick, curious glances, and then he disappeared. He walked right through the house and out the back and was not seen again.

The two female cousins came at once. They held the funeral on the second day, with the town coming to look at Miss Emily beneath a mass of bought flowers, with the crayon face of her father musing profoundly above the bier and the ladies sibilant and macabre; and the very old men—some in their brushed Confederate uniforms—on the porch and the lawn, talking of Miss Emily as if she had been a contemporary of theirs, believing that they had danced with her and courted her perhaps, confusing time with its mathematical progression, as the old do, to whom all the past is not a diminishing road but, instead, a huge meadow which no winter ever quite touches, divided from them now by the narrow bottle-neck of the most recent decade of years.

　　Already we knew that there was one room in that region above stairs which no one had seen in forty years, and which would have to be forced. They waited until Miss Emily was decently in the ground before they opened it.

　　The violence of breaking down the door seemed to fill this room with pervading dust. A thin, acrid pall as of the tomb seemed to lie everywhere upon this room decked and furnished as for a bridal: upon the valance curtains of faded rose color, upon the rose-shaded lights, upon the dressing table, upon the delicate array of crystal and the man's toilet things backed with tarnished silver, silver so tarnished that the monogram was obscured. Among them lay a collar and tie, as if they had just been removed, which, lifted, left upon the surface a pale crescent in the dust. Upon a chair hung the suit, carefully folded; beneath it the two mute shoes and the discarded socks.

　　The man himself lay in the bed.

　　For a long while we just stood there, looking down at the profound and fleshless grin. The body had apparently once lain in the attitude of an embrace, but now the long sleep that outlasts love, that conquers even the grimace of love, had cuckolded him. What was left of him, rotted beneath what was left of the nightshirt, had become inextricable from the bed in which he lay; and upon him and upon the pillow beside him lay that even coating of the patient and biding dust.

　　Then we noticed that in the second pillow was the indentation of a head. One of us lifted something from it, and leaning forward, that faint and invisible dust dry and acrid in the nostrils, we saw a long strand of iron-gray hair.

非线性叙事与象征
——福克纳《献给艾米丽的玫瑰》的哥特式解读

　　《献给艾米丽的玫瑰》(A Rose for Emily)是福克纳最著名的短篇小说。该小说最早发表于1930年4月份的《星期六晚邮报》(Saturday Evening Post),后收录于福克纳的短篇小说集《十三篇》(These Thirteen,1931),《小说集》(Collected Stories,1950)和《威廉·福克纳短篇小说集》(Selected Short Stories of William Faulkner,1961)中。

　　该小说共分五个小节,女主人公是居住在美国南方杰弗森小镇(Jefferson)上的艾米丽·格里尔森(Emily Grierson)小姐。她被当作南方小镇上最后的贵族和淑女:居住在曾经豪华的房子里,与父亲出门都坐高级马车,能写漂亮典雅的信笺,能教孩子们画画。但因为追求她的男青年都被父亲拒绝,这导致了艾米丽年过三十岁仍旧孑然一身。父亲死后,艾米丽遇见了北方佬荷默·伯隆(Homer Barron)。这个精力充沛、充满活力的男人很快俘获了艾米丽的芳心。而正当她决定对心上人托付终身之际,却发现自己根本无法留住这个男人的心。根植于南方贵族骨子里的清高个性扭曲了艾米丽的内心,她购买砒霜谋杀了自己的男友,而且与尸体同床共枕直到她去世。这个秘密直到故事的最后才被小镇上的居民们发现。

小说讲述的故事体现了美国南方哥特式文学的典型特征:破败的老房子,离群索居的女主人,怪异的种种迹象和到故事结尾才揭晓的谋杀。那么福克纳在这部作品里采用了什么方法来营造其南方哥特式文学的氛围?下面就从非线性叙事、叙述者的身份之谜、象征和隐喻、种族歧视以及贵族身份与死亡的反差这五个方面来探讨福克纳的叙事方法。

一、非线性叙事

在初次阅读这个故事的时候,读者们的第一个反应也许是恐怖或者厌恶,但福克纳采用了巧妙的文学技巧让他的作品引人入胜,其中之一就是时间顺序的悬疑性安排。

这个故事明显不是按照时间顺序讲述的,而是采用了时间上的插叙与倒叙,这可以让读者感受到作者在讲故事方面的天赋。故事里只提到了几个具体的时间,比如镇长沙多里斯上校(Colonel Sartoris)是在1894年免除了艾米丽的纳税义务,而艾米丽是在74岁的时候去世的。因此我们还是可以按照时间顺序重新安排故事的小节。

第4节:艾米丽出生;
第2节:艾米丽和她的父亲在镇上坐着精致的马车;
第2节:艾米丽的父亲去世了,而艾米丽3天后才接受父亲去世的事实;
第3节:荷默·伯隆来到了镇上,并开始追求艾米丽;
第4节:艾米丽购置了一套男士的银质盥洗用具和衣物;
第3节:艾米丽在药店买了砒霜;
第4节:荷默失踪了;
第2节:艾米丽的房子周围散发出腐臭味;
第1节:艾米丽去世了,镇上的邻居们去吊唁;
第5节:房门打开了,黑人男仆也离开了,人们发现了艾米丽的秘密;

如果按照事件发展的时间顺序来讲述整个故事,那么艾米丽为什么要购买砒霜以及房子怎么会有腐臭味就缺乏悬疑色彩了。

当然,这个故事的伟大之处不只是非线性的时间安排,还有福克纳是如何一步一步让读者发现这个所谓的贵族小姐最后成了一个"倒下的纪念碑"("fallen monument")。

二、叙述者的身份之谜

这个故事开始于艾米丽的葬礼,然后在人们发现荷默的尸体时戛然而止。那么给读者讲述这个故事的叙述者是谁?这个叙述者是男性还是女性?是上了年纪的人还是年轻人?叙述者对艾米丽的态度是同情还是谴责?

故事的第一句话就是:"艾米丽·格里尔森小姐过世了,全镇的人都去送丧"("When Miss Emily Grierson died, our whole town went to her funeral")。这里的"我们"显然是一个集体的叙述声音。但到了后来,叙述者的视角转换了,变成了单一的叙述者,因为这个叙述者显然了解一些其他人不知道的秘密。可以说,叙述者的身份之谜增加了故事的悬疑成分。

三、象征和隐喻

阅读该作品,我们也许会问:故事的标题为什么是献给艾米丽的玫瑰?玫瑰色和玫瑰花意味着什么?在故事的最后,人们进入艾米丽的卧室后,发现里面有"败了色的玫瑰色窗帘,玫瑰色的灯罩"("upon the valance curtains of faded rose color, upon the rose-shaded lights")。玫瑰当然象征着爱情。福克纳自己是这样解释标题的含义:"这只是一个没有自己生活的可怜女人,她的父亲把她关起来,在她的爱人也要离她而去时,她不得不杀了他,这就是'一朵给艾米丽的玫瑰花'。"

除了玫瑰花,小说里还有其他的象征和隐喻。比如在故事第一节的开头就是艾米丽·格里尔森小姐的去世,镇上的人们前去吊唁。通过对艾米丽生前所住房子的描述,可以看出美国南方小镇昔日的繁华和今日的破败的对比:

"It was a big, squarish frame house that had once been white, decorated with cupolas and spires and scrolled balconies in the heavily lightsome style of the seventies, set on what had once been our most select street. But garages and cotton gins had encroached and obliterated even the august names of that neighborhood..."

"一幢过去漆成白色的四方形大木屋,坐落在当年一条最考究的街道上,还装点着有十九世纪七十年代风味的圆形屋顶、尖塔和涡形花纹的阳台,带有浓厚的轻盈气息。可是汽车间和轧棉机之类的东西侵犯了这一带庄严的名字,把它们涂抹得一干二净。"

这栋房子的变化也是一个隐喻:象征着昔日美国南方贵族的体面生活,以及在南北战争之后南方小镇的日益没落。

后来在镇上的代表就纳税问题拜访她时,从对艾米丽房屋内部的描述可以看出这所房子成了女主人公自我封闭的象征:

"It smelled of dust and disuse—a close, dank smell. The Negro led them into the parlor. It was furnished in heavy, leather-covered furniture. When the Negro opened the blinds of one window, they could see that the leather was cracked; and when they sat down, a faint dust rose sluggishly about their thighs, spinning with slow motes in the single sun-ray."

"一股尘封的气味扑鼻而来,空气阴湿而又不透气,这屋子长久没有人住了。黑人领他们到客厅里,里面摆设的笨重家具全都包着皮套子。黑人打开了一扇百叶窗,这时,便更可看出皮套子已经坼裂;等他们坐了下来,大腿两边就有一阵灰尘冉冉上升,尘粒在那一缕阳光中缓缓旋转。"

房子里因为多年不见阳光,也不开门窗,导致空气不流通,灰尘也很多。这说明晚年的艾米丽离群索居,也隐喻了她因为保守自己的秘密而把自己的房子变成了一座坟墓。

四、种族歧视

种族歧视是美国南方文学中不可避免的主题之一。在该小说中,南方残存的蓄奴制痕迹无处不在。当时的镇长沙多里斯上校明知奴隶制已经取消并且黑人获得了选举权,仍旧颁布了黑人妇女不系围裙不得上街的命令。由此可见福克纳笔下的南方小镇种族歧视的严重性。

从对黑人的称呼上也可以看出对黑人的歧视。艾米丽有一个忠实伺候她的黑人男仆,从青年到老态龙钟的暮年,他始终在为格里尔逊家族默默付出。而在故事里,他虽然有自己的名字,但他只是被称为"黑人"("the Negro")或是"那个黑鬼"("that nigger of hers"),这些词语都具有非常强烈的种族歧视色彩。黑人男仆是那个时代背景下黑人奴隶群体生存状态的真实缩影。

而从整个黑人群体来看,南北战争结束后,广大的黑人民众虽然获得了政治上的平等,却依旧饱受奴役和歧视,小说里黑仆沉默的本质就是他的话语权被剥夺。而且即使黑人找到了工作,也仍然面临着经济上的剥削和工作上的不平等。在故事里,北方佬荷默·伯隆带着黑人来小镇上铺路,镇上的孩子们可以听到"他用不堪入耳的话责骂黑人,而黑人则随着铁镐的上下起落有节奏地哼着劳动号子"("hear him cuss the niggers, and the niggers singing in time to the rise and fall of picks.")。

在故事的第五节,邻居们来吊唁艾米丽时,黑人老仆人在打开门后,自己从后门走出,就消失了。黑人男仆去了哪里?他是不是获得了自由?故事虽然没有给出答案,但这无疑值得我们思考。

五、贵族身份与死亡的反差

故事中的艾米丽被当作是南方最后的贵族与淑女的象征,但她的谋杀秘密使得她与死亡联系在了一起。比如在故事的第二节里,邻居们抱怨艾米丽房子里散发出难闻的气味,斯蒂芬法官则认为不应该当着"贵妇"("a lady")的面说有难闻的气味。这里的"贵妇"一词在美国南方无疑意味着白人女性,艾米丽成了南方贵族妇女的象征,她的名誉则需要同样是贵族的白人男性去保护。而她和父亲的肖像画则充分说明了这种关系:

"We had long thought of them as a tableau, Miss Emily a slender figure in white in the background, her father a spraddled silhouette in the foreground, his back to her and clutching a horsewhip, the two of them framed by the back-flung front door."

"我们把这家人一直看作一幅画中的人物：身段苗条、穿着白衣的艾米丽小姐立在背后，她父亲叉开双脚的侧影在前面，背对艾米丽，手执一根马鞭，一扇向后开的前门恰好嵌住了他们俩的身影。"

这幅画展示了贵族父女之间的关系：父亲代表了家族的权威，而女儿则扮演着典雅而顺从的贵族小姐形象。

在故事的第三节里，当荷默·伯隆来到小镇并开始于艾米丽一起出行后，镇上的人们议论纷纷，认为艾米丽不应该与一个北方佬在一起，即她不应该忘了她的"贵族举止"（"noblesse oblige"）。这个法语词的使用说明镇里的那些邻居们正是以贵族身份自居，去评价艾米丽的有失体统。

而对晚年艾米丽样貌的描述则充满了死亡的气息：

"…a small, fat woman in black, with a thin gold chain descending to her waist and vanishing into her belt, leaning on an ebony cane with a tarnished gold head. Her skeleton was small and spare; perhaps that was why what would have been merely plumpness in another was obesity in her. She looked bloated, like a body long submerged in motionless water, and of that pallid hue."

"一个小模小样、腰圆体胖的女人，穿了一身黑服，一条细细的金表链拖到腰部，落到腰带里去了，一根乌木拐杖支撑着她的身体，拐杖头的镶金已经失去光泽。她的身架矮小，也许正因为这个缘故，在别的女人身上显得不过是丰满，而她却给人以肥大的感觉。她看上去像长久泡在死水中的一具死尸，肿胀发白。"

这无疑是对艾米丽的秘密的暗示：因为她长期和她已死的恋人待在一起，自己也变得像一具死尸了。这也与艾米丽所谓的贵族身份和淑女象征形成了巨大的反差。

在故事的最后，小镇上的人们在艾米丽布置的像新房的卧室床上发现了荷默已经腐烂的尸体，以及枕头旁边"一绺长长的铁灰色头发"（"a long strand of iron-gray hair"）。小说到这里戛然而止，但留给读者们的思考却有很多：艾米丽曾经给镇上的孩子们上过画画课，她的水平应该也不差，为什么后来没有孩子们去她那里学画画了？那个黑人男仆为什么在知道艾米丽毒杀了她的恋人并保存了其尸体后还是愿意伺候艾米丽直至去世？这些都是值得我们进一步阅读和思考的问题。

主要参考文献

福克纳.献给爱米丽的一朵玫瑰花[M]//福克纳.福克纳短篇小说集.陶洁，编.南京：译林出版社，2001.

福克纳.喧哗与骚动[M].李文俊，译.上海：上海译文出版社，2010.

FAULKNER W. Collected Stories[M]. New York:Vintage,1995.

FAULKNER W. The Essential Faulkner[M]. New York:Random House,2012.

思考题

(1) 故事标题中的"玫瑰"有哪些含义？

(2) 故事的场景是美国南方的小镇，如果故事发生在别的地方，会有何不同？

(3) 故事中的女性人物扮演着什么角色？

(4) 故事中的黑人男仆和艾米丽哪一个更孤独？他们各自孤独的原因是什么？他们有选择的权利么？

(5) 如果这个故事是一个回忆录，那么这是谁的回忆？

(6) 故事结尾中的灰色头发有何意义？

Chapter 9　Joy Luck Club
by Amy Tan
(excerpts)

 背景介绍

谭恩美(Amy Tan,1952—),美国当代华裔女作家,1952年出生于美国加利福尼亚州奥克兰,其父母是从中国大陆来的移民。在父亲去世后,随母亲移居瑞士。在此期间,谭恩美了解到其母亲在来美国之前曾在中国有过一段婚姻,并在上海留有子女。谭恩美在1987年随母亲返回中国,并见到了她同母异父的三个姐姐。根据这段经历,谭恩美创作了《喜福会》(*Joy Luck Club*, 1989)。

该小说讲述了旧金山四家华裔移民家庭的故事,四家人组织了一个叫"喜福会"的俱乐部,他们定期聚在一起打麻将,还轮流做东做中国菜招待大家。整本书也像打麻将一样分四章,每一章又分四节,一共十六小节。四位母亲(其中一位母亲吴宿愿在故事开始时已经去世,她的故事是由其女儿吴菁妹讲述的)和她们的四位女儿分别从自己的角度讲述她们在中国和美国的经历,以及她们母女之间因文化差异等原因导致的冲突和最后的认同经历。

《喜福会》一经出版即在美国受到好评。在1989年《纽约时报》畅销书排行榜连续九个月上榜;1989年获L. A. Times书籍奖及美国国家书籍奖;1990年获美国联邦俱乐部书籍奖和美国加州书评会最佳小说奖;1991年获美国最佳小说奖。《喜福会》被翻译成25种语言,并于1993年被改编为同名电影。

谭恩美的小说还包括《灶神之妻》(*The Kitchen God's Wife*, 1991)、《灵感女孩》(*The Hundred Secret Senses*, 1995)、《接骨师之女》(*The Bonesetter's Daughter*, 2001)、《沉没之鱼》(*Saving Fish from Drowning*, 2005)和《奇幻山谷》(*The Valley of Amazement*, 2013)等。这些作品多表现母女两代移民关系和华裔在美国面临的文化冲突。尽管谭恩美获得了诸多奖项,但是其作品也因为对中国传统文化细节描述的部分失实而受到争议。

Feathers From a Thousand LI Away

The old woman remembered a swan she had bought many years ago in Shanghai for a foolish sum. This bird, boasted the market vendor, was once a duck that stretched its neck in hopes of becoming a goose, and now look! —it is too beautiful to eat.

Then the woman and the swan sailed across an ocean many thousands of li wide, stretching their necks toward America. On her journey she cooed to the swan: "In America I will have a daughter just like me. But over there nobody will say her worth is measured by the loudness of her husband's belch. Over there nobody will look down on her, because I will make her speak only perfect American English. And over there she will always be too full to swallow any sorrow! She will know my meaning, because I will give her this swan—a creature that became more than what was hoped for."

But when she arrived in the new country, the immigration officials pulled her swan away from her, leaving the woman fluttering her arms and with only one swan feather for a memory. And then she had to fill out so many forms she forgot why she had come and what she had left behind.

Now the woman was old. And she had a daughter who grew up speaking only English and swallowing more Coca-Cola than sorrow. For a long time now the woman had wanted to give her daughter the single swan feather and tell her, "This feather may look worthless, but it comes from afar and carries with it all my good intentions." And she waited, year after year, for the day she could tell her daughter this in perfect American English.

Jing-Mei Woo: The Joy Luck Club

My father has asked me to be the fourth corner at the Joy Luck Club. I am to replace my mother, whose seat at the mah jong table has been empty since she died two months ago. My father thinks she was killed by her own thoughts.

"She had a new idea inside her head," said my father. "But before it could come out of her mouth, the thought grew too big and burst. It must have been a very bad idea."

The doctor said she died of a cerebral aneurysm. And her friends at the Joy Luck

Club said she died just like a rabbit: quickly and with unfinished business left behind. My mother was supposed to host the next meeting of the Joy Luck Club.

The week before she died, she called me, full of pride, full of life: "Auntie Lin cooked red bean soup for Joy Luck. I'm going to cook black sesame-seed soup."

"Don't show off," I said.

"It's not showoff." She said the two soups were almost the same, *chabudwo*. Or maybe she said *butong*, not the same thing at all. It was one of those Chinese expressions that means the better half of mixed intentions. I can never remember things I didn't understand in the first place.

My mother started the San Francisco version of the Joy Luck Club in 1949, two years before I was born. This was the year my mother and father left China with one stiff leather trunk filled only with fancy silk dresses. There was no time to pack anything else, my mother had explained to my father after they boarded the boat. Still his hands swam frantically between the slippery silks, looking for his cotton shirts and wool pants.

When they arrived in San Francisco, my father made her hide those shiny clothes. She wore the same brown-checked Chinese dress until the Refugee Welcome Society gave her two hand-me-down dresses, all too large in sizes for American women. The society was composed of a group of white-haired American missionary ladies from the First Chinese Baptist Church. And because of their gifts, my parents could not refuse their invitation to join the church. Nor could they ignore the old ladies' practical advice to improve their English through Bible study class on Wednesday nights and, later, through choir practice on Saturday mornings. This was how my parents met the Hsus, the Jongs, and the St. Clairs. My mother could sense that the women of these families also had unspeakable tragedies they had left behind in China and hopes they couldn't begin to express in their fragile English. Or at least, my mother recognized the numbness in these women's faces. And she saw how quickly their eyes moved when she told them her idea for the Joy Luck Club.

Joy Luck was an idea my mother remembered from the days of her first marriage in Kweilin, before the Japanese came. That's why I think of Joy Luck as her Kweilin story. It was the story she would always tell me when she was bored, when there was nothing to do, when every bowl had been washed and the Formica table had been wiped down twice, when my father sat reading the newspaper and smoking one Pall Mall cigarette after another, a warning not to disturb him. This is when my mother would take out a box of old ski sweaters sent to us by unseen relatives from Vancouver. She would snip the bottom of a sweater and pull out a kinky thread of yarn, anchoring it to a piece of cardboard. And as she began to roll with one sweeping rhythm, she would start her story. Over the years, she told me the same story, except for the ending, which grew darker, casting long shadows into her life, and eventually into mine.

"I dreamed about Kweilin before I ever saw it," my mother began, speaking Chinese. "I dreamed of jagged peaks lining a curving river, with magic moss greening the banks. At the tops of these peaks were white mists. And if you could float down this river and eat the moss for food, you would be strong enough to climb the peak. If you slipped, you would only fall into a bed of soft moss and laugh. And once you reached the top, you would be able to see everything and feel such happiness it would be enough to never have worries in your life ever again.

"In China, everybody dreamed about Kweilin. And when I arrived, I realized how shabby my dreams were, how poor my thoughts. When I saw the hills, I laughed and shuddered at the same time. The peaks looked like giant fried fish heads trying to jump out of a vat of oil. Behind each hill, I could see shadows of another fish, and then another and another. And then the clouds would move just a little and the hills would suddenly become monstrous elephants marching slowly toward me! Can you see this? And at the root of the hill were secret caves. Inside grew hanging rock gardens in the shapes and colors of cabbage, winter melons, turnips, and onions. These were things so strange and beautiful you can't ever imagine them.

"But I didn't come to Kweilin to see how beautiful it was. The man who was my husband brought me and our two babies to Kweilin because he thought we would be safe. He was an officer with the Kuomintang, and after he put us down in a small room in a two-story house, he went off to the northwest, to Chungking.

"We knew the Japanese were winning, even when the newspapers said they were not. Every day, every hour, thousands of people poured into the city, crowding the sidewalks, looking for places to live. They came from the East, West, North, and South. They were rich and poor, Shanghainese, Cantonese, northerners, and not just Chinese, but foreigners and missionaries of every religion. And there was, of course, the Kuomintang and their army officers who thought they were top level to everyone else.

"We were a city of leftovers mixed together. If it hadn't been for the Japanese, there would have been plenty of reason for fighting to break out among these different people. Can you see it? Shanghai people with north-water peasants, bankers with barbers, rickshaw pullers with Burma refugees. Everybody looked down on someone else.

It didn't matter that everybody shared the same sidewalk to spit on and suffered the same fast-moving diarrhea. We all had the same stink, but everybody complained someone else smelled the worst. Me? Oh, I hated the American air force officers who said habba-habba sounds to make my face turn red. But the worst were the northern peasants who emptied their noses into their hands and pushed people around and gave everybody their dirty diseases.

"So you can see how quickly Kweilin lost its beauty for me. I no longer climbed the peaks to say, How lovely are these hills! I only wondered which hills the Japanese had reached. I sat in the dark corners of my house with a baby under each arm, waiting with nervous feet. When the sirens cried out to warn us of bombers, my neighbors and I jumped to our feet and scurried to the deep caves to hide like wild animals. But you can't stay in the dark for so long. Something inside of you starts to fade and you become like a starving person, crazy-hungry for light. Outside I could hear the bombing. Boom! Boom! And then the sound of raining rocks. And inside I was no longer hungry for the cabbage or the turnips of the hanging rock garden. I could only see the dripping bowels of an ancient hill that might collapse on top of me. Can you imagine how it is, to want to be neither inside nor outside, to want to be nowhere and disappear?

"So when the bombing sounds grew farther away, we would come back out like newborn kittens scratching our way back to the city. And always, I would be amazed to find the hills against the burning sky had not been torn apart.

"I thought up Joy Luck on a summer night that was so hot even the moths fainted to the ground, their wings were so heavy with the damp heat. Every place was so crowded there was no room for fresh air. Unbearable smells from the sewers rose up to my second-story window and the stink had nowhere else to go but into my nose. At all hours of the night and day, I heard screaming sounds. I didn't know if it was a peasant slitting the throat of a runaway pig or an officer beating a half-dead peasant for lying in his way on the sidewalk. I didn't go to the window to find out. What use would it have been? And that's when I thought I needed something to do to help me move.

"My idea was to have a gathering of four women, one for each corner of my mah jong table. I knew which women I wanted to ask. They were all young like me, with wishful faces. One was an army officer's wife, like myself. Another was a girl with very fine manners from a rich family in Shanghai. She had escaped with only a little money. And there was a girl from Nanking who had the blackest hair I have ever seen. She came from a low-class family, but she was pretty and pleasant and had married well, to an old man who died and left her with a better life.

"Each week one of us would host a party to raise money and to raise our spirits. The hostess had to serve special *dyansyin* foods to bring good fortune of all kinds—dumplings shaped like silver money ingots, long rice noodles for long life, boiled peanuts for conceiving sons, and of course, many good-luck oranges for a plentiful, sweet life.

"What fine food we treated ourselves to with our meager allowances! We didn't notice that the dumplings were stuffed mostly with stringy squash and that the oranges were spotted with wormy holes. We ate sparingly, not as if we didn't have enough, but to protest how we could not eat another bite, we had already bloated ourselves from earlier in the day. We knew we had luxuries few people could afford. We were the lucky ones.

"After filling our stomachs, we would then fill a bowl with money and put it where everyone could see. Then we would sit down at the mah jong table. My table was from my family and was of a very fragrant red wood, not what you call rosewood, but *hong mu*, which is so fine there's no English word for it. The table had a very thick pad, so that when the mah jong *pai* were spilled onto the table the only sound was of ivory tiles washing against one another.

"Once we started to play, nobody could speak, except to say '*Pung!*' or '*Chr!*' when taking a tile. We had to play with seriousness and think of nothing else but adding to our happiness through winning. But after sixteen rounds, we would again feast, this time to celebrate our good fortune. And then we would talk into the night until the morning, saying stories about good times in the past and good times yet to come.

"Oh, what good stories! Stories spilling out all over the place! We almost laughed to death. A rooster that ran into the house screeching on top of dinner bowls, the same bowls that held him quietly in pieces the next day! And one about a girl who wrote love letters for two friends who loved the same man. And a silly foreign lady who fainted on a toilet when firecrackers went off next to her.

"People thought we were wrong to serve banquets every week while many people in the city were starving, eating rats and, later, the garbage that the poorest rats used to feed on. Others thought we were possessed by demons—to celebrate when even within our own families we had lost generations, had lost homes and fortunes, and were separated, husband from wife, brother from sister, daughter from mother. Hnnnh! How could we laugh, people asked.

"It's not that we had no heart or eyes for pain. We were all afraid. We all had our miseries. But to despair was to wish back for something already lost. Or to prolong what was already unbearable. How much can you wish for a favorite warm coat that hangs in the closet of a house that burned down with your mother and father inside of it? How long can you see in your mind arms and legs hanging from telephone wires and starving dogs running down the streets with half-chewed hands dangling from their jaws? What was worse, we asked among ourselves, to sit and wait for our own deaths with proper somber faces? Or to choose our own happiness?

"So we decided to hold parties and pretend each week had become the new year. Each week we could forget past wrongs done to us. We weren't allowed to think a bad thought. We feasted, we laughed, we played games, lost and won, we told the best stories. And each week, we could hope to be lucky. That hope was our only joy. And that's how we came to call our little parties Joy Luck."

My mother used to end the story on a happy note, bragging about her skill at the game. "I won many times and was so lucky the others teased that I had learned the trick of a clever thief," she said. "I won tens of thousands of *yuan*. But I wasn't rich. No. By then paper money had become worthless. Even toilet paper was worth more. And that made us laugh harder, to think a thousand-*yuan* note wasn't even good enough to rub on our bottoms."

I never thought my mother's Kweilin story was anything but a Chinese fairy tale. The endings always changed. Sometimes she said she used that worthless thousand-*yuan* note to buy a half-cup of rice. She turned that rice into a pot of porridge. She traded that gruel for two feet from a pig. Those two feet became six eggs, those eggs six chickens. The story always grew and grew.

And then one evening, after I had begged her to buy me a transistor radio, after she refused and I had sulked in silence for an hour, she said, "Why do you think you are missing something you never had?" And then she told me a completely different ending to the story.

"An army officer came to my house early one morning," she said, "and told me to go quickly to my husband in Chungking. And I knew he was telling me to run away from Kweilin. I knew what happened to officers and their families when the Japanese arrived. How could I go? There were no trains leaving Kweilin. My friend from Nanking, she was so good to me. She bribed a man to steal a wheelbarrow used to haul coal. She promised to warn our other friends.

"I packed my things and my two babies into this wheelbarrow and began pushing to Chungking four days before the Japanese marched into Kweilin. On the road I heard news of the slaughter from people running past me. It was terrible. Up to the last day, the Kuomintang insisted that Kweilin was safe, protected by the Chinese army. But later that day, the streets of Kweilin were strewn with newspapers reporting great Kuomintang victories, and on top of these papers, like fresh fish from a butcher, lay rows of people—men, women, and children who had never lost hope, but had lost their lives instead. When I heard this news, I walked faster and faster, asking myself at each step, Were they foolish? Were they brave?

"I pushed toward Chungking, until my wheel broke. I abandoned my beautiful mah jong table of *hong mu*. By then I didn't have enough feeling left in my body to cry. I tied scarves into slings and put a baby on each side of my shoulder. I carried a bag in each hand, one with clothes, the other with food. I carried these things until deep grooves grew in my hands. And I finally dropped one bag after the other when my hands began to bleed and became too slippery to hold onto anything.

"Along the way, I saw others had done the same, gradually given up hope. It was like a pathway inlaid with treasures that grew in value along the way. Bolts of fine fabric and books. Paintings of ancestors and carpenter tools. Until one could see cages of ducklings now quiet with thirst and, later still, silver urns lying in the road, where people had been too tired to carry them for any kind of future hope. By the time I arrived in Chungking I had lost everything except for three fancy silk dresses which I wore one on top of the other."

"What do you mean by 'everything'?" I gasped at the end. I was stunned to realize the story had been true all along. "What happened to the babies?"

She didn't even pause to think. She simply said in a way that made it clear there was no more to the story: "Your father is not my first husband. You are not those babies."

When I arrive at the Hsus' house, where the Joy Luck Club is meeting tonight, the first person I see is my father. "There she is! Never on time!" he announces. And it's true. Everybody's already here, seven family friends in their sixties and seventies. They look up and laugh at me, always tardy, a child still at thirty-six.

I'm shaking, trying to hold something inside. The last time I saw them, at the funeral, I had broken down and cried big gulping sobs. They must wonder now how someone like me can take my mother's place. A friend once told me that my mother and I were alike, that we had the same wispy hand gestures, the same girlish laugh and sideways look. When I shyly told my mother this, she seemed insulted and said, "You don't even know little percent of me! How can you be me?" And she's right. How can I be my mother at Joy Luck?

Chapter 9 Joy Luck Club *by Amy Tan*

"Auntie, Uncle," I say repeatedly, nodding to each person there. I have always called these old family friends Auntie and Uncle. And then I walk over and stand next to my father.

He's looking at the Jongs' pictures from their recent China trip. "Look at that," he says politely, pointing to a photo of the Jongs' tour group standing on wide slab steps. There is nothing in this picture that shows it was taken in China rather than San Francisco, or any other city for that matter. But my father doesn't seem to be looking at the picture anyway. It's as though everything were the same to him, nothing stands out. He has always been politely indifferent. But what's the Chinese word that means indifferent because you can't *see* any differences? That's how troubled I think he is by my mother's death.

"Will you look at that," he says, pointing to another nondescript picture.

The Hsus' house feels heavy with greasy odors. Too many Chinese meals cooked in a too small kitchen, too many once fragrant smells compressed onto a thin layer of invisible grease. I remember how my mother used to go into other people's houses and restaurants and wrinkle her nose, then whisper very loudly: "I can see and feel the stickiness with my nose."

I have not been to the Hsus' house in many years, but the living room is exactly the same as I remember it. When Auntie An-mei and Uncle George moved to the Sunset district from Chinatown twenty-five years ago, they bought new furniture. It's all there, still looking mostly new under yellowed plastic. The same turquoise couch shaped in a semicircle of nubby tweed. The colonial end tables made out of heavy maple. A lamp of fake cracked porcelain. Only the scroll-length calendar, free from the Bank of Canton, changes every year.

I remember this stuff, because when we were children, Auntie An-mei didn't let us touch any of her new furniture except through the clear plastic coverings. On Joy Luck nights, my parents brought me to the Hsus'. Since I was the guest, I had to take care of all the younger children, so many children it seemed as if there were always one baby who was crying from having bumped its head on a table leg.

"You are responsible," said my mother, which meant I was in trouble if anything was spilled, burned, lost, broken, or dirty. I was responsible, no matter who did it. She and Auntie An-mei were dressed up in funny Chinese dresses with stiff stand-up collars and blooming branches of embroidered silk sewn over their breasts. These clothes were too fancy for real Chinese people, I thought, and too strange for American parties. In those days, before my mother told me her Kweilin story, I imagined Joy Luck was a shameful Chinese custom, like the secret gathering of the Ku Klux Klan or the tom-tom dances of TV Indians preparing for war.

But tonight, there's no mystery. The Joy Luck aunties are all wearing slacks, bright print blouses, and different versions of sturdy walking shoes. We are all seated around the dining room table under a lamp that looks like a Spanish candelabra. Uncle George puts on his bifocals and starts the meeting by reading the minutes:

"Our capital account is $24,825, or about $6,206 a couple, $3,103 per person. We sold Subaru for a loss at six and three-quarters. We bought a hundred shares of Smith International at seven. Our thanks to Lindo and Tin Jong for the goodies. The red bean soup was especially delicious. The March meeting had to be canceled until further notice. We were sorry to have to bid a fond farewell to our dear friend Suyuan and extended our sympathy to the Canning Woo family. Respectfully submitted, George Hsu, president and secretary."

That's it. I keep thinking the others will start talking about my mother, the wonderful friendship they shared, and why I am here in her spirit, to be the fourth corner and carry on the idea my mother came up with on a hot day in Kweilin.

But everybody just nods to approve the minutes. Even my father's head bobs up and down routinely. And it seems to me my mother's life has been shelved for new business.

Auntie An-mei heaves herself up from the table and moves slowly to the kitchen to prepare the food. And Auntie Lin, my mother's best friend, moves to the turquoise sofa, crosses her arms, and watches the men still seated at the table. Auntie Ying, who seems to shrink even more every time I see her, reaches into her knitting bag and pulls out the start of a tiny blue sweater.

The Joy Luck uncles begin to talk about stocks they are interested in buying. Uncle Jack, who is Auntie Ying's younger brother, is very keen on a company that mines gold in Canada.

"It's a great hedge on inflation," he says with authority. He speaks the best English, almost accentless. I think my mother's English was the worst, but she always thought her Chinese was the best. She spoke Mandarin slightly blurred with a Shanghai dialect.

"Weren't we going to play mah jong tonight?" I whisper loudly to Auntie Ying, who's slightly deaf.

"Later," she says, "after midnight."

"Ladies, are you at this meeting or not?" says Uncle George. After everybody votes unanimously for the Canada gold stock, I go into the kitchen to ask Auntie An-mei why the Joy Luck Club started investing in stocks.

"We used to play mah jong, winner take all. But the same people were always winning, the same people always losing," she says. She is stuffing wonton, one chopstick jab of gingery meat dabbed onto a thin skin and then a single fluid turn with her hand that seals the skin into the shape of a tiny nurse's cap. "You can't have luck when someone else has skill. So long time ago, we decided to invest in the stock market. There's no skill in that. Even your mother agreed."

Auntie An-mei takes count of the tray in front of her. She's already made five rows of eight wonton each. "Forty wonton, eight people, ten each, five row more," she says aloud to herself, and then continues stuffing. "We got smart. Now we can all win and lose equally. We can have stock market luck. And we can play mah jong for fun, just for a few dollars, winner take all. Losers take home leftovers! So everyone can have some joy. Smart-hanh?"

I watch Auntie An-mei make more wonton. She has quick, expert fingers. She doesn't have to think about what she is doing. That's what my mother used to complain about, that Auntie An-mei never thought about what she was doing.

"She's not stupid," said my mother on one occasion, "but she has no spine. Last week, I had a good idea for her. I said to her, Let's go to the consulate and ask for papers for your brother. And she almost wanted to drop her things and go right then. But later she talked to someone. Who knows who? And that person told her she can get her brother in bad trouble in China. That person said FBI will put her on a list and give her trouble in the U. S. the rest of her life. That person said, You ask for a house loan and they say no loan, because your brother is a communist. I said, You already have a house! But still she was scared.

文化身份和母女关系的冲突与认同——解读《喜福会》

《喜福会》这部小说是典型的族裔文学作品。亚裔文学与非裔、印第安裔和拉丁裔文学都会探讨由于族裔身份引起的文化身份冲突等问题,即小说中的主人公如何看待其族裔身份在美国主流环境中面临的种族歧视和身份认同等问题。因此,华裔文学如何以西方人可以理解和接受的方式用英文再现中国传统文化以及中西文化差异是华裔文学作品中的主题之一。此外,《喜福会》还特别关注了华裔母女之间因为文化差异和母女关系导致的冲突问题。本文从中国文化传统的改写、歧视与反抗、母女两代人的冲突与认同以及族裔身份认同等几方面探讨该作品的艺术特色。

一、中国文化传统的改写

用英语向西方读者展示中国的传统文化,不可避免地会涉及对文化传统的改写。《喜福会》中有的改写是结合了故事中母女关系的主题。比如,在小说的每一章前面都有一个短的寓言故事:千里鹅毛、二十六道凶门、美国式解读、西天王母。这些寓言就体现了母女两代人对中国传统文化的理解差异。在第一章的寓言故事"千里鹅毛"中,老太太带着一根鹅毛远渡重洋来到美国,希望她的孩子能说完美的英语,能过得衣食无忧,却不料被移民局没收了。千里送鹅毛的故事来自《路史》中的记载。古代土官缅氏派遣缅伯高送天鹅给唐朝,过沔阳湖,鹅飞走了,只有一翎留了下来。缅伯高只好将这一翎作为礼物呈上,并说:"礼轻人意重,千里送鹅毛。"宋朝的苏轼、欧阳修、黄庭坚等人都有千里送鹅毛的诗句流传下来。这里可以说是华裔移民对千里鹅毛的一种解读。

但谭恩美对某些中国传统故事的改写显得过于夸张和残忍。在第一章第二节许安梅的故事《伤疤》里,许安梅讲述了自己的母亲因为嫁给别人做了三姨太,被娘家人嫌弃。在许安梅的外婆病重的时候,许安梅的母亲将自己胳膊上的肉割了一片下来给外婆做了一碗汤。割骨疗亲的故事在我国古代被认为是人衰老时血气也衰弱,需要补充血气,而用亲人尤其是晚辈亲人的肉或器官来补,是因为亲人间本身有血缘关系,特别是父母子女之间血气更是可以直接转移,所以被当作一种治疗方法。

千里鹅毛和割骨疗亲的故事在不熟悉中国传统文化的西方读者眼里会显得比较愚昧甚至残忍。但谭恩美并没有一味地描写中国传统的愚昧之处,她也描写了中国传统价值观的可取之处,这在母女两代人的冲突中显得尤为典型。

二、性别歧视与反抗

在以女性人物为主的《喜福会》里,不仅是在旧中国的女性面临着性别歧视问题,即使到了现代的美国,她们也会在婚姻和工作中面临性别歧视问题。故事里的母亲和女儿都在经历这些歧视的过程中实现了自我意识的觉醒和反抗。

在第一章第三节江林多的故事《红烛》里,江林多从小被指腹为婚,来给她相面的媒婆说她会是个好媳妇,因为她属马,会是个勤快的媳妇。属相被当作对性格和婚姻等命运判决的重要因素。这在拉丁裔女作家希斯内罗丝(Sandra Cisneros,1954—)的《芒果街上的小屋》(*The House on Mango Street*,1983)中也有类似的描述:女主人公在谈到自己名字的含义时也说到自己是在马年出生的,而在一些墨西哥男性的传统观念里,马年出生的女性会被认为是运气不好的。

在第三章第一节丽娜·圣克莱尔的故事《饭粒丈夫》里,丽娜与其丈夫哈罗德几乎在所有的家庭开支方面(甚至包括丽娜不喜欢养的猫和很少吃的冰激凌)都是 AA 制,而哈罗德的工资差不多是她的七倍。在母亲发现女儿和女婿的物品清单后，虽然女儿是以文化差异来解释，但在母亲的坚持和帮助下，丽娜最后还是鼓起勇气对哈罗德说明自己其实不吃冰激凌，将其从清单中划掉，并且表达了不想生活中所有事情都斤斤计较的想法。

三、母女两代人的冲突与认同

在四对母女的故事中，母女之间往往是从误解和冲突开始，而在故事最后达到了某种程度上的认同与和解。比如，在第二章第四节吴菁妹的故事《望女成凤》里，母亲希望她从小能努力练习钢琴，成为神童，从而更好地融入美国社会：

"My mother believed you could be anything you wanted to be in America. You could open a restaurant. You could work for the government and get good retirement. You could buy a house with almost no money down. You could become rich. You could become instantly famous."

"在美国，任何梦想都能成为事实。你可以做一切你想做的：开餐馆，或者在政府部门工作，以期得到很高的退休待遇。你可以不用付一个子的现金，就可以买到一栋房子。你有可能发财，也有可能出人头地。"

但吴菁妹小时候并不理解，认为在美国父母不应该逼迫自己的孩子。而直到母亲去世后，吴菁妹再次打开钢琴，回忆起小时候弹的曲子，这才意识到母亲对自己严格要求的含义。在第三章第四节吴菁妹的故事《最佳品质》里，在吴菁妹已经成年后，母亲送给她一块护身符，并且告诉吴菁妹虽然她也许在弹琴和下棋方面比不过别人家的孩子，但她拥有善良的品质，这时的吴菁妹理解了母亲对她的期待。

同样，在第二章第一节韦弗里·江小时候的故事《游戏规则》里，作为女儿的韦弗里从小就展示出了下棋的天赋。但她不愿意母亲把自己当战利品一样到处炫耀，因此和母亲产生了隔阂。韦弗里发现即使是在梦里也在和母亲下棋，深感焦虑不安的她只能选择逃避。到了第三章第二节韦弗里长大后的故事《四面八方》里，虽然韦弗里还是会就她的发型，吃饭要不要给小费等琐事与母亲意见不一致；而且她的美国男友在一家人吃饭时因中西餐桌礼仪的差异出了很多洋相，但到了故事最后，她也终于明白其实她的母亲只是在等待女儿敞开心扉。

四、族裔身份的认同

如何理解自己的华裔身份是故事中的女儿们始终要面临的问题：一方面，她们会因为自身的华裔身份在学习和工作时面临种族歧视的问题；另一方面，她们从小接受美国教育，能够说流利的英语，接受的是美国的价值观和生活方式。因此，她们如何解决自己的族裔身份认同问题是小说中的主题之一。

在最后一个故事，即第四章第四节吴菁妹的故事《团圆》里，吴菁妹在十五岁读高中的时候并不认为自己是中国人,但她的母亲却说这是她无法逃避的,因为这是与生俱来的。多年后,吴菁妹在从香港进入深圳的那一刻起,就觉得自己起了变化:

"I saw myself transforming like a werewolf, a mutant tag of DNA suddenly triggered, replicating itself insidiously into a syndrome, a cluster of telltale Chinese behaviors, all those things my mother did to embarrass me—haggling with store owners, pecking her mouth with a toothpick in public, being color-blind to the fact that lemon yellow and pale pink are not good combinations for winter clothes."

"我恍若看见自己像个狼人似的变了身,DNA 的突变体被激活,典型的中国式举止行为不知不觉地在我身上显现——所有那些母亲做来令我难堪的事,比如和商店老板讨价还价,在公共场合用牙签剔牙,色盲似的看不出柠檬黄和浅粉色不宜搭配做冬装。"

这里对典型中国人行为的描述当然有以偏概全的问题,但也可以看出这是一些西方人眼中的中国人的刻板印象。

作品还以吴菁妹的视角描写了当时广州的街景给她带来的文化冲击:

"I can see row after row of apartments, each floor cluttered with laundry hanging out to dry on the balcony... And then there is a building, its front laced with scaffolding made of bamboo poles held together with plastic strips. Men and women are standing on narrow platforms, scraping the sides, working without safety straps or helmets."

"我可以看到排排楼房连绵不断,每层楼的阳台都晾晒着衣服……接着前方出现一座尚未竣工的大楼,楼前的脚手架是用竹竿和塑料绳扎成的,男女工人们站在狭窄的脚手架上刮着墙皮,既没戴安全帽,也没系安全带。"

这里也是从西方人的视角来看待当时中国的发展状况和中西生活方式的差异(比如中国人是在阳台上晾衣服而不是用烘干设备)。

但是吴菁妹通过父亲的讲述,终于明白了她的中文名字的含义,也了解了为什么母亲会在从桂林逃难时不得不把两个女儿遗弃在路上。吴菁妹在上海与两位同母异父的姐姐相见时,她仿佛看到了自己的母亲。而这时,吴菁妹也终于明白自己身上的中国成分的含义了。《团圆》既是吴菁妹和其家人的团聚,也象征她对自己族裔身份的认同。

《喜福会》用英文书写了中国传统故事,女性面临的性别和种族歧视问题及她们的反抗,母女两代人的价值观冲突与和解,以及她们的族裔身份与认同经历。虽然从中国读者的视角来看,个别中国传统故事过于愚昧或残忍,但《喜福会》还是以中国传统故事中的大团圆作为结局:吴菁妹和她同母异父的两个妹妹相见了,吴菁妹也意识到中国是流淌在她血液中的家。可以说团圆实现了她们母亲的愿望,也实现了读者对华裔作品的期待。

主要参考文献

程爱民,张瑞华. 中美文化的冲突与融合:对《喜福会》的文化解读[J]. 国外文学,2001

(3):86-92.

顾悦.论《喜福会》中的创伤记忆与家庭模式[J].当代外国文学,2011(2):100-110.

何卫华.《喜福会》:"天鹅"之歌与政治隐喻[J].外语教学,2015(30):70-75.

刘昀.母女情深——论《喜福会》的故事环结构与母女关系主题[J].四川外语学院学报,2003,19(6):51-55.

陆薇.从话语的消失看《喜福会》中主体的重建[J].四川外语学院学报,2000(16.4):18-22.

谭恩美.喜福会[M].李军,章力,译.北京:外语教学与研究出版社,2016.

袁霞.从《喜福会》中的"美国梦"主题看东西文化冲突[J].外国文学研究,2003(3):82-85.

张瑞华.解读谭恩美《喜福会》中的中国麻将[J].外国文学评论,2001(1):95-100.

周晔.飞散、杂合与全息翻译——从《喜福会》看飞散文学写作特色及翻译理念[J].解放军外国语学院学报,2008,31(4):76-81.

HAMILTON P L. Feng Shui, Astrology, and the Five Elements: Traditional Chinese Belief in Amy Tan's *The Joy Luck Club*[J]. MELUS,1994,24(2):125-145.

HEUNG M. Daughter-Text/Mother-Text: Matrilineage in Amy Tan's *Joy Luck Club*[J]. Feminist Studies,1993,19(3):596-616.

SOURIS S. "Only Two Kinds of Daughters": Inter-Monologue Dialogicity in *The Joy Luck Club*[J]. MELUS,1994,19(2):99-123.

TAN A. The Joy Luck Club[M]. New York: Penguin Books, 2006.

XU B. Memory and the Ethnic Self: Reading Amy Tan's *The Joy Luck Club*[J]. MELUS,1994,19(1):3-18.

思考题

(1)在故事里的母女两代人中,你更喜欢哪一代?哪一代更为坚强?

(2)故事里对男性美国人是如何描写的?他们与华裔女友或妻子之间产生的分歧是中西文化差异导致的么?

(3)故事里有四对母女,她们之间的冲突和最后的和解有何共同点?

Part Ⅱ Poetry

Chapter 1　Sonnet 18：Shall I compare thee to a summer's day?

by William Shakespeare

 **背景介绍**

十四行诗起源于文艺复兴初期，为意大利诗人彼特拉克（Francesco Petrarch, 1304—1374）所首创，16世纪自意大利传入英国。在格律上，英诗中的十四行诗普遍采用抑扬格五音步（iambic pentameter）；在音韵上，十四行诗主要分为三种：彼特拉克体、斯宾塞体和莎士比亚体。其中莎士比亚体由三个四行诗和一个英雄双行体组成，其押韵格式多为 abab, cdcd, efef, gg。在内容上，每节都可以展开一个新的意义内容，通过末尾的偶句点明主题。

莎士比亚不仅是一代戏剧大师，其创作的十四行诗也脍炙人口，共有一百五十四首之多。一般认为，这些诗作的第一首至一百二十六首是赠给作者的朋友——一位英姿勃发的青年贵族。其中尤以第十八首影响力最大，广受好评。在诗中，莎士比亚不吝溢美之词，既赞誉了朋友的美貌，又表达了对诗歌艺术的信心。自然界的力量会磨蚀人的容颜，直至消灭人的肉身，而凝结在诗歌作品中的人类智慧，却可以跨越时空，达到永恒。

 **文本选读**

Sonnet 18：Shall I compare thee to a summer's day?
　　　　by William Shakespeare

Shall I compare thee to a summer's day?
Thou art more lovely and more temperate.
Rough winds do shake the darling buds of May,
And summer's lease hath all too short a date.

Sometime too hot the eye of heaven shines,
And often is his gold complexion dimm'd;

莎士比亚十四行诗第十八首：
　　我能否将你比作夏天？
　　　　威廉·莎士比亚

我能否将你比作夏天？
你比夏天更美丽温婉。
狂风将五月的蓓蕾凋残，
夏日的勾留何其短暂。

休恋那丽日当空，
转眼会云雾迷蒙；

And every fair from fair sometime declines,　　休叹那百花飘零，
By chance, or nature's changing course, untrimm'd;　　摧折于无常的天命；

But thy eternal summer shall not fade,　　唯有你永恒的夏日常新，
Nor lose possession of that fair thou ow'st.　　你的美貌亦毫发无损。
Nor shall Death brag thou wander'st in his shade,　　死神也无缘将你幽禁，
When in eternal lines to time thou grow'st.　　你在我永恒的诗中长存。

So long as men can breathe or eyes can see,　　只要世间尚有人吟诵我的诗篇，
So long lives this, and this gives life to thee.　　这诗就将不朽，永葆你的芳颜。

（朱生豪　译）

作品赏析

　　此诗在音韵上属于经典的莎士比亚体，韵式为：abab, cdcd, efef, gg。每一诗行十个音节，节奏上按轻重搭配构成五个音步，即抑扬格五音步。

　　该诗首句就采用问话体"我能否将你比作夏天？"不知道诗人此刻是在与友人交谈，还是在自言自语。舒缓的语气，将读者引入思考。英国所处地理纬度较高，夏天不炎热，是气候宜人的季节，赋予读者美好的联想：温暖的阳光，和煦的微风，娇艳的花朵，纷飞的蜜蜂，苍翠的群山以及人们在夏季独有的那份恬适与慵懒。"你比夏天更美丽温婉。"夏日已然如此美好，与朋友相比依旧显得黯然失色。读到此句，作为读者的我们不禁恍然大悟。原来夏日仅仅是个铺垫，用来衬托朋友更美丽、更温婉。

　　紧接着诗行的发展犹如平地之处有惊雷。一方面，"狂风"肆虐，摧残着"五月的蓓蕾"，不禁让人心生怜惜，感叹世间美好的事物在自然的伟力面前竟是如此不堪一击，转瞬即逝；另一方面，夏季天气多变，"丽日当头"转眼间便切换为"云雾迷蒙"。自然展现出神秘莫测的一面，令人敬畏。

　　"休叹那百花飘零，摧折于无常的天命"，面对"狂风"过境后"百花飘零"的残局，诗人难免悲从中来，认为是"nature's changing course"（自然界变化无常的天命）造成了人世间种种的遗憾。西方自古希腊时代起，人类就敬畏变幻无常的命运。东方的文学经典中也有"天道常变易，运数杳难寻"这样的诗句来感慨世事无常，造化弄人。至此，读者不禁会联想到诗人所歌颂的那位朋友。随着凋零的花朵被自然的力量摧残殆尽，那个曾经比夏天更美丽、更温婉的朋友在自然界的风暴中是否也面临在劫难逃的宿命呢？

　　第三节诗人笔锋一转，只"but"一词便一扫笼罩在读者心中忧虑叹惋的阴霾。诗歌基调亦由沉重转为明快，前后对比，更加凸显"你永恒夏日"的弥足珍贵。纵然"百花飘零"，但"你的美貌亦毫发无损"；"无常的天命"摧折百花，但"死神"对"你"却束手无策，只因"你在我永恒的诗中长存"。这最后一句犹如神来之笔，画龙点睛，点明诗人真实意图

不仅在于赞美朋友、歌颂友谊,更是为了褒扬诗歌不朽的力量。

　　诗歌最后两行进一步阐释缘由,诗人赞颂的朋友已融进了诗人的创作,从这个意义上说,诗人赋予了朋友永恒的生命力。只要诗人坚信自己的诗篇能成为经典,为世人传诵,朋友便在一次次诵读中永葆青春,在一代代读者心中鲜活灿烂。如此一来,诗人将朋友的美丽化为动人诗篇,而动人的诗篇又延续朋友的美丽,一人一诗,互相成全。最后,诗人又以诗咏诗,极大地提升了诗歌意境,升华了诗歌主题,成为传世佳作,也应验了诗人所说的"你在我永恒的诗中长存"。

思考题

　　(1)诗人为何选择将友人与夏天相比,而非春天、秋天或冬天?

　　(2)第一节中的"summer"与第三节中的"summer"所指是否一致? 如有不同,区别在哪里?

　　(3)该诗的本意是赞颂朋友,希望朋友的美在诗人的诗中永生,为何诗人却没有直接描绘朋友的美而是用大量笔墨描写短暂易逝的夏日?

延伸阅读

Sonnet 75 from Amoretti

by Edmund Spenser

One day I wrote her name upon the strand,
But came the waves and washed it away:
Again I wrote it with a second hand,
But came the tide, and made my pains his prey.

"Vain man," said she, "that dost in vain assay,
A mortal thing so to immortalize;
For I myself shall like to this decay,
And eke my name be wiped out likewise."

"Not so,"(quod I) "let baser things devise,
To die in dust, but you shall live by fame:
My verse your vertues rare shall eternize,
And in the heavens write your glorious name:

Where whenas death shall all the world subdue,
Our love shall live, and later life renew."

Chapter 2　Elegy Written in a Country Churchyard

by Thomas Gray

 背景介绍

英国诗人托马斯·格雷在 1750 年创作了《墓畔哀歌》并于 1751 年公开发表。本诗的创作灵感部分源于格雷在另一位诗人 Richard West 去世(1742 年)后引发的一连串思索。全诗以平静、沉思般的语气探讨了"死亡"和"对死者的追思和缅怀"这两大主题。诗篇的叙述者通过思量这些默默无闻的墓中人的生平经历,内心泛起一丝丝涟漪。作为最广为人知的英文诗篇之一,《墓畔哀歌》中的诗句被后来者广为借鉴和引用,其中一些表达已然成为英语中的习语,亦或是被引用作为其他小说(*Far from the Madding Crowd*)或者电影(*The Paths of Glory*)的标题。

 文本选读

Elegy Written in a Country Churchyard 　　　　by Thomas Gray	墓畔哀歌 托马斯·格雷

The curfew tolls the knell of parting day,　　　　晚钟响起来一阵阵给白昼报丧,
The lowing herd wind slowly o'er the lea,　　　　牛群在草原上迂回,吼声起落,
The plowman homeward plods his weary way,　　耕地人累了,回家走,脚步跟跄,
And leaves the world to darkness and to me.　　 把整个世界留给了黄昏与我。

Now fades the glimm'ring landscape on the sight,　苍茫的景色逐渐从眼前消退,
And all the air a solemn stillness holds,　　　　一片肃穆的寂静盖遍了尘寰,
Save where the beetle wheels his droning flight,　只听见嗡嗡的甲虫转圈子纷飞,
And drowsy tinklings lull the distant folds;　　　昏沉的铃声催眠着远处的羊栏。

Save that from yonder ivy-mantled tow'r　　　　只听见常春藤披裹的塔顶底下,

Chapter 2 Elegy Written in a Country Churchyard *by Thomas Gray*

The moping owl does to the moon complain
Of such, as wand'ring near her secret bow'r,
Molest her ancient solitary reign.

Beneath those rugged elms, that yew-tree's shade,
Where heaves the turf in many a mould'ring heap,
Each in his narrow cell for ever laid,
The rude forefathers of the hamlet sleep.

The breezy call of incense-breathing Morn,
The swallow twitt'ring from the straw-built shed,
The cock's shrill clarion, or the echoing horn,
No more shall rouse them from their lowly bed.

For them no more the blazing hearth shall burn,
Or busy housewife ply her evening care:
No children run to lisp their sire's return,
Or climb his knees the envied kiss to share.

Oft did the harvest to their sickle yield,
Their furrow oft the stubborn glebe has broke;
How jocund did they drive their team afield!
How bow'd the woods beneath their sturdy stroke!

Let not Ambition mock their useful toil,
Their homely joys, and destiny obscure;
Nor Grandeur hear with a disdainful smile
The short and simple annals of the poor.

The boast of heraldry, the pomp of pow'r,
And all that beauty, all that wealth e'er gave,
Awaits alike th' inevitable hour.
The paths of glory lead but to the grave.

Nor you, ye proud, impute to these the fault,

一只阴郁的柢枭向月亮诉苦，
怪人家无端走进它秘密的住家，
搅扰它这个悠久而僻静的领土。

峥嵘的榆树底下，扁柏的荫里，
草皮鼓起了许多零落的荒堆，
各自在洞窟里永远放下了身体，
小村里粗鄙的父老在那里安睡。

香气四溢的晨风轻松的呼召，
燕子从茅草棚子里吐出的呢喃，
公鸡的尖喇叭，使山鸣谷应的猎号
再不能唤醒他们在地下的长眠。

在他们，熊熊的炉火不再会燃烧，
忙碌的管家妇不再会赶她的夜活；
孩子们不再会"牙牙"的报父亲来到，
为一个亲吻爬倒他膝上去争夺。

往常是：他们一开镰就所向披靡，
顽梗的泥板让他们犁出了垄沟；
他们多么欢欣地赶牲口下地！
他们一猛砍，树木就一棵棵低头！

"雄心"别嘲讽他们实用的操劳，
家常的欢乐，默默无闻的命运；
"豪华"也不用带着轻蔑的冷笑，
来听讲穷人的又短又简的生平。

门第的炫耀，有权有势的煊赫，
凡是美和财富所能赋予的好处，
前头都等待着不可避免的时刻：
光荣的道路无非是引导到坟墓。

骄傲人，你也不要怪这些人不行，

If Mem'ry o'er their tomb no trophies raise,	"怀念"没有给这些人建立纪念堂,
Where thro' the long-drawn aisle and fretted vault	没有让悠长的廊道、雕花的拱顶,
The pealing anthem swells the note of praise.	洋溢着洪亮的赞美歌,进行颂扬。
Can storied urn or animated bust	栩栩的半身像,铭刻了事略的瓮碑,
Back to its mansion call the fleeting breath?	难道能恢复断气,促使还魂?
Can Honour's voice provoke the silent dust,	"荣誉"的声音能激发沉默的死灰?
Or Flatt'ry soothe the dull cold ear of Death?	"献媚"能叫死神听软了耳根?
Perhaps in this neglected spot is laid	也许这一块地方,尽管荒芜,
Some heart once pregnant with celestial fire;	就埋着曾经充满过灵焰的一颗心;
Hands, that the rod of empire might have sway'd,	一双手,本可以执掌到帝国的王笏,
Or wak'd to ecstasy the living lyre.	或者出神入化地拨响了七弦琴。
But Knowledge to their eyes her ample page	可是"知识"从不曾对他们展开
Rich with the spoils of time did ne'er unroll;	它世代积累而琳琅满目的书卷;
Chill Penury repress'd their noble rage,	"贫寒"压制了他们高贵的襟怀,
And froze the genial current of the soul.	冻结了他们从灵府涌出的流泉。
Full many a gem of purest ray serene,	世界上多少晶莹皎洁的珠宝
The dark unfathom'd caves of ocean bear:	埋在幽暗而深不可测的海底;
Full many a flow'r is born to blush unseen,	世界上多少花吐艳而无人知晓,
And waste its sweetness on the desert air.	把芳香白白地散发给荒凉的空气。
Some village-Hampden, that with dauntless breast	也许有乡村汉普顿在这里埋身,
The little tyrant of his fields withstood;	反抗过当地的小霸王,胆大、坚决;
Some mute inglorious Milton here may rest,	也许有缄口的米尔顿,从没有名声;
Some Cromwell guiltless of his country's blood.	有一位克伦威尔,并不曾害国家流血。
Th' applause of list'ning senates to command,	要博得满场的元老雷动的鼓掌,
The threats of pain and ruin to despise,	无视威胁,全不顾存亡生死,
To scatter plenty o'er a smiling land,	把富庶,丰饶遍播到四处八方,
And read their hist'ry in a nation's eyes,	打从全国的笑眼里读自己的历史——
Their lot forbade: nor circumscrib'd alone	他们的命运可不许:既不许罪过

Their growing virtues, but their crimes confin'd;	有所放纵,也不许发挥德行;
Forbade to wade through slaughter to a throne,	不许从杀戮中间涉登宝座
And shut the gates of mercy on mankind,	从此对人类关上仁慈的大门;

The struggling pangs of conscious truth to hide,	不许掩饰天良在内心的发作,
To quench the blushes of ingenuous shame,	隐瞒天真的羞愧,恬不红脸;
Or heap the shrine of Luxury and Pride	不许用诗神的金焰点燃了香火
With incense kindled at the Muse's flame.	锦上添花去塞满"骄""奢"的神龛。

Far from the madding crowd's ignoble strife,	远离了纷纭人世的勾心斗角,
Their sober wishes never learn'd to stray;	他们有清醒愿望,从不学糊涂,
Along the cool sequester'd vale of life	顺着生活的清凉僻静的山坳,
They kept the noiseless tenor of their way.	他们坚持了不声不响的正路。

Yet ev'n these bones from insult to protect,	可是叫这些尸骨免受到糟踏,
Some frail memorial still erected nigh,	还是有脆弱的碑牌树立在近边,
With uncouth rhymes and shapeless sculpture deck'd,	点缀了拙劣的韵语、凌乱的刻划,
Implores the passing tribute of a sigh.	请求过往人就便献一声婉叹。

Their name, their years, spelt by th' unletter'd muse,	无闻的野诗神注上了姓名、年份,
The place of fame and elegy supply:	另外再加上地址和一篇悼词;
And many a holy text around she strews,	她在周围撒播了一些经文,
That teach the rustic moralist to die.	教训乡土道德家怎样去死。

For who to dumb Forgetfulness a prey,	要知道谁甘愿舍身哑口的"遗忘",
This pleasing anxious being e'er resign'd,	坦然撇下了忧喜交织的此生,
Left the warm precincts of the cheerful day,	谁离开风和日暖的明媚现场
Nor cast one longing, ling'ring look behind?	而能不依依地回头来顾盼一阵?

On some fond breast the parting soul relies,	辞世的灵魂还依傍钟情的怀抱,
Some pious drops the closing eye requires;	临闭的眼睛需要尽哀的珠泪,
Ev'n from the tomb the voice of Nature cries,	即使坟冢里也有"自然"的呼号
Ev'n in our ashes live their wonted fires.	他们的旧火还点燃我们的新灰。

For thee, who mindful of th' unhonour'd Dead	至于你,我关心这些默默的陈死人,

Dost in these lines their artless tale relate;
If chance, by lonely contemplation led,
Some kindred spirit shall inquire thy fate,

Haply some hoary-headed swain may say,
"Oft have we seen him at the peep of dawn
Brushing with hasty steps the dews away
To meet the sun upon the upland lawn.

"There at the foot of yonder nodding beech
That wreathes its old fantastic roots so high
His listless length at noontide would he stretch,
And pore upon the brook that babbles by.

"Hard by yon wood, now smiling as in scorn,
Mutt'ring his wayward fancies he would rove,
Now drooping, woeful wan, like one forlorn,
Or craz'd with care, or cross'd in hopeless love.

"One morn I miss'd him on the custom'd hill,
Along the heath and near his fav'rite tree;
Another came; nor yet beside the rill,
Nor up the lawn, nor at the wood was he;

"The next with dirges due in sad array
Slow thro' the church-way path we saw him borne.
Approach and read (for thou canst read) the lay,
Grav'd on the stone beneath yon aged thorn."

THE EPITAPH

Here rests his head upon the lap of Earth
A youth to Fortune and to Fame unknown.
Fair Science frown'd not on his humble birth,
And Melancholy mark'd him for her own.

用这些诗句讲他们质朴的故事,
假如在幽思的引导下,偶然有缘分,
一位同道来问起你的身世——

也许会有白头的乡下人对他说,
"我们常常看见他,天还刚亮,
就用匆忙的脚步把露水碰落,
上那边高处的草地去会晤朝阳;

"那边有一棵婆娑的山毛榉老树,
树底下隆起的老根盘错在一起,
他常常在那里懒躺过一个中午,
悉心看旁边一道涓涓的小溪。

"他转游到林边,有时候笑里带嘲,
念念有词,发他的奇谈怪议,
有时候垂头丧气,像无依无靠,
像忧心忡忡或者像情场失意。

"有一天早上,在他惯去的山头,
灌木丛,他那棵爱树下,我不见他出现;
第二天早上,尽管我走下溪流,
上草地,穿过树林,他还是不见。

"第三天我们见到了送葬的行列,
唱着挽歌,抬着他向坟场走去——
请上前看那丛老荆棘底下的碑碣,
(你是识字的)请念念这些诗句":

墓　　铭

这里边,高枕地膝,是一位青年,
生平从不曾受知于"富贵"和"名声";
"知识"可没轻视他出身的微贱,
"清愁"把他标出来认作宠幸。

Large was his bounty, and his soul sincere,	他生性真挚,最乐于慷慨施惠,
Heav'n did a recompense as largely send:	上苍也给了他同样慷慨的报酬:
He gave to Mis'ry all he had, a tear,	他给了"坎坷"全部的所有,一滴泪;
He gain'd from Heav'n ('twas all he wish'd) a friend.	从上苍全得了所求,一位朋友。
No farther seek his merits to disclose,	别再想法子表彰他的功绩,
Or draw his frailties from their dread abode,	也别再把他的弱点翻出了暗窖
(There they alike in trembling hope repose)	(他们同样在颤抖的希望中休息)。
The bosom of his Father and his God.	那就是他的天父和上帝的怀抱。

(卞之琳 译)

一、韵律和形式赏析

《墓畔哀歌》是运用经典的"英雄四行体"("heroic quatrain")所作的挽歌。英雄四行体指的是每个诗节有四行,每行均为五音步抑扬格(iambic pentameter),且韵脚的模式也是规范的 abab, cdcd, efef, ⋯依此类推。18 世纪的诗人尤其注重格律的规范,以第一节为例,每行均由十个音节以一抑一扬(一弱读一强读)交替构成。为了保持五音步抑扬格的规范,第二行中的"over"这一双音节词汇也进行了压缩,变为单音节形式"o'er"。诸如此类的词中省略(syncope)在本诗中数次出现,如后文的"tow'r"(tower),"pow'r"(power)等。纵观全诗,格雷始终保持了格律的严谨规范,鲜有"违背"格式的诗行出现。

> The **cur**few **tolls** the **knell** of **part**ing **day**,   (a)
> The **low**ing **herd** wind **slow**ly **o'er** the **lea**,   (b)
> The **plow**man **home**ward **plods** his **wear**y **way**,   (a)
> And **leaves** the **world** to **dark**ness **and** to **me**.   (b)

《墓畔哀歌》的标题中尽管包含了挽歌(elegy)一词,但该作品从严格意义上来说并非是一个典型的挽歌。挽歌是写给逝者的抒情诗,以表达对某人离去的哀思。而此诗并未明确地追思某一位死者(Richard West 的去世虽被视作创作动机之一,但全诗中只字未提),涉及的多是广大默默无闻的乡村凡人(obscure rustic people)。诗文中也缺少一些典型的挽歌体元素,如祈祷(invocation)、哀悼者(mourner)、花朵等。并且诗人也并未突出强调"失去"(loss)这一经典主题。所以,更应该将此诗理解为格雷以"挽歌"之名对人生中所经历的亲友的离世、自己终有一死的命运以及"生命"与"死亡"这些宏大命题的一种沉思。

二、内容解读

第一部分：本诗的前三节(1~12行)交代了本诗的场景——远离喧嚣的郊区墓地。格雷描绘了一番夜幕降临、万物平息的凄美之景。诗人运用大量的视觉和听觉的意象来表现其孤身一人在一片静谧之中踱步沉思。尤其是听觉上的表述："晚钟报丧"的声响("curfew tolls the knell")、"甲虫纷飞的嗡嗡声"("beetle wheels his droning flight")、"昏沉的铃声"("drowsy tinklings")和"猫头鹰的诉苦"("moping owl does to the moon complain")，这些微弱的声响更是反衬出了周围的一片寂静，唯有动物的"窃窃私语"和钟声、铃声依稀可辨。头韵(alliteration)的运用和听觉意象的描绘相得益彰。尤其是第二节中的"solemn stillness"，"s"这一齿擦音(sibilance)的反复使用，好似在说"Shush, Shush! Don't make a sound."

第二部分：本诗的第四至七节(13~28行)点出了在"树下""荫里""荒堆""洞窟"这些意象之中"安睡"的墓中人——"小村里粗鄙的父老"("The rude forefathers of the hamlet")。对于这些普通人来说，死亡剥夺了他们生活中点滴的快乐：晨风、鸟语、妻子的关照和孩子的嬉戏。第七节中特别描写了墓中人生前的劳作带给他们"欢欣"，同时也赋予了他们成就感。格雷在全诗中大量使用单音节词汇以贴近他所描写的主体对象(obscure rustic people)的日常表达习惯，如第五节中"No more shall rouse them from their lowly bed."和第6节中"Or clime his knees the envied kiss to share."

第三部分：本诗的第八至十一节(29~44行)作者话锋转向了上层阶级的人们(也可能暗含了此诗的所有读者)。"门第"("heraldry")、"权势"("pow'r")、"美貌"("beauty")、"财富"("wealth")无法阻止死亡这一不可避免的时刻(inevitable hour)和终点。同时，诗人还用了许多富人缅怀逝者时的典型具体的意象："纪念堂"("trophies")、"廊道"("aisle")、"拱顶"("vault")、"赞美歌"("anthem")、"半身像"("animated bust")等所有的虚饰也无法挽回逝去的生命。这四节中，有五个非行首的词首字母却用了大写"Ambition""Grandeur""Mem'ry""Honour""Flatt'ry"表示强调："雄心"勃勃、"奢靡"考究者莫要蔑视；"怀念"无需物质的虚饰，且"荣誉"和"献媚"在死神面前也是无济于事。格雷在第九节和第十一节中用到了排比结构来重点强调死亡的不可避免和不可逆转，"The boast of heraldry"和"The pomp of pow'r"词组结构形成排比。两个设问"Can storied urn..."和"Can Honor's voice..."句型排比。

第四部分：本诗的第十二至十九节(45~76行)呈现了全诗的中心观点：穷人(或无名之辈)有着和上流社会的人(或风云人物)同样的潜质，只是外在环境没有给他们施展才华的际遇。这些墓中人的心中也许曾"充满灵焰"("pregnant with celestial fire")，若非"贫寒"("Chill Penury")的限制，致使他们终日忙于生计而无暇求知("Knowledge")，或许他们也能成就一番事业。为了进一步证明中心观点，诗人先是用暗喻(metaphor)将他们比作深埋海底的"珠宝"("gem")和无人知晓的"花朵"("flow'r")，继而引典文豪

"Milton"和领袖"Cromwell"以提出墓中也许有具备同等才能但无用武之地者。这些"凡夫俗子"的生活中反倒没有"杀戮"（"slaughter"）、谎言或"骄奢"（"Luxury and Pride"），他们"远离了纷纭人世的勾心斗角"（"Far from the madding crowd's ignoble strife"），"清醒"（"sober"）且"安静"（"noiseless"）地走着自己的"正路"。

第五部分：本诗的第二十至二十三节（77～92 行）随着"Yet"一词的转折，诗人再次将目光投向墓地。墓碑上"拙劣的韵语、凌乱的刻划"（"uncouth rhymes and shapeless sculpture"）依然是人们对平凡逝者的一种缅怀。因为无论贵贱，谁也不甘被人"遗忘"（"forgetfulness"），离开时也不免会"依依地回头来顾盼"（"cast one longing, ling'ring look behind"）。真正的死亡其实是被全然地遗忘，倘若自己的身世和作品能留存在他人的记忆中，这便是生命以另一种形式得到了延续。

第六部分：本诗的第二十四至二十九节（93～116 行）过渡到诗人想象自己离世后"他人"对其身世的评述。第二十四节中的人称代词具有一定的迷惑性，"For thee"和"thy fate"实际上指诗人自己的身世。继而从第二十五节开始，格雷虚构了一位"白头的乡下人"（"hoary-headed swain"）向路人介绍自己的一生。在白发老者的叙述中，格雷似乎是一位游荡者，在树下溪边像一个"无依无靠"（"forlorn"）又"忧心忡忡"（"craz'd with care"）的失意恋人一般，"念念有词，阐发他的奇谈怪议"（"Mutt'ring his wayward fancies he would rove"）。从诗人这部分的措辞（diction）不难看出，格雷自己眼中的诗人形象是这样一个敏感、孤寂、冥思而又带有一丝忧伤的形象。白发老者这一形象的创造也透射出诗人对于死亡和记忆的理解。死亡将我们从主体变为客体，而死者（生命的主体）希望自己的一生可以被他人缅怀（变为记忆的客体）。所以，诗人创造出一个新的主体（白发老者）来讲述和追忆客体（诗人自己）的生平经历，并邀请读者们留意下文中诗人的墓志铭。

第七部分：本诗的最后三节（117～128 行）是诗人格雷自己的"墓志铭"（"Epitaph"）。格雷笔下的自己出身平凡（"*A youth to Fortune and to Fame unknown*"），一方面承恩"知识"（"*Fair Science*"），另一方面又饱受"坎坷"（"*Mis'ry*"），但是他"生性真挚"（"*his soul sincere*"）因而得到了上苍的"眷顾"（"*recompense*"）。最后一节，无疑表达了作者希望死亡为自己带来的是一种平静，他终将回归上帝的怀抱，而此生的"是非功与过，无需后人说"。

思考题

(1) 托马斯·格雷对于贫富贵贱持有什么样的观点？他在诗篇末段提到自己时，把自己归入了"普通人"还是"上层人"？

(2) 格雷是他的父母所生的十二个孩子中唯一免受夭折存活下来的。他人生中所目睹的死亡如何影响本诗的创作？

(3) 挽歌（elegy）似乎理应是充满哀伤和不舍之情，本诗是否旨在给读者带来忧伤和思念的情绪？

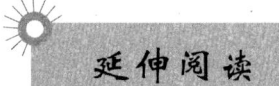

Annabel Lee

by Edgar Allan Poe

It was many and many a year ago,
In a kingdom by the sea,
That a maiden there lived whom you may know
By the name of Annabel Lee;
And this maiden she lived with no other thought
Than to love and be loved by me.

I was a child and she was a child,
In this kingdom by the sea,
But we loved with a love that was more than love-
I and my Annabel Lee-
With a love that the winged seraphs of heaven
Coveted her and me.

And this was the reason that, long ago,
In this kingdom by the sea,
A wind blew out of a cloud, chilling
My beautiful Annabel Lee;
So that her highborn kinsman came
And bore her away from me,
To shut her up in a sepulchre
In this kingdom by the sea.

The angels, not half so happy in heaven,
Went envying her and me-
Yes! - that was the reason (as all men know,
In this kingdom by the sea)
That the wind came out of the cloud by night,
Chilling and killing my Annabel Lee.

But our love it was stronger by far than the love
Of those who were older than we-
Of many far wiser than we-
And neither the angels in heaven above
Nor the demons down under the sea
Can ever dissever my soul from the soul
Of the beautiful Annabel Lee;

For the moon never beams, without bringing me dreams
Of the beautiful Annabel Lee;
And the stars never rise, but I feel the bright eyes
Of the beautiful Annabel Lee;
And so, all the night-tide, I lie down by the side
Of my darling- my darling-my life and my bride,
In the sepulchre there by the sea,
In her tomb by the sounding sea.

Chapter 3　She dwelt among untrodden ways
by William Wordsworth

 背景介绍

　　威廉·华兹华斯(William Wordsworth,1770—1850,简称华兹华斯),英国浪漫主义时期诗人,是"湖畔诗人"的领袖。他年轻时一度对法国革命怀有巨大的热情,然而战争使得华兹华斯的爱情遭受重挫。他精神上一度萎靡不振,从此开始远离政治,选择隐居乡间,寄情山水,专注于诗歌创作,在大自然里寻找慰藉。华兹华斯认为"所有的好诗都是强烈情感的自然流露"("the spontaneous overflow of powerful emotion"),主张诗人"选用人们真正用的语言"来写"普通生活里的事件和情境"。华兹华斯将自己的诗歌理念融入了自己的创作中,自然界的千姿百态以及各式各样的乡村人物,都经由他的想象进入其作品。《她居住在人迹罕到的地方》是华兹华斯著名的爱情诗《露西组诗》中的一篇。作品语言上质朴清新,感情上唯美真挚,主题上宁静的自然之美与淡雅的人性之美相互辉映,是一篇意境丰富的诗歌佳作。

 文本选读

| She dwelt among the untrodden ways | 她居住在人迹罕到的地方 |
| by William Wordsworth | 威廉·华兹华斯 |

She dwelt among the untrodden ways
Beside the springs of Dove,
A Maid whom there were none to praise
And very few to love;

A violet by a mossy stone
Half hidden from the eye!
—Fair as a star, when only one
Is shining in the sky.

她居住在人迹罕到的地方,
在鸽泉的近旁,
这姑娘没有人称赞,
也很少有人把她爱上。

一朵半隐半现的紫罗兰,
开放在长满青苔的石头旁!
美俏得像颗孤星一样,
闪耀在天上。

She lived unknown, and few could know	她活着时默默无闻，
When Lucy ceased to be;	她死去时，知者甚罕；
But she is in her grave; and, oh,	但如今露西已进入坟墓，
The difference to me!	啊，这对我就大大两样！

（秦希廉　译）

华兹华斯的浪漫主义思想——《露西组诗》的自然朴素之美

作为英国最早的浪漫主义诗人之一，华兹华斯深受卢梭"真正的美源于自然"观念的影响，形成了自己独特的自然观。在他看来，与人类社会相对立的自然才是真、善、美的化身。华兹华斯崇尚大自然之美，厌恶冷酷无情的城市工业文明，向往幽静无争的田园世界。他的自然主题诗歌清新淡雅，寓情于景，所描写的自然风光中也寄托了人生哲理。

本篇诗歌《她住在人迹罕至的地方》是著名的《露西组诗》中的一篇。作品语言质朴清新，感情上唯美真挚，是一篇意境丰富的诗歌佳作。露西是诗人心中的理想女子，也是他的精神寄托，主题上宁静的自然之美与淡雅的人性之美相互辉映。诗中美丽却少人问津的女子，纯洁、高尚、超凡脱俗。"A violet by a mossy stone"，"Fair as a star"，她像紫罗兰一样半遮半掩，像星星一样闪烁。诗中的露西无法考证是否确有其人，也许露西是一位远离世俗的如花般的女子，自开自落；也许露西是诗人心中的恋人，她独属于诗人心底最美好的念想；更或许露西是诗人内心的被女性化了的自己。最后无可替代的露西消逝，诗人的心从此天翻地覆，或许暗指诗人遭受的挫折。

一、语言朴素清新，情感自然流露

这首短诗总共有三节，有着很强的音乐效果。每个诗节中，第二行与第四行押韵，如"Dove"和"love"，"eye"和"sky"，"be"和"me"。韵律整齐，这种格律由民歌体发展而来，形式上与诗人的自然主题相统一。诗中元音使用较多，放缓诗歌节奏，呈现出画面般的静态美。

第一节"the untrodden way"，"the springs of Dove"等点明了露西的生活环境幽静，远离世俗喧嚣。泉水冠以鸽子之名，鸽子赋予人平静与祥和之感。露西生活在这样一个淡泊、典雅的环境中，这份安谧与淳朴无疑也契合了作者精神世界的追求。"A Maid whom there were none to praise, And very few to love"，"这姑娘没有人称赞，也很少有人把她爱上。"，这么淡雅美丽的姑娘居然无人赏识，表达了诗人的惋惜之情。

从全诗来看，诗人选词简单朴素，并无华丽辞藻的堆砌，这正是他语言观的体现。华兹华斯所处的18世纪古典主义盛行,文坛多强调行文华丽,偏重高雅、委婉的词汇,诗歌从形式到内容显得过于矫饰。华兹华斯非常反对这种语言风格,倡导抛弃新古典主义时期陈旧的词句,推动浪漫文学的发展,使用"一种更淳朴和有力的"民间语言,从而表达某种真情实感。本诗是华兹华斯的一首经典抒情诗,描述远离喧嚣的普通田园人家的生活,展示了唯美的意境,蕴含了诗人真切的情感,这也正反映了诗人"所有的好诗都是强烈情感的自然流露"的诗歌理念。

二、人与自然融合,人文思想彰显

"A violet by a mossy stone","Fair as a star",半遮半掩的苔石旁的紫罗兰,闪耀夜空的明亮星星,这看似不相关甚至矛盾的一对意象是诗人有意而为之,展现了诗人丰富的想象力。华兹华斯强调诗人的想象力,认为想象可以"使日常的东西在不平常的状态下呈现在心灵面前"。露西的美、紫罗兰的美、星星的美,实现了人与自然之物的融合,与"天人合一"的理念相通。然而,紫罗兰与孤单的星星虽然展示了露西的美丽,但却是一种稍显凄凉、悲壮的美。此外,"She lived unknown",她无人知晓,无人欣赏。露西的美丽与现实世界的冷酷对比强烈,暗示了美丽姑娘的不幸命运,令读者动容。

女性和大自然是华兹华斯作品中重要的元素,露西并非上流社会的贵族小姐,而是僻静郊区普通人家的姑娘。华兹华斯诗中的主角多是远离俗世的普通人物,如高原上的刈麦女、体衰却仍为生活而奔波的捞水蛭人、纯真无邪的农家儿童等。在真实的生活体验中,在与自然近距离接触的环境下,这些平凡的人身上有着返璞归真的人性,一种纯洁的未被扭曲的人性。

在诗歌最后一节,"But she is in her grave",露西长眠于地下,与诗篇开头美丽幽静的景致描写形成反差,让读者感到悲恸。但是在诗人眼里,露西的死亡却未必是一种悲情的安排。诗人热爱自然,提倡人类应该顺从自然法则,既然死亡是不可避免的自然规律,就应当坦然面对。也许诗歌当中所用到的紫罗兰与星星的意象,正是诗人对露西归宿的某种伏笔。死后的露西肉体归于尘土,化作紫罗兰;而灵魂升天,变成夜空中一颗闪亮的星。通过这种安排,露西与自然融为一体,在自然的轮回演绎中获得了永恒。在《露西组诗》的其他诗篇中,诗人华兹华斯也同样表达了这样一种人与自然和谐统一的观点。简单的诗句中蕴含着生命的真谛,给予读者很大的启发。

思考题

(1)诗人使用了紫罗兰和星星两种意象,有什么内涵?
(2)中国也有田园派诗人,他们的诗歌与华兹华斯的诗歌有何异同?
(3)现在很多人想要离开繁忙喧嚣的城市,前往宁静偏远的郊区生活,你怎么看待这种选择?
(4)试从华兹华斯的自然观分析,在现代社会,人与自然应该怎样和谐相处?

■ Chapter 3　She dwelt among untrodden ways *by William Wordsworth*

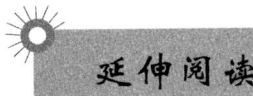

The Solitary Reaper

by William Wordsworth

Behold her, single in the field,
Yon solitary Highland Lass!
Reaping and singing by herself;
Stop here, or gently pass!
Alone she cuts and binds the grain,
And sings a melancholy strain;
O listen! for the Vale profound
Is overflowing with the sound.

No Nightingale did ever chant
More welcome notes to weary bands
Of travellers in some shady haunt,
Among Arabian sands:
A voice so thrilling ne'er was heard
In spring-time from the Cuckoo-bird,
Breaking the silence of the seas
Among the farthest Hebrides.

Will no one tell me what she sings? —
Perhaps the plaintive numbers flow
For old, unhappy, far-off things,
And battles long ago:
Or is it some more humble lay,
Familiar matter of to-day?
Some natural sorrow, loss, or pain,
That has been, and may be again?

Whate'er the theme, the Maiden sang
As if her song could have no ending;

I saw her singing at her work,
And o'er the sickle bending;—
I listened, motionless and still;
And, as I mounted up the hill,
The music in my heart I bore,
Long after it was heard no more.

Chapter 4　Ulysses
by Alfred Tennyson

 背景介绍

　　《尤利西斯》是维多利亚时期桂冠诗人之一的阿尔弗雷德·丁尼生在1833年创作，并于1842在其广受好评的《诗歌》第二卷中收录和发表。本诗的创作动机和丁尼生的剑桥挚友——诗人 Arthur Henry Hallam 的去世密切相关。全诗借用尤利西斯这一神话原型，通过描绘尤利西斯对于平淡乏味的家庭生活的不满，和其再启征程、扬帆远航的英勇决定，来抒发诗人自身"烈士暮年，壮心不已"的豪情壮志。面对岁月的流逝和命运的坎坷，英雄的心依旧坚强如故，且将不断地"奋斗、探索、寻求，永不屈服"。

 文本选读

Ulysses	尤利西斯
by Alfred Tennyson	阿尔弗雷德·丁尼生

It little profits that an idle king,　　　　　　这太无谓——当一个闲散的君主
By this still hearth, among these barren crags,　安居家中，在这个嶙峋的岛国，
Match'd with an aged wife, I mete and dole　　我与年老的妻子相匹，颁布着
Unequal laws unto a savage race,　　　　　　不公的法律，治理野蛮的种族，——
That hoard, and sleep, and feed, and know not me.　他们吃、睡、收藏，而不理解我。

I cannot rest from travel: I will drink　　　　　我不能停歇我的跋涉；我决心
Life to the lees: All times I have enjoy'd　　　　饮尽生命之杯。我一生都在
Greatly, have suffer'd greatly, both with those　体验巨大的痛苦、巨大的欢乐，
That loved me, and alone, on shore, and when　有时与爱我的伙伴一起，有时却独自一个；
Thro' scudding drifts the rainy Hyades　　　　不论在岸上或海上，当带来雨季的毕
　　　　　　　　　　　　　　　　　　　　宿星团催动
Vext the dim sea: I am become a name;　　　激流滚滚，扬起灰暗的海波。我已经变
　　　　　　　　　　　　　　　　　　　　成这样一个名字，

For always roaming with a hungry heart
Much have I seen and known; cities of men
And manners, climates, councils, governments,
Myself not least, but honour'd of them all;
And drunk delight of battle with my peers,
Far on the ringing plains of windy Troy.
I am a part of all that I have met;
Yet all experience is an arch wherethro'
Gleams that untravell'd world whose margin fades
For ever and for ever when I move.

How dull it is to pause, to make an end,
To rust unburnish'd, not to shine in use!
As tho' to breathe were life! Life piled on life
Were all too little, and of one to me
Little remains: but every hour is saved
From that eternal silence, something more,
A bringer of new things; and vile it were
For some three suns to store and hoard myself,
And this gray spirit yearning in desire
To follow knowledge like a sinking star,
Beyond the utmost bound of human thought.

This is my son, mine own Telemachus,
To whom I leave the sceptre and the isle,—
Well-loved of me, discerning to fulfil
This labour, by slow prudence to make mild
A rugged people, and thro' soft degrees
Subdue them to the useful and the good.
Most blameless is he, centred in the sphere
Of common duties, decent not to fail
In offices of tenderness, and pay
Meet adoration to my household gods,
When I am gone. He works his work, I mine.

由于我如饥似渴地漂泊不止，
我已见识了许多民族的城
及其风气、习俗、枢密院、政府，
而我在他们之中最负盛名；
在遥远而多风的特洛亚战场，
我曾陶醉于与敌手作战的欢欣。
我自己是我全部经历的一部分；
而全部经验，也只是一座拱门，
尚未游历的世界在门外闪光，
而随着我一步一步的前进，它的边界也
不断向后退让。

最单调最沉闷的是停留，是终止，
是蒙尘生锈而不在使用中发亮！
难道说呼吸就能算是生活？
几次生命堆起来尚嫌太少，
何况我唯一的生命已余年无多。
唯有从永恒的沉寂之中抢救每个小时，
让每个小时带来
一点新的收获。最可厌的是
把自己长期封存、贮藏起来，
让我灰色的灵魂徒然渴望
在人类思想最远的边界之外
追求知识。像追求沉没的星星。

这是我的儿子忒勒玛科斯，
我给他留下我的岛国和王杖，
他是我所爱的，他有胆有识，
能胜任这一工作；谨慎耐心地
教化粗野的民族，用温和的步骤
驯化他们，使他们善良而有用。
他是无可指责的，他虽年少，
在我离去后他会担起重任，
处理好那些需要谨慎应付的事务
并对我家的佑护神表示崇敬。
他和我，将各做各的工作。

There lies the port; the vessel puffs her sail:
There gloom the dark, broad seas. My mariners,
Souls that have toil'd, and wrought, and thought
    with me—
That ever with a frolic welcome took
The thunder and the sunshine, and opposed
Free hearts, free foreheads—you and I are old;
Old age hath yet his honour and his toil;
Death closes all: but something ere the end,
Some work of noble note, may yet be done,
Not unbecoming men that strove with Gods.
The lights begin to twinkle from the rocks:
The long day wanes: the slow moon climbs: the deep
Moans round with many voices. Come, my friends,
'T is not too late to seek a newer world.
Push off, and sitting well in order smite
The sounding furrows; for my purpose holds
To sail beyond the sunset, and the baths
Of all the western stars, until I die.
It may be that the gulfs will wash us down:
It may be we shall touch the Happy Isles,
And see the great Achilles, whom we knew.
Tho' much is taken, much abides; and tho'
We are not now that strength which in old days
Moved earth and heaven, that which we are, we are;
One equal temper of heroic hearts,
Made weak by time and fate, but strong in will

To strive, to seek, to find, and not to yield.

海港就在那边,船儿已经扬帆,
大海黑暗一片。我的水手们——
与我同辛劳、同工作、同思想的人,

对雷电和阳光永远同等欢迎。
并用自由的心与头颅来抗争,——
你们和我都已老了,但老年
仍有老年的荣誉、老年的辛劳;
死亡终结一切,但在终点前
我们还能做一番崇高的事业,
使我们配称为与神斗争的人。
礁石上的灯标开始闪光了,
长昼将尽,月亮缓缓攀登,
大海用无数音响在周围呻唤。
来呀,朋友们,探寻更新的世界
现在尚不是为时过晚。开船吧!
坐成排,划破这喧哗的海浪,
我决心驶向太阳沉没的彼方,
超越西方星斗的浴场,至死方止。
也许深渊会把我们吞噬,
也许我们将到达琼岛乐土,
与老朋友阿喀琉斯会晤。
尽管已达到的多,未知的也多啊,
虽然我们的力量已不如当初,
已远非昔日移天动地的雄姿,
但我们仍是我们,英雄的心
尽管被时间消磨、被命运削弱,我们
的意志坚强如故,
坚持着奋斗、探索、寻求,而不屈服。

(飞白 译)

一、韵律赏析

从格律上看,《尤利西斯》属于无韵诗(blank verse)。无韵诗(亦名"白体诗")每行用五个长短格音步——十个音节组成,每首诗行数不拘,不压韵。当然,诗人在最后四行设计了"aabb"的韵脚以增强诗篇的终结感和强调中心句的表意。全诗的音步类型主要采用抑扬格(iambic),即一个弱读音节后跟一个重读音节,但其中也穿插了不少扬扬格(spondee)的使用,即两个重读音节的连续使用。以最后两行为例:"Made weak(扬扬格)by time and fate, but strong in will/To strive(抑扬格), to seek(抑扬格), to find(抑扬格), and not to yield."五音步抑扬格的无韵诗体在英文诗歌和戏剧中被广泛使用,原因之一是这种格律更贴近日常用语。而作者偶尔插入的"扬扬格"让诗篇有了更丰富的韵律和跌宕起伏的情感表达。扬扬格可以放缓诗歌的"步调"从而强调出表意的转折、加强或是内心的冲突和挣扎。岁月("time")无情、命运("fate")无常,诗人的英雄之心("heroic hearts")无奈被时光"消磨"("made weak"),但是他的意志始终坚强如故("strong in will")。可见,倒数第二行以"扬扬格"开头,很好地为最后一行中激情澎湃的"青云之志"作出铺垫。

二、形式特色

《尤利西斯》主要运用戏剧独白,即全诗有一个叙述者(一般不是诗人本身),在特定场景下进行叙述,从而与一个或者多个听众进行沟通和交流。此诗的叙述者是尤利西斯,听众在家人(前两节)、臣民(第三节)和即将共同踏上新征程的水手们(第四节)中循序切换。通过诗人对独白者的语言的选择和控制,一个鲜活的人物形象跃然纸上,使得诗歌的表意和人物更有感染力。《尤利西斯》的语言在选词上朴实无华,但气势上恢宏澎湃,如"I will drink/Life to the lees"以及"for my purpose holds/To sail beyond the sunset, and the baths/Of all the western stars, until I die."这两句中用到的无非是日常生活中的一些通俗词汇"lees"(酒渣),"sunset"(日落),"stars"(星辰),但作者(或者说叙述者)用它们抒发了想要"饮尽生命之杯"和驶向天涯海角"至死方止"的雄心。本诗另一个突出的语言特色是跨行连续(enjambment)这一手法的运用。跨行连续指一个句子、短语或思想从上一行延续到下一行的这种行间"转移"。上述两例均为跨行连续,此诗中的其他例子也随处可见:

> ··· All times I have enjoy'd
> Greatly, have suffer'd greatly, both with those
> That loved me, and alone, on shore, and when
> Thro' scudding drifts the rainy Hyades
> Vext the dim sea; ···

第七至十一行,每行末均与下一行连贯在一起。跨行连续手法的运用能加快诗篇的节奏和表意的强度。读者能感受到动作之间连接紧密,事件推进节奏紧凑。尤利西斯在此回忆了自己跌宕起伏的一生——经历了各种挑战、痛苦和壮举。通过戏剧独白和跨行连续的使用,读者脑中很清晰地浮现出一位务实质朴、不甘寂寞、雄心满怀的暮年英雄形象。

三、内容解读

首先,诗歌的题目就直接点出了"尤利西斯"这个神话原型。Ulysses(又称 Odysseus)是神话传说中希腊西部伊塔卡岛(Ithaca)国王,曾参加特洛伊战争。荷马史诗《奥德赛》讲述了希腊英雄奥德赛(尤利西斯)在特洛伊战争取胜后返航途中的历险故事。利用木马计攻陷特洛伊城后,奥德赛不顾海神波塞冬的咒语启航回家,一路上历尽劫难,在海上又漂泊了十年,最终与妻子重聚。《奥德赛》第十一章中先知提瑞西阿斯(Tiresias)预测,在回到伊塔卡岛后,尤利西斯将再次开启一段新的和谜一般的旅程,最终将平静地死去。所以,诗人丁尼生对尤利西斯晚年的生活进行合理的想象,同时借神话英雄的艺术形象抒发自身心中感慨。作为本诗的叙述者,尤利西斯的文学原型和人物背景为诗篇中尤利西斯"忆往昔峥嵘岁月"和"而今迈步从头越"提供了重要的背景支撑。

在第一节诗中,第一人称叙述者"我"言简意赅地表达了对"安居乐业"的不满。诗人此节中用到了两个意象"still hearth"(平静的炉火)和"barren crags"(贫瘠的峭壁),对它们的含义加以分析不难看出,平静的不仅仅是家中的炉火,更是指曾经激荡于主人公心中的火焰几乎消失殆尽,而贫瘠的可能一方面是岛国的土地,同样也是统治岛国的乐趣。第三行中"mete and dole"字面意义是"测量和发放",多与日用品及补给品搭配,而这里用于搭配法律,而且是"unequal laws",由此可窥见国王对于"法制"所表达出的讽刺。而岛上的子民更是同"savage race"一般的愚民,终日只知道满足近乎原始的生存需求,丝毫不懂"我"的雄心壮志。

自然,在第二节中,尤利西斯开始向"不懂他的"大众或听众介绍他的往昔经历和勃勃野心。一句"I will drink/Life to the lees"宣告了主人翁渴望丰富多彩的人身旅程。"我"曾经历巨大的痛苦("have suffer'd greatly"),也曾体会极大的快乐("have enjoy'd/Greatly")。"当带来雨季的毕宿星团催动激流滚滚,扬起灰暗的海波"("scudding drifts the rainy Hyades/Vext the dim sea"),"我"依然勇往直前。因为这些壮举,"我"已然"青史留名"("I am become a name")。接下来,尤利西斯表现出他对于航海的渴望不限于旅程中的挑战,他的所见所闻更是可以满足他"如饥似渴的心"("hungry heart")。接着,作者选用了一系列意象来描绘对未知领域的探索,正如穿过一道"拱门"("arch")可以看到"尚未游历的世界"("untravell'd world")闪耀出吸引人的"光芒"("gleams")。而随着探索的脚步,这个世界的边际不断地"退让"("margin fades")。诗人用"铁剑"作暗喻,指出"蒙尘生锈而不在使用中发亮"("To rust unburnish'd, not to shine in use!")是人生最为沉闷无趣的格局。最后,尤利西斯表达出英雄暮年的感怀,死亡这一"永恒的沉寂"("eternal silence")留给他的时日无多,所以他更是需要争分夺秒地去追逐知识,正如去追求一颗"沉没的星星"("a sinking star")。

第三节中,尤利西斯话锋一转,似乎对岛上的臣民介绍了他的继任者忒勒玛科斯

(Telemachus)。老国王对儿子的能力给予了充分的肯定,他"无可指责"("blameless")的儿子凭借其"谨慎耐心"("slow prudence")和"温和的步骤"("soft degrees")定能不辱使命。这样"我"走了之后,我们父子将各司其职("He works his work, I mine.")。

终于,尤利西斯介绍完自己的心志和后继者,第四节诗篇来到了"直挂云帆济沧海"的部分,戏剧独白的对象也转变为"我"的水手们。诗人在最后一节中运用了大量的意象描绘了一幅波澜壮阔的图景:thunder, sunshine, long day, slow moon,(moaning) voices, sounding furrows, baths of stars, 等等。叙述者在这些意象的辅助下,激昂地表达了对自由、老年、死亡以及意志这些重大主题的看法。尤利西斯和水手们将"用自由的心与头颅来抗争"("and opposed/Free hearts, free foreheads")一切不测风云;将用行动和勇气证明"老年仍有老年的荣誉、老年的辛劳"("Old age hath yet his honour and his toil");将"决心驶向太阳沉没的彼方,超越西方星斗的浴场,至死方止"("To sail beyond the sunset, and the baths/Of all the western stars, until I die.");更将用坚定的意志不断"奋斗、探索、寻求,而不屈服"("To strive, to seek, to find, and not to yield")。

思考题

(1)戏剧独白的形式是否助益于本诗的艺术表达?

(2)本诗第三节,看起来与前后的风格和主题关联不紧密。第三节在诗篇中是否有存在的价值和意义?

(3)初读此诗,大多读者会被尤利西斯的青云之志所打动,称赞其英雄之心。诗篇是否同样表现出他的性格弱点或者缺陷?

延伸阅读

When I am dead, my dearest

by Christina Rossetti

When I am dead, my dearest,
Sing no sad songs for me;
Plant thou no roses at my head,
Nor shady cypress tree:
Be the green grass above me
With showers and dewdrops wet;
And if thou wilt, remember,
And if thou wilt, forget.

I shall not see the shadows,

I shall not feel the rain;

I shall not hear the nightingale

Sing on, as if in pain:

And dreaming through the twilight

That doth not rise nor set,

Haply I may remember,

And haply may forget.

Chapter 5 "Hope" is the Thing with Feathers-(314)

by Emily Dickinson

 背景介绍

  《"希望"是长着羽毛的东西》这首诗是美国十九世纪著名女诗人艾米莉·狄金森的代表作之一，包含信仰与生命两大主题。该诗采用作者一贯的创作风格，简朴的文字及紧凑的内容向读者呈现了一幅"希望"这只长着羽毛的小鸟一路抵御寒风暴雨，跃过大海寒地，始终引吭高歌，温暖人心的画面。面临如此恶劣的环境，小鸟依旧意志坚定，既不接受一丝馈赠，也没有丝毫妥协。这就是希望的力量——始终激励人斗志昂扬，奋勇前行。这首短诗看似写鸟，实则蕴含深刻的人生哲理，给读者留下了无尽的思考。

 文本选读

"Hope" is the Thing with Feathers-(314) by Emily Dickinson	"希望"是长着羽毛的东西-(314) 艾米莉·迪金森
"Hope" is the thing with feathers - That perches in the soul - And sings the tune without the words - And never stops - at all -	"希望"是长着羽毛的东西 它栖息在灵魂里 唱着无词的歌儿 永远都不会停息
And sweetest - in the Gale - is heard - And sore must be the storm - That could abash the little Bird That kept so many warm -	在狂风中我听见这最甜蜜的乐曲 疼痛一定是风暴本身 它能使小鸟局促不安 它拥有那么多温暖
I've heard it in the chillest land - And on the strangest Sea -	我曾听见它啊 在最寒冷的土地上

Chapter 5 "Hope" is the Thing with Feathers-(314) by Emily Dickinson

Yet - never - in Extremity,
It asked a crumb - of me.

也在最陌生的海域
是的,即使身处绝境
它从未向我索取过一点一滴。

(饶蕾 译)

  这首诗在形式上体现了诗人独特的创作风格,譬如,该诗在大写字母的使用上打破常规,诗行中有些名词并非居于句首却仍以大写字母开头(例如,第二节第一行中的"Gale",最后一节第二、三行中的"Sea"与"Extremity");另外,诗人放弃传统的标点,大量使用破折号(例如每行结尾的短破折号的重复出现,意在语音、语意上的停顿间歇,有一种舒缓流畅的音乐节奏感;第一节与第三节中双破折号将"at all"和"never"与其他成分隔开,既起一种强调的作用又达到前后呼应的效果,最后一行中破折号兼有停顿和强调的效果)。该诗在节奏韵律上也不循常规,以不规则的格律体现"颂歌"经书的形式。每行大都由5至9个音节组成,且每节的第二句都由6个音节组成,运用最简单的"轻、重"音步搭配,按抑扬格三音步构成诗行,但是第一句却是扬抑格,以此突出中心词"Hope"。全诗从每节来看基本上采用第二、四句押韵的形式,即 abcb 的格律形式,双数行押韵(除了第一节"soul"与"all"不押韵,后面两节中"storm"与"warm""sea"与"me"押韵),单数行随意(如第二节 heard 与 bird 押韵)。全诗从整体上来看,似又松散地押 ab-bb 韵律,比如第一节第三行结尾的"words"与第二节中"heard"和"bird"押韵,第三节中"sea""extremity"与"me"押韵。诗人这种散漫不羁的写作风格既是她诗歌特色所在,也是她内心情感独白。

  除了韵律上的非传统,通俗易懂的词汇也是这首诗的一大特色。诗中出现的名词,如"gale"(狂风),"Storm"(风暴),"bird"(小鸟),"land"(陆地),"sea"(大海)等都是人们常见的自然景象,这一连串的名词使读者不经意间置身于自然的万千变换之中,有身临其境之感。该诗大多选用日常生活中常用的单音节动词,简单有趣,如"perches"(栖息),"sings"(唱歌),"stops"(停留),"kept"(使……保持),"asked"(询问)等,这些动词使得"希望"这个无形抽象的概念具体化和形象化。艾米莉·狄金森善于通过奇特的想象,将一个抽象的概念用实际的可感触的具象表现出来,立意新颖,感情真挚,细细品来别有一番风味。

  狄金森的诗作通常没有标题,首句往往被当作标题。诗人的每首诗都被编了号,这首诗编号为 314。全诗以"Hope"一词开篇,道出该诗的主题,开门见山,直抒胸襟。"Hope is the thing with feathers -."是诗人巧用暗喻的修辞手法将希望比作一只长满羽毛的小鸟。接着第一节中"perches""sings"及"stops"这三个动词便清晰地引出了小鸟这个意象,它栖息在灵魂建筑的天地里,唱着生命不竭之歌。这里,小鸟在自己的世界里永不停歇地歌唱,正如诗人在自己的一方天地里坚持不懈地埋头写诗一样。作者将自己的希望投射在小鸟身上,赋予小鸟顽强的毅力,无畏的精神,乐此不疲地做着自己喜欢的事情。此时的小鸟就是诗人的写照,携着希望,带着信仰,永不停息。

第二节作者笔锋一转,画风突变,赋予整首诗跳跃的节奏感和别样的画面感。狂风暴雨越激烈,小鸟的歌声越甜美。此节中形容词对比鲜明,如"sweetest"(最甜美的)与"sore"(恼火的,酸痛的),"little"(小的)与"warm"(温暖的)。"sweetest"后省略了"sound",语意未尽,耐人寻味;"sore"句中运用了倒装,凸显了强调的意蕴。在险恶的环境下,小鸟可能稍显不安,但小鸟的精神常在,歌声依旧,予人温暖。诗人通过小鸟这个意象,表达自己的希冀——像小鸟一样怀揣希望,克服重重困难坚持自己的创作梦想。最后一行"kept"这个词一语双关,既表明诗人坚持诗歌创作的决心,也表明诗人希望自己的文字始终温暖人心。

在第三节中,诗歌叙述的情节达到高潮,小鸟的形象被刻画得淋漓尽致。希望这只小鸟历经狂风暴雨,始终一路歌唱,哪怕在最严寒的土地、最陌生的海域,依旧不停歇,歌声越发美妙。尽管饥饿至极,也不接受一丝馈赠与回报。第一行与第二行中的"chillest land"(最严寒的田地)与"strangest sea"(最陌生的海洋)这两个使用了形容词最高级的短语描绘了更加恶劣的环境,与第二节中的"gale"(狂风)与"storm"(暴风雨)在语意上形成一种递进的关系。这些意象渲染了大自然的冷酷无情,又何尝不是诗人眼中人类社会世态炎凉的写照。诗人过着孤寂单调的隐居生活,面对现实世界的束缚,也渴望像小鸟一样自由自在,怀揣希望,展翅翱翔。面对理想和现实的矛盾,诗人在诗的结尾表达了自己的决心。第三行的"yet"(然而)让读者眼前一亮,诗人也在一瞬间确认了自己的答案。第三行中"never"与第一节最后一行"never at all"前后首尾呼应,再次体现小鸟顽强的生命与崇高的信仰。全诗不断重复使用"and"和"that",既起到语意连贯的作用,又不断推动情节的发展,层层递进,发人深省。

思考题

(1)诗人为什么将希望比作小鸟?
(2)诗的第二节第四行开头的单词"that"具体指代什么?
(3)该诗最后以"me"结尾,有何深意?

延伸阅读

One Word Is Too Often Profaned(TO—)
by Percy Bysshe Shelly

One word is too often profaned
For me to profane it,

Chapter 5 "Hope" is the Thing with Feathers-(314) *by Emily Dickinson*

One feeling too falsely disdained
For thee to disdain it;
One hope is too like despair
For prudence to smother,
And pity from thee more dear
Than that from another,

I can give not what men call love,
But wilt thou accept not
The worship the heart lifts above
And the Heavens reject not, —
The desire of the moth for the star,
Of the night for the morrow,
The devotion to something afar
Form the sphere of our sorrow?

Chapter 6　He Wishes for the Cloths of Heaven
by William Butler Yeats

 **背景介绍**

　　《他冀求天国的锦缎》是爱尔兰诗人威廉·巴特勒·叶芝早期的一首诗歌,发表于1899年,收录在诗人的第三卷诗集《苇间风》中。全诗简短精要,语言质朴动人,诗人对心爱之人至真至纯的爱直击人心。开篇诗人向我们描述了他心中最美好的事物——天国的锦缎,金色银色的光线织就,湛蓝、灰暗又漆黑的锦缎,一如作者纯粹又深沉的爱。但诗人笔锋陡转,无奈感叹自己除怀有梦想外一贫如洗,强烈的反差让读者对诗人倍感怜惜。诗人用卑微的口吻深情告白,愿将仅有的梦想铺在心爱之人脚下,只求心爱之人轻踏于上。如此真挚的情感深深感染着读者的心,读过之人无不为诗人的爱所折服,满心怜惜也随之化为感动和崇尚。

 **文本选读**

He Wishes for the Cloths of Heaven
　　　by William Butler Yeats

Had I the heaven's embroidered cloths,
Inwrought with golden and silver light,
The blue and the dim and the dark cloths
Of night and light and the half-light,
I would spread the cloths under your feet;
But I, being poor, have only my dreams;
I have spread my dreams under your feet;
Tread softly because you tread upon my dreams.

他冀求天国的锦缎
　　威廉·巴特勒·叶芝

假如我有天国的锦绣绸缎,
那用金色银色的光线织就,
黑夜、白天、黎明和傍晚,
湛蓝、灰暗、和漆黑的锦缎,
我就把那锦缎铺在你脚下;
可我,一贫如洗,只有梦;
我把我的梦铺在了你脚下;
轻点,因为你踏着我的梦。

（傅浩　译）

 **作品赏析**

　　全诗总共八行,除了第三、四行是跨句行(enjambment),即两行结合起来表达一个

完整的意思,剩下的诗行都是结句行(end-stopped line)。本诗靠传统的韵律来体现节奏感,整体上为抑扬格五音步。全诗的押韵格式为abab,bcbc。除第四、第五行外,其他押韵的两行韵脚都是完全相同的词,分别为"cloths"(锦缎)、"light"(光线)、"feet"(脚步)、"dreams"(梦)。除此之外,本诗还运用了头韵与腹韵,如第四行"the dim and the dark"、第五行的"night and light and the half-light",使得诗歌蕴含音乐美和节奏美,读起来声情交融、音义一体,具有很强的表现力和感染力,让读者在丝丝入耳的诗歌中体会诗人的款款深情。

这首诗基调忧郁,但情真意切,字里行间,情意绵延。全诗较多地使用单音节词,如动词"had"(有)、"spread"(铺展)、"tread"(踩、踏),形容词"blue"(湛蓝的)、"dim"(灰暗的)、"dark"(漆黑的)、"poor"(贫穷的),且用词多有重复,如"cloths"在诗中出现四次,"light"出现三次,"feet""spread""dreams"各出现两次。这些简单的词串联起来却表达着诗人最真切的爱意,正如叶芝的诗风——汲取浪漫主义和唯美主义的抒情而不流于铺张,融合现代派的新颖和奇幻而不艰深晦涩。

全诗前五行都围绕着锦缎这一意象展开,第一行诗人用天国的锦绣绸缎引出诗歌话题,第二行开始描述此锦缎,那是金色银色的光线织就的锦缎,而金色银色象征着高贵、幸福,由此可见诗人渴望给予心爱之人世间美好之物,希望给她带来幸福。

第三、四行更进一步描述天国的锦缎,在黑夜、白天、黎明和傍晚泛着不同颜色光彩的锦缎,蕴含了作者更深的诗意。诗人选用的颜色不是鲜艳的红、黄、紫等,而是湛蓝、灰暗、漆黑。蓝是天空和海洋的颜色,既给人一种宁静和纯粹的感觉,又代表着忧郁和沮丧,正如诗人的爱,宁静纯粹,却可望而不可得;灰色有阴郁和低落之意;黑色则象征痛苦和沮丧。这三种颜色,从黎明到白天,再从黄昏到夜晚,色调变暗加深,如同诗人越爱越伤,渐入谷底的心情。黑夜、白天、黎明和傍晚,实则整天整夜,诗人分开来写,使得我们阅读的心理时间延长,如此既体现出作者每时每刻的爱意,更显示出诗人已经占满还要溢出的爱。这天国的锦缎,既是诗人想要献给心爱之人美好并能让她感到幸福的事物,又承载着诗人对心爱女子深沉而纯粹的爱。

如此珍贵的锦缎,诗人并非是作为礼物赠送给心爱之人,亦非量裁成衣裳让心爱之人披在身上,而是如第五行中所说:我就把那锦缎铺在你脚下。盛宴之中,红毯铺地,俊才靓女,玉叶金柯,拾级而上,而诗人心爱之人脚下铺的却是天国的锦缎,足以衬托出诗人心中的她地位至高,形象圣洁。相比之下,诗人却卑微如尘埃。第六行中的转折表达了诗人的无奈,"可我,一贫如洗,只有梦",他清楚自己穷困交加的处境——一无所有,唯有梦想,但并未说明梦想为何。

假若诗人继续幻想,心爱之人走在天国的锦缎之上,锦缎铺就的路想必是通往诗人与心爱之人相契与共、琴瑟和鸣的世界。但诗人不敢有此奢求,只能将此作为一个无法实现的梦。美梦虽能满足内心一时的欢愉,但终究太脆弱易碎。梦醒的权利操纵在心爱之人手中,她的只言片语便可以彻底粉碎诗人沉浸于其中的梦。如果美梦注定要醒,诗人只求心爱之人能让他醒得慢些。

　　此处的梦,也许不仅仅是睡梦,也代表了作者最真诚的心与最脆弱的自尊。诗人将自己的梦想铺在心爱之人脚下,实际上是将自己最致命、最脆弱却又最宝贵的心与自尊交予心爱之人。她的每一步、每一个动作,都牵引着诗人的神经,触动着作者的内心。诗人但求心爱之人怜悯自己那颗爱她爱得无可救药的心,对他的深情温柔以待。

　　如果说梦想指明了一个人生命的意义,那么追求梦想即是找寻生命的意义。而对于诗人来说,能够俘获爱人的芳心,从而得到永恒不朽的爱,已然构成了诗人生命的全部意义。因此,诗人不仅仅是请求心爱之人轻轻地踏在自己的美梦与爱她的心灵之上,更是请求心上人给自己多一些爱她的权利,给自己的生命更多的意义。

思考题

(1) 诗中"天国的锦缎"有何象征意义?
(2) 为什么诗人笔下金色银色的光线织就的锦缎却是湛蓝、灰暗和漆黑的?
(3) 你认为诗人的梦指的是什么?

延伸阅读

When You Are Old
by William Butler Yeats

When you are old and grey and full of sleep,
And nodding by the fire, take down this book,
And slowly read, and dream of the soft look
Your eyes had once, and of their shadows deep;

How many loved your moments of glad grace,
And loved your beauty with love false or true;
But one man loved the pilgrim Soul in you,
And loved the sorrows of your changing face;

And bending down beside the glowing bars,
Murmur, a little sadly, how Love fled
And paced upon the mountains overhead,
And hid his face amid a crowd of stars.

Chapter 7 Stopping by Woods on a Snowy Evening

by Robert Frost

《雪夜林边小立》是美国诗人罗伯特·弗洛斯特最著名的一首抒情诗。全诗语言平淡质朴,节奏流畅舒缓,描绘了诗人在新英格兰冬日雪花纷飞的傍晚赶车行至一片幽静的树林时,被林间的雪景吸引而驻足观望、流连忘返的经历。夜晚的雪林静谧安详,万籁俱寂的天地间,唯有小马摇动颈上铃铎发出的叮当声以及微风伴着雪花轻轻拂过的声音。止步不前的诗人此刻正思绪万千,人群中分外孤独的诗人逃离尘世,此刻却寻到了另一种孤独。短暂休憩中的诗人面临着永久安睡的诱惑,但随着铃铎声响,诗人清教徒的意识恍然觉醒。他毅然选择回归社会履行未尽的义务,实现未完成的梦想。

Stopping by Woods on a Snowy Evening
　　　by Robert Frost

雪夜林边小立
　　　罗伯特·弗洛斯特

Whose woods these are I think I know,
His house is in the village though.
He will not see me stopping here,
To watch his woods fill up with snow.

我想我认识树林的主人
他家住在林边的农村;
他不会看见我暂停此地,
欣赏他披上雪装的树林。

My little horse must think it queer,
To stop without a farmhouse near,
Between the woods and frozen lake,
The darkest evening of the year.

我的小马准抱着个疑团:
干嘛停在这儿,不见人烟,
在一年中最黑的晚上,
停在树林和冰湖之间。

He gives his harness bells a shake,

它摇了摇颈上的铃铎,

To ask if there is some mistake.	想问问主人有没有弄错。
The only other sound's the sweep,	除此之外唯一的声音
Of easy wind and downy flake.	是风飘绒雪轻轻拂过。
The woods are lovely, dark and deep.	树林真可爱,既深又黑,
But I have promises to keep,	但我有许多诺言不能违背,
And miles to go before I sleep.	还要赶多少路才能安睡,
And miles to go before I sleep.	还要赶多少路才能安睡。

(飞白 译)

作品赏析

这首《雪夜林边小立》靠传统的韵律和节段来体现节奏感。全诗共分4小节,每小节4行,用抑扬格4音步的格律写成,即一个弱读音节后跟一个重读音节。诗的韵律结构是:aaba,bbcb,ccdc,dddd,即每节的第一、二、四行押韵,第三行却改韵使其和下一节同韵。也就是说,第一节第三行最后一个词"here",决定了第二节第一、二、四行的韵("queer""neer""year");第二节第三行最后一词"lake",决定了第三节第一、二、四行的韵("shake""mistake""flake");同样,第三节第三行最末一词"sweep",又决定了第四节第一、二、四行的韵("deep""keep""sleep")。这样,节与节之间似有一钩,相互扣连,构成不断的韵链。诗人在向前推进中写作,伴随着主题而产生了运动美和节奏美。如果第四节第三行出现新韵e,那么,按照前面的规律,这首诗就应该继续写下去(eefe,…)。为了圆满结束这首诗,第四节第三、四行重复应当是最佳选择,这样既避免了一种诗句未完、难以收尾的缺憾感,又通过重复使得最后一节的4行全压尾韵,以和谐统一之美收拢全诗。

除了音韵优美,朴实无华的选词也是这首诗的一大特色。诗中出现的名词,如"woods"(树林)、"snow"(雪)、"house"(房舍)、"village"(村庄)、"farmhouse"(农舍)、"little horse"(小马)、"lake"(湖泊)等都是人们身边常见的事物。诗中出现的动词,如"think"(想)、"know"(知道)、"see"(看见)、"stop"(停下)、"watch"(观看)、"fill up"(填满)、"ask"(问)、"have"(有)、"keep"(保留、履行)、"go"(去、走)、"sleep"(睡觉)等,俱是英语中最常用的单音节词。罗伯特·弗洛斯特的诗句没有复杂的句子结构,没有渲染夸张,没有刻意的雕琢修饰,质朴的语言往往蕴含着深刻的寓意。

在第一节中,诗人在首行表明自己认识树林的主人。"I think"的使用一方面放缓了诗歌的节奏,另一方面为"树林的主人"的解读提供了另外一种可能性。诗人在喧嚣的尘世中,终日为生计而奔波辛劳。而作为诗人的他,内心深处一定构想过一处属于自己的桃花源。只有在那里,他才可以从纷繁复杂的现实世界中逃遁出来,寻找到内心短暂的宁静。诗人雪夜驾车途经的这篇树林,也许正契合了诗人心中桃花源的想象,是诗人曾在梦中千回百转流连之所。因此尽管夜黑雪急,诗人仍旧不由自主停下了赶路的脚步,于心中久违之地欣赏披着雪装的树林。此刻的邂逅虽是初见,却如旧识。从这个意义上来说,树林的主人或许就是诗人自己。"林边的农村"不过是诗人此时心中的幻象,自然不会有人看到诗人暂停于此。

诗人陶醉于美景之时,小马则心生疑惑。小马在此处象征着一类人,相较精神世界,他们更加关注现实需求。因此,小马不能明白诗人为何停留于这荒无人烟的地方。此刻诗人孤独的内心是多么渴求安宁,哪怕那份安宁会转瞬即逝;诗人疲惫了,他多么希望能卸下所有重担,抛开尘世的一切纷扰短暂回归自然,哪怕现实随时会将他拉回。诗人的心境是小马所不能理解的。也正是因为孤独,在人群中无法获得理解的诗人,转而寻求大自然的慰藉。因为,在人群中,孤独是一个人的落寞,而在大自然中,孤独才是一个人的狂欢。于是,在最黑的夜晚,诗人停留于树林与冰湖之间。黑无疑象征着死亡的神秘,而白则象征着孤独的苍白无力。这一黑一白两种色调互相映衬,黑让白更为清冷,白使黑更加深邃。幽深的树林远离尘世,隔离人群,处于树林中的诗人正在面对死亡的诱惑,而冰湖透出的寒意将死亡渲染得更加冰冷,也更为彻底。这条路的两头正连着两个对立的世界,通往冰湖,也就意味着永远安睡。死亡,可怕又美丽,因为它会剥夺你只有活着才能领略到的美和感受到的快乐,同时又消除你承受的所有痛苦与忧愁。因此,痛苦与忧愁越多,死亡的诱惑也就越大。但若转身离去,便意味着重返那纷纷扰扰的人世间。何去何从,诗人正在面临抉择。

第三节中,寒风徐徐吹,雪花纷纷舞。诗人在寂静的音和纯一的色中与大自然融为一体。而小马摇动颈上的铃铎,正是这突如其来的铃铛声打破雪天的寂静,也打破诗人的思绪,将诗人拉回现实。而此处诗人选用小马这一意象,是因为动物有着最本能的直觉。诗人沉溺于雪景之时,小马却嗅到了危险的气息,故不安地摇动铃铎。在小马的提醒下,诗人作为清教徒的意识也已觉醒,他已经做出了选择。清教徒向来奉守回馈社会,承担社会责任的信条,因此诗人才在第四节中说:"The woods are lovely, dark and deep. But I have promises to keep, And miles to go before I sleep." 尽管雪林迷人,但诗人还有诺言不能违背,安睡之前还有路程要赶。"promises"正是作者未尽的义务,而"miles"的意义更为丰富,既蕴含了诗人要履行的社会责任,又包括了诗人追求的人生理想。诗歌结尾两句重复,一来表达诗人追求理想的坚定,二则启发读者思考自己的人生之路。

思考题

(1)诗人为何选择使用第一人称?

(2)诗人在最后一节中提到"但我有许多诺言不能违背",这个"promise"是特指,还是泛指?

(3)最后一节中,"dark""deep"与"lovely"同时出现是否显得矛盾?有何象征意义存在?

The Road Not Taken

by Robert Frost

Two roads diverged in a yellow wood,
And sorry I could not travel both
And be one traveler, long I stood
And looked down one as far as I could
To where it bent in the undergrowth;

Then took the other, as just as fair,
And having perhaps the better claim,
Because it was grassy and wanted wear;
Though as for that the passing there
Had worn them really about the same,

And both that morning equally lay
In leaves no step had trodden black.
Oh, I kept the first for another day!
Yet knowing how way leads on to way,
I doubted if I should ever come back.

I shall be telling this with a sigh
Somewhere ages and ages hence:
Two roads diverged in a wood, and I -
I took the one less traveled by,
And that has made all the difference.

Chapter 8　l(a

by E. E. Cummings

背景介绍

　　卡明斯(1894—1962)是美国现代著名诗人、画家、评论家、作家和剧作家。他属于先锋派艺术家,深受现代艺术中的印象主义、立体主义和文学领域的意象主义、未来主义风格影响。作为一位现代主义诗人,卡明斯对现代诗歌语言进行了实验性探索,在词汇、句法和语法的使用上大胆打破规则。卡明斯在发表的诗歌里常使用小写字母,如用"i"替代"I",在署名时也总是用小写的"e. e. cummings"以此弱化诗人的存在感。由于兼具作为画家的禀赋,卡明斯在诗歌创作时尤其注重语言的视觉效果,排版上追求形式与内容的统一,作品常呈现出诗中有画、画中有诗的特征,因此他的诗作被誉为"视觉诗",赋予读者耳目一新的阅读体验。

文本选读

　　l(a

　　by E. E. Cummings

l(a	孤(一
le	片
af	树
fa	叶
	飘
l1	落
	了)
s)	零
one	零
l	
iness	

（周诗羽　译）

作品赏析

  这首著名的落叶诗其实是一幅动态的诗画。诗人将 a leaf falls(一片树叶飘落了)一句话插入 loneliness(孤独)一个词中,又把这四个单词拆开,排成垂直的一列,模拟一片叶子从树枝上飘下,随风翩跹,轻盈盘旋,最终簌然落地的整个过程,亦诗亦画,诗画结合。诗人正是通过这一片落叶的飘零洞悉出人世间生老病死的自然法则,既感伤秋的悲凉,又慨叹死的孤寂。

  从视觉上,每一诗行皆由一个或少数几个字母排列而成,形单影只的字母正与一片落叶的形象相符,"l"正如落叶的叶柄,"(a"则似叶面,叶子在风中翻转,"af"与"fa"正体现出树叶在空中随风摇曳、左右晃动的姿态。错落组合的字母又像是树叶在时缓时急的风中时慢时快地舞动,因而交替出现的背影或侧颜。排成竖列的字母形象上犹如空中垂直飘落的树叶,给人一种孤独寂寥的感觉,又巧妙呼应"loneliness"一词。全诗唯一完整的单词"one"蕴意着"独自、孤单","l"与"I"相近,"("将"l"与"a"分离,恰似"我"被迫分离,随后,"leaf"与"leave"谐音,既指树叶离开枝头,又暗指世间的生离死别,而离别总是多愁。"fall"一词既可为动词,意为"下落",又可作名词,意为"秋天"。古今中外,秋天难免带给我们萧瑟孤寂之感。"loneliness"一词被拆散,并嵌入"a leaf falls"中,诗人用蒙太奇的手法将抽象的孤独与具体的落叶合二为一,也因为此种交叉,使得孤独贯穿始终,让整首诗就像一片有灵魂的落叶,用身体的每一个部位向我们诠释孤独。此外,诗中四处留白代表落叶下落速度减缓的情态,每一次迟疑恰似不同人生阶段过渡的挣扎徘徊,第一处正是婴幼儿阶段的无意识,第二处是轻狂放纵的青少年步入成熟稳重的中年之前的茫然若迷,第三处则是中年进入老年的无所适从,最后一处便是人们面对死亡的怅然若失。人如落叶,必然叶落归根。

  从听觉上,/f/与/s/两音,一个模拟微风拂拂,落叶轻微颤动的呼呼声,另一个则模拟飕飕吹过的风声。流音/l/在诗中反复出现,贯穿始终,正代表树叶下坠全过程中人们不易察觉的细微风声。最开始,落叶离开枝头,随后与拂拂微风共舞(/f/音两次出现)。风力减弱,落叶停止翻转。停留片刻("ll"象征),又径直飘落,飕飕之风也透过枝桠吹过,树叶似乎踉跄一下("("象征),又翻转叶身(one 象征),继续下落。最后落地一瞬间,树叶与地面轻微摩擦,发出微弱沙沙声("ss"象征)。萧萧落叶,飕飕秋风,从听觉触发秋的悲凉,声色转换,视听交融,令读者不禁感叹秋的悲凉,更感伤老年迟暮,死之将临的悲戚。

思考题

  (1)请从这首诗中找出更多细节,说明诗人是如何向读者传达孤独这一主题的。

  (2)这首诗中的标点符号和声音的运用有何特殊之处?

  (3)这首诗中的空格有什么寓意?诗歌的形式是如何强化主题的?

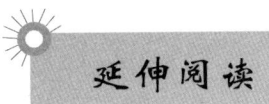

延伸阅读

Somewhere I Have Never Travelled, Gladly Beyond
by e. e. Cummings

somewhere i have never travelled, gladly beyond
any experience, your eyes have their silence:
in your most frail gesture are things which enclose me,
or which i cannot touch because they are too near

your slightest look easily will unclose me
though i have closed myself as fingers,
you open always petal by petal myself as Spring opens
(touching skilfully, mysteriously) her first rose

or if your wish be to close me, i and
my life will shut very beautifully, suddenly,
as when the heart of this flower imagines
the snow carefully everywhere descending;

nothing which we are to perceive in this world equals
the power of your intense fragility: whose texture
compels me with the colour of its countries,
rendering death and forever with each breathing

(i do not know what it is about you that closes
and opens; only something in me understands
the voice of your eyes is deeper than all roses)
nobody, not even the rain, has such small hands

Part Ⅲ Drama

Chapter 1　Richard Ⅲ
by William Shakespeare
(*excerpts*)

背景介绍

　　《理查三世》是英国剧作家威廉·莎士比亚大约于1591年创作的历史剧(第一四开本中的完整标题为 *The Tragedy of King Richard the Third*),同时也是"伊丽莎白时期演出场次最多的莎士比亚历史剧"。作品讲述了国王理查三世夺取王位的过程和其短暂的统治。该剧是莎士比亚所著的第一组四联剧中的最后一部,前三部分别是《亨利六世》的上、中、下篇(*Henry Ⅵ, Part1～Part3*)。主人公理查三世是莎翁笔下颇为独特且广为人知的重要人物形象之一,其影响力不逊色于踌躇的丹麦王子、妒忌的黑人将军、篡位的国王夫妇和昏聩的落魄父王。从篇幅来说,《理查三世》是第一四开本(the First Quarto)中第二长的戏剧(仅次于《哈姆雷特》)。全剧共分五幕,第一幕从理查描述哥哥爱德华四世的即位开始,理查对歌舞升平的太平盛世表达了不满,决心以歹徒自诩,谋划弑君篡位。同时,他恳求并成功说服亨利六世之子爱德华的寡妻安夫人(Lady Ann)嫁给自己这个"杀死了她丈夫和她父王的人"。为了顺利夺取王位,理查命人除掉了哥哥克莱伦斯。第二幕中,爱德华四世去世,理查三世与自己的侄子爱德华五世会面,并将年轻的爱德华五世及其弟约克公爵监禁在伦敦塔,以避免他们同自己争夺王位。第三幕中,在勃金汉(Buckingham,理查的侄子)的帮助下,理查试图证明自己是王位最合适的人选。为此,他处死了所有的反对者,并晓以利害说服其他的勋爵接受他即位。第四幕,理查加冕后拒绝兑现其承诺赏赐给勃金汉的爵位和财产,勃金汉深感性命堪忧,于是和里奇蒙德(Richmond,未来的亨利七世)相继发动叛乱,理查的王位和声望变得风雨飘摇。第五幕,理查三世和里奇蒙德在博斯沃斯原野交战。战前,理查梦到了他曾杀害的那些人的幽灵,心中也生出忏悔之意。最终,理查三世战败,里奇蒙德即位成为亨利七世,玫瑰战争结束。

文本选读

Character Lists(*In the order of appearance in the following excerpts*)
Duke of Gloucester, [afterwards **King Richard Ⅲ**], *brothers to the King*

Duke of Clarence, *brothers to the King*
Sir Robert Brakenbury, *Lieutenant of the Tower*
Sir Richard Ratcliff, *allies of King Richard Ⅲ*
Sir William Catesby, *allies of King Richard Ⅲ*

ACT I SCENE I (abridged)　　London. A street.
　　　　　[*Enter GLOUCESTER, solus*]
GLOUCESTER　　Now is the winter of our discontent
　　Made glorious summer by this sun of York;
　　And all the clouds that lower'd upon our house
　　In the deep bosom of the ocean buried.
　　Now are our brows bound with victorious wreaths;
　　Our bruised arms hung up for monuments;
　　Our stern alarums chang'd to merry meetings,
　　Our dreadful marches to delightful measures.
　　Grim-visag'd war hath smooth'd his wrinkled front;
　　And now, instead of mounting barbed steeds
　　To fright the souls of fearful adversaries,
　　He capers nimbly in a lady's chamber
　　To the lascivious pleasing of a lute.
　　But I, that am not shaped for sportive tricks,
　　Nor made to court an amorous looking-glass;
　　I, that am rudely stamp'd, and want love's majesty
　　To strut before a wanton, ambling nymph;
　　I, that am curtail'd of this fair proportion,
　　Cheated of feature by dissembling nature,
　　Deform'd, unfinish'd, sent before my time
　　Into this breathing world, scarce half made up,
　　And that so lamely and unfashionable
　　That dogs bark at me as I halt by them;
　　Why, I, in this weak piping time of peace,
　　Have no delight to pass away the time,
　　Unless to spy my shadow in the sun
　　And descant on mine own deformity:
　　And therefore, since I cannot prove a lover,

Chapter 1 Richard Ⅲ *by William Shakespeare*

To entertain these fair well-spoken days,

I am determined to prove a villain

And hate the idle pleasures of these days.

Plots have I laid, inductions dangerous,

By drunken prophecies, libels and dreams,

To set my brother Clarence and the king

In deadly hate the one against the other:

And if King Edward be as true and just

As I am subtle, false and treacherous,

This day should Clarence closely be mew'd up,

About a prophecy, which says that 'G'

Of Edward's heirs the murderer shall be.

Dive, thoughts, down to my soul: here

Clarence comes.

[*Enter CLARENCE, guarded, and BRAKENBURY*]

Brother, good-day; what means this armed guard

That waits upon your grace?

CLARENCE　　His majesty

Tendering my person's safety, hath appointed

This conduct to convey me to the Tower.

GLOUCESTER　　Upon what cause?

CLARENCE　　Because my name is George.

GLOUCESTER　　Alack, my lord, that fault is none of yours;

He should, for that, commit your godfathers:

O, belike his majesty hath some intent

That you shall be new-christen'd in the Tower.

But what's the matter, Clarence? may I know?

CLARENCE　　Yea, Richard, when I know; for I protest

As yet I do not: but, as I can learn,

He hearkens after prophecies and dreams;

And from the cross-row plucks the letter G.

And says a wizard told him that by G

His issue disinherited should be;

And, for my name of George begins with G,

It follows in his thought that I am he.

These, as I learn, and such like toys as these

Have moved his highness to commit me now.

GLOUCESTER　　Why, this it is, when men are ruled by women:

'Tis not the king that sends you to the Tower:

My Lady Grey his wife, Clarence, 'tis she

That tempers him to this extremity.

Was it not she and that good man of worship,

Anthony Woodville, her brother there,

That made him send Lord Hastings to the Tower,

From whence this present day he is deliver'd?

We are not safe, Clarence; we are not safe.

CLARENCE　　By heaven, I think there's no man is secure

But the queen's kindred and night-walking heralds

That trudge betwixt the king and Mistress Shore.

Heard ye not what an humble suppliant

Lord hastings was to her for his delivery?

GLOUCESTER　　Humbly complaining to her deity

Got my lord chamberlain his liberty.

I'll tell you what; I think it is our way,

If we will keep in favour with the king,

To be her men and wear her livery:

The jealous o'erworn widow and herself,

Since that our brother dubb'd them gentlewomen.

Are mighty gossips in this monarchy.

BRAKENBURY　　I beseech your graces both to pardon me;

His majesty hath straitly given in charge

That no man shall have private conference,

Of what degree soever, with his brother.

GLOUCESTER　　Even so; an't please your worship, Brakenbury,

You may partake of any thing we say:

We speak no treason, man: we say the king

Is wise and virtuous, and his noble queen

Well struck in years, fair, and not jealous;

We say that Shore's wife hath a pretty foot,

A cherry lip, a bonny eye, a passing pleasing tongue;

And that the queen's kindred are made gentle-folks:

How say you sir? Can you deny all this?

BRAKENBURY With this, my lord, myself have naught to do.

GLOUCESTER Naught to do with mistress Shore! I tell thee, fellow,

He that doth naught with her, excepting one,

Were best he do it secretly, alone.

BRAKENBURY What one, my lord?

GLOUCESTER Her husband, knave: wouldst thou betray me?

BRAKENBURY I beseech your grace to pardon me, and withal

Forbear your conference with the noble duke.

CLARENCE We know thy charge, Brakenbury, and will obey.

GLOUCESTER We are the queen's abjects, and must obey.

Brother, farewell: I will unto the king;

And whatsoever you will employ me in,

Were it to call King Edward's widow sister,

I will perform it to enfranchise you.

Meantime, this deep disgrace in brotherhood

Touches me deeper than you can imagine.

CLARENCE I know it pleaseth neither of us well.

GLOUCESTER Well, your imprisonment shall not be long;

Meantime, have patience.

CLARENCE I must perforce. Farewell.

Exeunt CLARENCE, BRAKENBURY, and Guard.

GLOUCESTER Go, tread the path that thou shalt ne'er return.

Simple, plain Clarence! I do love thee so,

That I will shortly send thy soul to heaven,

If heaven will take the present at our hands.

But who comes here? the new-deliver'd Hastings?

*　　*　　*　　*

ACT V SCENE IV(*abridged*) Inside his tent, KING RICHARD Ⅲ

[*The Ghosts vanish*]

[*KING RICHARD Ⅲ starts out of his dream*]

KING RICHARD Ⅲ Give me another horse: bind up my wounds.

Have mercy, Jesu! --Soft! I did but dream.

O coward conscience, how dost thou afflict me!

The lights burn blue. It is now dead midnight.
Cold fearful drops stand on my trembling flesh.
What do I fear? myself? there's none else by:
Richard loves Richard; that is, I am I.
Is there a murderer here? No. Yes, I am:
Then fly. What, from myself? Great reason why:
Lest I revenge. What, myself upon myself?
Alack. I love myself. Wherefore? for any good
That I myself have done unto myself?
O, no! alas, I rather hate myself
For hateful deeds committed by myself!
I am a villain: yet I lie. I am not.
Fool, of thyself speak well: fool, do not flatter.
My conscience hath a thousand several tongues,
And every tongue brings in a several tale,
And every tale condemns me for a villain.
Perjury, perjury, in the high'st degree
Murder, stem murder, in the direst degree;
All several sins, all used in each degree,
Throng to the bar, crying all, Guilty! guilty!
I shall despair. There is no creature loves me;
And if I die, no soul shall pity me:
Nay, wherefore should they, since that I myself
Find in myself no pity to myself?
Methought the souls of all that I had murder'd
Came to my tent; and every one did threat
To-morrow's vengeance on the head of Richard.

[*Enter RATCLIFF.*]

RATCLIFF	My lord!
KING RICHARD III	'Zounds! who is there?
RATCLIFF	Ratcliff, my lord; 'tis I. The early village-cock

Hath twice done salutation to the morn;
Your friends are up, and buckle on their armour.

KING RICHARD III   O Ratcliff, I have dream'd a fearful dream!
What thinkest thou, will our friends prove all true?

RATCLIFF	No doubt, my lord.
KING RICHARD Ⅲ	O Ratcliff, I fear, I fear,--
RATCLIFF	Nay, good my lord, be not afraid of shadows.
KING RICHARD Ⅲ	By the apostle Paul, shadows to-night

  Have struck more terror to the soul of Richard

  Than can the substance of ten thousand soldiers

  Armed in proof, and led by shallow Richmond.

  It is not yet near day. Come, go with me;

  Under our tents I'll play the eaves-dropper,

  To see if any mean to shrink from me.

[Exeunt.]

* * * *

ACT V SCENE IV Another part of the field.

  [<i>Alarum: excursions. Enter NORFOLK and forces fighting; to him CATESBY</i>]

CATESBY	Rescue, my Lord of Norfolk, rescue, rescue!

  The king enacts more wonders than a man,

  Daring an opposite to every danger:

  His horse is slain, and all on foot he fights,

  Seeking for Richmond in the throat of death.

  Rescue, fair lord, or else the day is lost!

[Alarum. Enter KING RICHARD Ⅲ]

KING RICHARD Ⅲ	A horse! a horse! my kingdom for a horse!
CATESBY	Withdraw, my lord; I'll help you to a horse.
KING RICHARD Ⅲ	Slave, I have set my life upon a cast,

  And I will stand the hazard of the die:

  I think there be six Richmonds in the field;

  Five have I slain to-day, instead of him.

  A horse! a horse! my kingdom for a horse!

[Exeunt.]

 作品赏析

灵魂挣扎的悲剧英雄——理查三世双重精神"扭曲"的悲剧性

  威廉·莎士比亚的著名历史剧《理查三世》围绕主人公格罗斯特公爵(Duke of

Gloucester，继位后史称"理查三世")夺取王位的历程及其统治和战争展开。理查三世是莎翁基于历史人物进行的又一伟大文学塑造。他笔下这位身体畸形、心灵扭曲、阴险狡诈、残忍暴戾的君王吸引了中外数代读者，至今仍保有其独特的"魅力"。在众多读者眼中，理查三世是暴君和魔鬼的化身，其走向王权的道路中充斥着阴谋诡计和冷血谋杀。但是仅仅将其视作一个"穷凶极恶"之人未免有失偏颇。倘若超越单纯的伦理道德判断，而采用悲剧性视角来剖析其挣扎的灵魂，或许我们同样可以将理查三世定义为一位悲剧英雄(Tragic Hero)。

一、悲剧和悲剧人物

古希腊哲学思想家亚里士多德在其美学经典巨作《诗学》(*Poetics*)中首次对悲剧进行了全面的论述，并将悲剧定义为："悲剧是对一个严肃、完整、有一定长度的行动的模仿。它的媒介是通过"装饰"的语言以不同的形式用于剧的不同部分，它的模仿方式是借助人们的行动，而不是叙述，通过引发怜悯和恐惧使这些情感得到疏泄。"这也正是悲剧的独特魅力所在，其引发的"恐惧""怜悯"等情绪会使受众心中萌生出一种"崇高感"。而受众心中的这些情绪往往和悲剧人物紧密相连，对于悲剧人物的界定也许不能用"善/恶""好/坏"这样简单的二元对立来划分。正如亚里士多德在描述悲剧人物时的叙述："这些人不具十分的美德，也不是十分的公正，他们之所以遭受不幸，不是因为本身的罪恶或邪恶，而是因为犯了某种错误。"悲剧人物既非圣贤亦非恶魔，而是一个介于善恶之间，且在诸多"好"的品质上超出一般人的角色。朱光潜先生同样说过："从审美意义上去理解，一个穷凶极恶的人如果在他的邪恶当中表现出超乎常人的坚毅和巨人般的力量，也可以成为悲剧人物"。

第一四开本中的《理查三世》的完整英文标题为 *The Tragedy of King Richard the Third*，由此可见莎士比亚最初就是基于历史事件和人物在塑造一部悲剧。这部悲剧中，最具有悲剧色彩的人物不是那些被理查三世冷血铲除的"异己"，而是这位灵魂挣扎的国王本身。他除了残暴，同时体现出了坚毅、勇敢和抗争等品质。他的"过失"在于权欲的过度膨胀和获取权利的手段残酷，最终也导致了他众叛亲离、惨死战场的结局。因此他也是一位介于好人与坏人之间或是"善恶兼备"的一位"悲剧英雄"。

二、人物悲剧性的动因——理查三世的双重精神"扭曲"

亚里士多德指出悲剧有六大要素："情节(Plot)、性格(Characters)、思想(Thought)、言词(Diction)、形象(Spectacle)和歌曲(Melody)"。对于作品中人物的悲剧性而言，其性格和思想是引向其悲剧命运的主要内因。理查三世的性格孤僻和思想扭曲，不少读者会单向地将理查三世的精神扭曲看作是魔鬼一般的穷凶极恶。但是倘若超出褒贬而从广义上来理解"扭曲"一词也可以理解为对于"常态"或是"平衡状态"的一种"背离"。理查三世身上我们或许可以看到两种维度的背离：一方面是负面的"恶魔般的堕落"，另一方面是正向的"英雄式的升华"。

理查三世"恶魔般的堕落"的动因之一在全文开篇著名的独白中就有所交代——"我既被卸除了一切匀称的身段模样,欺人的造物者又骗去了我的仪容,使得我残缺不全,不等我生长成形,便把我抛进这喘息的人间"("I, that am curtail'd of this fair proportion,/ Cheated of feature by dissembling nature,/ Deform'd, unfinish'd, sent before my time/ Into this breathing world, scarce half made up")。他与生俱来的畸形躯壳使得他"不适于调情弄爱"("not shaped for sportive tricks"),更无法"在嫡娜的仙姑面前昂首阔步"("want love's majesty/To strut before a wanton ambling nymph")。既然无法享受眼下"歌舞升平"("piping time of peace")的欢愉,他只得"口中念念有词,埋怨我这废体残形"("descant on my own deformity")。因此他早已暗下决心"以歹徒自许,专事仇视眼前的闲情逸致了"("I am determined to prove a villain/And hate the idle pleasures of these days")。继而,理查三世设下一系列的阴谋圈套,通过冷血谋杀先后铲除了他通往王位的"绊脚石"。他先后处死了十二人,包括几位年轻的王子、他的哥哥Clarence和强娶的安夫人(Lady Ann)。其"恶魔般的堕落"因其追逐权利过程中的残忍暴行变得昭然若揭。

但是,正如前文所提及,作为一个悲剧人物,理查德有着明显的"过失"——过度膨胀的权欲。但是在这贪婪的人性背后隐藏着他内心的一种"补偿机制",而他极端化的补偿手段背后却能窥探到一些"英雄式的升华"。对于自己的废体残形,理查三世在开头的独白中的确表露出了一些自怨自艾的情绪,但是他并未选择逃避、沉沦甚至是放弃这条看似没有价值的生命,而是决心倾其所有且"不择手段"地来证明自己的价值并赢得他人的认可。从心理补偿的角度,这是一种自我保护和自我突破;从需求层次的角度,这也是对"自我实现"(Self-Actualization)的追求;从性格特点的角度,这同样是一种不向命运低头的倔强和坚毅。造物主没有给他君临天下的堂堂仪表,而在前作《亨利六世下篇》(第三幕第二场)中当时的格罗斯特就曾表达"我就不能不把幸福寄托在我所梦想的王冠上面。"("I'll make my heaven to dream upon the crown.")然而面对自己的梦想他感到过迷失,"好比一个迷失在荆棘丛中的人,一面披荆斩棘,一面被荆棘刺伤;一面寻找出路,一面又迷失路途,没法走到空旷的地方,却拼命要把这地方找到。我一定要摆脱这些困苦,不惜用一柄血斧开出路。"("And I,--like one lost in a thorny wood,/That rends the thorns and is rent with the thorns,/Seeking a way and straying from the way;/Not knowing how to find the open air,/But toiling desperately to find it out,--/Torment myself to catch the English crown;/And from that torment I will free myself,/Or hew my way out with a bloody axe.")由此可以看出理查三世在迷途中的悲剧色彩和对于自我实现的渴望与坚毅。此外,在该剧第五幕第三场中,读者也能够感受到理查三世尚未完全泯灭的良心。在他的梦境中,惨遭其荼毒的人以超自然的鬼魂形式出现,控诉他的罪行并诅咒他的命运。他从梦中惊醒,说道:"呵,良心是个懦夫,你惊扰得我好苦!"("O coward conscience, how dost thou afflict me!")接着他内心中产生一系列矛盾的自我剖析,"呀! 我其实恨我自己,因为我自己干下了可恨的罪行。我是个罪犯。不对,我在乱说了;我不是个罪犯。"("Alas, I rather hate myself/ For hateful deeds committed by myself! / I am a villain. Yet I lie, I am not.")一方面他的良心激发自我疚责,另一方面他的野心又驱使自我逃避。最后,在第五幕第四场中,他豪迈地喊出了"一匹马! 一匹马! 我的王位换一匹马!"("A horse! A horse! My kingdom for a horse!")此时,战阵中的他,对一匹战马的渴望已然超越了王位,超越了权力,他一心只想再度上马迎敌,宁死不降。在战场上理查三世没有丝毫的怯懦,而是表现出了英勇的气节。

总之,《理查三世》的悲剧不仅仅是畸形躯壳的悲剧,也是精神世界"恶魔和英雄"并存的双重扭曲的悲剧。极端化的"自我实现"愿望和残酷的"心理补偿"方式增添了主人公的悲剧性色彩。同时,也令读者心中交织着憎恶、恐惧、怜悯、惋惜等一系列复杂而又能激发崇高感的情绪。

主要参考文献

莎士比亚. 莎士比亚全集[M]. 朱生豪,等译. 北京:人民文学出版社,1995.

亚里士多德. 诗学[M]. 罗念生,译. 上海:上海人民出版社,2006.

杨晓莲. 超越中的悲剧人物——试论《理查三世》的悲剧性[J]. 外国文学研究,1993(3):59-63.

朱光潜. 悲剧心理学[M]. 合肥:安徽教育出版社,2008.

邹广胜,龚丽可. 论理查三世的悲剧心理[J]. 当代外国文学,2018(1):108-117.

思考题

(1)剧中多次用到了戏剧旁白和独白,为何理查三世会频繁地把秘密透露给观众? 这对于他的人物形象塑造产生了什么效果?

(2)剧中为何会多次出现预言性的梦境和诅咒? 这些语言如何影响了我们的阅读感悟?

(3)文学经典作品中塑造了许多的畸形人形象,还有哪些著名的畸形人,他们所经历的精神扭曲和理查三世有何异同?

Chapter 2 Hamlet
by William Shakespeare
(excerpts)

 背景介绍

  《哈姆雷特(Hamlet)》是由威廉·莎士比亚于 1599 年至 1602 年间创作的一部悲剧作品，被公认为莎士比亚的代表作。该剧刻画了复杂的人性、蕴含了深刻的悲剧意义，也因此代表了整个西方文艺复兴时期文学的最高成就。《哈姆雷特》同《麦克白》《李尔王》和《奥赛罗》一起组成莎士比亚"四大悲剧"。

  戏剧讲述了丹麦王子哈姆雷特对谋杀其父、骗娶其母并阴谋篡取王位的叔叔克劳狄斯进行复仇的故事。在哈姆雷特近乎孤军奋战的复仇过程中，他始终表现出犹豫彷徨的特征，导致他在行动上多次出现延宕不决并因此错失了复仇锄奸的良机。究竟是什么因素导致了哈姆雷特的犹豫呢？有评论家认为这是一出性格悲剧，哈姆雷特性格上软弱，气质上忧郁，最终使得他面对复仇任务时显得患得患失；也有评论家认为这部剧继承了古希腊悲剧传统，是一部典型的命运悲剧。哈姆雷特与神秘莫测的命运进行的抗争，不过有如蚍蜉撼树般无力。随着 20 世纪初弗洛伊德提出俄狄浦斯情结，导致哈姆雷特犹豫的原因又有了新的阐释。这种源自于精神分析学的解读将有助于我们对人性展开更深入的探究。

 文本选读

Act Ⅰ Scene Ⅱ （abridged）

HAMLET
O, that this too too solid flesh would melt
Thaw and resolve itself into a dew!
Or that the Everlasting had not fix'd
His canon 'gainst self-slaughter! O God! God!
How weary, stale, flat and unprofitable,

Seem to me all the uses of this world!

Fie on't! ah fie!'tis an unweeded garden,

That grows to seed; things rank and gross in nature

Possess it merely. That it should come to this!

But two months dead; nay, not so much, not two:

So excellent a king; that was, to this,

Hyperion to a satyr; so loving to my mother

That he might not beteem the winds of heaven

Visit her face too roughly. Heaven and earth!

Must I remember? why, she would hang on him,

As if increase of appetite had grown

By what it fed on: and yet, within a month--

Let me not think on't --Frailty, thy name is woman! --

A little month, or ere those shoes were old

With which she follow'd my poor father's body,

Like Niobe, all tears:--why she, even she--

O, God! a beast, that wants discourse of reason,

Would have mourn'd longer--married with my uncle,

My father's brother, but no more like my father

Than I to Hercules: within a month:

Ere yet the salt of most unrighteous tears

Had left the flushing in her galled eyes,

She married. O, most wicked speed, to post

With such dexterity to incestuous sheets!

It is not nor it cannot come to good:

But break, my heart; for I must hold my tongue.

ACT III SCENE I (abridged)

HAMLET

To be, or not to be: that is the question:

Whether 'tis nobler in the mind to suffer

The slings and arrows of outrageous fortune,

Or to take arms against a sea of troubles,

And by opposing end them? To die: to sleep;

No more; and by a sleep to say we end
The heart-ache and the thousand natural shocks
That flesh is heir to, 'tis a consummation
Devoutly to be wish'd. To die, to sleep;
To sleep: perchance to dream: ay, there's the rub;
For in that sleep of death what dreams may come
When we have shuffled off this mortal coil,
Must give us pause: there's the respect
That makes calamity of so long life;
For who would bear the whips and scorns of time,
The oppressor's wrong, the proud man's contumely,
The pangs of despised love, the law's delay,
The insolence of office and the spurns
That patient merit of the unworthy takes,
When he himself might his quietus make
With a bare bodkin? who would fardels bear,
To grunt and sweat under a weary life,
But that the dread of something after death,
The undiscover'd country from whose bourn
No traveller returns, puzzles the will
And makes us rather bear those ills we have
Than fly to others that we know not of?
Thus conscience does make cowards of us all;
And thus the native hue of resolution
Is sicklied o'er with the pale cast of thought,
And enterprises of great pith and moment
With this regard their currents turn awry,
And lose the name of action.--Soft you now!
The fair Ophelia! Nymph, in thy orisons
Be all my sins remember'd.

Act III Scene IV (abridged)

The Queen's closet
Enter QUEEN MARGARET and POLONIUS

LORD POLONIUS

He will come straight. Look you lay home to him:

Tell him his pranks have been too broad to bear with,

And that you grace hath screen'd and stood between

Much heat and him. I'll sconceme even here.

Pray you, be round with him.

HAMLET

[Within]Mother,mother,mother!

QUEEN GERTRUDE

I'll warrant you,

Fear me not:withdraw,I hear him coming.

POLONIUS hides behind the arras

Enter HAMLET

HAMLET

Now, mother, what's the matter?

QUEEN GERTRUDE

Hamlet, thou hast thy father much offended.

HAMLET

Mother, you have my father much offended.

QUEEN GERTRUDE

Come, come, you answer with an idle tongue.

HAMLET

Go, go, you question with a wicked tongue.

QUEEN GERTRUDE

Why, how now, Hamlet!

HAMLET

What's the matter now?

QUEEN GERTRUDE

Have you forgot me?

HAMLET

No, by the rood, not so:

You are the queen, your husband's brother's wife;

And--would it were not so! --you are my mother.

QUEEN GERTRUDE

Nay, then, I'll set those to you that can speak.

HAMLET

Come, come, and sit you down; you shall not budge;

You go not till I set you up a glass

Where you may see the inmost part of you.

QUEEN GERTRUDE

What wilt thou do? thou wilt not murder me?

Help, help, ho!

LORD POLONIUS

[Behind] What, ho! help, help, help!

HAMLET

[Drawing] How now! a rat? Dead, for a ducat, dead!

Makes a pass through the arras

LORD POLONIUS

[Behind] O, I am slain!

Falls and dies

QUEEN GERTRUDE

O me, what hast thou done?

HAMLET

Nay, I know not:

Is it the king?

QUEEN GERTRUDE

O, what a rash and bloody deed is this!

HAMLET

A bloody deed! almost as bad, good mother,

As kill a king, and marry with his brother.

QUEEN GERTRUDE

As kill a king!

HAMLET

Ay, lady, 'twas my word.

Lifts up the array and discovers POLONIUS

Thou wretched, rash, intruding fool, farewell!

I took thee for thy better: take thy fortune;

Thou find'st to be too busy is some danger.

Leave wringing of your hands: peace! sit you down,

And let me wring your heart; for so I shall,

If it be made of penetrable stuff,

If damned custom have not brass'd it so

That it is proof and bulwark against sense.

QUEEN GERTRUDE

What have I done, that thou darest wag thy tongue

In noise so rude against me?

HAMLET

Such an act

That blurs the grace and blush of modesty,

Calls virtue hypocrite, takes off the rose

From the fair forehead of an innocent love

And sets a blister there, makes marriage-vows

As false as dicers' oaths:O, such a deed

As from the body of contraction plucks

The very soul, and sweet religion makes

A rhapsody of words:heaven's face doth glow:

Yea, this solidity and compound mass,

With tristful visage, as against the doom,

Is thought-sick at the act.

QUEEN GERTRUDE

Ay me, what act,

That roars so loud, and thunders in the index?

HAMLET

Look here, upon this picture, and on this,

The counterfeit presentment of two brothers.

See, what a grace was seated on this brow;

Hyperion's curls;the front of Jove himself;

An eye like Mars, to threaten and command;

A station like the herald Mercury

New-lighted on a heaven-kissing hill;

A combination and a form indeed,

Where every god did seem to set his seal,

To give the world assurance of a man:

This was your husband. Look you now, what follows:

Here is your husband;like a mildew'd ear,

Blasting his wholesome brother. Have you eyes?
Could you on this fair mountain leave to feed,
And batten on this moor? Ha! have you eyes?
You cannot call it love; for at your age
The hey-day in the blood is tame, it's humble,
And waits upon the judgment; and what judgment
Would step from this to this? Sense, sure, you have,
Else could you not have motion; but sure, that sense
Is apoplex'd; for madness would not err,
Nor sense to ecstasy was ne'er so thrall'd
But it reserved some quantity of choice,
To serve in such a difference. What devil was't
That thus hath cozen'd you at hoodman-blind?
Eyes without feeling, feeling without sight,
Ears without hands or eyes, smelling sans all,
Or but a sickly part of one true sense
Could not so mope.
O shame! where is thy blush? Rebellious hell,
If thou canst mutine in a matron's bones,
To flaming youth let virtue be as wax,
And melt in her own fire: proclaim no shame
When the compulsive ardour gives the charge,
Since frost itself as actively doth burn
And reason panders will.

QUEEN GERTRUDE

O Hamlet, speak no more:
Thou turn'st mine eyes into my very soul;
And there I see such black and grained spots
As will not leave their tinct.

HAMLET

Nay, but to live
In the rank sweat of an enseamed bed,
Stew'd in corruption, honeying and making love
Over the nasty sty,--

QUEEN GERTRUDE

O, speak to me no more;

These words, like daggers, enter in mine ears;

No more, sweet Hamlet!

HAMLET

A murderer and a villain;

A slave that is not twentieth part the tithe

Of your precedent lord; a vice of kings;

A cutpurse of the empire and the rule,

That from a shelf the precious diadem stole,

And put it in his pocket!

QUEEN GERTRUDE

No more!

HAMLET

A king of shreds and patches,--

俄狄浦斯情结——困扰哈姆雷特"犹豫"症的解读

在《哈姆雷特》这部戏剧中,丹麦王子哈姆雷特是一个充满浪漫主义悲情色彩的艺术舞台形象。他忧郁感伤,耽于幻想,回避现实,最终走向了悲剧的结局。他在思想上显得犹豫不决,在复仇行动上一再拖延耽搁。一个典型的例子是自父亲的亡魂向他昭示后,他就一再坚定决心要杀死叔父为父复仇。在其叔父祷告之时,哈姆雷特就意识到这是一个绝好的复仇时机,他最终还是在行动上退缩了,并找出一个极为牵强的理由"等候一个更残酷的机会"来为自己辩解。此种自我矛盾的忧郁性格始终贯穿于哈姆雷特的整个复仇过程中。而究其原因,可以说很大程度上源自哈姆雷特身上潜藏的俄狄浦斯情结。

俄狄浦斯是古希腊戏剧家索福克勒斯创作的著名悲剧《俄狄浦斯王》中的主角。当神谕显示他注定将杀父娶母,俄狄浦斯选择了放逐自己,远走他乡,以逃避预言里可怕的罪恶。但他的抗争无法摆脱宿命,俄狄浦斯仍旧一步步坠入了命运为其布下的陷阱并最终走向毁灭。虽然俄狄浦斯在主观上并无意恋母娶母,他阴差阳错犯下的弥天大罪却在客观上导致他成为了文学作品中第一个杀父娶母的人。19世纪末20世纪初,奥地利心理学家,精神分析学的奠基人弗洛伊德对俄狄浦斯的故事进行了分析并创造性地提出"俄狄浦斯情结"(Oedipus complex)。在剧中,"To be or not to be"的问题一再困扰着哈姆雷特,他肩负复仇使命却时时刻刻陷入犹豫彷徨不能自拔,令哈姆雷特痛苦的根源正是深藏于他内心的俄狄浦斯情结。

  首先,在第一幕第二场中,对于年轻的王子哈姆雷特来说,人生中不幸的打击接踵而至——父亲猝死,王位丢失,母亲改嫁。在城堡大厅里,国王与王后轮番劝慰他放下笼罩在身上的忧郁,接受眼前的事实。而哈姆雷特只是一味敷衍搪塞。无比压抑的他通过一段独白表达了内心真实的想法:

> "That it should come to this!
> But two months dead: nay, not so much, not two:
> So excellent a king; that was, to this,
> Hyperion to a satyr; so loving to my mother
> That he might not beteem the winds of heaven
> Visit her face too roughly. Heaven and earth!
> …
> A little month; or ere thoes shoes were old
> With which she follow'd my poor father's body,
> Like Niobe, all tears: why she, even she,—
> O God! a beast, that wants discourse of reason,
> Would have mourn'd longer,—married with my uncle,
> My father's brother, but no more like my father
> Than I to Hercules: within a month,
> Ere yet the salt of most unrighteous tears
> Had left the flushing in her galled eyes,
> She married. O! most wicked speed, to post
> With such dexterity to incestuous sheets.
> …"

  在这段独白中,哈姆雷特赞美父亲完美如天神,贬低叔父丑恶似妖魔,而对母亲的改嫁则表现出异乎寻常的排斥和痛恨。归根结底,这些都是哈姆雷特潜意识中恋母情结的外化体现。他的父亲是一位人人崇敬的高贵的君王,更是俘获母亲芳心的男人。由于恋母情结的作祟,哈姆雷特一直以父亲这一完美形象作为自身的楷模,而潜意识下取代父亲的想法被理性和道德伦理观念抑制着,他只能将父亲视为自己意志的体现。在一定程度上,父亲的形象即是自己的形象,对父亲的赞美就是对自身的褒扬。父亲的去世意味着潜抑机制的消失,而此时,叔父的横刀夺爱使得哈姆雷特潜意识中将他视为情敌。因此,在尚不知道叔父谋害父亲这一真相之时,叔父在哈姆雷特眼中已经被打上了"丑怪(satyr)"的标签,显得尤为可憎。在亚洲、非洲、美洲一些国家长期流行过嫁给小叔子这种收继婚俗。即便在当时新教盛行的欧洲,这种例子也并不少见,可见母亲的改嫁并非乱伦之举。可是哈姆雷特却认定母亲的行为罪不可恕。母亲在自己心中是圣洁、忠贞、高贵、无私宛如天使一般的存在，母亲的改嫁则标志着这一完美形象的彻底崩塌。哈姆雷特心中追求完美女性的理想也随之破灭。因此，身陷痛苦和绝望中的哈姆雷特才会在这段独白中对母亲的改嫁表现出极度的痛恨和强烈的谴责。

其次，在第三幕第四场中，哈姆雷特在王后寝宫中继续毫不留情地指责母亲的再嫁行为：

"Such an act

That blurs the grace and blush of modesty,

Calls virtue hypocrite, takes off the rose

From the fair forehead of an innocent love

And sets a blister there, makes marriage-vows

As false as dicers' oaths：O, such a deed

As from the body of contraction plucks

The very soul, and sweet religion makes

A rhapsody of words：heaven's face doth glow：

Yea, this solidity and compound mass,

With tristful visage, as against the doom,

Is thought-sick at the act."

根据这段独白不难看出，父亲的意外去世固然让哈姆雷特悲伤，然而令他念念不忘的始终是母亲改嫁这一事实。王后并未参与谋害国王的阴谋，她对先王的死亡真相一无所知，从某种程度上讲，无辜的母亲也是阴谋的受害者。但哈姆雷特不但没有同情自己处于弱势地位的母亲，反而内心无比愤懑。在他看来，母亲嫁给杀人凶手罪不容赦。在恋母情结的驱使下，他对母亲的爱已经到了异常狂热的地步，他决不能接受叔父占有自己心爱的母亲。于是，他用最下贱的字眼来咒骂叔父：

"A murderer and a villain；

A slave that is not twentieth part the tithe

Of your precedent lord；a vice of kings；

A cutpurse of the empire and the rule,

That from a shelf the precious diadem stole,

And put it in his pocket！"

哈姆雷特对母亲的诘责之词也愈发激烈：

"Nay, but to live

In the rank sweat of an enseamed bed,

Stew'd in corruption, honeying and making love

Over the nasty sty,——"

讽刺和挖苦已不能倾泻哈姆雷特内心的苦楚，他索性泼妇骂街般地恣意谩骂以发泄心中的愤懑,其用词之污秽令人难以想象竟出自一个高贵的王子之口。究其原因,人生多重的不幸纷至袭来,年轻的王子内心的积郁在不断地积累和发酵。在王后寝宫与母亲独处的这样一个特定场景下,哈姆雷特内心的俄狄浦斯情结再一次被唤醒,仿佛导火索般引燃了他的情绪。他对于母亲的情感是复杂矛盾的,痛恨中交织着爱恋。恨的根源在于哈姆雷特潜意识中认为母亲的改嫁不仅是对父亲的背叛,更是对自己的背叛,而对母亲的爱越深,被背叛的感觉也就越强烈,由此产生的恨意越浓,说出的话也就越极端。并且父亲去世后,他本可以在心理上得到某种满足,即便自己依旧无法光明正大地表示对母亲的爱,但至少母亲的爱会全部倾注在自己身上,然而叔父克劳狄斯的横亘插足扼杀了他所有的期待,得到母亲的愿望一再破灭令他自身陷入极度失望和痛苦之中,这种极端消极的情绪又束缚自己的行动,最终导致复仇事宜一再拖延。

最后,在第三幕第一场,哈姆雷特道出了该剧中脍炙人口的经典独白:又一次表现出了俄狄浦斯情结对其复仇行动的影响:

"To be, or not to be: that is the question:
Whether 'tis nobler in the mind to suffer
The slings and arrows of outrageous fortune,
Or to take arms against a sea of troubles,
And by opposing end them?
..."

从俄狄浦斯情结的角度看,哈姆雷特在这段独白中表现出的摇摆不定的立场源自于他在潜意识中想要杀死自己父亲的特殊心理,而毒死父亲并霸占母亲的叔父实现了哈姆雷特长久以来压抑在心底的欲望。从这个意义上说,叔父就成了哈姆雷特潜意识里的黑色替身。默然忍受命运暴虐的毒箭意味着忍受叔父篡夺王位、霸占母亲的锥心事实;而挺身反抗人世无涯的苦难便意味着完成任重道远的复仇,而复仇就是杀死潜意识中的自己,所以才是一种苦难。两难相权,导致年轻的王子无法做出选择。哈姆雷特杀死躲在窗帘后面的波隆尼尔时果断决绝,也曾毫不手软地设计除掉叔父派去谋杀他的两个大臣,然而唯独面对与自己有着深仇大恨的克劳狄斯就是不能痛下杀手。在俄狄浦斯情结的束缚下,哈姆雷特的行动能力丧失了,杀死克劳狄斯为父亲报仇的敌意也在自我谴责中衰退了,这才导致了他行动的延宕不决。

总之,哈姆雷特的俄狄浦斯情结是导致他复仇犹豫不决的主因。复仇便意味着自我否定。哈姆雷特在自我谴责与自我惩罚中挣扎,并对人生和爱情产生怀疑乃至绝望。他悲悯人世间的苦难,又恐惧未知的死亡。在种种犹疑之中,复仇这一伟大的事业也渐渐失去了行动的意义。

主要参考文献

陈达. 恋母情结——以弗洛伊德的观点解读哈姆雷特[J]. 重庆工商大学学报(社会科学版),2006(3):114-116.

李克."恋母情结"与哈姆雷特[J]. 广西社会科学,2001(5):88-90.

虞佳. 论哈姆雷特的三大情结[J]. 文化艺术研究,2010(1):134-142.

郑金霞. 由"to be, or not to be: that is a question"看哈姆雷特的恋母情结[J]. 时代文学(下半月),2011(2):147-148.

思考题

(1)莎士比亚在戏剧中将哈姆雷特塑造得忧郁感伤、犹豫不决,你怎样看待这样一个男性形象?

(2)"To be, or not to be: that is the question..."这一段独白运用了哪些修辞手法?

(3)你怎样看待戏剧《哈姆雷特》中的女性角色?

Chapter 3　Death of a Salesman
by Arthur Miller
（excerpts）

《推销员之死》是美国剧作家阿瑟·米勒1949年出版的一部两幕剧。这部剧作展现了小人物的生存困境,批评了物欲横流的商业社会,戳穿了"美国梦"的泡沫。米勒以及剧中主角"威利·罗曼"(Willy Loman)从此成为家喻户晓的人物。《推销员之死》在演出之后立即大受好评并赢得了1949年的普利策奖。主人公威利是一个美国社会中的小人物。他在推销员的岗位上已经工作了三十余年,梦想像自己的榜样——推销员辛格曼那样获得成功。事与愿违的是,他为公司辛苦奔波了大半辈子,最后却落得被新老板解雇的下场。他的家庭中也充斥着谎言,威利的儿子比夫和哈皮只是两个不务正业的投机者,并不是他想象中的有为青年。梦想与现实的巨大落差使得威利经常精神恍惚,冷酷的现实最终打碎了威利所有关于成功的幻想,只能选择自杀来为家人换取保险赔偿金。荒谬的是,他不知道自杀并不属于理赔范围。这部剧作的悲剧性不仅体现在威利的结局,真正的悲剧是小人物追求一生的梦想的破灭。威利无望的生活与富丽堂皇的"美国梦"形成鲜明对照,折射出残酷的生活现实中人类的生存危机。

ACT ONE

...

Light has risen on the boys' room. Unseen, WILLY is heard talking to himself, "Eighty thousand miles," and a little laugh. BIFF gets out of bed, comes downstage a bit, and stands attentively. BIFF is two years older than his brother, HAPPY, well built, but in these days bears a worn air and seems less self-assured. He has succeeded less, and his dreams are stronger and less acceptable than HAPPY's. HAPPY is tall, powerfully made. Sexuality is like a visible color on him, or a scent that many women have discovered. He, like his brother, is lost, but in a different way, for he has never allowed himself to turn his face toward defeat and is thus more confused and hard-skinned, although seemingly more content.

HAPPY (*getting out of bed*): He's going to get his licence taken away if he keeps that up. I'm getting nervous about him, y'know, BIFF?

BIFF: His eyes are going.

HAPPY: No, I've driven with him. He sees all right. He just doesn't keep his mind on it. I drove into the city with him last week. He stops at a green light and then it turns red and he goes. (*He laughs.*)

BIFF: Maybe he's color-blind.

HAPPY: Pop? Why, he's got the finest eye for color in the business. You know that.

BIFF (*sitting down on his bed*): I'm going to sleep.

HAPPY: You're not still sour on Dad, are you, BIFF?

BIFF: He's all right, I guess.

WILLY (*underneath them, in the living-room*): Yes, sir, eighty thousand miles—eighty-two thousand! BIFF: You smoking?

HAPPY (*holding out a pack of cigarettes*): Want one?

BIFF (*taking a cigarette*): I can never sleep when I smell it.

WILLY: What a simonizing job, heh!

HAPPY (*with deep sentiment*): Funny, BIFF, y'know? Us sleeping in here again? The old beds. (*He pats his bed affectionately.*) All the talk that went across those two beds, huh? Our whole lives. BIFF: Yeah. Lotta dreams and plans.

HAPPY (*with a deep and masculine laugh*): About five hundred women would like to know what was said in this room.

(*They share a soft laugh.*)

BIFF: Remember that big Betsy something—what the hell was her name—over on Bushwick Avenue?

HAPPY (*combing his hair*): With the collie dog!

BIFF: That's the one. I got you in there, remember?

HAPPY: Yeah, that was my first time—I think. Boy, there was a pig! (*They laugh, almost crudely.*) You taught me everything I know about women. Don't forget that.

BIFF: I bet you forgot how bashful you used to be. Especially with girls.

HAPPY: Oh, I still am, BIFF.

BIFF: Oh, go on.

HAPPY: I just control it, that's all. I think I got less bashful and you got more so. What happened, BIFF? Where's the old humor, the old confidence? (*He shakes BIFF's knee. BIFF gets up and moves restlessly about the room.*) What's the matter?

BIFF: Why does Dad mock me all the time?

HAPPY: He's not mocking you, he—

BIFF: Everything I say there's a twist of mockery on his face. I can't get near him.

HAPPY: He just wants you to make good, that's all. I wanted to talk to you about Dad for a long time, BIFF. Something's—happening to him. He—talks to himself.

BIFF: I noticed that this morning. But he always mumbled.

HAPPY: But not so noticeable. It got so embarrassing I sent him to Florida. And you know something? Most of the time he's talking to you.

BIFF: What's he say about me?

HAPPY: I can't make it out.

BIFF: What's he say about me? HAPPY: I think the fact that you're not settled, that you're still kind of up in the air...

BIFF: There's one or two other things depressing him, HAPPY.

HAPPY: What do you mean?

BIFF: Never mind. Just don't lay it all to me.

HAPPY: But I think if you got started—I mean—is there any future for you out there?

BIFF: I tell ya, Hap, I don't know what the future is. I don't know—what I'm supposed to want.

HAPPY: What do you mean?

BIFF: Well, I spent six or seven years after high school trying to work myself up. Shipping clerk, salesman, business of one kind or another. And it's a measly manner of existence. To get on that subway on the hot mornings in summer. To devote your whole life to keeping stock, or making phone calls, or selling or buying. To suffer fifty weeks of the year for the sake of a two-week vacation, when all you really desire is to be outdoors, with your shirt off. And always to have to get ahead of the next fella. And still—that's how you build a future.

HAPPY: Well, you really enjoy it on a farm? Are you content out there?

BIFF (*with rising agitation*): Hap, I've had twenty or thirty different kinds of job since I left home before the war, and it always turns out the same. I just realized it lately. In Nebraska when I herded cattle, and the Dakotas, and Arizona, and now in Texas. It's why I came home now, I guess, because I realized it. This farm I work on, it's spring there now, see? And they've got about fifteen new colts. There's nothing more inspiring or—beautiful than the sight of a mare and a new colt. And it's cool there now, see? Texas is cool now, and it's spring. And whenever spring comes to where I am, I suddenly get the feeling, my God, I'm not gettin' anywhere! What the hell am I doing, playing around with horses, twenty-eight dollars a week! I'm thirty-four years old, I oughta be makin' my future. That's when I come running home. And now, I get here, and I don't know what to do with myself. (*After a pause*) I've always made a point of not wasting my life, and everytime I come back here I know that all I've done is to waste my life.

HAPPY: You're a poet, you know that, BIFF? You're a— you're an idealist!

BIFF: No, I'm mixed up very bad. Maybe I oughta get married. Maybe I oughta get stuck into something. Maybe that's my trouble. I'm like a boy. I'm not married, I'm not in business, I just—I'm like a boy. Are you content, Hap? You're a success, aren't you? Are you content?

HAPPY: Hell, no!

BIFF: Why? You're making money, aren't you?

HAPPY (*moving about with energy, expressiveness*): All I can do now is wait for the merchandise manager to die. And suppose I get to be merchandise manager? He's a good friend of mine, and he just built a terrific estate on Long Island. And he lived there about two months and sold it, and now he's building another one. He can't enjoy it once it's finished. And I know that's just what I would do. I don't know what the hell I'm workin' for. Sometimes I sit in my apartment—all alone. And I think of the rent I'm paying. And it's crazy. But then, it's what I always wanted. My own apartment, a car, and plenty of women. And still, goddammit, I'm lonely.

BIFF (*with enthusiasm*): Listen, why don't you come out West with me?

HAPPY: You and I, heh?

BIFF: Sure, maybe we could buy a ranch. Raise cattle, use our muscles. Men built like we are should be working out in the open.

HAPPY (*avidly*): The Loman Brothers, heh?

BIFF (*with vast affection*): Sure, we'd be known all over the counties!

HAPPY (*enthralled*): That's what I dream about, BIFF. Sometimes I want to just rip my clothes off in the middle of the store and outbox that goddam merchandise manager. I mean I can outbox, outrun, and outlift anybody in that store, and I have to take orders from those common, petty sons-of-bitches till I can't stand it any more.

BIFF: I'm tellin' you, kid, if you were with me I'd be HAPPY out there.

HAPPY (*enthused*): See, BIFF, everybody around me is so false that I'm constantly lowering my ideals...

BIFF: Baby, together we'd stand up for one another, we'd have someone to trust.

HAPPY: If I were around you—

BIFF: Hap, the trouble is we weren't brought up to grub for money. I don't know how to do it.

HAPPY: Neither can I!

BIFF: Then let's go!

HAPPY: The only thing is—what can you make out there?

BIFF: But look at your friend. Builds an estate and then hasn't the peace of mind to live in it.

HAPPY: Yeah, but when he walks into the store the waves part in front of him. That's fifty-two thousand dollars a year coming through the revolving door, and I got more in my pinky finger than he's got in his head.

BIFF: Yeah, but you just said—

HAPPY: I gotta show some of those pompous, self-important executives over there that Hap Loman can make the grade. I want to walk into the store the way he walks in. Then I'll go with you, BIFF. We'll be together yet, I swear. But take those two we had tonight. Now weren't they gorgeous creatures?

BIFF: Yeah, yeah, most gorgeous I've had in years.

HAPPY: I get that any time I want, BIFF. Whenever I feel disgusted. The only trouble is, it gets like bowling or something. I just keep knockin' them over and it doesn't mean anything. You still run around a lot?

BIFF: Naa. I'd like to find a girl—steady, somebody with substance.

HAPPY: That's what I long for. BIFF: Go on! You'd never come home.

HAPPY: I would! Somebody with character, with resistance! Like Mom, y'know? You're gonna call me a bastard when I tell you this. That girl Charlotte I was with tonight is engaged to be married in five weeks. (*He tries on his new hat.*)

BIFF: No kiddin'!

HAPPY: Sure, the guy's in line for the vice-presidency of the store. I don't know what gets into me, maybe I just have an overdeveloped sense of competition or something, but I went and ruined her, and furthermore I can't get rid of her. And he's the third executive I've done that to. Isn't that a crummy characteristic? And to top it all, I go to their weddings! (*Indignantly, but laughing*) Like I'm not supposed to take bribes. Manufacturers offer me a hundred-dollar bill now and then to throw an order their way. You know how honest I am, but it's like this girl, see. I hate myself for it. Because I don't want the girl, and, still, I take it and—I love it!

BIFF: Let's go to sleep.

HAPPY: I guess we didn't settle anything, heh?

BIFF: I just got one idea that I think I'm going to try.

HAPPY: What's that?

BIFF: Remember Bill Oliver?

HAPPY: Sure, Oliver is very big now. You want to work for him again?

BIFF: No, but when I quit he said something to me. He put his arm on my shoulder, and he said, "BIFF, if you ever need anything, come to me."

HAPPY: I remember that. That sounds good.

BIFF: I think I'll go to see him. If I could get ten thousand or even seven or eight thousand dollars I could buy a beautiful ranch.

HAPPY: I bet he'd back you. 'Cause he thought highly of you, BIFF. I mean, they all do. You're well liked, BIFF. That's why I say to come back here, and we both have the apartment. And I'm tellin' you, BIFF, any babe you want ...

BIFF: No, with a ranch I could do the work I like and still be something. I just wonder though. I wonder if Oliver still thinks I stole that carton of basketballs.

HAPPY: Oh, he probably forgot that long ago. It's almost ten years. You're too sensitive. Anyway, he didn't really fire you.

BIFF: Well, I think he was going to. I think that's why I quit. I was never sure whether he knew or not. I know he thought the world of me, though. I was the only one he'd let lock up the place. WILLY (*below*): You gonna wash the engine, BIFF?

HAPPY: Shh!

(BIFF *looks at* HAPPY, *who is gazing down, listening.* WILLY *is mumbling in the parlor.*)

HAPPY: You hear that?

(*They listen.* WILLY *laughs warmly.*)

BIFF (*growing angry*): Doesn't he know Mom can hear that?

WILLY: Don't get your sweater dirty, BIFF!

(*A look of pain crosses* BIFF's *face.*)

HAPPY: Isn't that terrible? Don't leave again, will you? You'll find a job here. You gotta stick around. I don't know what to do about him, it's getting embarrassing.

WILLY: What a simonizing job!

BIFF: Mom's hearing that!

WILLY: No kiddin', BIFF, you got a date? Wonderful!

HAPPY: Go on to sleep. But talk to him in the morning, will you?

BIFF (*reluctantly getting into bed*): With her in the house. Brother!

HAPPY (*getting into bed*): I wish you'd have a good talk with him.

(*The light on their room begins to fade.*)

BIFF (*to himself in bed*): That selfish, stupid...

HAPPY: Sh... Sleep, BIFF.

(*Their light is out. Well before they have finished speaking, WILLY's form is dimly seen below in the darkened kitchen. He opens the refrigerator, searches in there, and takes out a bottle of milk. The apartment houses are fading out, and the entire house and surroundings become covered with leaves. Music insinuates itself as the leaves appear.*)

存在主义视角解读威利·洛曼的悲剧

阿瑟·米勒(1915—2005)的《推销员之死》是美国戏剧史上的三大悲剧之一。我国学者对该剧的解读主要围绕"美国梦"、资本主义社会的弊端、威利·洛曼的悲剧形象、米勒的悲剧观、心理分析等研究方向展开。从萨特的存在主义哲学视角分析该剧本，可以更深刻地理解造成主人公威利悲剧人生的根源，揭示他如何拒绝接受真实的自我，放弃通过自由选择来赋予生存以意义，继而逃避为自己的行为负责，最终落入幻想与现实之间的狭小缝隙无法动弹。威利的悲剧启示我们，尽管人类存在于一个荒诞而虚无的世界，在异化力量的挤压下面临生存困境，人仍可以通过自由选择赋予生活以意义和价值。不管在怎样的社会中我们都要坚守内心的选择，积极为自己的行为负责。

存在主义(Existentialism)又称"萨特的存在主义""无神论存在主义"，是20世纪30年代末40年代初在法德出现的现代主义流派，"二战"后进入美国。存在主义是20世纪上半叶最具代表性的哲学思潮。哲学家海德格尔在《存在与时间》中第一次使用存在主义这一名称，他认为人类存在于一个荒诞的世界，面对的是虚无和孤独。早期的传统观念里有一些广为接受的假设：人是具有理性的动物，赖以生存的世界至少是部分可知的；在有秩序的社会结构里，人是其中的一个组成部分；人类身处逆境也不会丧失自己的英雄气概与尊严。20世纪40年代后，以让·保罗·萨特(Jean-Paul Sartre)和艾伯特·加缪(Albert Camus)等为代表的存在主义哲学不认同传统的信仰，相反地，他们认为人类不过是被抛到一个无意义的世界里："每个人都是沦落异乡的孤独的生灵；这个陌生的世界里不存在固有的人类真理、价值标准与任何意义。人生只不过是对生存目标和存在意义的徒劳的探索过程,人生本自虚无,并终将化为虚无;人生的存在是件既痛苦又荒诞的事"。就像西西弗斯每天把沉重的石头推到陡峭的山上,再眼看着这个大石头滚到山脚,永远地重复这个毫无意义的动作。

存在主义理论的集大成者萨特主要阐述了三个哲学命题:"存在先于本质""世界是荒谬的,人生是痛苦的"和"自由选择"。与笛卡尔"我思故我在"强调主体的理性不同,萨特认为自我存在是首要的。我不存在,则一切都不存在。人本身不具有什么本质特征,人的本质是由人根据自由意志做出的选择所塑造的,即自我决定本质。萨特解释为"人首先存在着,遇到他自身,涌现在世界上,然后才给自己定性"。其次,萨特眼中的世界是荒谬的,不存在什么上帝或者道德准则,人与人之间的关系充满了冲突。无论贫穷还是富裕,都只是这个冷酷世界里的一个孤独的人。存在主义世界观迎合了"二战"后人们感觉所有信仰已分崩离析的恐惧不安以及之后机器化大生产造成的心理危机。后者在米勒生活的美国尤为明显。战后的美国凭借先进科技实现了经济的腾飞,机器大生产带来劳动生产率的大幅提高的同时,还导致了劳动力的过剩。与机器相比,人的价值变得微不足道,人类面临着被自己创造出的机器所奴役的困境。被社会中的异化现象困扰的许多美国作家在存在主义思想中找到了共鸣。最后,"自由选择"是存在主义思想中极为重要的概念。自由是存在主义的核心。萨特提出,如果存在确实先于本质,那么人就永远不能"参照一个已知的或特定的人性来解释自己的行动"或做出选择,换言之,长期统治人们思想的决定论是不存在的——人是绝对自由的。无论面对何种状况,人都可以按照个人意志做出自由选择。另一方面,人的选择不仅塑造自身的特性,还会影响其他人。既然人的行为是自由选择的结果,他对自己的存在和选择就负有全部责任,而不是推诿给某种神灵或规则。从这个意义上说,绝对自由地选择就必须要绝对地负责。因此,自由可能成为一种负担,用萨特的话说,"人是被判决为自由的(we are condemned to be free)",它是人"最荒谬又最严酷的义务"。当人们想逃避时就会创造一些理论来说服自己,证明人并不能自由地选择,因此我们也无需为自己的行为负上全部责任。

阿瑟·米勒的剧作多以美国底层社会的小人物为主角,真实展现普通人的命运,曾被誉为"美国的良心"。米勒的创作深受古希腊悲剧和易卜生戏剧的影响,前者使他认识到悲剧产生的根源往往来自于人们自身的缺陷,后者的社会问题剧则启发他思考现代人的生存状况。《推销员之死》中威利·罗曼的悲剧一定程度上正是源于他无法正确认识自我,为了逃避自由选择可能带来的责任而采取自欺,逐渐走向了孤独与幻灭的不归路。

大部分评论家把资本主义社会对普通人的剥削与压迫看作是导致威利人生悲剧的主要原因,但是如果把这部剧作简单看成是对"美国梦"的控诉则太过流于表面。在萨特的存在主义理论的观照下,我们可以发现威利终其一生都未能正视真实自我,立志做一名推销员不是基于忠于本心的自由选择,而是受到外界影响。威利把自己的处处碰壁多归结于外部原因,常常抱怨世道变了或者运气欠佳,不愿承认自己可能并不适合这个工作,同时也不愿正视两个儿子的真实情况,试图逃避对自己和对他人的责任。威利自身的问题很大程度上造成了他们一家的悲剧。

威利的一生都在为做一名成功的推销员这个目标奔波,直到自杀的时候仍然挂念着他的梦想,幻想会有很多客户和推销员来参加他的葬礼。选择推销员作为终身职业看起来是威利为了实现自身价值而做出的自由选择,但是于他而言至关重要的这一职业其实与本性相悖,是源于他想象中的所谓成功和体面。存在主义认为人是自由的,人具有主体性,这当然不是说人可以完全脱离外部环境而独立存在,而是坚信人不是必须顺应社会或者被动接受。威利从一开始就没有正确认识自我,仅仅因为看到老推销员大卫·辛格曼的成功范例就认为这是一份在世人眼里有前途的工作,希望能够获得社会定义的所谓的成功。实际上,从威利想象中与本的对话以及与两个儿子的交流中,我们不难发现威利很擅长手工活,喜爱自然,可能更适合去西部或者做个工匠。威利也多次跟本和琳达提到想离开城市,带着孩子回到美妙的大自然中去。遗憾的是,受商业社会的价值观影响,威利认为有出息的人必须在商界打拼,无法接受真实的自我,因此放弃自由选择,违背本性规划了不适合自己的人生,并为自己幻想出一个受人欢迎的推销员形象。正是因为一开始就已经丢掉了自我,只是一个"空心人",所以威利非常依赖于其他人的评价,把"好人缘"看作是推销员最重要的特质。

"His name was Dave Singleman. And he was eighty-four years old, and he'd drummed merchandise in thirty-one states. And old Dave, he'd go up to his room, y'understand, put on his green velvet slippers—I'll never forget—and pick up his phone and call the buyers, and without ever leaving his room, at the age of eighty-four, he made his living. And when I saw that, I realized that selling was the greatest career a man could want. 'Cause what could be more satisfying than to be able to go, at the age of eighty-four, into twenty or thirty different cities, and pick up a phone, and be remembered and loved and helped by so many different people? Do you know? When he died—and by the way he died the death of a salesman, in his green velvet slippers in the smoker of the New York, New Haven, and Hartford, going into Boston—when he died, hundreds of salesmen and buyers were at his funeral. Things were sad on a lotta trains for months after that. *He stands up. Howard has not looked at him.* In those days there was personality in it, Howard. There was respect, and comradeship, and gratitude in it. Today, it's all cut and dried, and there's no chance for bringing friendship to bear—or personality. You see what I mean? They don't know me any more."

"他名叫大卫·辛格曼,八十四岁了,在三十一个州里招揽买卖。要明白,老大卫走到自己房里,穿上绿丝绒拖鞋——我永远忘不了——拿起电话机就给买主通话,一步也用不着出门,在八十四岁高龄,照样过日子。我看到这件事,才明白做推销员是理想中最好的职业。因为,活到八十四岁,还能去二三十个城市,拿起电话机,就有那么多三教九流的人记得他,喜欢他,帮助他,有什么能比这更叫人称心的事啊?你知道吗?他死的时候——顺便说一句,他临死前还是个推销员呢——穿着绿丝绒拖鞋,坐在从纽约经纽黑文和哈特福德开到波士顿的火车吸烟车厢里。他死了以后,几百个推销员和买主都来参加他的葬礼。从此一连好几个月不少火车上都是一片伤心景象。(他站起身。霍华德没对他看)想当年,大家可讲人品呢,霍华德。大家讲尊重,讲交情,讲知恩报德。到如今,样样都按死规矩!办事,也没机会再谈什么交情啦,也不谈什么啦。你懂得我的意思吗?人家再也不认识我了。"

这段话解释了威利坚持要做一个推销员的原因。十八九岁就开始跑推销的威利很早就怀疑过自己做这行是否有前途,原打算去阿拉斯加找金矿的他遇到传奇推销员辛格曼后立刻改变了想法,从此坚信这是"理想中最好的职业"。从他的回忆中我们发现,威利认为做推销员是最好职业不是因为自己具备相关才能,也不是因为热爱这份工作。最主要的原因是在他眼中,做一名成功的推销员依靠的是好人缘而不是辛勤工作。威利始终认为这个职业靠的就是大家讲交情,如果能受欢迎,那么就会成为大家眼中的体面人,受尊重,甚至年纪大了也能凭着人缘轻轻松松赚钱。可见威利选择做一名推销员不是出于实现梦想,也不是因为能够胜任,而是看中了它的体面和舒服。他把别人的成功简单归结于好人缘,并根据自己的主观臆断总结出成功的秘诀就是受人欢迎,还把这套成功学教给了两个儿子,一定程度上导致他们从小夸夸其谈,轻视实干。当威利向新老板霍华德抱怨业绩不佳是因为世道变了,大家都不讲交情时,后者的反应说明威利的成功学一开始就立不住脚:"本来就是这么回事嘛,威利。"

萨特认为,当人们想要逃避责任时往往会采用自欺的方法,否定自己本来的样子,伪装出符合自己角色的形象。顺应主流价值观成了一名推销员之后,威利经常吹嘘自己的能力和业绩,告诉家人公司有多离不开他,在新英格兰地区他多有威风,"巡警都把我的汽车当成自己汽车来爱护。"年老体衰面临开不出单子,只能靠佣金过活的窘境时,他依然抛不开自己想象出来的形象,把生活不如意归因于外部原因——商业社会的人情冷漠,老主顾和老东家的离开等,幻想有朝一日时来运转,上天可以赐予他们一家做大买卖的机会。对于两个儿子比夫和哈比,威利也一直在逃避自己教育不当的责任。威利从小向他们灌输人格魅力比才干更重要的观念,嘲笑查理和伯纳德只会勤奋工作,坚信比夫和哈比进入商界后一定能凭借好人缘获得成功。比夫数学不及格无法毕业的时候威利一边大骂老师,一边让他找同学要考试答案。看到两个儿子偷东西,威利不仅不制止,反而夸他们有胆识。在他的影响下,两个儿子游手好闲,工作不顺时也编造种种谎言来骗威利夫妇。当发现寄予厚望的比夫和哈比并不是他心目中的青年才俊后,威利没有反省自己的问题,勇敢承担起重建家人关系的责任,反而觉得是老天不公平,社会没有给两个儿子干大事的机会。比夫在遭遇种种挫折后看清自己不适合从商,也渐渐发现父亲并不具备成为一名优秀推销员的条件:"我们跟城市这个疯人院不是一路!我们应当到旷野里去做搅拌水泥的活,或者——或者做木匠活。"可惜威利不愿面对现实,宁愿守着虚幻的梦想,在白日梦中无法自拔。

　　威利始终无法接受真实的自己,不愿承认自己要为工作的失败和家庭的分裂负责,在心理重压下出现幻觉,沉浸在对过去的回忆中,常常自言自语,被周围人当作精神错乱的人。威利回忆的内容主要是与现实相比更幸福更有希望的一些事情,例如业绩最佳的那个月;比夫和哈比崇拜他,兴冲冲地给他洗车的欢乐场景;还有与哥哥本的对话。从心理分析的角度我们不难发现本很有可能是威利虚构出的另一个自己,代表了他向往的生活:闯荡世界发大财。每当在现实遇到困难时,威利就会和本对话,幻想如果当时和本一起离开城市,现在自己应该也成了富翁。由此可见,威利依旧把梦想无法实现的原因归结于外部环境,沉溺于过去是因为他无法把握现在,更没法改变未来,只能诉诸于过去。

　　很多评论家把威利的自杀归结于他的"美国梦"的破灭。确实,威利已经连自我都丢失了,还如何能在本就残酷的人生中找到意义和价值呢?值得注意的是,我们不应把《推销员之死》简单看成剧作家米勒对挤压人性的商业社会的抨击,从而过分夸大外部环境对威利一家的影响。威利的悲剧启示我们,面对日益恶化的生存状况,人们还是拥有自由选择的机会,有可能通过自己的选择为人生赋予意义。

主要参考文献

密勒 A.推销员之死[M].英若诚,译.北京:中国对外翻译出版公司,1999.

M. H.艾布拉姆斯,杰弗里·高尔特·哈珀姆.文学术语词典(中英对照 第10版)[M].吴松江,路雁,朱金鹏,等编译.北京:北京大学出版社,2014.

萨特.存在主义是一种人道主义[M].周煦良,汤永宽,译.上海:上海译文出版社,2005.

CENTOLA S R. Compromise as Bad Faith: Arthur Miller's *A View from the Bridge* and William Inge's *Come Back, Little Sheba*[J]. Midwest Quarterly,1986,28(1):100-113.

MILLER A. Death of a Salesman[M]. Penguin, 1986.

思考题

(1) 通过阅读选段,你认为比夫和哈比是什么样的人?他们与父亲威利的关系如何?
(2) 你认为哪些原因导致了威利一家的悲剧?
(3) 威利的妻子林达在这部剧作中是什么形象?她需要为威利的悲剧负责任吗?
(4) 试结合历史背景比较分析《推销员之死》与《了不起的盖茨比》中"美国梦"的异同。

Chapter 4 Waiting for Godot

by Samuel Beckett

(excerpts)

 背景介绍

塞缪尔·贝克特(Samuel Beckett,1906—1989)是爱尔兰小说家、评论家、荒诞派戏剧的重要代表人物。荒诞派戏剧是对西方现代派文学中"荒诞文学"的发展,是战后西方社会思想意识通过舞台艺术最具代表性的反映,"荒诞"观集中体现了西方世界普遍性的精神危机和悲观情绪。《等待戈多》(*Waiting for Godot*)是荒诞派戏剧中里程碑式的作品。戏剧表现的是"什么也没有发生,谁也没有来,谁也没有去"的悲剧。虽然《等待戈多》在质疑"自我"的不存在,但是同时又在探索和寻找"自我",这种绝望中的希望也鼓励了很多人。1969年,贝克特因为"具有新奇形式的小说、戏剧作品,使现代人从贫困的境地得到了振奋"而获诺贝尔文学奖。

 文本选读

A country road. A tree.

Evening.

Estragon, sitting on a low mound, is trying to take off his boot. He pulls at it with both hands, panting.

He gives up, exhausted, rests, tries again.

As before.

Enter Vladimir.

ESTRAGON:

(*giving up again*). Nothing to be done.

VLADIMIR:

(*advancing with short, stiff strides, legs wide apart*). I'm beginning to come round to that opinion. All my life I've tried to put it from me, saying Vladimir, be reasonable, you haven't yet tried everything. And I resumed the struggle. (*He broods, musing on the struggle. Turning to Estragon.*) So there you are again.

ESTRAGON: Am I?

VLADIMIR: I'm glad to see you back. I thought you were gone forever.

ESTRAGON: Me too.

VLADIMIR: Together again at last! We'll have to celebrate this. But how? (*He reflects.*) Get up till I embrace you.

ESTRAGON: (*irritably*). Not now, not now.

VLADIMIR: (*hurt, coldly*). May one inquire where His Highness spent the night?

ESTRAGON: In a ditch.

VLADIMIR: (*admiringly*). A ditch! Where?

ESTRAGON: (*without gesture*). Over there.

VLADIMIR: And they didn't beat you?

ESTRAGON: Beat me? Certainly they beat me.

VLADIMIR: The same lot as usual?

ESTRAGON: The same? I don't know.

VLADIMIR: When I think of it... all these years... but for me... where would you be... (*Decisively.*) You'd be nothing more than a little heap of bones at the present minute, no doubt about it.

ESTRAGON: And what of it?

VLADIMIR: (*gloomily*). It's too much for one man. (*Pause. Cheerfully.*) On the other hand what's the good of losing heart now, that's what I say. We should have thought of it a million years ago, in the nineties.

ESTRAGON: Ah stop blathering and help me off with this bloody thing.

VLADIMIR: Hand in hand from the top of the Eiffel Tower, among the first. We were respectable in those days. Now it's too late. They wouldn't even let us up. (*Estragon tears at his boot.*) What are you doing?

ESTRAGON: Taking off my boot. Did that never happen to you?

VLADIMIR: Boots must be taken off every day, I'm tired telling you that. Why don't you listen to me?

ESTRAGON: (*feebly*). Help me!

VLADIMIR: It hurts?

ESTRAGON: (*angrily*). Hurts! He wants to know if it hurts!

VLADIMIR: (*angrily*). No one ever suffers but you. I don't count. I'd like to hear what you'd say if you had what I have.

ESTRAGON: It hurts?

VLADIMIR: (*angrily*). Hurts! He wants to know if it hurts!

ESTRAGON: (*pointing*). You might button it all the same.

VLADIMIR: (*stooping*). True. (*He buttons his fly.*) Never neglect the little things of life.

ESTRAGON: What do you expect, you always wait till the last moment?

VLADIMIR: (*musingly*). The last moment ... (*He meditates.*) Hope deferred makes the something sick, who said that?

ESTRAGON: Why don't you help me?

VLADIMIR: Sometimes I feel it coming all the same. Then I go all queer. (*He takes off his hat, peers inside it, feels about inside it, shakes it, puts it on again.*) How shall I say? Relieved and at the same time... (*he searches for the word*) ... appalled. (*With emphasis.*) AP-PALLED. (*He takes off his hat again, peers inside it.*) Funny. (*He knocks on the crown as though to dislodge a foreign body, peers into it again, puts it on again.*) Nothing to be done. (*Estragon with a supreme effort succeeds in pulling off his boot. He peers inside it, feels about inside it, turns it upside down, shakes it, looks on the ground to see if anything has fallen out, finds nothing, feels inside it again, staring sightlessly before him.*) Well?

ESTRAGON: Nothing.

VLADIMIR: Show me.

ESTRAGON: There's nothing to show.

VLADIMIR: Try and put it on again.

ESTRAGON: (*examining his foot*). I'll air it for a bit.

VLADIMIR: There's man all over for you, blaming on his boots the faults of his feet. (*He takes off his hat again, peers inside it, feels about inside it, knocks on the crown, blows into it, puts it on again.*) This is getting alarming. (*Silence. Vladimir deep in thought, Estragon pulling at his toes.*) One of the thieves was saved. (*Pause.*) It's a reasonable percentage. (*Pause.*) Gogo.

ESTRAGON: What?

VLADIMIR: Suppose we repented.

ESTRAGON: Repented what?

VLADIMIR: Oh ... (*He reflects.*) We wouldn't have to go into the details.

ESTRAGON: Our being born?

Vladimir breaks into a hearty laugh which he immediately stifles, his hand pressed to his pubis, his face contorted.

VLADIMIR: One daren't even laugh any more.

ESTRAGON: Dreadful privation.

VLADIMIR: Merely smile. (*He smiles suddenly from ear to ear, keeps smiling, ceases as suddenly.*) It's not the same thing. Nothing to be done. (*Pause.*) Gogo.

ESTRAGON: (*irritably*). What is it?

VLADIMIR: Did you ever read the Bible?

ESTRAGON: The Bible ⋯ (*He reflects.*) I must have taken a look at it.

VLADIMIR: Do you remember the Gospels?

ESTRAGON: I remember the maps of the Holy Land. Coloured they were. Very pretty. The Dead Sea was pale blue. The very look of it made me thirsty. That's where we'll go, I used to say, that's where we'll go for our honeymoon. We'll swim. We'll be happy.

VLADIMIR: You should have been a poet.

ESTRAGON: I was. (*Gesture towards his rags.*) Isn't that obvious?

Silence.

VLADIMIR: Where was I ⋯ How's your foot?

ESTRAGON: Swelling visibly.

VLADIMIR: Ah yes, the two thieves. Do you remember the story?

ESTRAGON: No.

VLADIMIR: Shall I tell it to you?

ESTRAGON: No.

VLADIMIR: It'll pass the time. (*Pause.*) Two thieves, crucified at the same time as our Saviour. One—

ESTRAGON: Our what?

VLADIMIR: Our Saviour. Two thieves. One is supposed to have been saved and the other ⋯ (*he searches for the contrary of saved*) ⋯ damned.

ESTRAGON: Saved from what?

VLADIMIR: Hell.

ESTRAGON: I'm going.

He does not move.

VLADIMIR: And yet ⋯ (*pause.*) ⋯ how is it-this is not boring you I hope-how is it that of the four Evangelists only one speaks of a thief being saved. The four of them were there -or thereabouts-and only one speaks of a thief being saved. (*Pause.*) Come on, Gogo, return the ball, can't you, once in a while?

ESTRAGON: (*with exaggerated enthusiasm*). I find this really most extraordinarily interesting.

VLADIMIR: One out of four. Of the other three, two don't mention any thieves at all and the third says that both of them abused him.

ESTRAGON: Who?

VLADIMIR: What?

ESTRAGON: What's all this about? Abused who?

VLADIMIR: The Saviour.

ESTRAGON: Why?

VLADIMIR: Because he wouldn't save them.

ESTRAGON: From hell?

VLADIMIR: Imbecile! From death.

ESTRAGON: I thought you said hell.

VLADIMIR: From death, from death.

ESTRAGON: Well what of it?

VLADIMIR: Then the two of them must have been damned.

ESTRAGON: And why not?

VLADIMIR: But one of the four says that one of the two was saved.

ESTRAGON: Well? They don't agree and that's all there is to it.

VLADIMIR: But all four were there. And only one speaks of a thief being saved. Why believe him rather than the others?

ESTRAGON: Who believes him?

VLADIMIR: Everybody. It's the only version they know.

ESTRAGON: People are bloody ignorant apes.

He rises painfully, goes limping to extreme left, halts, gazes into distance off with his hand screening his eyes, turns, goes to extreme right, gazes into distance. Vladimir watches him, then goes and picks up the boot, peers into it, drops it hastily.

VLADIMIR: Pah!

He spits. Estragon moves to center, halts with his back to auditorium.

ESTRAGON: Charming spot. (*He turns, advances to front, halts facing auditorium.*) Inspiring prospects. (*He turns to Vladimir.*) Let's go.

VLADIMIR: We can't.

ESTRAGON: Why not?

VLADIMIR: We're waiting for Godot.

ESTRAGON: (*despairingly*). Ah! (*Pause.*) You're sure it was here?

VLADIMIR: What?

ESTRAGON: That we were to wait.

VLADIMIR: He said by the tree. (*They look at the tree.*) Do you see any others?

ESTRAGON: What is it?

VLADIMIR: I don't know. A willow.

ESTRAGON: Where are the leaves?

VLADIMIR: It must be dead.

ESTRAGON: No more weeping.

VLADIMIR: Or perhaps it's not the season.

ESTRAGON: Looks to me more like a bush.

VLADIMIR: A shrub.

ESTRAGON: A bush.

VLADIMIR: A—. What are you insinuating? That we've come to the wrong place?

ESTRAGON: He should be here.

VLADIMIR: He didn't say for sure he'd come.

ESTRAGON: And if he doesn't come?

VLADIMIR: We'll come back tomorrow.

ESTRAGON: And then the day after tomorrow.

VLADIMIR: Possibly.

ESTRAGON: And so on.

VLADIMIR: The point is—

ESTRAGON: Until he comes.

VLADIMIR: You're merciless.

ESTRAGON: We came here yesterday.

VLADIMIR: Ah no, there you're mistaken.

ESTRAGON: What did we do yesterday?

VLADIMIR: What did we do yesterday?

ESTRAGON: Yes.

VLADIMIR: Why... (*Angrily.*) Nothing is certain when you're about.

ESTRAGON: In my opinion we were here.

VLADIMIR: (*looking round*). You recognize the place?

ESTRAGON: I didn't say that.

VLADIMIR: Well?

ESTRAGON: That makes no difference.

VLADIMIR: All the same... that tree... (*turning towards auditorium*) that bog...

ESTRAGON: You're sure it was this evening?

VLADIMIR: What?

ESTRAGON: That we were to wait.

VLADIMIR: He said Saturday. (*Pause.*) I think.

ESTRAGON: You think.

VLADIMIR: I must have made a note of it. (*He fumbles in his pockets, bursting with miscellaneous rubbish.*)

ESTRAGON: (*very insidious*). But what Saturday? And is it Saturday? Is it not rather Sunday? (*Pause.*) Or Monday? (*Pause.*) Or Friday?

VLADIMIR: (*looking wildly about him, as though the date was inscribed in the landscape*). It's not possible!

ESTRAGON: Or Thursday?

VLADIMIR: What'll we do?

ESTRAGON: If he came yesterday and we weren't here you may be sure he won't come again today.

VLADIMIR: But you say we were here yesterday.

ESTRAGON: I may be mistaken. (*Pause.*) Let's stop talking for a minute, do you mind?

VLADIMIR: (*feebly*). All right. (*Estragon sits down on the mound. Vladimir paces agitatedly to and fro, halting from time to time to gaze into distance off. Estragon falls asleep. Vladimir halts finally before Estragon.*) Gogo! … Gogo! … GOGO!

Estragon wakes with a start.

ESTRAGON: (*restored to the horror of his situation*). I was asleep! (*Despairingly.*) Why will you never let me sleep?

VLADIMIR: I felt lonely.

ESTRAGON: I had a dream.

VLADIMIR: Don't tell me!

ESTRAGON: I dreamt that—

VLADIMIR: DON'T TELL ME!

ESTRAGON: (*gesture toward the universe*). This one is enough for you? (*Silence.*) It's not nice of you, Didi. Who am I to tell my private nightmares to if I can't tell them to you?

VLADIMIR: Let them remain private. You know I can't bear that.

ESTRAGON: (*coldly.*) There are times when I wonder if it wouldn't be better for us to part.

VLADIMIR: You wouldn't go far.

ESTRAGON: That would be too bad, really too bad. (*Pause.*) Wouldn't it, Didi, be really too bad? (*Pause.*) When you think of the beauty of the way. (*Pause.*) And the goodness of the wayfarers. (*Pause. Wheedling.*) Wouldn't it, Didi?

VLADIMIR: Calm yourself.

ESTRAGON: (*voluptuously.*) Calm ··· calm ··· The English say cawm. (*Pause.*) You know the story of the Englishman in the brothel?

VLADIMIR: Yes.

ESTRAGON: Tell it to me.

VLADIMIR: Ah stop it!

ESTRAGON: An Englishman having drunk a little more than usual proceeds to a brothel. The bawd asks him if he wants a fair one, a dark one or a red-haired one. Go on.

VLADIMIR: STOP IT!

Exit Vladimir hurriedly. Estragon gets up and follows him as far as the limit of the stage. Gestures of Estragon like those of a spectator encouraging a pugilist. Enter Vladimir. He brushes past Estragon, crosses the stage with bowed head. Estragon takes a step towards him, halts.

ESTRAGON: (*gently.*) You wanted to speak to me? (*Silence. Estragon takes a step forward.*) You had something to say to me? (*Silence. Another step forward.*) Didi ···

VLADIMIR: (*without turning*). I've nothing to say to you.

ESTRAGON: (*step forward*). You're angry? (*Silence. Step forward*). Forgive me. (*Silence. Step forward. Estragon lays his hand on Vladimir's shoulder.*) Come, Didi. (*Silence.*) Give me your hand. (*Vladimir half turns.*) Embrace me! (*Vladimir stiffens.*) Don't be stubborn! (*Vladimir softens. They embrace. Estragon recoils.*) You stink of garlic!

VLADIMIR: It's for the kidneys. (*Silence. Estragon looks attentively at the tree.*) What do we do now?

ESTRAGON: Wait.

VLADIMIR: Yes, but while waiting.

ESTRAGON: What about hanging ourselves?

VLADIMIR: Hmm. It'd give us an erection.

ESTRAGON: (*highly excited*). An erection!

VLADIMIR: With all that follows. Where it falls mandrakes grow. That's why they shriek when you pull them up. Did you not know that?

ESTRAGON: Let's hang ourselves immediately!

VLADIMIR: From a bough? (*They go towards the tree.*) I wouldn't trust it.

ESTRAGON: We can always try.

VLADIMIR: Go ahead.

ESTRAGON: After you.

VLADIMIR: No no, you first.

ESTRAGON: Why me?

VLADIMIR: You're lighter than I am.

ESTRAGON: Just so!

VLADIMIR: I don't understand.

ESTRAGON: Use your intelligence, can't you?

Vladimir uses his intelligence.

VLADIMIR: (*finally*). I remain in the dark.

ESTRAGON: This is how it is. (*He reflects.*) The bough... the bough... (*Angrily.*) Use your head, can't you?

VLADIMIR: You're my only hope.

ESTRAGON: (*with effort*). Gogo light—bough not break—Gogo dead. Didi heavy—bough break—Didi alone. Whereas—

VLADIMIR: I hadn't thought of that.

ESTRAGON: If it hangs you it'll hang anything.

VLADIMIR: But am I heavier than you?

ESTRAGON: So you tell me. I don't know. There's an even chance. Or nearly.

VLADIMIR: Well? What do we do?

ESTRAGON: Don't let's do anything. It's safer.

VLADIMIR: Let's wait and see what he says.

ESTRAGON: Who?

VLADIMIR: Godot.

ESTRAGON: Good idea.

VLADIMIR: Let's wait till we know exactly how we stand.

ESTRAGON: On the other hand it might be better to strike the iron before it freezes.

VLADIMIR: I'm curious to hear what he has to offer. Then we'll take it or leave it.

ESTRAGON: What exactly did we ask him for?

VLADIMIR: Were you not there?

ESTRAGON: I can't have been listening.

VLADIMIR: Oh…Nothing very definite.

ESTRAGON: A kind of prayer.

VLADIMIR: Precisely.

ESTRAGON: A vague supplication.

VLADIMIR: Exactly.

ESTRAGON: And what did he reply?

VLADIMIR: That he'd see.

ESTRAGON: That he couldn't promise anything.

VLADIMIR: That he'd have to think it over.

ESTRAGON: In the quiet of his home.

VLADIMIR: Consult his family.

ESTRAGON: His friends.

VLADIMIR: His agents.

ESTRAGON: His correspondents.

VLADIMIR: His books.

ESTRAGON: His bank account.

VLADIMIR: Before taking a decision.

ESTRAGON: It's the normal thing.

VLADIMIR: Is it not?

ESTRAGON: I think it is.

VLADIMIR: I think so too.

Silence.

ESTRAGON: (*anxious*). And we?

VLADIMIR: I beg your pardon?

ESTRAGON: I said, And we?

VLADIMIR: I don't understand.

ESTRAGON: Where do we come in?

VLADIMIR: Come in?

ESTRAGON: Take your time.

VLADIMIR: Come in? On our hands and knees.

ESTRAGON: As bad as that?

VLADIMIR: Your Worship wishes to assert his prerogatives?

ESTRAGON: We've no rights any more?

Laugh of Vladimir, stifled as before, less the smile.

VLADIMIR: You'd make me laugh if it wasn't prohibited.

ESTRAGON: We've lost our rights?

VLADIMIR: (*distinctly*). We got rid of them.

Silence. They remain motionless, arms dangling, heads sunk, sagging at the knees.

ESTRAGON: (*feebly*). We're not tied? (*Pause.*) We're not—

VLADIMIR: Listen!

They listen, grotesquely rigid.

ESTRAGON: I hear nothing.

VLADIMIR: Hsst! (*They listen. Estragon loses his balance, almost falls. He clutches the arm of Vladimir, who totters. They listen, huddled together.*) Nor I.

Sighs of relief. They relax and separate.

ESTRAGON: You gave me a fright.

VLADIMIR: I thought it was he.

ESTRAGON: Who?

VLADIMIR: Godot.

ESTRAGON: Pah! The wind in the reeds.

VLADIMIR: I could have sworn I heard shouts.

ESTRAGON: And why would he shout?

VLADIMIR: At his horse.

Silence.

ESTRAGON: (*violently*). I'm hungry!

VLADIMIR: Do you want a carrot?

ESTRAGON: Is that all there is?

VLADIMIR: I might have some turnips.

ESTRAGON: Give me a carrot.

(*Vladimir rummages in his pockets, takes out a turnip and gives it to Estragon who takes a bite out of it. Angrily.*) It's a turnip!

VLADIMIR: Oh pardon! I could have sworn it was a carrot.

(*He rummages again in his pockets, finds nothing but turnips.*) All that's turnips. (*He rummages.*) You must have eaten the last. (*He rummages.*) Wait, I have it. (*He brings out a carrot and gives it to Estragon.*) There, dear fellow.

(*Estragon wipes the carrot on his sleeve and begins to eat it.*) Make it last, that's the end of them.

ESTRAGON: (*chewing*). I asked you a question.

VLADIMIR: Ah.

ESTRAGON: Did you reply?

VLADIMIR: How's the carrot?

ESTRAGON: It's a carrot.

VLADIMIR: So much the better, so much the better. (*Pause.*) What was it you wanted to know?

ESTRAGON: I've forgotten. (*Chews.*) That's what annoys me. (*He looks at the carrot appreciatively, dangles it between finger and thumb.*) I'll never forget this carrot. (*He sucks the end of it meditatively.*) Ah yes, now I remember.

VLADIMIR: Well?

ESTRAGON: (*his mouth full, vacuously*). We're not tied?

VLADIMIR: I don't hear a word you're saying.

ESTRAGON: (*chews, swallows*). I'm asking you if we're tied.

VLADIMIR: Tied?

ESTRAGON: Ti-ed.

VLADIMIR: How do you mean tied?

ESTRAGON: Down.

VLADIMIR: But to whom? By whom?

ESTRAGON: To your man.

VLADIMIR: To Godot? Tied to Godot! What an idea! No question of it. (*Pause.*) For the moment.

ESTRAGON: His name is Godot?

VLADIMIR: I think so.

ESTRAGON: Fancy that. (*He raises what remains of the carrot by the stub of leaf, twirls it before his eyes.*) Funny, the more you eat the worse it gets.

VLADIMIR: With me it's just the opposite.

ESTRAGON: In other words?

VLADIMIR: I get used to the muck as I go along.

ESTRAGON: (*after prolonged reflection*). Is that the opposite?

VLADIMIR: Question of temperament.

ESTRAGON: Of character.

VLADIMIR: Nothing you can do about it.

ESTRAGON: No use struggling.

VLADIMIR: One is what one is.

ESTRAGON: No use wriggling.

VLADIMIR: The essential doesn't change.

ESTRAGON: Nothing to be done. (*He proffers the remains of the carrot to Vladimir.*) Like to finish it?

A terrible cry, close at hand. Estragon drops the carrot. They remain motionless, then together make a sudden rush towards the wings. Estragon stops halfway, runs back, picks up the carrot, stuffs it in his pocket, runs to rejoin Vladimir who is waiting for him, stops again, runs back, picks up his boot, runs to rejoin Vladimir. Huddled together, shoulders hunched, cringing away from the menace, they wait.

在无望中守候希望——解读荒诞剧《等待戈多》

《等待戈多》这部戏剧中情节简单,两个流浪汉爱斯特拉冈(Estragon)和弗拉季米尔(Vladimir)等待身份不明的"戈多",而"戈多"却迟迟不来。实际上他们也不知道"戈多"是谁,他们好像很熟悉,但是好像又不认识,自己也不知道为什么要等待。然而,两个主人公仍然无聊地等待下去,并且一边等,一边用各种毫无意义的手段打发时光。他们头脑混乱,对话和举止行为都毫无逻辑,都极度害怕孤独。第二天,两人仍然在等待"戈多",模模糊糊回忆起昨日的场景,继续重复之前的对话。整个过程中,没有跌宕起伏的情节,没有剧烈的人物冲突,没有明确的原因和结果。故事发生在混乱虚无的乡间小路上,只有一棵树,毫无生机。故事情节简单枯燥,一遍遍地循环重复,无异于什么都没发生。看似毫无创新,实际上将人们内心的枯燥、迷茫、无助等淋漓尽致地表现出来了。作品大胆地呈现了极其荒诞的剧情和人物形象,着重表现的是人的心态、心理活动过程以及心理障碍。多种荒诞元素:剧情、人物、场景、语言对话、行为举止等,使作品具有张力和可读性,成为经典作品之一。

一、人物形象怪异荒诞

两个流浪汉爱斯特拉冈和弗拉季米尔作为主要角色贯穿全剧,后面上场的波卓(Pozzo)和幸运儿(Lucky)由原来的主仆关系转变为互相帮扶的瞎子和哑巴。剧中角色稀少,并且举止行为都无法用正常人的思维来解读。与其他作家不同,贝克特作品中的人物形象通常不是光鲜优雅的上层人物,而是来源于社会底层不起眼的小人物,如病态丑恶的流浪汉、瘪三、残疾者、老人,等等。作者有意将生活的残酷、不堪、无奈、挣扎等呈现在读者面前。剧中的大人物——大家心中叨念、口里传诵的"戈多",始终没有出现,没有人知道他是谁,也为剧情添加了神秘的色彩。

剧中人物形象怪异荒诞,但仍各具特点。弗拉季米尔属于思考派,注重思想、偏重精神。他活泼、积极,总是提起话头,爱分析,说话带点哲理味。弗拉季米尔喜欢脱帽子,"He takes off his hat again, peers inside it.(他又脱下帽子,向帽内窥视)",他对帽子似乎有特殊的依赖性。帽子代表身份、礼仪、地位,脱掉帽子的意象代表剧中人物失去了的独立思考能力。爱斯特拉冈比较冷漠,内心消极,好吃贪睡。他以脱靴子作为出场,并且在剧中不停地穿靴子、脱靴子,如"sitting on a low mound, is trying to take off his boot""tears at his boot""Taking off my boot""Estragon with a supreme effort succeeds in pulling off his boot""then goes and picks up the boot""runs back, picks up his boot"等。靴子暗示了爱斯特拉冈属于行动派,注重实际,偏于客观肉体。他讲求实际,擅长行动,一直不停吃和睡。但是脱靴子似乎暗示了放弃行动。在读者看来,不停地脱帽子和脱靴子似乎都是强迫症,两人用这种强迫行为来缓解内心的焦虑,但实际上并无意义。两人相依为命,却又漠不关心,渴望改变,却缺乏实际行动。

戏剧开端介绍场景,"country road"和"tree","树"的意向和"等待"的意向两者相结合,共同寓意两个主要人物弗拉基米尔和埃斯特拉冈似乎有所追求,却因长期被动等待机会的到来而陷入迷惘和惰性而无法自拔的人生。这样的人生是一个怪异而尴尬的循环,最终因丧失对机遇的敏感和反应力而走向"等待着等待"的结局。

二、绝望中隐含的希望

作为贯穿全剧的中心线索"戈多"朦胧虚无,决定着所有人物的命运。虽然一直未透露"戈多"指谁,未明了"戈多"什么时候到来,这个始终缺席的角色却一直牵引着众人的心。有人认为"戈多"代指"上帝";有人解读为"死亡";还有人认为剧中后期上场的人物Pozzo就是戈多。对于"戈多"接受度较高的解释是代指"上帝",名字Godot或许是God字面上的变形,他似乎能带人脱离绝望,但却始终不曾现身;予人以希望的同时,又令人感受到无尽的绝望。曾有人问作者贝克特"戈多"究竟是什么,贝克特回复到"我要是知道,早在戏里说出来了"。总之,对于"戈多"的身份,就像"一千个读者眼中的一千个哈姆雷特"一样。总之,身份不明的"戈多"让此剧保持悬而未决的结局和没有定解的意义。

爱斯特拉冈和弗拉季米尔的等待有没有意义呢?如同"百年孤独",亦或像希腊神话中的西西弗斯不断重复、永无止境地往陡山上推巨石,付出努力却永远徒劳无结果。西西弗斯是否存在其他选择我们不得而知,爱斯特拉冈和弗拉季米尔除了等待又能做些什么改变呢?他们的等待是被迫的还是主动自愿的?现实生活中,人们一生都在等待,这是一种本质特性的存在。《等待戈多》这部剧揭示了"人类在一个荒诞的宇宙中的尴尬处境",人与外部的客观世界是处在一种无法感知的隔绝状态。但是,本剧中一个客观事实是,爱斯特拉冈和弗拉季米尔从未放弃等待。"等待戈多"是一种状态,作为某种驱动力,鼓励人们坚持下去,忍受枯燥乏味、重复毫无新意的日子。不放弃就有希望,但是消极的等待不会有意义,爱斯特拉冈和弗拉季米尔或许只有真正行动起来,才能抛开幻想的泡沫,从而打开一个全新的世界。

主要参考文献

王思媛.从《等待戈多》中的主题意象看现代人的精神窘境[D].武汉:武汉大学,2017.

思考题

(1) 作者使用了什么艺术手法来塑造人物形象?
(2) 剧中两个流浪汉的角色代表的是哪类社会群体?
(3) 你认为,他们会继续等待戈多吗?
(4) 剧中角色各种"毫无意义"的重复动作是出于什么背景或原因?

Chapter 5　M. Butterfly
by David Henry Hwang
（excerpts）

《蝴蝶君》是第一部由华裔剧作家创作并在美国乃至世界范围内获得广泛认可的美国戏剧。这部剧的灵感来自于20世纪60年代发生在一个中国京剧演员与法国外交人员之间的真实故事。剧中主角宋丽玲的原型时佩璞当时在一次演出中扮演京剧《梁祝》里的祝英台，给法国驻华大使馆低级职员布尔西科留下深刻印象。时佩璞对布尔西科谎称自己是女儿身，从小被当作男孩子抚养，并与之相恋。两人以夫妻身份生活多年，布尔西科还将时佩璞及领养儿子时度度以家属身份带回法国。1983年，时佩璞在法国被判间谍罪，其男儿身的秘密暴露，与布尔西科18年恋情告终。这一离奇的案件轰动了法国，美国记者也争相报道。美籍华裔剧作家黄哲伦从《纽约时报》上看到这个新闻时，敏锐地发现了其中呼之欲出的种族刻板印象，随后基于这个故事，以歌剧《蝴蝶夫人》作为颠覆的原型创作出《蝴蝶君》剧本，探索东方与西方、民族与种族、性别与政治、身份与认同等重大文化命题。该剧本自从20世纪80年代诞生以来，多次登上百老汇的舞台，并获得托尼奖最佳戏剧奖，后来又被改编为电影。

黄哲伦在剧中塑造了一个用西方传统观念看待东方的主人公——法国外交官加利马尔。看过歌剧《蝴蝶夫人》后，他爱上了在舞台上扮演蝴蝶夫人的中国演员宋丽玲，认为她就是自己理想中的东方女人。20年后，当年的法国外交官被指控泄漏情报，被捕后他才发现深爱的蝴蝶夫人竟然是个男扮女装的间谍，在绝望中，加利马尔自尽身亡。

Scene 6

German ambassadors house. Beijing. 1960.

The upstage special area now becomes a stage. Several chairs face upstage, representing seating for some twenty guests in the parlor. A few "diplomats"—Renee,

Marc, Toulon—*in formal dress enter and take seats.*

Gallimard also sits down, but turns towards us and continues to talk. Orchestral accompaniment on the tape is now replaced by a simple piano. Song picks up the death scene from the point where Butterfly uncovers the hara-kiri knife.

Gallimard: The ending is pitiful. Pinkerton, in an act of great courage, stays home and sends his American wife to pick up Butterfly's child. The truth, long deferred, has come up to her door.

Song, playing Butterfly, sings the lines from the opera in her own voice—which though not classical, should be decent.

Song: "Con onor muore/ chi non puo serbar/ vita con onore."

Gallimard(Simultaneously): "Death with honor/ Is better than life/ Life with dishonor/."

The stage is illuminated; we are now completely within an elegant diplomat's residence. Song proceeds to play out an abbreviated death scene. Everyone in the room applauds. Song, shyly, takes her bows. Others in the room rush to congratulate her. Gallimard remains with us.

Gallimard: They say in opera the voice is everything. That's probably why I'd never before enjoyed opera. Here... here was a Butterfly with little or no voice—but she had the grace, the delicacy... I believed this girl. I believed her suffering. I wanted to take her in my arms-so delicate, even I could protect her, take her home, pamper her until she smiled.

Over the course of the proceeding speech, Song has broken from the upstage crowd and moved directly upstage of Gallimard.

Song: Excuse me. Monsieur...?

Gallimard turns upstage, shocked.

Gallimard: Oh! Gallimard. Mademoiselle...? A beautiful...

Song: Song Liling.

Gallimard: A beautiful performance.

Song: Oh, please.

Gallimard: I usually-

Song: You make me blush. *I'm* no opera singer at all.

Gallimard: I usually don't like Butterfly.

Song: I can't blame you in the least.

Gallimard: I mean, the story-

Song: Ridiculous.

Chapter 5 M. Butterfly *by David Henry Hwang*

Gallimard: I like the story, but... what?

Song: Oh, you like it?

Gallimard: I... what I mean is, I've always seen it played by huge women in so much bad makeup.

Song: Bad makeup is not unique to the West.

Gallimard: But, who can believe them?

Song: And you believe me?

Gallimard: Absolutely. You were utterly convincing. *It's* the first time—

Song: Convincing? As a Japanese woman? The Japanese used hundreds of our people for medical experiments during the war, you know. But I gather such an irony is lost on you.

Gallimard: No! I was about to say, it's the first time I've seen the beauty of the story.

Song: Really?

Gallimard: Of her death. It's a... a pure sacrifice. He's unworthy, but what can she do? She loves him... so much. It's a very beautiful story.

Song: Well, yes, to a Westerner.

Gallimard: Excuse me?

Song: It's one of your favorite fantasies, isn't it? The submissive Oriental woman and the crud white man.

Gallimard: Well, I didn't quite mean ...

Song: Consider it this way: what would you say if a blonde homecoming queen fell in love with a short Japanese businessman? He treats her cruelly, then goes home for three years, during which time she prays to his picture and turns down marriage from a young Kennedy. Then, when she learns he has remarried, she kills herself. Now, I believe you would consider this girl to be a deranged idiot, correct? But because it's an Oriental who kills herself for a Westerner—ah! you find it beautiful.

Silence.

Gallimard: Yes... well... I see your point,...

Song: I will never do Butterfly again, Monsieur Gallimard. If you wish to see some real theatre, come to the Peking Opera sometime. Expand your mind.

Song walks offstage.

Gallimard (To us): So much for protecting her in my big Western arms.

从《蝴蝶夫人》到《蝴蝶君》——从后殖民视角解读《蝴蝶君》

剧名 M. Butterfly 中缩略语字母 M. 在法语里既是"夫人"(Madam)的缩写,也是"先生"(Monsieur)的缩写。这个指意模糊的剧名一来表明了此剧与久演不衰的西方经典歌剧《蝴蝶夫人》之间的紧密联系;二来呼应了剧中主角宋丽玲的性别不明。《蝴蝶夫人》(Madam Butterfly)是意大利作曲家普契尼于 1904 年改编的一部具有东方色彩的歌剧,被称为"世界十大歌剧作品之一"。该剧讲述了一个美丽的日本女子无怨无悔地爱上薄情的美国军官。故事发生在 1900 年前后的日本长崎市。日本姑娘巧巧桑("巧巧"是日语"蝴蝶"的音译,"桑"是表敬称的音译)为了爱情脱离家庭,毅然嫁给美国海军军官平克顿,并在丈夫回国后独守三年。忠贞不渝的巧巧桑等来的却是背信弃义的平克顿和他新娶的美国妻子。得知平克顿回来只是准备带走自己给他生的儿子后,蝴蝶夫人悲痛万分,自尽身亡。

后殖民理论(Postcolonialism Theories)研究英格兰、西班牙、法国等欧洲国家在历史、文化、政治、文学以及话语模式上不同于其旧有的殖民地的差别(也包括种族之间的差别)。按照后殖民主义的观点,西方的思想和文化以及其文学的价值与传统,总是被认为居于世界文化的主导地位;与之相对照的是,非西方的第三世界或东方的传统则被排挤到了边缘地带,或不时地扮演一种相对于西方的"他者"(other)的角色。其代表人物爱德华·赛义德将文学与政治紧密结合起来,提出"东方主义"(Orientalism)。爱德华·赛义德在专著《东方主义》导言中开宗明义地指出:"东方几乎就是一个欧洲人的发明,它自古以来就是一个充满浪漫传奇色彩和异国情调的、萦绕着人们的记忆和视野的、有着奇特经历的地方。"对自我的肯定往往是通过对"他者"的否定来完成的,每个社会,每种文化都有它的"他者"。正如西方需要东方,尤其把西方的文明与东方的野蛮,西方的强大与东方的软弱,西方的男性化与东方的女性化……相对照。

美丽脆弱,温顺忠贞,向白人男子寻求保护的东方女子是一种广为流传的关于东方的刻板形象。普契尼的"蝴蝶夫人"就代表了西方难以割舍的东方情结。亚洲女性被比喻为供人赏玩的蝴蝶,只能依附骑士般的西方男性,为了爱不惜牺牲自己。表面上凄美的爱情故事实质上影射了某个时期东西方的关系:民族之间的强与弱,主宰与顺从。该剧的成功很大程度上归功于迎合了西方社会看待东方女子的固定模式;另一方面,《蝴蝶夫人》的推广强化了东方人软弱、愚昧的刻板印象。

抱着颠覆传统亚洲女性被动顺从形象的初衷,黄哲伦的《蝴蝶君》在题材上依然沿用原有的故事,但剧中东西方的角色却发生了明显的易位:剧中的男主人公加利马尔不再是《蝴蝶夫人》中平克顿那样阳光潇洒,充满男性魅力的美国海军军官形象,变成了文弱敏感、有些同性恋倾向的法国外交官。性格强势的白人妻子和情人都无法满足他的自尊心,而宋丽玲让他看到了幻想中的羞涩娇弱的亚洲女子,从而萌生了强烈的保护欲和占有欲。在刚刚看完宋丽玲的演出后,加利马尔把她比作蝴蝶:

"Here...here was a Butterfly with little or no voice-but she had the grace, the delicacy... I wanted to take her in my arms-so delicate, even I could protect her, take her home, pamper her until she smiled."(Act One, Scene Six)

但是这只蝴蝶把他玩弄于股掌之上,最后还无情打破了他的幻想,加利马尔自己反倒成了脆弱的蝴蝶。剧终,他穿上蝴蝶夫人的和服,戴上蝴蝶夫人的面具选择了自杀,而这正是《蝴蝶夫人》中巧巧桑的结局。

其次,宋丽玲不再是柔弱无力的巧巧桑。她(他)以男扮女装的手法掩盖了自己的真实性别和身份,利用加利马尔的心理精心布下陷阱诱他入局。长达20年的情人关系中加利马尔一直以为他控制着宋丽玲,直到最后才明白宋丽玲操控了他。这只"中国蝴蝶"不再是被动的、沉默的。《蝴蝶君》中对东西权力关系的质疑多出自于她(他)口。

"Consider it this way: what would you say if a blonde homecoming queen fall in love with a short Japanese businessman? He treats her cruelly, then goes home for three years, during which time she prays to his picture and turns down marriage from a young Kennedy. Then, when she learns he has remarried, she kills herself. Now, I believe you would consider this girl to be a deranged idiot, correct? But because it's an Oriental who kills herself for a Westerner-ah! -you find it beautiful."(Act One, Scene Six)

这里宋丽玲直指《蝴蝶夫人》中爱情故事的荒谬之处,抨击西方观众脑中根深蒂固的种族偏见。与加利马尔一样,观众关于东方主义的幻想被颠覆了。

《蝴蝶君》解构了东方女子被看作蝴蝶夫人的刻板印象,颠倒了原有的东西方权力关系,发出了"与西方中心主义相对立的他者的声音,对原有的东西方关系中潜在运作的文化霸权与权力关系进行了一次惊人的倒置。"此剧中东方主义幻想的破灭体现出重新审视东西方关系的必要性。在多元文化的背景下,东西方更应该相互尊重,相互理解。正如黄哲伦在后记里所说:"我把它(《蝴蝶君》)看成是对各方的一个请求,希望它能穿透我们各自的层层累积的文化和性别误识,为了我们相互的利益,从同为人类的共同的平等的立场出发,真诚看待对方。"

主要参考文献

王宁. 东方主义、后殖民主义和文化霸权主义批判——爱德华·赛义德的后殖民主义理论剖析[J]. 北京大学学报(哲学社会科学版),1995(2):54-62.

ABRAMS M H, Geoffrey Galt Harpham. A Glossary of Literary Terms[M]. Ninth ed., Florence: Cengage Learning, 2015.

HWANG D H. M. Butterfly[M]. New York: Plume, 1993.

SAID E W. Orientalism[M]. Vancouver:Vintage Books,2003.

思考题

(1)《蝴蝶君》中宋丽玲是一个怎样的人物形象？试从剧本中举例说明。

(2)宋丽玲利用西方男子对东方女性的幻象给了加利马尔所代表的西方社会致命一击，你认为这是一个积极正面的中国男人形象吗？

(3)东方(Oriental)和西方(Occidental)仅仅是地理概念吗？

Part IV Prose

Chapter 1 Of Studies

by Francis Bacon

 背景介绍

弗朗西斯·培根(1561—1626),是英国文艺复兴时期著名的哲学家、散文家,被称为"英国唯物主义的第一个创始人",也是实验科学和近代归纳法的创始人。培根出生于伦敦一个新贵族家庭,12岁入剑桥大学三一学院,担任过女王的特别法律顾问以及宫廷首席检察官,后来遭陷害而脱离政治生涯,从此专心从事文学创作和著述活动。他的主要作品有 *Novum Organum*《新工具》、*Essays*《论说文集》、*The Interpretation of Nature*《自然的解释》、*Great Instauration*《伟大的复兴》等。培根的作品和思想理念对英国的思想史、近代哲学史和科学史都产生了深远的影响。

《论读书》选自培根的 *Essays*《论说文集》,该文集从哲学家的角度思考广泛的人生问题,篇幅不长但风格活泼易懂,体现了作者对人生的通透理解,是文艺复兴以来欧洲古典人文主义价值观和政治理想的集中体现。文集总共包含58篇,涵盖社会、人生、真理、爱情、友谊、学习等多个方面,短小精悍,充满了哲理和趣味。《论读书》这篇随笔展现了作者对读书治学的独到见解,其风格古朴典雅,简洁明快,语言整齐有气势,发人深省。全文逻辑严谨,立论分明,体现了培根缜密的哲学思维和科学素养,堪称论证的典范。

文本阅读

Studies serve for delight, for ornament, and for ability. Their chief use for delight, is in privateness and retiring; for ornament, is in discourse; and for ability, is in the judgment and disposition of business. For expert men can execute, and perhaps judge of particulars, one by one; but the general counsels, and the plots and marshalling of affairs, come best, from those that are learned.

To spend too much time in studies is sloth; to use them too much for ornament is affection; to make judgment wholly by their rules, is the humor of a scholar. They perfect nature, and are perfected by experience: for natural abilities are like natural plants, that need pruning, by study; and studies themselves, do give forth directions too much at large, except they be bounded in by experience.

Crafty men contemn studies, simple men admire them, and wise men use them; for they teach not their own use; but that is a wisdom without them, and above them, won by observation. Read not to contradict and confuse; nor to believe and take for granted; nor to find talk and discourse; but to weigh and consider.

Some books are to be tasted, others to be swallowed, and some few to be chewed and digested; that is, some books are to be read only in parts; others to be read, but not curiously; and some few to be ready wholly, and with diligence and attention. Some books also may be read by deputy, and extracts made of them bothers; but that would be only in the less important arguments, and the meaner sort of books; else distilled books are like common distilled waters, flashy things.

Reading makes a full man; conference a ready man; and writing an exact man. And therefore, if a man writes little, he had need have a great memory; if he confer little, he had need have a present wit; and if he read little, he had need have much cunning, to seem to know, that he doth not.

Histories make men wise; poets witty; the mathematics subtle; natural philosophy deep; moral grave; logic and rhetoric able to contend. Abeunt studia in mores. Nay, there is no stand or impediment in the wit, but may be wrought out by fit studies; like as diseases of the body, may have appropriate exercises. Bowling is good for the stone and reins; shooting for the lungs and breast; gentle walking for the stomach; riding for the head; and the like. So if a man's wit be wandering, let him study the mathematics; for in demonstrations, if his wit be called away never so little, he must begin again. If his wit be not apt to distinguish or find differences, let him study the schoolmen; for they are cymini sectors. If he be not apt to beat over matters, and to call up one thing to prove and illustrate another, let him study the lawyers' cases. So every defect of the mind, may have a special receipt.

作品赏析

本篇散文其实只有一段,为了方便阅读分成若干段落。《论读书》开篇点题,概括了全文的主旨,介绍读书的目的为"delight(消遣)""ornament(装点)""ability(增进才能)"。文章接下来概述了不同的读书目的在生活中各类场合的应用。段尾通过对比"expert men(专于一技者)"和"those that are learned(博学之士)"的区别,指出"唯有博学之士方能纵观全局,通权达变",再次重申了读书的重要性。

第二段,作者警示了读书方法不同会导致相反的效果,不可过度沉溺,不可过多炫耀,不可仅凭教条进行论断。读书应该与经验互为补充"perfected by experience",相得益彰,如中国古人所言"读万卷书,行万里路""尽信书不如无书"。拓展来看,即为理论与实践之间的辩证关系。排比短句的使用使意义更加连贯,增强了气势。

第三段展示了不同的人对于读书的态度,充满劝导意味的警示句,语言上同样采用对称的排比句式,一气呵成,节奏明快。

第四段"Some books are to be tasted, others to be swallowed, and some few to be chewed and digested"使用排比结构和省略,指明了对待不同的书,我们应该持有不同的阅读方式。所有的书并非同等重要,如果不加以区分,就会导致事倍功半。因此,阅读书籍前,学习者应有所选择。"else distilled books are, like common distilled waters, flashy things.",此句使用了比喻修辞,把经过提炼的书比喻为"distilled waters 蒸馏水",使得抽象的"distilled books"生动具体,通俗易懂。

第五段中首句是脍炙人口的名言:"Reading makes a full man; conference a ready man; and writing an exact man"(读书使人充实,讨论使人机智,笔记使人准确)。该句采用并列句式,后面的两个短句省略了谓语动词"makes",使得句子显得简练。该段随后使用了三个结构一致、形式工整的条件从句,通过反证法再次强调了在学习过程中读书、讨论、笔记都是不可或缺的重要环节。

第六段"Histories make men wise; poets witty; the mathematics subtle; natural philosophy deep; moral grave; logic and rhetoric able to contend."(读史使人明智,读诗使人聪颖,算数使人缜密,自然哲学使人深刻,伦理使人庄重,逻辑与修辞使人善辩)"是广为流传的经典佳句。本段阐释了不同的书籍对于人们性格塑造所产生的影响。论述上采用举例论证,正如"stone and reins(肾脏),lungs and breast(胸肺),stomach(肠胃),head(头脑)"这些身体部位的疾病可以通过"Bowling(滚球),shooting(射箭),gentle walking(散步),riding(骑马)"等锻炼方式加以矫正,心智上的缺陷也是可以通过专门的药方加以治愈。正如"You are what you read",书籍就是我们的精神食粮,能够陶冶个性,改善心智。

培根的这篇《论读书》结构整齐严谨,语言简洁明快,比喻形象贴切,排比对称工整。作者善于利用句子结构的重复和音节韵律的变化加强论述效果,阐述读书学习的重要性,读罢仍有意犹未尽之感。培根的散文关注社会现实,其中许多看法和观点都源自于作者自身的生活经验,充满哲理和睿智,给读者以深刻的启迪。

主要参考文献

程梅.英语散文精品赏析[M].天津:南开大学出版社,2005.

金春伟.Of Studies 的文体赏析[J].齐齐哈尔大学学报(哲学社会科学版),2005(5):118-120.

罗选民,张少雄,张跃军.英美文学赏析教程:诗歌、戏剧与散文卷[M].北京:清华大学出版社,2016.

余健明,肖惜.英语名篇名段背诵精华[M].广州:华南理工大学出版社,2008.

朱立华.英语经典名篇赏析[M].天津:南开大学出版社,2007.

思考题

（1）在《论读书》这篇散文中，培根使用了哪些修辞手法？试举例分析。

（2）培根在文中提倡的读书方法，哪个最适合你的学习？

（3）试比较培根的作品与现当代中国散文，风格有什么不同？

（4）培根的劝学与中国古代哲学家的劝学思想相比（如孔子、荀子等），各有什么特点？

Chapter 2　Walden
by Henry David Thoreau
(*excerpts*)

 背景介绍

《瓦尔登湖》是美国作家亨利·戴维·梭罗所著的一本著名的散文集,记录了梭罗在瓦尔登湖畔一间小木屋里独居两年多的生活,详细描绘了他的所见所闻和富有哲理的思考。为了证明人类生活并不需要依赖于过多的物质享受,梭罗隐居在美国马萨诸塞州东部康科德镇的瓦尔登湖畔,开荒种地,自给自足。他崇尚自然,每天在林中观察动物和植物,与森林、鸟虫等对话,记录湖水的涨落,晚上则在小木屋中写下自己的观察和思考。《瓦尔登湖》共由18篇散文组成,梭罗在散文集中把两年多的生活压缩成一年,用四季更替来象征人类的发展。他追求精神生活,关注灵魂的成长,以实际行动告诉世人:大部分人所追求的舒适生活其实并非必需品,精神上的满足并不来源于物质追求。梭罗在文学创作和生活实践中都有一个贯穿始终的主张,那就是回归自然,尊重自然界中的万事万物。在生态失衡和环境恶化日趋严重的工业社会,瓦尔登湖已成为人与自然和谐共处的象征。这本散文集开创了自然主义文学和环境保护主义思潮,是美国文学非小说著作中最受读者欢迎的书籍,在1985年《美国遗产》评选的"10本构成美国人性格的书"中名列榜首。

 文本选读

Where I Lived, and What I Lived For

At a certain season of our life we are accustomed to consider every spot as the possible site of a house. 1 I have thus surveyed the country on every side within a dozen miles of where I live. In imagination I have bought all the farms in succession, for all were to be bought, and I knew their price. I walked over each farmer's premises, 2 tasted his wild apples, discoursed on husbandry with him, took his farm at his price, at any price, mortgaging it to him in my mind; even put a higher price on it,—took everything but a deed of it,—took his word for his deed, for I dearly love to talk,—cultivated it, and him too to some extent, I trust, and withdrew when I had enjoyed it long enough, leaving him to carry it on. This experience entitled me to be regarded as a sort of real-estate broker by my friends. Wherever I sat, there I might live, and the landscape radiated from me accordingly. What is a house but a sedes, a seat? —better if a country seat. I discovered many a site for a house not likely to be soon improved, which some might have thought too far from the village, but to my eyes the village was too far from it. Well, there I might live, I said; and there I did live, for an hour, a summer and a winter life; saw how I could let the years run off, buffet the winter through, and see the spring come in. The future inhabitants of this region, wherever they may place their houses, may be sure that they have been anticipated. An afternoon sufficed to lay out the land into orchard, woodlot, and pasture, and to decide what fine oaks or pines should be left to stand before the door, and whence each blasted tree could be seen to the best advantage; and then I let it lie, fallow perchance, for a man is rich in proportion to the number of things which he can afford to let alone.

My imagination carried me so far that I even had the refusal of several farms,—the refusal was all I wanted,— but I never got my fingers burned by actual possession. The nearest that I came to actual possession was when I bought the Hollowell place, and had begun to sort my seeds, and collected materials with which to make a wheelbarrow to carry it on or off with; but before the owner gave me a deed of it, his wife—every man has such a wife—changed her mind and wished to keep it, and he offered me ten dollars to release him. Now, to speak the truth, I had but ten cents in the world, and it surpassed my arithmetic to tell, if I was that man who had ten cents, or who had a farm, or ten dollars, or all together. However, I let him keep the ten dollars and the farm too, for I had carried it6 far enough; or rather, to be generous, I sold him the farm for just what I gave for it, and, as he was not a rich man, made him a present of ten dollars, and still had my tencents, and seeds, and materials for a wheelbarrow left. I found thus that I had been a rich man without any damage to my poverty. But I retained the landscape, and I have since annually carried off what it yielded without a wheelbarrow. With respect to landscapes,

"I am monarch of all I survey,

My right there is none to dispute."

I have frequently seen a poet withdraw, having enjoyed the most valuable part of a farm,9 while the crusty farmer supposed that he had got a few wild apples only. Why, the owner does not know it for many years when a poet has put his farm in rhyme,10 the most admirable kind of invisible fence, has fairly impounded it, milked it, skimmed it, and got all the cream, and left the farmer only the skimmed milk.

The real attractions of the Hollowell farm, to me, were: its complete retirement, being about two miles from the village, half a mile from the nearest neighbor, and separated from the highway by a broad field; its bounding on the river, which the owner said protected it by its fogs from frosts in the spring, though that was nothing to me; the gray color and ruinous state of the house and barn, and the dilapidated fences, which put such an interval between me and the last occupant; the hollow and lichen-covered apple trees, gnawed by rabbits, showing what kind of neighbors I should have; but above all, the recollection I had of it from my earliest voyages up the river, when the house was concealed behind a dense grove of red maples, through which I heard the housedog bark. I was in haste to buy it, before the proprietor finished getting out some rocks, cutting down the hollow apple trees, and grubbing up some young birches which had sprung up in the pasture, or, in short, had made any more of his improvements. To enjoy these advantages I was ready to carry it on; like Atlas,11 to take the world on my shoulders,—I never heard what compensation he received for that,—and do all those things which had no other motive or excuse but that I might pay for it and be unmolested in my possession of it; for I knew all the while that it would yield the most abundant crop of the kind I wanted if I could only afford to let it alone. But it turned out as I have said.

All that I could say, then, with respect to farming on a large scale, (I have always cultivated a garden,) was, that I had had my seeds ready. Many think that seeds improve with age. I have no doubt that time discriminates between the good and the bad; and when at last I shall plant, I shall be less likely to be disappointed. But I would say to my fellows, once for all, as long as possible live free and uncommitted. It makes but little difference whether you are committed to a farm or the county jail.

...

When first I took up my abode in the woods, that is, began to spend my nights as well as days there, which, by accident, was on Independence Day, or the fourth of July, 1845, my house was not finished for winter, but was merely a defence against the rain, without plastering or chimney, the walls being of rough weather-stained boards, with wide chinks, which made it cool at night. The upright white hewn studs and freshly planed door and window casings gave it a clean and airy look, especially in the morning, when its timbers were saturated with dew, so that I fancied that by noon some sweet gum would exude from them. To my imagination it retained throughout the day more or less of this auroral character, reminding me of a certain house on a mountain which I had visited the year before. This was an airy and unplastered cabin, fit to entertain a travelling god, and where a goddess might trail her garments. The winds which passed over my dwelling were such as sweep over the ridges of mountains, bearing the broken strains, or celestial parts only, of terrestrial music. The morning wind forever blows, the poem of creation is uninterrupted; but few are the ears that hear it. Olympus is but the outside of the earth everywhere.

The only house I had been the owner of before, if I except a boat, was a tent, which I used occasionally when making excursions in the summer, and this is still rolled up in my garret; but the boat, after passing from hand to hand, has gone down the stream of time. With this more substantial shelter about me, I had made some progress toward settling in the world. This frame, so slightly clad, was a sort of crystallization around me, and reacted on the builder. It was suggestive somewhat as a picture in outlines. I did not need to go out doors to take the air, for the atmosphere within had lost none of its freshness. It was not so much within doors as behind a door where I sat, even in the rainiest weather. The Harivansa says, "An abode without birds is like a meat without seasoning.' Such was not my abode, for I found myself suddenly neighbor to the birds; not by having imprisoned one, but having caged myself near them. I was not only nearer to some of those which commonly frequent the garden and the orchard, but to those wilder and more thrilling songsters of the forest which never, or rarely, serenade a villager,— the wood-thrush, the veery, the scarlet tanager, the field-sparrow, the whippoorwill, and many others.

...

I went to the woods because I wished to live deliberately, to front only the essential facts of life, and see if I could not learn what it had to teach, and not, when I came to die, discover that I had not lived. I did not wish to live what was not life, living is so dear; nor did I wish to practice resignation, unless it was quite necessary. I wanted to live deep and suck out all the marrow of life, to live so sturdily and Spartan-like[64] as to put to rout all that was not life, to cut a broad swath and shave close, to drive life into a corner, and reduce it to its lowest terms, and, if it proved to be mean, why then to get the whole and genuine meanness of it, and publish its meanness to the world; or if it were sublime, to know it by experience, and be able to give a true account of it in my next excursion. For most men, it appears to me, are in a strange uncertainty about it, whether it is of the devil or of God, and have somewhat hastily concluded that it is the chief end of man here to "glorify God and enjoy him forever."

Still we live meanly, like ants; though the fable tells us that we were long ago changed into men; like pygmies we fight with cranes; it is error upon error, and clout upon clout, and our best virtue has for its occasion a superfluous and evitable wretchedness. Our life is frittered away by detail. An honest man has hardly need to count more than his ten fingers, or in extreme cases he may add his ten toes, and lump the rest. Simplicity, simplicity, simplicity! I say, let your affairs be as two or three, and not a hundred or a thousand; instead of a million count half a dozen, and keep your accounts on your thumb nail. In the midst of this chopping sea of civilized life, such are the clouds and storms and quick sands and thousand-and-one items to be allowed for, that a man has to live, if he would not founder and go to the bottom and not make his port at all, by dead reckoning, and he must be a great calculator indeed who succeeds. Simplify, simplify. Instead of three meals a day, if it be necessary eat but one; instead of a hundred dishes, five; and reduce other things in proportion. Our life is like a German Confederacy, made up of petty states, with its boundary forever fluctuating, so that even a German cannot tell you how it is bounded at any moment. The nation itself, with all its so called internal improvements, which, by the way, are all external and superficial, is just such an unwieldy and overgrown establishment, cluttered with furniture and tripped up by its own traps, ruined by luxury and heedless expense, by want of calculation and a worthy aim, as the million households in the land; and the only cure for it as for them is in a rigid economy, a stern and more than Spartan simplicity of life and elevation of purpose. It lives too fast. Men think that it is essential that the Nation have commerce, and export ice, and talk through a telegraph, and ride thirty miles an hour, without a doubt, whether they do or not; but whether we should live like baboons or like men, is a little uncertain. If we do not get out sleepers, and forge rails, and devote days and nights to the work, but go to tinkering upon our lives to improve them, who will build railroads? And if railroads are not built, how shall we get to heaven in season? But if we stay at home and mind our business, who will want railroads? We do not ride on the railroad; it rides upon us. Did you ever think what those sleepers are that underlie the railroad? Each one is a man, an Irish-man, or a Yankee man. The rails are laid on them, and they are covered with sand, and the cars run smoothly over them. They are sound sleepers, I assure you. And every few years a new lot is laid down and run over; so that, if some have the pleasure of riding on a rail, others have the misfortune to be ridden upon. And when they run over a man that is walking in his sleep, a supernumerary sleeper in the wrong position, and wake him up, they suddenly stop the cars, and make a hue and cry about it, as if this were an exception. I am glad to know that it takes a gang of men for every five miles to keep the sleepers down and level in their beds as it is, for this is a sign that they may sometime get up again.

Why should we live with such hurry and waste of life? We are determined to be starved before we are hungry. Men say that a stitch in time saves nine, and so they take a thousand stitches to-day to save nine to-morrow. As for work, we haven't any of any consequence. We have the Saint Vitus' dance, and cannot possibly keep our heads still. If I should only give a few pulls at the parish bell-rope, as for a fire, that is, without setting the bell, there is hardly a man on his farm in the outskirts of Concord, notwithstanding that press of engagements which was his excuse so many times this morning, nor a boy, nor a woman, I might almost say, but would forsake all and follow that sound, not mainly to save property from the flames, but, if we will confess the truth, much more to see it burn, since burn it must, and we, be it known, did not set it on fire,80—or to see it put out, and have a hand in it, if that is done as handsomely; yes, even if it were the parish church itself. Hardly a man takes a half hour's nap after dinner, but when he wakes he holds up his head and asks, "What's the news?" as if the rest of mankind had stood his sentinels. Some give directions to be waked every half hour, doubtless for no other purpose; and then, to pay for it, they tell what they have dreamed. After a night's sleep the news is as indispensable as the breakfast. "Pray tell me anything new that has happened to a man anywhere on this globe,"—and he reads it over his coffee and rolls, that a man has had his eyes gouged out this morning on the Wachito River; never dreaming the while that he lives in the dark unfathomed mammoth cave of this world, and has but the rudiment of an eye himself.

...

梭罗的生态主义思想——生态批评视域中的《瓦尔登湖》

生态批评(Ecocriticism)起源于20世纪90年代的美国,领军人物之一威廉·霍沃思这样描述生态批评家的特征:"生态批评家是评价记叙人类文明对自然之影响的作品的人,他歌颂大自然,谴责掠夺自然的人,同时还呼吁人类采取行动来逆转掠夺者对自然造成的破坏。"作为现代生态文学的先驱和环境保护意识的倡导者,亨利·戴维·梭罗在《瓦尔登湖》《河上一周》《湎因森林》等一系列关于自然的著作中集中阐述了富有哲理的生态主义思想,突出强调人类应尊重自然,回归自然,与自然和谐共处。在梭罗看来,与自然亲密接触可以使人类获得精神上的满足,提升道德修养,深刻理解生活的真谛。梭罗的自然观与人生哲学对于生活在环境问题严峻,生存压力日益增大的现代社会的我们具有重要的借鉴意义。

一、尊重自然,善待一切生命

梭罗生活的19世纪中叶是美国社会高度发展时期,人们享受了工业文明带来的种种便利。启蒙运动解放了宗教的束缚,人们意识到自己不是匍匐在上帝面前的奴仆,而是具有理性光辉的个体。经济和科技的发展鼓励人们发挥主观能动性,探索未知,改造世界。人被看作地球的中心、万物的灵长,征服自然、改造自然的人类中心主义观念在这一时期颇为流行。人类对待自然的态度导致了以破坏生态环境为代价的工业发展模式,砍伐树木、开采矿产、排放废气等行为都反映出人类以自然界的主宰的身份肆意妄行。梭罗对这种现象持坚定的否定态度,他认为人类与动植物一样都只是自然的一份子,人类并不比自然界中的其他生物高级。人与自然应该是平等的,共同构成一个完整和谐的整体。

"I wish to speak a word for Nature, for absolute freedom and wildness, as contrasted with a freedom and culture merely civil—to regard man as an inhabitant, or a part and parcel of Nature, rather than a member of society. I wish to make an extreme statement, if so I may make an emphatic one, for there are enough champions of civilization: the minister and the school committee and every one of you will take care of that."

"我想为伟大的自然讨个公道,因为它比世俗化的人类文明多了一种自由和狂野之美。我们应该视人类为大自然的居民,或者自然的一个组成部分,而不是社会的一员。如果这样说让大家觉得惊诧,请原谅我只是为了强调自己的观点。因为世俗的文明有很多人拥护——政府官员、学校委员会的委员以及你们每一个人,因此少我一人也没多大关系。"

梭罗把人类与自然界中的其他生物均看成是地球的组成部分,因此都是地位平等的生物。在《瓦尔登湖》中,梭罗充满感情地描述各种动植物,把它们形容成自己的好邻居。他认为从长远效益来看,人类必须与大自然和谐相处。梭罗的生态主义思想与生态批评中的生态整体主义不谋而合。王诺在《欧美生态文学》中指出,生态整体主义强调的是"把人类的物质欲望、经济的增长、对自然的改造和扰乱限制在能为生态系统所承受、吸收、降解和恢复的范围内。这种限制为的是生态系统的整体利益,而生态系统的整体利益与人类的长远利益和根本利益是一致的。"人类不可能脱离生态系统而生存,社会发展的历史已经充分证明了以人类为中心的生态观仅考虑到眼前利益,损害了人类长远的也是根本的利益。

基于此种尊重自然,平等对待各种生命形式的理念,梭罗指出自然界里的一切存在都是有理由的,反对人类以自己的标准去判断其他物种的价值,按照是否具有经济效益来划分其他物种。诸如为了获取板材而砍伐森林,为了捕猎快感而杀害动物,为了种植

粮食而开垦荒地之类的改造大自然的人类活动,在梭罗眼中是缺乏道德的侵略行为。他在《瓦尔登湖》中多次表述对伐木的反感:

"But I was interested in the preservation of the venison and the vert more than the hunters or woodchoppers, and as much as though I had been the Lord Warden himself; and if any part was burned, though I burned it myself by accident, I grieved with a grief that lasted longer and was more inconsolable than that of the proprietors; nay, I grieved when it was cut down by the proprietors themselves. I would that our farmers when they cut down a forest felt some of that awe..."

"我比猎者或伐木者更关心野味和森林保护,仿佛我自己便是护林官一样;假若它有一部分给烧掉了,即便是我自己不小心烧掉的,我也要大为悲伤,比任何一个森林主本人都要哀痛得更长久,而且更无法释怀。当它被森林主砍掉的时候我也十分悲痛。我希望我们的农夫在砍伐一片森林的时候,能够感觉到那种恐惧……"

在梭罗笔下,人、动物和植物都是平等的生命。所谓"高等"与"低等","有用"与"无用",完全是人类从主观利益出发人为划分的。人类同其他物种一样,只是地球这个整体中普通的一分子。那么,我们人类应该如何认识自身的位置,如何处理与大自然的关系呢?生活在19世纪的梭罗以自己的实际行动给出了答案:人类必须尊重自然,敬畏一切生命形式,善待我们的这些邻居。

二、物质简朴、精神丰富的生活方式

梭罗热爱自然,亲近自然,但他选择去瓦尔登湖生活并不是因为厌倦了工业文明,从而隐居山野,根本原因是要证明现代物质文明带来的所谓"舒适"不是人类生活的必需品,只要精神富有,即使将物质需求降到最低限度,人们依然可以过得逍遥自在。在梭罗生活的时代,工业文明迅速发展,生活质量大幅提高,人们享受着物质带来的便利时也日渐受到物质的束缚。为了满足物质欲望,追赶流行的生活方式,人们不得不终日奔波,辛苦劳作。但是金钱和享乐无法改善人的精神生活,物质丰富、精神贫乏成为当时美国人的普遍生存状态。在梭罗眼中,一味追逐物质财富会使人忘记生命的意义,金钱至上和享乐主义的人生观是肤浅和荒谬的。财富不仅没能给人们带去幸福和满足,反而成了束缚他们的枷锁:"我看见年轻的人,我的邻居,不幸的是他们生下来就继承了田地、庐舍、谷仓、牛羊和农具;得到他们倒是容易,要摆脱他们的束缚却困难得多。"不管是富可敌国的大资本家,还是勉强温饱的贫民,都有可能变成物质的奴隶。

梭罗主张简单朴素的生活方式,指出生活的必需品实际极为有限,人们追逐的大多数物品其实并没有自己想象得那么重要。世人关注的大多是那些琐碎的个人利益和感官享受,而梭罗认为这不是真正的生活。梭罗关注的是人的精神世界,物质简朴、精神丰富的生活才是他的理想。那么,如何去寻求真正的生活意义呢?梭罗在《瓦尔登湖》里给出的建议是"简朴!简朴!简朴!(Simplicity! Simplicity! Simplicity!)"。梭罗的人生观与当今社会推崇的极简生活和"断舍离"概念具有相似的思想来源。自然环境和社会生态的恶化,再加上发展带来的生存竞争,人们早已感到不堪重负,内心渴望摆脱物欲和执念,过一种清爽自由的生活。

为了实践理想中的简朴生活,梭罗在美国独立纪念日七月四号这天开始了瓦尔登湖畔的独居,抛弃不必要的物质累赘,以满足基本生活需求为标准,依靠自己的劳动获取食物等生活资料。简单的生活没有使他觉得了无生趣,与大自然的亲密接触给予他巨大的精神慰藉,使他能够自由地探索自己的思想和灵魂。梭罗的实践证明人可以过一种物质简朴而精神富有的生活,而生活的真理就是"简单"。正如在《瓦尔登湖》的结束语中所说:

"I learned this, at least, by my experiment; that if one advances confidently in the direction of his dreams, and endeavors to live the life which he has imagined, he will meet with a success unexpected in common hours. He will put some things behind, will pass an invisible boundary; new, universal, and more liberal laws will begin to establish themselves around and within him…In proportion as he simplifies his life, the laws of the universe will appear less complex, and solitude will not be solitude, nor poverty poverty, nor weakness weakness."

"至少我从这个实验中了解到:一个人若能自信地向他梦想的方向行进,努力经营他向往的生活,他是可以获得意想不到的成功的。他会越过一条看不见的界线,把一些事物抛在后面;新的、更广大的、更自由的规律会开始围绕着他,并且在他的内心里建立起来……他自己的生活越简单,宇宙的规律也就越显得简单,寂寞将不再是寂寞,贫困将不再是贫困,软弱将不再是软弱。"

三、回归自然,天人合一

梭罗的自然观建立在爱默生开创的美国超验主义思潮的基础上。超验主义是1836年到美国内战之间盛行于新英格兰地区的哲学和文学思潮。其领导人是美国思想家爱默生,梭罗是重要成员之一。超验主义观点强调人的主观能动性,主张人能超越感觉和理性而直接认识真理;主张人是神圣的,赞美人性中的神性,认为人可以通过精神与上帝直接交流。超验主义反对当时影响广泛的加尔文教关于"人性恶""命定论"等教条的宣传,不同意机械唯物主义轻视人的智慧、把人看作机器的论断,对刚开始在美国社会流行的物质主义和消费主义倾向也持怀疑态度。热爱自然,相信自己,自力更生,反对权威,重视与自己心灵的交流等都是超验主义倡导的观点。

梭罗继承了爱默生的主要思想,相信人可以通过主体感知去理解自然,在与自然的交流中获得启示与灵感。与爱默生把自然看作是神秘的"隐喻",主张人类去自然中探索"超灵",与"上帝"对话的理念不同的是,梭罗相信自然界本身就是神圣的,是宇宙精神的象征。自然不仅具有抚慰情感、启迪人心的作用,人还可以在与自然的交流中完善自我,提升修养，实现个人精神与宇宙精神的统一。在瓦尔登湖独居的两年多时间里，梭罗饶有兴致地观察身边的一切：记录湖水在不同天气状况下变幻的颜色，观看小老鼠寻找面包屑的过程，倾听鸟儿在林间自由地歌唱……他在大自然中从清晨待到黄昏，边观察边沉思，他认为这样做可以"使有限的生命得到无限延伸"：

"I grew in those seasons like corn in the night, and they were far better than any work of the hands would have been. They were not time subtracted from my life, but so much over and above my usual allowance."

"我在这样的季节中生长，好像玉米生长在夜间一样，这比任何手上的劳动好得不知多少了。这样做不是从我的生命中减去了时间，而是在我通常的时间里增添了许多，还超产了许多。"

梭罗意识到工业社会中人类精神世界日渐荒芜，忙于追逐外在物质的人们本末倒置，忽视与自己心灵的沟通。梭罗关于人与自然和谐统一的观点与东方文化中"天人合一"理念有异曲同工之妙。他以自己在瓦尔登湖的体验呼吁人们回归自然，融入自然，与自然合而为一得到升华。梭罗在《瓦尔登湖》一书中反复阐述自然的灵性：自然界是生命之源，也是人类的精神之源。我们应该学习大自然那样"朴素和健康，放松紧锁的双眉，让每一缕生命之光照耀全身"。

梭罗许多保护自然的想法与当代社会盛行的环保主义理念非常相似，他尊重自然、回归自然的观点和广阔的生态情怀超越了时代的局限，许多人认为他是人类历史上第一位自然主义者与环境保护主义者。《瓦尔登湖》一书集中体现了梭罗丰富的生态哲学。诸如自然万物平等、尊重自然、回归自然、重精神轻物质、崇尚简朴等思想深刻影响了被誉为"自然主义文学之父"的约翰·巴勒斯(John Burroughs)、"环保运动领袖"约翰·缪尔(John Muir)等后来者。随着工业化进程带来的恶果日益显现，梭罗的名声在进入二十世纪后不断攀升。他的作品不仅得到美国人的高度评价，在世界范围内也影响巨大。其著作《瓦尔登湖》被广泛看作物质生活中难得的精神食粮。海德格尔曾说，人应该"诗意地栖居在大地上"。瓦尔登湖早已不再是一个具体的地点，它象征着一种人与自然和谐相处的理想生活方式。

主要参考文献

梭罗 H D. 瓦尔登湖[M]. 徐迟, 译. 上海: 上海译文出版社, 1982.

王诺. 欧美生态文学[M]. 北京: 北京大学出版社, 2003.

张晶. 从超验自然观到生态哲学——梭罗的个人主义及其对西方环境保护主义思潮的建构[J]. 理论月刊, 2010(5): 52-54.

BUELL L. The Environmental Imagination: Thoreau—Nature Writing, and the Formation of American Culture[M]. Cambridge: Harvard University Press, 1995.

GLOTFELTY C & Fromm Harold. The Ecocriticism Reader: Landmarks in Literary Ecology

[M]. Athens：University of Georgia Press，1996.

THOREAU H D. Walden[M]. London：F. Watts，1969.

思考题

(1)你认为梭罗倡导的简朴生活是怎样的生活？

(2)梭罗为什么要选择 7 月 4 号开始在瓦尔登湖畔的生活？有何寓意？

(3)试结合当今中国社会的现状分析梭罗的生态思想的现实意义。

(4)梭罗在《瓦尔登湖》中大量引用东方文化经典，请找出其中涉及中国文化的部分并评价梭罗的解读。

Chapter 3　Three Days to See

by Helen Keller

(excerpts)

 背景介绍

　　Helen Keller(海伦·凯勒,1880—1968),美国著名女作家、教育家、慈善家、社会活动家。在一岁多时因患急性充血症而丧失视力和听力,海伦以惊人的毅力克服重重困难,并于1899年入读哈佛大学。大学期间她以自己如何战胜病残的经历写下了《我的人生故事》,给许多残疾人带来了希望和鼓励。86年的漫长岁月中海伦生活在无光、无声的世界里,在此期间,海伦突破了识字关、语言关、写作难关,先后学会了英、法、德、拉丁、希腊五种语言并完成了14本著作。代表作有:《假如给我三天光明》《我的人生故事》《石墙故事》。她致力于为残疾人造福,建立了许多慈善机构,1964年荣获"总统自由勋章",次年入选美国《时代周刊》评选的"二十世纪美国十大偶像"之一。马克·吐温说过,19世纪出了两个了不起的人物,拿破仑和海伦·凯勒。

　　本篇散文节选自同名书 *Three Days to See*,也是海伦·凯勒的一部自传。这部书中,作者以一个身残志坚的柔弱女子的视角,告诫身体健全的人们应热爱生活,珍惜生命。在文中,作者采用第一人称写作,希望在这假想的三天时间里,能看见自己的老师、朋友;能去参观自然史和艺术博物馆;能看看纽约城和日常世界;最后还要去看一场戏剧。三天的活动,内容涉及生活的各个方面,既表现了作者对生活中美的追求,也表达了作者对人类创造的高度赞美。*Three Days to See* 曾经发表在美国《大西洋月刊》上,同名书也多次荣登畅销榜。

 文本选读

　　All of us have read thrilling stories in which the hero had only a limited and specified time to live. Sometimes it was as long as a year, sometimes as short as 24 hours. But always we were interested in discovering just how the doomed hero chose to spend his last days or his last hours. I speak, of course, of free men who have a choice, not condemned criminals whose sphere of activities is strictly delimited.

　　Such stories set us thinking, wondering what we should do under similar circum-

Chapter 3 Three Days to See *by Helen Keller*

stances. What events, what experiences, what associations should we crowd into those last hours as mortal beings? What happiness should we find in reviewing the past, what regrets?

Sometimes I have thought it would be an excellent rule to live each day as if we should die tomorrow. Such an attitude would emphasize sharply the values of life. We should live each day with a gentleness, a vigor, and a keenness of appreciation which are often lost when time stretches before us in the constant panorama of more days and months and years to come. There are those, of course, who would adopt the Epicurean motto of "Eat, drink, and be merry," but most people would be chastened by the certainty of impending death.

In stories the doomed hero is usually saved at the last minute by some stroke of fortune, but almost always his sense of values is changed. he becomes more appreciative of the meaning of life and its permanent spiritual values. It has often been noted that those who live, or have lived, in the shadow of death bring a mellow sweetness to everything they do.

Most of us, however, take life for granted. We know that one day we must die, but usually we picture that day as far in the future. When we are in buoyant health, death is all but unimaginable. We seldom think of it. The days stretch out in an endless vista. So we go about our petty tasks, hardly aware of our listless attitude toward life.

The same lethargy, I am afraid, characterizes the use of all our faculties and senses. Only the deaf appreciate hearing, only the blind realize the manifold blessings that lie in sight. Particularly does this observation apply to those who have lost sight and hearing in adult life. But those who have never suffered impairment of sight or hearing seldom make the fullest use of these blessed faculties. Their eyes and ears take in all sights and sounds hazily, without concentration and with little appreciation. It is the same old story of not being grateful for what we have until we lose it, of not being conscious of health until we are ill.

I have often thought it would be a blessing if each human being were stricken blind and deaf for a few days at some time during his early adult life. Darkness would make him more appreciative of sight; silence would tech him the joys of sound.

Now and then I have tested my seeing friends to discover what they see. Recently I was visited by a very good friends who had just returned from a long walk in the woods, and I asked her what she had observed. "Nothing in particular, " she replied. I might have been incredulous had I not been accustomed to such reposes, for long ago I became convinced that the seeing see little. How was it possible, I asked myself, to walk for an hour through the woods and see nothing worthy of note? I who cannot see find hundreds of things to interest me through mere touch.

I feel the delicate symmetry of a leaf. I pass my hands lovingly about the smooth skin of a silver birch, or the rough, shaggy bark of a pine. In the spring I touch the branches of trees hopefully in search of a bud the first sign of awakening Nature after her winter's sleep. I feel the delightful, velvety texture of a flower, and discover its remarkable convolutions; and something of the miracle of Nature is revealed to me. Occasionally, if I am very fortunate, I place my hand gently on a small tree and feel the happy quiver of a bird in full song. I am delighted to have the cool waters of a brook rush thought my open finger. To me a lush carpet of pine needles or spongy grass is more welcome than the most luxurious Persian rug. To me the page ant of seasons is a thrilling and unending drama, the action of which streams through my fingertips.

At times my heart cries out with longing to see all these things. If I can get so much pleasure from mere touch, how much more beauty must be revealed by sight. Yet, those who have eyes apparently see little. the panorama of color and action which fills the world is taken for granted. It is human, perhaps, to appreciate little that which we have and to long for that which we have not, but it is a great pity that in the world of light the gift of sight is used only as a mere convenience rather than as a means of adding fullness to life.

If I were the president of a university I should establish a compulsory course in "How to Use Your Eyes". The professor would try to show his pupils how they could add joy to their lives by really seeing what passes unnoticed before them. He would try to awake their dormant and sluggish faculties.

...

The First Day

On the first day, I should want to see the people whose kindness and gentleness and companionship have made my life worth living. First I should like to gaze long upon the face of my dear teacher, Mrs. Anne Sullivan Macy, who came to me when I was a child and opened the outer world to me. I should want not merely to see the outline of her face, so that I could cherish it in my memory, but to study that face and find in it the living evidence of the sympathetic tenderness and patience with which she accomplished the difficult task of my education. I should like to see in her eyes that strength of character which has enabled her to stand firm in the face of difficulties, and that compassion for all humanity which she has revealed to me so often.

...

The Second Day

The next day-the second day of sight - I should arise with the dawn and see the thrilling miracle by which night is transformed into day. I should behold with awe the magnificent panorama of light with which the sun awakens the sleeping earth. This day I should devote to a hasty glimpse of the world, past and present. I should want to see the pageant of man's progress, the kaleidoscope of the ages. How can so much be compressed into one day? Through the museums, of course. Often I have visited the New York Museum of Natural History to touch with my hands many of the objects there exhibited, but I have longed to see with my eyes the condensed history of the earth and its inhabitants displayed there - animals and the races of men pictured in their native environment; gigantic carcasses of dinosaurs and mastodons which roamed the earth long before man appeared, with his tiny stature and powerful brain, to conquer the animal kingdom; realistic presentations of the processes of development in animals, in man, and in the implements which man has used to fashion for himself a secure home on this planet; and a thousand and one other aspects of natural history.

...

The Third Day

The following morning, I should again greet the dawn, anxious to discover new delights, for I am sure that, for those who have eyes which really see, the dawn of each day must be a perpetually new revelation of beauty.

This, according to the terms of my imagined miracle, is to be my third and last day of sight. I shall have no time to waste in regrets or longings; there is too much to see. The first day I devoted to my friends, animate and inanimate. The second revealed to me the history of man and Nature. Today I shall spend in the workaday world of the present, amid the haunts of men going about the business of life. And where can one find so many activities and conditions of men as in New York? So the city becomes my destination.

...

At midnight my temporary respite from blindness would cease, and permanent night would close in on me again. Naturally in those three short days I should not have seen all I wanted to see. Only when darkness had again descended upon me should I realize how much I had left unseen. But my mind would be so crowded with glorious memories that I should have little time for regrets. Thereafter the touch of every object would bring a glowing memory of how that object looked.

Perhaps this short outline of how I should spend three days of sight does not agree with the program you would set for yourself if you knew that you were about to be stricken blind. I am, however, sure that if you actually faced that fate your eyes would open to things you had never seen before, storing up memories for the long night ahead. You would use your eyes as never before.

Everything you saw would become dear to you. Your eyes would touch and embrace every object that came within your range of vision. Then, at last, you would really see, and a new world of beauty would open itself before you.

I who am blind can give one hint to those who see -- one admonition to those who would make full use of the gift of sight: Use your eyes as if tomorrow you would be stricken blind. And the same method can be applied to the other senses. Hear the music of voices, the song of a bird, the mighty strains of an orchestra, as if you would be stricken deaf tomorrow. Touch each object you want to touch as if tomorrow your tactile sense would fail. Smell the perfume of flowers, taste with relish each morsel, as if tomorrow you could never smell and taste again. Make the most of every sense: glory in all the facets of pleasure and beauty which the world reveals to you through the several means of contact which Nature provides. But of all the senses, I am sure that sight must be the most delightful.

海伦·凯勒的《假如给我三天光明》流畅自然，让读者如沐春风而又深受启发。不同于其他的说理和劝导性散文，这篇散文用轻松而又理性的笔调表达了作者对美丽世界的向往。虽然场景描述都是源自于作者的虚拟想象，但是字里行间流露出的情感真挚自然，令读者深受感染。

文章层次分明，逻辑清晰。开头几段通过预设一位时日不多的主人公带动读者的感情和思考。"as long as a year（长达一年）"，"as short as twenty-four hours（短至一日）"，相对于整个人生过程，最后时刻都显得太短，弥足珍贵。这样的故事不禁让我们陷入思考，"what we should do under similar circumstances?""what associations should we crowd into those last hours as mortal beings?""what happiness should we find in reviewing the past, what regrets?"在相似的情况下，我们该怎么办？作为终有一死的人，在那最终的几个小时内，会充满一些什么样的遭遇、什么样的感受、什么样的联想呢？我们回顾往事，会找到哪些幸福、哪些遗憾呢？作者一连串地发问，引出人们经常思考的哲学问题：人生的意义究竟是什么？人的一生应当怎样度过才体现价值？

接下来，作者提到"it would be an excellent rule to live each day as if we should die tomorrow"，秉持一种原则，即把每天都当作最后一天来度过，这样的人生态度能"emphasize sharply the values of life（更凸显生命的价值）"。总之，即将失去生命的人比其

他人更加热爱生活。被拯救的故事中的主人公们,"becomes more appreciative of the meaning of life and its permanent spiritual values(更重视生命的意义和精神上的追求)"。

然而,与之形成鲜明对比的是,大多数人"take life for granted",认为生命是理所当然的,认为死亡还很遥远。"When we are in buoyant health, death is all but unimaginable. We seldom think of it."拥有健康体魄之时,人们总觉着死亡还很遥远。但事实上,"死亡和明天,你永远不知道哪个先到来"。"So we go about our petty tasks, hardly aware of our listless attitude toward life(我们总是把时间浪费在无意义的事情上,意识不到自己对生活的倦怠和冷漠态度)"。

"The same lethargy, I am afraid, characterizes the use of all our faculties and senses",其中characterizes是一个动词,意为"以……为特点",即我们可能用同样的懒散态度利用自己的本能和感官。"Only the deaf appreciate hearing, only the blind realize the manifold blessings that lie in sight(只有失聪之人更珍惜听力,唯有失明之人更能看清幸福)",身残之人与普通人的态度截然相反,形成了鲜明的对比,健康的人反而更容易忽视生命的可贵之处。

"it would be a blessing if each human being were stricken blind and deaf for a few days at some time during his early adult life. Darkness would make him more appreciative of sight; silence would tech him the joys of sound."如果每个人早年曾经失聪失明,也不失为一件幸运之事,因为黑暗之中更加珍爱光明的美好,寂静之中更会享受声音的美妙。失聪失明之后,人们会更加用心体会生命的可贵之处。

在文章中,作者多次使用体格健全的人来和自己作对比。在树林里散步后,朋友看到的是"nothing in particular(无特别之处)",没有任何值得关注的东西,这令作者深感震惊。不过因为早已习惯了这样的回答,这样一个难堪的结果倒也在作者的预料之中,"I became convinced that the seeing see little."海伦早已坚信,视力完好之人不如盲人看到的多。正如中国的《道德经》里所说,"五色令人目盲,五音令人耳聋,五味令人口爽,驰骋畋猎令人心发狂,难得之货令人行妨",即"缤纷的色彩使人眼睛昏花,变幻的音响使人耳朵发聋,丰腴的美食使人口味败坏,驰骋打猎令人心意狂荡,珍奇财宝令人行为不轨"。作者想要告诉读者,要珍爱生命,充分利用身体感官去感受世界的美好,珍惜自己所拥有的一切。海伦是这样想的,也是这样实践的。在森林里,她仅靠触摸,就感受到了树叶的完美对称、白桦树光滑的树皮、松树粗糙的树干,她寻找嫩芽、抚摸花朵、倾听小鸟歌唱、感受清凉的溪水和松针青草。大自然的馈赠让她欣喜不已,她感恩这个色彩缤纷、生机勃勃的世界。

"If I were the president of a university I should establish a compulsory course in 'How to Use Your Eyes'",字里行间将作者希望人们用心对待生活的殷切心情表露得淋漓尽致。"假如给我三天光明,我会……"。海伦展开丰富的想象,给读者呈现了一个

清晰美好的世界,一个我们自认为熟悉但却陌生的世界。

"On the first day, I should want to see the people whose kindness and gentleness and companionship have made my life worth living."第一天,海伦想透过心灵之窗看到那些鼓励她生活下去的善良、温厚的人们。她尤其迫不及待地想见到亲爱的莎莉文老师,由此可见海伦是心怀感恩之情的善良之人。"In the night of that first day of sight, I should not be able to sleep, so full would be my mind of the memories of the day."第一天结束之时,我甚至会激动地无法入眠,心中充满了对于这一天的美好回忆。

The second day of sight - I should arise with the dawn and see the thrilling miracle by which night is transformed into day. I should behold with awe the magnificent panorama of light with which the sun awakens the sleeping earth."第二天,海伦要在黎明之时起身,欣赏黑夜变为白昼的动人奇迹。她怀着敬畏之心,仰望壮丽的曙光全景,看太阳唤醒沉睡的大地。看完日出,海伦开启探索之旅,她奔向城市,去参观那些有名的博物馆,观察大自然的过去与现在,领略这个世界的人文与艺术。栩栩如生的描写使读者面前呈现一位快乐奔跑的少女,她满怀着对这个世界的向往、感激与欣赏。

"I should again greet the dawn""I shall spend in the workaday world of the present, amid the haunts of men going about the business of life"。最后一天,海伦渴望拥抱现实世界,去体验工作的繁忙和生活的气息,感受忙忙碌碌的人们真实的生活状态。"Everything you saw would become dear to you. Your eyes would touch and embrace every object that came within your range of vision."所有这些目光所及之物,都将成为回味一生的美好记忆。

"I who am blind can give one hint to those who see -- one admonition to those who would make full use of the gift of sight: Use your eyes as if tomorrow you would be stricken blind."最后,海伦用自身的例子告诉读者,要好好珍惜自己的感官,不辜负生命中的美好。作者的真情流露深深地感染了读者,作为体格健全之人,我们有何理由不去好好体验这充满魅力的世界呢?

《假如给我三天光明》以自传体散文的形式,真实记录了作者平凡又伟大的一生,展现了作者对从未见过、听过的世界的丰富想象,散发着浓郁的生命气息。普通人通常不懂得珍惜自己先天的禀赋,虽然视听健全,却可能什么都看不见,什么都听不见。而对于双目失明、双耳失聪的作者海伦而言,她仅凭双手的感知就发现了这个世界如此多的美好。同时,她对世界充满憧憬,并且时刻心怀感恩。她不断通过倾诉自己的经历、分享自己的感悟让更多人及时醒悟。中国古语记载"左丘失明,厥有国语;孙子膑脚,兵法修列"。许多诸如左丘、孙膑、海伦这样身陷严重残疾的人没有辜负生命的美好,而是力所能及地实现自己的价值,倾诉对生活的热爱。海伦所呈现出的顽强的生命意识给读者带来强烈震撼的同时,也给予读者深深的启迪与思考。

主要参考文献

刘璐.《假如给我三天光明》的生命意识研究[J].佳木斯大学社会科学学报,2017,35(1):116.

朱立华.英语经典名篇赏析[M].天津:南开大学出版社,2007.

思考题

(1)根据选文,人们通常是怎样利用自己的感官的?

(2)在你的生活中,你最珍惜的是什么?为什么?

(3)如果你遭遇了一些重大挫折,将会怎样应对?

Chapter 4　Youth

by Samuel Ullman

 背景介绍

作者缪尔·厄尔曼(1840—1924)出生于德国,儿时随家人移居美国,青年时曾参加过南北战争。作为教育家和社会活动家,他积极倡导所有的孩子,无论是白人还是黑人,都有平等接受教育的权利。厄尔曼年逾七旬才开始写作,其中最著名的代表作就是散文"Youth"(青春)。1917年该作品自问世以来,就产生了强烈而持续的轰动效应。成千上万的读者把它抄下来随身诵读,众多的世界名人也将其视为座右铭。美国的麦克阿瑟将军在指挥整个太平洋战争期间,办公桌上始终摆着装有短文《青春》复印件的镜框,文中的许多词句常被他在谈话或开会作报告时引用。松下公司的创始人松下幸之助说:"多年来,《青春》始终是我的座右铭。"为了纪念这位作者,位于伯明翰的阿拉巴马大学成立了缪尔·厄尔曼博物馆,为游客展示该作者的作品和生平事迹。

 文本选读

　　Youth is not a time of life; it is a state of mind; it is not a matter of rosy cheeks, red lips and supple knees; it is a matter of the will, a quality of the imagination, a vigor of the emotions; it is the freshness of the deep springs of life.

　　Youth means a temperamental predominance of courage over timidity, of the appetite for adventure over the love of ease. This often exists in a man of sixty more than a boy of twenty. Nobody grows old merely by a number of years. We grow old by deserting our ideals.

　　Years may wrinkle the skin, but to give up enthusiasm wrinkles the soul. Worry, fear, self-distrust bows the heart and turns the spirit back to dust.

　　Whether sixty or sixteen, there is in every human being's heart the lure of wonder, the unfailing child-like appetite of what's next, and the joy of the game of living. In the center of your heart and my heart there is a wireless station; so long as it receives messages of beauty, hope, cheer, courage and power from men and from the infinite, so long are you young.

When the aerials are down, and your spirit is covered with snows of cynicism and the ice of pessimism, then you've grown old, even at twenty, but as long as your aerials are up, to catch the waves of optimism, there is hope you may die young at eighty.

作品赏析

《青春》这篇抒情散文短小凝练。作者用流畅的文笔和轻松自如的语言,告诉读者要珍惜时间,即使身在年老之时,也要保持积极、健康的生活态度。前三个段落从"知"的角度定义青春,揭示其品质特质。后两个段落中,作者从"行"的角度,告诉读者怎样才能让青春永久。全文逻辑清晰,层次结构合理,内容饱含哲理。

首段集中使用了对比手法,以"否定+肯定"结构的转折句式 Youth is not…it's…作为开篇并贯穿全段,句式中两个相反的意思互为衬托以凸显作者的观点,这种写作手法别具风格,令读者过目难忘。段落内排比句式的运用使得语义更加连贯,行文颇有气势。本段中作者赋予青春多重的阐释,指出青春的内涵是"a state of mind(心态)""It is a matter of the will, a quality of the imagination, vigor of the emotions; it is the freshness of the deep spring of life.(青春是毅力、激情、创意;青春是生命涌泉的清澈、激扬)"。隐喻修辞的使用增强了语言的表现力,令抽象的道理显得具象生动。

第二段承接首段,进一步深化了自己的见解,对青春的涵义做了更深入的阐释。作者比较了完全不同的人生状态:courage vs. timidity, adventure vs. ease, old vs. young。"This often exits in a man of sixty more than a boy of twenty","青春所蕴含的锐勇和进取,二十岁的后生身上具备,而六旬长者则更多见。"这种观点的确新颖独特,与中文里的"老骥伏枥,志在千里"有异曲同工之妙。"Nobody grows merely by the number of years. We grow old by deserting our ideals",衰老并非因为年龄,而是因为丢弃了梦想,"ideals"与首段的"state of mind"相呼应。

第三段承上启下,短短两句话便道出青春永存的真谛,也为后面两段做好了铺垫。"enthusiasm"与前段的"ideals"语意相同,指积极向上的热情与理想信念。作为对比,"worry, fear, self-distrust(烦忧、惶恐、丧失自信)"指消极的心态。时间易逝,青春年华固然珍贵,而作者更看重"enthusiasm(激情)"。光阴荏苒只是令肌肤生出皱纹,而一旦丧失热情和信念,人的灵魂则转向衰颓腐朽。当烦忧、惶恐、丧失自信扭曲人的心灵之时,灵魂甚至先于肉体归于尘土。由此可见,乐观进取的心态才是青春的代名词,青春的真谛在于始终以积极的态度面对生活。

第四段,作者从生活实践的角度回答了如何让青春长存。"lure of wonders, the unfailing childlike appetite of what's next and the joy of the game of living,"即"人对未知的向往,孩子般的好奇心以及生活本身的乐趣"是人人皆备的特性,这三种特性鼓励人们扬起心中的天线去接收人间与上天发出的美好、希望、快乐、勇气和力量。"A wireless station(无线电波)"是作者的妙笔,用来喻指人人心中皆有的不服老的心态以及对青春的不倦追求。巧妙的修辞,容易引起读者的共鸣。

第五段中,作者使用对照的修辞手法,生动活泼地向读者展现了"when the aerials are down(天线垂下)"和"your aerials are up(天线竖起)"这两种生命状态,强调了希望、乐观在保持青春时的重要作用。"aerials(天线)"显然是作者使用的隐喻,岁月易逝,年龄渐长,但对人生的孜孜追求却可以抵挡岁月的侵蚀,这才是青春永驻的关键。如果玩世不恭,自暴自弃,即使正值年轻岁月,也是"垂垂老矣"。

主要参考文献

庞绍波.我对 Samuel Ullman 的散文《Youth》一文的赏析[J].科技咨询导报,2006(18):223.

苏慧,王占斌.塞缪尔·厄尔曼散文 Youth 的点评与欣赏[J].语文学刊:外语教育教学,2009(6):82.

思考题

(1)人类变老是一种不可逆转的自然现象,应该怎样保持年轻的心态?

(2)作为一名年轻的大学生,怎样才能使大学生活难忘而且更有意义?

(3)在你看来,年轻人最理想的生活是什么样子?

(4)时光飞逝,每个人都终将老去,你觉着自己的晚年生活会是怎样的?